DOWN & OUT IN MANHATTAN

DOWN & OUT IN MANHATTAN

A FINANCIAL THRILLER

JUSTIN CALLAHAN

DOWN & OUT IN MANHATTAN

Printed by CreateSpace

Copyright © 2012, 2016 by Justin Callahan

Cover and interior design by Maria Fernandez

All rights reserved. No part of this book may be reproduced in whole or in part without written permission from the publisher, except by reviewers who may quote brief excerpts in connection with a review in a newspaper, magazine, or electronic publication; nor may any part of this book be reproduced, stored in a retrieval system, or transmitted in any form or by any means electronic, mechanical, photocopying, recording, or other, without written permission from the author.

Library of Congress Cataloging-in-Publication Data is available.

ISBN-13: 978-1-49934-205-5
ISBN-10: 1-49934-205-5

10 9 8 7 6 5 4 3 2 1

In Loving Memory of
Sheila MacGill Callahan

DOWN & OUT IN MANHATTAN

NEW YORK CITY
LATE FALL, 1989

Ten dollars for the well they were charging at Roebling's that year. That was forty dollars a round, and my turn would come three times. Toss in a cab ride, tips, dinner; it was a day's work spent on a night out, two-fifty for a Tuesday. It just wasn't worth my money, my time, or the damage to my liver. And to make matters worse I was in the midst of an epiphany: I was not in love with Susan and never would be. It was depressing, but at least I now knew why. It had nothing to do with who she was and everything to do with who she wasn't. I slapped my Amex on the bar, straightened my tie, and shot my cuffs. Even in the midst of an epiphany you've got to represent. Susan and Cheryl excused themselves to go to the ladies room.

They weren't even gone a minute before my buddy Brad, who was a close talker, invaded my personal space and declared in a confidential tone, "My card's maxed out, brother. It's going to be declined."

I looked at him in disgust. "What? Are you planning to wash dishes?"

He hooked his thumbs in his red suspenders. "I don't think it's an option. I don't think they have dishes."

"Right," I agreed warily, "So what is your plan?"

"You are." He grinned. "You think you can help me out till Friday?"

I let half the air escape from my chest. "What do you do with all your money, anyway? I mean, you're a stockbroker, right?"

He made a point of checking the time on his gold Rolex before saying, "I got habits. Clothes, restaurants, cabs, rent. Like that."

"Yeah, no problem," I said, my attention diverted by two men tooling up to the bar. Roebling's was in The South Street Seaport, in the old Fulton Fish Market building. Back in the Eighties it was pretty popular and you never knew who was going to show up. I mean it could be the guys from the mailroom, or the owner of the company. Tonight it was the boss, or at least my boss: Arnold Norton, Senior Partner at the investment-banking firm of Walsh Dahmer. I hardly knew the guy, and he hardly knew me, but he knew I worked for him, and when our eyes locked we nodded at each other. I didn't recognize the man he was with, but he too looked somehow familiar.

Brad nodded his head at the new arrivals. "Who's that?" he asked.

"My boss, don't try to pitch him any stock."

"You really think I'd do that?"

"Remember, I know you. Say, you recognize the other guy?"

Brad scoped him, "Well," he said, "he doesn't look like anybody famous." He pitched his head back and forth like a questing dog. "You know the other guy, your boss. He looks a bit like you. Older, but like you."

"Yeah, I'm not getting that," I responded, studying the nut bowl through which I was picking.

"You should send them a drink. Score some points on your next review," Brad suggested.

Susan, who I'd been dating for six months, and Cheryl, who Brad had been dating for six hours, returned from their bathroom foray on that note, and Cheryl posed the question, "Send who a drink?"

"See the guy over there?" Brad asked.

"There are guys everywhere," Cheryl observed.

"Older guy, brown suit, next to the big guy in the blue blazer," Brad clarified.

"Okay," Cheryl agreed dubiously.

"That's Jack's boss. I think Jack should buy the guy a drink." Brad tapped his finger on his forehead.

Susan flipped her hair and studied her reflection in the mirror, "You really should, Jack," she agreed. "That kind of thing can help your career, schmoozing the boss."

I thought about it, and it made sense, so I flagged down the bartender. Mr. Norton barely even looked in my direction, and I wondered if I'd overstepped. After a few minutes the big familiar guy took his leave. Then Mr. Norton disappeared too, or at least I thought he did. About a half hour later he reappeared at my elbow, martini glass in hand.

"Hey," he said, "you're Cole, the analyst, right?"

I was half in the bag, or I'd never have been flip, but I responded, "You're Norton, the boss, right?"

"You'd never talk that way to me in the office," he said, but with a lazy smile, like he was one of the boys.

I introduced him to Brad, Cheryl, and Susan; Brad slipped him a business card. Norton made polite conversation with the group, bought a round, and then began to talk me slowly away and into a corner of the room. When we reached an empty table he sat and pointed me to a chair.

He leaned forward, staring keenly at my face. It was unsettling. Finally he said, "Betcha wondering why the boss corralled you over here."

"Well, now that you mention it, I am curious. I mean, we've never really spoken before, but it is convivial. Do you come here often?"

Norton chuckled low in his throat. "Years ago, back when Old Man Walsh had my job, and my department was small enough, I made a point to get to know everyone who worked under me. I found it to be a good practice, but these days I just don't get the same opportunity."

Now I understood; he was getting in touch with the common man. What I said was, "I can certainly understand how difficult it would be to maintain that tradition now."

He waved his hand dismissively, "I only explain, because I find it embarrassing that in the entire three years you've worked for us, we've never had a conversation." I noticed that, conversation or not, he knew how long I'd been with the firm, my name, and my job function. This was a company with two thousand employees.

"I never felt I had any claim on your time, sir. And I'm flattered that you're giving me some of it now," I responded like a good little brown nose.

"It's foolish not to go after the boss's time," Norton cut in sharply. "It is a well established fact that to get ahead in business, you've got to suck up to the boss. And there is no way you can achieve that without imposing on his time."

I didn't mean to, but I frowned. "I believe hard work speaks for itself."

He fixed me with a hard stare. "Hard work speaks in whispers, enough to keep you from getting fired, but not enough to get you ahead."

The advice was starting to feel almost paternal and I was smart enough to realize that would be a good vibe for the boss to feel toward me. So I said, "How's that?" just to encourage him along.

"It's like this," he answered, "when you work hard you think you create credit for yourself, and your supervisor does notice. The thing is, it's just not human nature to promote someone else's interests at the expense of your own. Bottom line, your boss takes credit for your work. Now you want to get ahead, you have to leapfrog the idiot you're reporting to, and get the ear of his boss. That's how you get ahead." He grinned.

I grinned back, trying to model his facial expression. "That's interesting. Counterintuitive, but interesting. What other advice do you have?"

"On getting ahead?" I could tell he had all kinds of advice, that I just had to choose a category, like he was an advice vending machine.

"Right," I answered eagerly.

He closed his eyes and feigned a few seconds of deep thought. "It depends. Different people have different styles, different motivations. You have to discover what motivates you, that which you hope to achieve and why."

"That's easy, I want to be successful."

He raised a bushy eyebrow. "And are you?"

"Not yet," I conceded.

"Success means different things to different people, Jack." He glanced quickly over his shoulder before returning his attention to me. "You need to define success for yourself."

I caught myself staring at his hands. They were wrapped around a martini glass, and his nails were long, maybe an inch off the tips, and sharp, but not effete. Here was this respectable, middle-aged man in a Brooks Brothers suit, and there were those claws, like the tip off to the alien under the human costume. He saw me notice, the loathing in my face, and he responded to it—not through words, instead an odd look crossed his face. He looked somehow pleased and the same time violating, like he was looking into the deepest parts of me, and amused by my childish repugnance.

I recovered. "Okay," I said, "how would you define it?"

He made a point of looking over my shoulder at the bar again for a moment. "Success is achieving that for which no price is too great, paying a price above gold or power, flesh or God."

I thought for a moment. I could tell he wanted reflection; Norton wanted his question taken seriously. It wouldn't have been good to answer him right away.

He gestured to the waitress for another round. I sighed noiselessly and decided to bare my soul to the man with the claws. "My mother, she's the only family I've ever known, she has Alzheimer's. I have her in a private home. If you've ever seen the public ones you'd recognize that I had no choice. The thing is, over the past few years, it's drained almost all of my resources, and I'm not sure how I'm going to pay for it this month. I guess

I'd pay just about any price to take care of her properly, to make her comfortable."

"So that's it?" His eyes burned into mine. "That's your price, to pay any price?"

I laughed nervously. "I guess. I might want a few other baubles too. Why are you asking me?"

"Because some prices are high, not in treasure, but in spirit. Many are willing to pay a price in blood, sweat, and tears, but it takes a special kind of man to pay a price in conscience, in spirit. I want to know if you are one of those men."

I lifted my glass and sucked down the dregs. "Let me spin it around on you, Mr. Norton."

He reached forward and placed a hand on my shoulder. "Call me Arnold."

"Right, Arnold," I agreed. "How about you. Is there something for which you would pay the price of the spirit?"

He gave my shoulder a squeeze. "Absolutely. The firm, I have already paid the price many times and would do so again. Now let me ask you: If given the opportunity, are you ready to pay the price?"

I looked past Norton to where Brad and the girls were laughing and drinking at the bar, then focused back on the boss sitting across from me. There was really only one correct answer. "I am," I said.

The waitress delivered our drinks and Norton stood up from the table. I stood with him and he took my hand, holding it for a long time while he stared a little intently at me. "Your mother," he finally said, "what is her first name?"

"Monique."

"French?"

"Her parents were French Canadian. I think she spoke French, though I only heard her do it a few times."

Norton lifted his glass from the tabletop, "Monique Cole? I seem to remember a Monique Cole who worked for the firm back in the late Sixties. Could it be the same one?"

I'm pretty sure I gave him a funny look, but I recovered quickly. "My mom worked for a company called W. D. Palmer."

"Well, back then, Jack, the firm was called W. D. Palmer. Walsh Dahmer & Palmer."

He looked a little shaken and I nodded at him, a bit confused at his sudden change in expression. Then he recovered and said, "Well, good night, Jack."

I nodded again and looked away. When I turned back he was gone.

ONE

The next afternoon was the day before Thanksgiving. I sat in my tiny office towering thirty-eight floors above Wall Street, peering out the narrow window to the sweeping landscape below, watching the gray skyline and pondering the events of the night before. My head was a bit thick and my mind a bit fuzzy.

I hadn't gotten very deep into my thoughts when my phone rang. I didn't ordinarily answer my own phone, I shared a secretary with another analyst, but she was taking advantage of the holiday and hadn't come into work. My back was to the phone and it was on the opposite end of the room, but I didn't have to take a single step to answer it. My office was that small.

I swallowed and tried to pump out a crisp tone. "Finance, Jack Cole speaking."

"Hi Jack, Arnold Norton."

"Good afternoon Mr. Norton. What can I do for you, sir?" I put the suck up machine in high gear, marveling at how quickly this was going.

"I hope you have already. How's that profile on Homer Industries coming along?" He sounded friendly, solicitous, and I guessed I hadn't embarrassed myself too badly the night before.

"I finished it fifteen minutes ago. Did you want me to run it up to your office?" God, I sounded almost perky. I was making myself sick.

He chuckled, "That's not necessary, Jack. I'll tell you what though. Tomorrow's Thanksgiving, but you *are* planning to be in the office on Friday. Aren't you?"

I hadn't been, but there was no way I'd admit to that now. "Yes, sir," I replied.

"Good. Look Jack, I think it's time we got you off the bench and out on the field with some of the players. What do you think of that? Are you ready for a challenge?"

"Absolutely," I replied in a tone of voice that I hoped sounded like a warm handshake. Now I was shocked. A couple of drinks the night before and I was being invited into the club. This was definitely what I wanted. I wanted to make deals and money, not crunch numbers for the rest of my life.

"Outstanding, Jack. That's what I hoped you would say. Make a reservation at Chez Pierre for a party of four at 12:30 on Friday. Tell them you want my usual table. You'll be lunching with me, Neil Grunley, and John Petersen. We'll discuss Homer Industries, so bring the profile with you."

"Yes sir, Mr. Norton."

"I told you, you can call me Arnold. Have a happy Thanksgiving and I'll see you Friday."

I leaned back in my chair, marveling at the opportunity that seemed to be jumping at me out of thin air. Someone rapped at the door: John from the mailroom handed me the usual stack. The third envelope down was from payroll. It contained a bonus check for $9,000, roughly four months of care for Mom. I turned it over in my hand, wondering what it was all about. The date on the check was November 22. Someone had written that check this morning. Apparently Norton wanted me to have that money because of the conversation about my mother we'd had at Roebling's the night before.

The phone rang again.

"Jack Cole."

"Hi Jack, its Sue." The voice cut through the wire, confronting me and I winced.

I sighed because I wanted her to hear it. "Hi, Sue."

"Don't sound so happy to hear from me, it'll go to my head."

"I just don't want to have an argument."

"Then you've made your decision?"

"It's not a decision. I would love to spend Thanksgiving with you and your family. But I can't. If I don't spend Thanksgiving with my mom, no one will."

"Your mom? I've met your mom, Jack. That's not your mom, that's just a body. Your mom left her body a long time ago. She's not even going to know you're there, and my parents are expecting you."

Her words darted out at me. It made it easier to say what I had to.

"Sue, your parents don't even like me. I'm going to spend tomorrow with my mom. If that makes you unhappy there's really nothing I can do about it. I'm sorry."

I heard an angry sniff, and the line went dead. I hung up the phone and then picked the receiver back up. I held it for a minute, considering. No way, I decided. If Sue really cared about me, she would understand about this. No way I was going to cave. It was one of the reasons for which I had come to my epiphany the night before: How could I love a woman who didn't understand something as basic as this? But, of course, this was not the only reason I had come to my epiphany. Truthfully, I had been in love once upon a time. I had realized at Roebling's the night before that even now, a decade later, I was still in love. It was the reason that none of my relationships over the past ten years had worked out.

The phone rang again. "Jack Cole."

"Hey, it's Brad. Got a minute?"

"What's up?"

"There's a new strip club just opened on the East Side, near the Fifty-Ninth Street Bridge. Supposed to be first rate in every way and guess who got VIP tickets?"

"I'm going to say you?"

"Bingo. I'm going up there tonight with Pat and Pete. You in?"

My opinion on strip clubs is this: I don't pay for it, I definitely don't pay to not get it, and I think it's a little degrading, both for the objectified women and for the men with their weird, pack sex mentality. "Not really my style, Brad. You know that." I said.

"You gotta live it up a little, Jack. You know, smell the roses? Besides, I was planning to true up with you a couple of days early. I just got a big ass commission check. How much do I owe you?"

"Five-fifty, including last night," I answered quickly.

"Well, I'm willing to pay it all back tonight, but only if you come to the club."

"I don't know, tomorrow's Thanksgiving and . . ."

He cut me off. "You gotta stop and smell the roses buddy, come on!"

I knew he was pacing around the desk where he spent the whole day pitching stock, and he was in the zone. Probably tossing a baseball up and down too. There was no way he was going to take no for an answer, and I wanted that five-fifty. If I didn't get it tonight, I'd be lucky to see it before the New Year. So in the end I reluctantly agreed to meet up with the guys at American Trash, a pseudo biker bar on First Avenue. When I arrived they were already there, drinking from beer buckets and boring the bartender stiff. Brad had brought along Pete Frankel, an aggressive broker who did pretty well for himself and liked to flash his cash. In fact that was probably the reason why the tough, cute chick behind the bar was tolerating them in the first place. The other guy was Pat Cairn, who worked in Brad's boiler room during the day while attending law school at night. They were okay guys; we went out drinking together pretty regularly, and played poker a couple of times a month.

Brad was excited about his VIP passes, "Check it out," he exclaimed, carefully drying a small area of the damp bar top before laying the gaudy, gold-colored, cardboard passes gently down on the wood. "These are hard to get. I mean it's the grand opening! Anyway right off the bat, free admission—a twenty dollar savings!" He slapped his hand on the stack of gold passes, "First lap dance free—another twenty dollar savings! A free drink, and unlimited access to the VIP room where there are going to be celebrities out the ass!"

"Wow, that's really something," I said just to be polite.

"Yeah, each one is like a fifty dollar gift card. I got it from a client." He pushed the tip of his nose to one side with his forefinger, indicating his client was connected. He waited till he was sure the bartender and a couple of chicks sitting close by would notice, and then he pulled out a thick wad of cash; peeled off five hundred and fifty dollars, and dropped the stack in front of me like it was a tip.

I snatched it up before it disappeared like fairy gold. "Thanks, pal," I said, and then I ordered a round for the boys.

I was surprised when the passes worked as advertised and we got our free admission, bypassing a line of freezing hopefuls. We went directly into the VIP room where there actually was a celebrity in attendance, even though it was only Mason Reiss, a TV show midget from the Seventies. Our free drink turned out to be a glass of cheap champagne, which I turned down in lieu of a black and soda that I had to pay for. We grabbed a table near a small stage and watched a cute redhead writhe around a pole. Then, while the other guys began discussing their options, I saw another dancer out of the corner of my eye, and something in the way she moved was achingly familiar.

I was certain, except I still wasn't sure. Quietly I slipped away from the table. I needed a closer look. If it was her, I didn't wish to be seen, so I moved in the shadows. The problem was that getting close enough to be sure also meant getting close enough for her to see me. But considering the circumstances, I knew where her journey had to end.

I left the VIP room and there she was, up on the stage. I felt jealous, titillated, sad, and elated, all in a mixture. My darkest fantasy and my greatest anxiety had both come to life. My most quiet need and most secret wish. It was the girl who broke my heart. The one I never forgot. The one whose memory kept me from committing to Sue, or anyone else.

My time with Lisa seemed all at once like yesterday, and a long time ago. Looking back I could see the seeds of its destruction came before the relationship even started. You see, I finished high school with no money for college, not even part time City College, and I desperately sought the college experience. I made a decision to work for a year and save money, and I did that in the South Street Seaport working as a bar back. The job didn't pay much, but what it did do was expose me to all the Wall Street guys, with their bravado and cash. Fortunately, they also had bad habits that I learned to cater to, selling them coke, marijuana, ecstasy. I'm sure it sounds bad, but a mind is a terrible thing to waste, and I needed the money to further my education. To make a long story short, I made a nice pile, got accepted to Hofstra University on Long Island, and retired from a life of crime. So when the summer ended, I packed some bags and hopped the LIRR to Hempstead.

After the second or third week I met Lisa Clement. Big brown eyes, long auburn hair, high cheekbones, all on top of an impossibly curvy body encased in tight striped shorts and a lavender

T-shirt. I never, in my wildest dreams, would have thought that a girl like her would take a second look at me, but she did.

It was a mixer outdoors in back of the dorm, and when we started talking it was like the whole world slipped away. We waited a month before we made love. I could have pushed it, but she was my first and I didn't. And so it went; all year we were inseparable. On winter break I went to Saratoga to meet her family. That summer when we had to go our separate ways, her upstate, and me back to the city, we talked by phone every day and made time to visit one another. I helped her buy a car.

For me, though, it was always bittersweet, because I knew from the first moment I fell for her how it would end. That knowing created a self-fulfilling prophecy. My fall was fueled by jealousy, possessiveness, anxiety, and paranoia. At the end of the third semester I ran out of money and had to leave Hofstra and my fairytale romance behind. We kept at it by phone for a little while, but the emotional distance grew almost as fast as the physical distance, and I grew more frustrated and jealous. I think I suffocated her in my paranoia.

When I last went up to visit her my conduct could not have been more pessimistic, or more controlling. As she drove me to the station at the end of my time, she said we were through and left me standing by a snow bank on the side of the road, heartbroken. My pride never let me look back, though my heart ached for her, and my soul yearned.

Now there she was, dancing on the stage at Golden Dreams, what my Buddy Brad was calling Fantasy Island, dancing for all the world to see. I wanted to pull her off the stage, wrap her in my coat, and take her home, where I could nurse her soul. But, I was now a thirty-year-old man, not a nineteen- or twenty-year-old kid. I had to tread carefully, and decide what was best to be done.

I kept out of her line of sight, made my way to the exit, and left without saying goodbye to Brad and the guys. I needed to be alone. I emerged from the club and into the shadow of the Queens-borough Bridge, where I paused to look at the billboard advertising the dancers. I found Lisa's head shot and underneath it was listed the name Charlotte C. I stood there for a long moment in front of the sign thinking about the name. Thinking perhaps it wasn't her after all, that I'd been mistaken. It only took a moment till I shook myself clear. Of course it was a stage name. It even made sense on some level to me. For some reason I remembered her telling me about her favorite book as a child, *Charlotte's Web.*

I took Second Avenue and hiked Uptown past the Roosevelt Island Tram. As I passed the original TGI Fridays on Second Avenue I saw white snow falling from the night sky, and I wrestled with my feelings. Lisa a stripper—it went against everything I knew of her. Not that she'd been a prude. In fact she had been a girl of healthy appetite. Of course, many years had passed and people change.

I had been so long simultaneously tortured and sustained by the memory. This was my chance for closure, the reality to cure my long withdrawal. By the time my footsteps landed me on my doorstep I had decided. I would accept this night as the closest thing to closure I was likely to get, avoid her, and attempt to move on with my life.

The entrance to my apartment let into the kitchen. I draped my jacket over the chair and sat in the dark. In that dark moment

I had a realization; I'd never gone back after her because I didn't think I was good enough. My fantasy had always been to create a titanic success of myself, and only then sweep her off her feet. But here I was again, in my tiny one bedroom on First Avenue, with the late bills for my mother's nursing home sitting unopened on a secondhand desk. The view from my window was an alley where the Chinese restaurant downstairs dumped their trash. That was why, after ten years of self-pity, I'd never gone after what I truly wanted. I was comfortable with mediocrity. I was afraid of success, and all that was about to change. It was time, I decided, to seize the day.

Detective Sgt. Nat Weston pulled up in front of 875 Park Avenue, parked his ten-year-old blue Oldsmobile and got out. A liveried doorman rushed out of the vestibule and stared. Nat was a tall, middle-aged, African-American in a green army jacket and Yankee baseball cap. Certainly not decked out like the average visitor to 875 Park Avenue.

"You can't park there," the doorman barked.

Nat brushed past him and entered the lobby, the doorman trailing in his wake. "Can I help you?"

Nat stared, considering. It'd been an odd call. He'd been helping his wife in the kitchen when it came. The chief himself wanted him to check out a murder scene on Park Avenue. It was Thanksgiving and someone else should have gone. In fact, a whole lot of other people should have gone, but it was going to be just him and a German detective from Interpol together with some techs and the body snatchers. Everything was to be kept quiet.

"Five B, I'm expected," Nat finally said.

The doorman looked at him like he doubted it. "You're still gonna have to move the car."

Nat shook his head.

"I have to keep the space clear for taxis."

Finally Nat flashed his gold shield. "Maybe, if you'd been even a little polite. Now ring Five B for me"—Nat squinted at the man's nametag—"Tony."

Tony sighed and picked up the house phone, "Your name?"

"Detective Weston."

Nat got off the elevator on the fifth floor. There was only one apartment and there was none of the usual hurly burly that characterizes a crime scene. In fact just one person waited for him at the door, a short, broad-shouldered man in an expensive suit.

"Detective Weston," he smiled, holding out his hand, "I'm Helmut Steger. Thank you for being prompt."

Nat took his hand. "Pleasure Helmut. You're the guy from Interpol?"

"Yes." He answered crisply.

Nat leaned up against the doorjamb. "What's up, Helmut?"

Helmut Steger looked quickly behind himself, and then peered past Nat down the hall before answering. "There has been a murder. We cannot have publicity because it might harm our case. We do need a report, a file here in New York, just in case. That is what you're here for, not to investigate, just to make a report."

"So I've been told," said Nat breezily.

Helmut stepped back from the threshold. "Why don't you come inside?"

Nat stepped into a round foyer with five doors leading off from different points along the circumference. One led off into a long hall on one side, and one off into a long hall on the other.

Another led into a sitting room, and yet another into a dining room. The fifth was closed. There were two other men in the apartment, and they were dusting, not for fingerprints like you might expect, but actually dusting.

The body was in the third bedroom down the south hall. It was a man in his late fifties, well dressed. Marks ringed his neck and the corpse smelled like he'd been dead for some time. The really freaky thing about the body was the hands, which had been cut off and the stumps cauterized. Lying next to the tub were a hacksaw and blowtorch.

"Where are the hands?"

Helmut shrugged.

"The murderers used those to take off the hands?"

Helmut nodded.

"I got a hacksaw just like that in my toolbox at home."

"Yes the tools are very common. There's nothing to be learned from them."

"You want to tell me what's going on here?"

Helmut stared at him for a good, long minute. "Would you care for a cup of coffee, Mr. Weston?"

Nat nodded slowly at him. "I would, Mr. Steger.

They left the bathroom and Helmut called out to one of his men in German. A few minutes later, they were being served coffee in the library.

Nat stirred his coffee, steaming in a delicate china cup. "Why are your men cleaning the apartment?"

Helmut waived his hand in the air as if to dismiss the thought that he knew Nat was having. "We've already gleaned all the evidence from the site we are likely to. And as I've said before, the investigation is being kept quiet. If we don't restore everything to normalcy, neighbors will talk."

Nat placed the thin cup deliberately down into the saucer on the table between them. "Who owns this apartment, and whose body is that lying in the bathroom?"

Helmut, as if modeling Nat's behavior, made the same series of deliberate moves with his own coffee cup, pushing the cup and saucer into the center of the table before answering. "It is a corporate apartment owned by Boycelander Bank. Boycelander is a private bank based in Zurich. The body belongs, or rather, belonged to, Wolfgang Dieter."

Nat leaned forward across the table. "So who killed him?"

Helmut leaned back. "You mean, who do I think killed him?"

"What's the point in beating around the bush, Helmut? You know they won't let me put it in the report anyway, and we both know you already know or you wouldn't be here."

The German laughed. "That's fair. And who knows, maybe if I give you some information you can keep your eyes open for me."

"That'll work."

Helmut closed his eyes for a few seconds before he began to speak. "I think Dieter was killed because he was passing information to watchdog groups about certain financial transactions which have the potential of being far more damaging than some of the recent public revelations. In terms of who killed him, I believe it to be a man who was born with the name of Roget Voltan about fifty-five years ago in the village of Givenchy, France."

Nat smirked. "That sounds kinda melodramatic. Who do you think Voltan is working for?"

"More coffee?" Nat shook his head, and Helmut poured himself another cup. "It's what he does for a living. I've been tracking Voltan for a long time. See, I'm something of a hunter as, I imagine, are you. And Roget Voltan would be my biggest prize. And that too is the reason I'm willing to give you more information than I probably should."

Nat leaned in close again. "Why's that?"

Helmut leaned in to meet him. "I think this Voltan is poaching in your territory. So I want you to keep your eyes open for him."

"You're going to have to tell me more about him."

"Voltan joined the French Foreign Legion at an early age. He served in North Africa and got kicked out after ten years. That's hard to do, getting kicked out of the Foreign Legion."

"So why'd he get kicked out?"

"He was a killer, and he became an embarrassment."

"What type of people did he kill?"

"Always men, never women. It was so long ago that I have little other information. The type of man was usually tough, the tough guys in the Arab towns. But of course, it's possible that even then the killings were political."

"So then what happened to him?"

"He worked for various governments as an assassin."

"My mother always said, find what you're good at," Nat mused.

Helmut gave him a strained smile and continued. "That's another reason why the investigation has to be kept quiet. He could be very embarrassing to a lot of people."

"So you're saying this murder here is political?"

"No. Voltan also works as what you might call a corporate hit man. A lot of Swiss banks and investment banking firms. I'm not going to say it happens a lot, but then there are not a lot of guys out there who specialize in this type of thing, so Voltan keeps busy."

"If you know about him, why are you having so much trouble catching him?"

"The difficult thing about Voltan is that he is a very intuitive man. He is intuitive when he is hunting his prey and he is intuitive when he is being hunted by police. In fact there are many members of law enforcement who refuse to hunt him, and there are some who have been tasked with that assignment who have ended up dead."

Nat's eyes narrowed. "He kills policemen?"

"I believe he has, when they have gotten too close."

"You believe? Why do you say that?"

"Remember the hands, Nat?"

"I remember the absence of the hands, Helmut."

"There has been more than one policeman who has disappeared only to have his fingerprints show up at a crime scene hundreds, if not thousands of miles from his home."

"You think he saves the hands from his victims to plant prints?"

"That, Detective Weston, is how do you say? His modus operandi."

"So how do I fit in to all this, Helmut?"

"I think he's active in New York now. You've seen his modus operandi today. You may come in contact with his work again. When you do I want you to call me at this number." He handed Nat a card. "I don't want you to discuss anything with anybody but me. When you call, ask for Eva Schmidt, she is my niece. She'll get a message to me and I'll call back."

Nat put the card in his pocket. "Why don't you want me to say anything? Why all the secrecy?"

"Let us say that there are a lot of people who would not want the things that Voltan knows to see the light of day and that makes him very powerful." Helmut leaned forward, staring intently into Nat's eyes, "He's a very dangerous man, Mr. Weston. Even as I search for him now, he is, in turn, hunting me."

I entered her room off an institutional corridor. The room smelled of astringent, maybe Witch Hazel. I'd come to associate the smell with my visits to her. She sat upright on the bed staring at a small television showing the Macy's Thanksgiving Day Parade. I stood for a moment in the door, looking through the room to the window beyond. Mother's view was bleak and gray, naked trees and empty lots leading to red brick housing projects, beneath an overcast sky.

"Hi, Mom," I said, placing my bags of Thanksgiving food on the table.

She squinted. "Do I know you?"

This part was always the toughest. She didn't know me anymore, but she'd get used to me during the visit.

I kissed her on the forehead and she smiled. "You remember me, Mom. It's Jack," her smile widened.

She rolled her eyes at me. "Can you help me get out of here? I want to go home but they won't let me."

I ignored this part. I always did. I stroked her long white hair. It was still beautiful, her hair, still streaked with blonde. She was much too young to have reached this dead end.

I was unpacking dinner when she began to point excitedly at the television. When I looked over the Cat in the Hat balloon was floating across the screen.

"You used to love that so much." She grinned at me, and in that moment I knew that she knew who I was.

I jumped on the spark and quickly quoted my favorite line to her from the book, the part when the fish says that the cat should not be about when your mother is out.

It was the right thing to do: She laughed, her blue eyes clearer than they had been in years and she said, "So much like your father, that cat . . ."

"My father!" I could barely keep myself from exclaiming. Even before her affliction she had always refused to talk about my father.

She looked startled. "Yes, your father he was very much like that cat, and your grandmother, she certainly could have played the part of the fish in the pot!"

I sucked in a deep breath of air. I knew the window, if it really was open, could slam shut at the slightest touch. "My father," I said softly, "What was his name?"

"His name?" she repeated. The familiar look of confusion passing over her face like a lunar eclipse. Then her eyes brightened again momentarily, "You know I met him at W. D. Palmer, at a party . . ." Her voice trailed off.

I sat down and took her hand, searching for more, but the moment was gone. Abruptly, she fell back against the pillows, gasping for air, her eyeballs rolling up in the back of her head. I jumped up and pushed the nurse call button.

Later, sitting in the ER drinking coffee, I began to let the memories back in. For five years I'd refused to think about how bad it had gotten before she'd gone into the nursing home. Once I thought about it, I realized that she'd begun to deteriorate even before I left for college.

She'd always been a cheerful, confident woman, at least until about the time of my sixteenth birthday. I hadn't really noticed it then, but in hindsight, I knew. It began in subtle ways, with an uncharacteristic moodiness and bad temper. By the time I went away to college, she was having memory lapses, which at the time I had just thought was a natural part of aging.

When she didn't show up for my college graduation ceremony I knew something was very wrong. I must have reminded her a dozen times leading up to it. I even called her the day before. While everyone else in my class left commencement to celebrate with their relatives, I went to the nearest phone and called home. She answered after two rings and when I asked her what happened, she said "What graduation?" That was when I knew, profoundly, that she had a problem.

I rushed home to find her sitting in the dark, the place a mess. She was crying, and told me she'd never forgive herself for missing my high school graduation.

I didn't bother to correct her, to tell her I'd graduated high school five years before. I held her in my arms and cried with her.

The next day I took her to the doctor. That night I took her home, cleaned the apartment, put her to bed and began going through her affairs. She hadn't been paying the bills, even though there was some money in the bank, so I took care of that and, a few days later, called the doctor to discuss the test results.

The man was very nice, but also very concerned. He showed me images he'd taken of her brain, particularly an area he called the neritic plaque, and a growth he called a neurofibrillary tangle. He told me that these pathological changes in her brain were consistent with Alzheimer's disease, or senile dementia, for which there was no known cure. He gave me a phone number for someone in social services and wished me luck.

I tried to take care of her at home, but I had no family or network to help me and I had to work. I got her into a day-care program, and found a job for myself. Then for two years, every evening after work, I'd pick her up from the center and take her home, and all the while her condition deteriorated. In the end she didn't even recognize me. I was spiritually and mentally exhausted when I finally made the decision to commit her to a full time nursing home. The guilt of it almost destroyed me. I took my two-week vacation from work, and they came to get her on the first Friday. Something inside of me had died that day.

Friday morning as I prepared for my lunch meeting with the Masters of the Universe, reception buzzed to tell me I had a call from a doctor. I didn't recognize the name, but I was sure it had to do with my mom. I'd been in the emergency room of Peninsula Hospital in Queens all night and I'd yet to sleep.

"Jack Cole."

"Jack, this is Dr. Schafer, I'm a colleague of Dr. Kling, your mother's GP."

"Is everything okay?"

"Well it is, and it isn't."

"What does that mean?"

"I understand you were there yesterday when your mother had her heart episode?"

"Yes."

"Well, the thing is, hmm. Under the circumstances, especially with an individual in your mother's condition, where she has difficulty communicating, we run a series of tests, just as a standard procedure. Look, there's no easy way of saying this, Jack. Your mother is in the mid stages of pancreatic cancer.

"What?" I just felt numb.

"Yes, I'm sorry. The thing is I believe we have a good chance of helping her; it is probably operable at this stage. Anyway, I'm going to need you to fill out some paperwork. Let me put you on the phone with my secretary, Barbara."

The line emptied and I just sort of sat there with my stomach churning. After a couple of minutes a woman's voice came on the line, "Hello, Jack Cole?"

"Yes, Barbara?"

"Yes Jack. When can you come down to the office?"

"Is tomorrow morning good for you?"

"No, we'll be closed, how about Monday, eight A.M.?"

"Fine, what do I need to bring?"

"I've already had your mom's paperwork sent down from Dr. Kling's office. She's on Medicare, correct?"

"Yes."

"Is there any supplemental coverage?"

"No."

"Okay, Jack. Medicare will only cover eighty percent of what they consider to be reasonable expenses, in the end that may only add up to sixty percent. The operation and post-op will cost an estimated thirty thousand. On Monday I'm going to need you to bring some ID, so you can sign the consent forms, and a check for six thousand so we can get started, that or we can explore public or indigent options."

My stomach turned. "No, I'll figure something out. I'll be there, but the money, probably later in the week. I have to jump through some hoops.

"Okay, bye for now. Have a good weekend."

The line went dead. A good weekend? Shit! Man, sometimes everything goes bad at once. My head was spinning. I really had to start making money fast, and that lunch meeting with Norton, already the most important thing in my life, was suddenly even more important.

I arrived at Chez Pierre and was greeted with icy civility by the Maître d'.

"I'm a bit early," I told him. "We have a reservation for twelve-thirty under Norton."

The ice broke and the man smiled, rubbing his pudgy hands together, "Arnold Norton?"

"Yes." I handed him my trenchcoat and decided to wait at the bar and grab a quick drink before the bosses arrived. Not that I was prone to drinking that early in the day, but I was nervous as hell and needed to take the edge off. So I grabbed a seat at the bar, quaffed a quick scotch, drinking it neat and chasing it with a Perrier. I paid the bill and was done, just as the three horsemen of the apocalypse were checking their coats at the front door.

Once seated at a quiet table in the back of the establishment, I scanned the faces of my three companions. At thirty I was by far the youngest. The others were all about the same age, middle to late fifties. They were all senior partners, and Mr. Petersen was also the company's chief legal counsel and a former Harvard Law School professor.

Mr. Grunley leaned forward. He had a lean, tan face and long, brown fingers, which he steepled under his chin like the Grinch as he spoke.

"Jack, even though this is the first opportunity we've had to speak with one another; I've had my eye on you since the first day you joined the firm. That was some damn fine work you did on the NatCon account, and I understand you recently finished your MBA." He leaned back in his seat waiting for a reply.

My hands were sweating, and my heart was sitting firmly at the bottom of my stomach. A lot depended on this man's good will. Even so, my hope was tempered with doubt. I doubted very much, for instance, that Grunley had ever cast a paternal eye on me, and my doings.

What I said was, "I appreciate your good opinion, and hope that I continue to justify it. I understand I was invited here today to discuss Homer Industries. I've taken the liberty of bringing four copies of the completed profile with me." As I reached into my briefcase for them, a harried waitress approached the table.

Mr. Grunley ordered a Dewar's and soda and when the others followed suit, I jumped on the bandwagon. But when the waitress launched into a recital of the daily specials, Grunley cut her off with a curt gesture. "Just get us the drinks. We'll let you know when we want to hear the specials." He turned to me, waving the profile I'd just handed him in the air. "I'm not going to read this whole damn thing right this minute, so why don't you give us a quick overview."

God he was rude. I cleared my throat and launched into my prepared speech.

"Homer Industries is a midsized firm based in Homerville Ohio. For the past hundred years it has been a closely held family corporation. It went public last year, but fifty-one percent of the voting stock is still held by John and Winston Homer, grandsons of the founder, Richard Homer.

"Originally the firm made iron products used to build warships for the navy. Over the years it has diversified, and now makes many different types of metal products for a wide range of vendors. The company has three factories, all in the vicinity of Homerville, and employs over five thousand workers, represented by three different unions. Last year the firm made a pre-tax profit in excess of twenty million dollars. It has net assets of over one hundred million."

"Mr. Petersen nodded around the table, "Well, you gentlemen hungry?"

Grunley crooked his finger imperiously at the waitress. "We'll hear those specials now, sweetheart." He said in a cloying, sickly sweet voice.

After we ordered, Mr. Norton looked over at me with his cold fish eyes, "What can you tell us about the pension fund that Homer controls?"

"It's solvent, not an issue."

They all stared at me in a way that made me feel vaguely uncomfortable. It seemed as if I were supposed to say something more, but for the life of me I couldn't figure out what. I waited, and finally Mr. Norton broke the silence.

"We want to know, specifically, how much is in the fund and whether it's over- or underfunded."

I flipped through the profile and looked up the information. "It has assets in excess of one hundred million dollars, and the pension benefit obligation is overfunded."

The masters of the universe leaned back and smiled at me.

"What's the average trading price on its common stock?" Mr. Petersen asked, lifting his drink.

"Around thirty dollars a share."

Petersen and Norton locked eyes for a fleeting second and I thought I saw Norton nod at him, but barely perceptible. Then

Petersen continued. "After we take our initial position we're going to want you to make certain the stock is pushed to retail clients, you might want to tip off some brokers. You think you could arrange that?"

I thought of my friend Brad Seaman, and his merry band of friends in the brokerage industry, "I think I could work that out."

The three other men around the table beamed, "That's the kind of can-do attitude we look for, Jack." Said Mr. Norton, like a principal at commencement. "The Homer brothers are in town this week. We'd like you to pitch them on the deal, and then we want you to set the whole thing up. Get together with Ed Bloomfield in accounting on the details, but we are not going to offer more than thirty dollars a share." He stared, waiting for a response, and when none was forthcoming he continued, "Jack, this is worth six figures to you. No bullshit. All that is required from you is absolute loyalty and discretion."

I was a little shocked. I mean I knew it was illegal, though it was really just a venal sin, insider trading. I mean, everybody knew how money was made on the street, especially during the 'Go Go Eighties,' and man, I needed that money. Try living in Manhattan and taking care of a mother with Alzheimer's.

TWO

The day was coming to a close and so was the ratio analysis I was performing on the Homer financial statements. I scrolled down a Lotus menu and saved the spreadsheet. In spite of the bittersweet quality of the day, I felt satisfied, but something in the back of my mind also told me to cover my ass. I realized that in all the hullabaloo of the day I hadn't received a memo, nothing in writing. Of course given the nature of their plans they wouldn't want anything in writing. I rebooted the computer and saved a file in journal form, recounting the day's events. I put a copy on disk and then deleted the original from the computer.

The sober business out of the way, I crowded all the negative thoughts from my mind. I put my worries about Mom in a separate room in my mind, shut the door, and finally allowed myself the luxury of really feeling good, optimistic . . . hopeful. In my mind I was singing the theme song to *The Jeffersons*; I was "Moving On Up." I was about to get my piece of the pie and I wanted to share how good it tasted. I hadn't talked to Susan since we'd had our disastrous Thanksgiving conversation, and though my emotions were muddled and mixed, I decided to invite her to dinner. Quickly, I dialed her office number.

"Hi, this is Susan." She sounded upbeat, that sexy lilt that I liked in her voice

After our last interaction I wasn't sure how I'd be received so I let my tone of voice sound a bit playful. "Hi Sue, its Jack."

She laughed softly, "That's funny, I was just thinking about you."

"Anything good?"

"Just playing around with a theory."

"Really, how's that?"

"I think I didn't see you yesterday, even after dinner, because you lie low on Thanksgiving, and as soon as I realized why, I forgave you."

"Okay, I'll bite, why do you think I lie low on Thanksgiving?"

"Because you're really a turkey!" She shouted fast and loud into the phone, and then she started laughing.

I waited for her to settle down. "Can I buy you dinner tonight?"

"Hold on a sec, let me check my calendar." She left me on hold for a full minute. "Sure, I'm free. What time?"

"Meet me in the bar at Giacomino's at seven."

"I'll see you there."

I pushed my mother completely out of my mind. I'd visit her on Sunday, I'd pay for her on Monday, but I needed a little time away.

At five thirty I left my office, walking on air. Despite rush hour crowds I managed to snag a cab, yet another sign of what I thought was good luck.

I had an hour and a half to make it uptown, take a shower, and get changed to meet Susan. Even so I told the driver to let me off on Seventy-second and Third, nine blocks from where I lived. I've always loved walking, especially in Manhattan. For me, a stroll through Manhattan is like being inside a kaleidoscope that never creates the same pattern twice.

It was cold, but with little of the cruel wind which is characteristic of New York winters. I looked up at the darkening, gray sky and thought about what photographers call the magic hour, before turning up my collar and setting off through the rush hour crowd.

When I reached the corner of Seventy-eighth and Third, a tall, lean black man emerged from under the awning of a supermarket and stepped directly into my path. He was dressed in tattered clothing with a dirty green overcoat on top. He wore only one shoe with the other foot swathed in rags. I had only a moment to take this in before the man screamed in my face.

"Yo man! You got a quarter?"

I shook my head and pushed past him, I only got a few feet before the man followed me yelling; "Yo! Yo!"

When I reached the next corner he got in front of me, blocking my path. He stared hatefully into my eyes, "Yo man, I'm talking to you!" I stared back. I didn't like what I saw—an angry, desperate, homeless man confronting me in my "safe" middle class neighborhood. I looked right and left as other well-dressed, middle class people passed by without a glance.

I put a little street in my voice, "What you want?"

"Don't fucking ignore me when I'm talking to you!"

"I'm listening, what do you want?"

He reached out and pushed me, "Gimme a dollar, mother-fucker!"

My heart raced, my hands shook, I was both scared and angry. It was too much. He shoved me again. I tried to move on but he pushed closer, his warm, reeking breath pressed against my face in a dense cloud of stink. In that moment I knew I was running out of choices. The man wasn't going to just let me go my way. I looked around for help but no one looked back. This was my problem. He reached out to push me again, and I slammed him with a hard right cross, turning my hips into it and closing my fist at the last possible second. He went down like a felled tree. Now, all of a sudden people were looking. The street felt strangely hushed. I walked slowly away, feeling bad about what I'd been forced to do.

I got to Giacomino's at five after seven, with maybe a little guilt in tow because I hadn't been thinking much of Susan since my chance sighting of Lisa. I stood in the vestibule and scanned the crowded bar. I spotted her and stood for a moment, watching. At twenty-six she was a tall, youthful, leggy blonde with full sensuous lips, and at this moment she sat between two men at the bar, holding court. That was annoying. She was there to meet me; she didn't have to flirt with other men while she waited. Unless, of course, she was trying to get under my skin, I wouldn't have done it to her, unless, of course, I was trying to get under her skin. But hey, we were two different people, I could either let it pass or create an argument. In the meantime, I thought, it was another reason to cut her loose.

I walked straight up and bent to kiss her cheek, and she was laughing, taking me in through the corner of her eye, judging what effect her behavior was having on me. The boys looked sidelong at me, disappointed.

"Hi, been waiting long?"

She took my hand, "I got here a little early, but these gentlemen have been entertaining me," she indicated the two on either side. "Jack, this is Scott and David."

I took note of their cheap suits and shook hands, "Thanks for keeping an eye on her for me." One of them was still pretty obviously ogling her, and I gave her hand a tug. "Ready to grab a table?" I asked.

Scott, the fellow on my left, a tall, husky, man in his early thirties with sandy blonde hair suggested, "Why don't you let us buy you a drink?"

I glanced at Susan and she nodded, so I said, "Sure, Black Label on the rocks."

"What line are you in?" asked Dave, a slim, dark man with a mustache.

"Jack's in investment banking. Aren't you, Jack?" Susan answered like I was her prize pig.

"Really, what firm are you with?" Scott asked, handing me my drink.

"Walsh Dahmer."

"I'm impressed." Scott handed me a business card. "Dave and I sell copiers. We've got the best prices in town, whether you buy or lease."

"You think the subways will go on strike tomorrow?" Susan asked.

Scott snorted. "Make it tough to get to work on Monday, but I don't think the MTA should give in to them. I mean most of these guys didn't even finish high school, and they're bitching about having to pay a portion of their health care costs. I mean, these unions are killing our economy, they get a job and they think they're in for life, like they're Supreme Court judges or something. They oughta fire the whole bunch of them! What do you think, Jack?" Scott sounded like a man on a soapbox.

This talk of health care and partial coverage made me think about my mother and her eighty percent coverage, and the doctor who needed up-front cash. I looked at the copier salesman. "I don't really have an opinion."

Dave smiled, and said to his buddy, "You're probably right, Scott, but I bet you'd feel different if you were the one who got downsized."

"Maybe but I'm the type of guy who'd always find a way to make myself useful."

I was tired of the conversation, "You ever see *Death of a Salesman*?" I asked.

"What?" Scott sounded confused.

"Nothing, let me buy you guys a drink, and I think Susan and I are going to take our table now." I dropped my Amex on the bar and asked the bartender for a round and Susan's tab.

Once at the table, even though I knew it would start an argument, I laid into Susan> "Why do you always have to do that?"

"What?" she asked, the smile fading from her lips.

"Why do you have to start conversations with other men at bars?"

"You were late. And I didn't start a conversation with them. They started it with me. Besides, no matter what you may think, you do not own me. There's no ring on my finger, and I'll talk to whomever I please. If I decide I want to sleep with someone else, I'll do that too!"

I cringed. Her voice was loud, and I was sure it carried to the neighboring tables. Once I had found her earthy bluntness charming and edgy. Now, ever since my epiphany, I just found it coarse and embarrassing. If I were honest, it really didn't matter to me all that much, but I couldn't leave it hanging. I was expected to respond in a wounded way and I wasn't going to disappoint, if for no other reason, than it would make the sex better later. My epiphany hadn't cured my desire for that.

"We've been going out together for almost six months, doesn't that count for something?"

She considered me a moment, and looking back I wonder if she couldn't see right through me just like I thought I could do her. But her face softened, "All right, I'm sorry. I'll try and be more sensitive. Let's order, I'm starving."

"What are you going to have? They say the Salad Nicosia is excellent."

"You know I'm not one of those salad eating bitches. I'm going to have the surf and turf. Did you expect to get off with a cheap date? And what do you think, a bottle of chardonnay?"

"I guess I'll have the same, but what do you say to a bottle of Möet? I think we have something to celebrate."

She gave me a sour look, "I hope you're not planning to propose."

"Fuck you."

She laughed, "Then what's to celebrate? Did you get your first grown up tooth?"

I outlined the day's events, leaving out the questionable details and the news about mom. I knew she wouldn't be sympathetic. After the Moet we had a bottle of Grigich Hills Chardonnay, and by the time the cognac and coffee arrived I was drunk, and then my beeper went off. (This was in the dark days before cell phones.) When I squinted at it in the candlelight I saw it was work, and I stood up. "I have to call my office."

I found the phone near the restroom and dialed the number for Mr. Norton's direct line. He picked up on the first ring. My stomach was doing flip-flops as I concentrated on not sounding as drunk as I felt. "Good evening Mr. Norton, Jack Cole here." I stifled a hiccup, "You beeped me?"

"Hi Jack," his voice was warm and friendly, "I told you to call me Arnold. I have good news for you. I mentioned that the Homers would be in town this week, didn't I?"

"Yes sir, you did." I hiccupped again and tried to cover it with a cough.

"Well, my secretary managed to get in touch with Winston Homer and tomorrow night you and Ed Bloomfield will have dinner with him and his brother, to pitch them on the project. What do you say to that?"

"That's fantastic—"

"Right. Now, I know its Saturday tomorrow, but under the circumstances, I didn't think you'd mind. So get a good night's sleep. I don't want you to do anything else tomorrow but concentrate on the details of this thing. Oh, and I want you to touch base with Ed Bloomfield, so get with him first thing in the morning. Any questions?"

"No, that's great. I'll get right on it."

"Good. Be in my office first thing in the morning and we'll go over some issues. And Jack, try a piece of lemon with bitters and sugar on top."

"Excuse me?"

Norton chuckled, "For your hiccups. I'm sure the bartender, wherever you are, has those things. Good night." The line went dead.

THREE

Norton had it right about the hiccups, and it made me wish he'd given me some advice for the hangover, because when I got to the office the next morning I felt terrible. I logged on and checked my e-mail. Only one message, it was from Ed Bloomfield, wanting to get together before the meeting.

I sipped a large cup of black coffee, let the reviving caffeine seep slowly into my pores, and thought about Ed. Ed Bloomfield was a real accounting nerd—always squinting at you from behind thick glasses like he was skeptical of your bottom line. And while I definitely needed to huddle up with Ed, having been told as much by The Boss, I still felt drunk. And Ed was the kind of guy to pick up on that. He was detail oriented. Couldn't be helped though; I popped a couple of aspirin and dialed his extension.

"Good morning, Ed Bloomfield speaking."

I winced: his voice oozed sunshine. "Morning Ed. It's Jack Cole."

"Jack, how are you? You sound a bit hoarse. Rough night?" Picking apart the details.

I faked a cough into the receiver, "I might be coming down with a cold."

"Not good. You should start a daily regimen of wheat grass and vegetable juice. I've been doing it for years and haven't had a cold since."

"How wonderful. In the meantime, you wanted to grab a little face time before the meeting?" I've always found corporate speech annoying and would only use it for the purpose of mockery, but Ed didn't seem to notice.

"Yes."

"Conference room near the coffee lounge, five minutes."

I downed my coffee, grabbed the Homer profile, and headed out the door.

The conference room at Walsh Dahmer is immense: a long table holding thirty-eight chairs dominates the room. It's intended to intimidate. The walls were replete with painted portraits of the firm's founders, like an English baronial hall. James Dahmer's eyes seemed to follow me around the oak paneled room, and it was creepy. Ed was already there, seated at the far end of the table, eating fruit salad and drinking green tea.

I sat next to him and spread out the file. "Ed, how are you? Can you tell me why you're involved here?"

He spluttered into his tea. "Why shouldn't I be?"

"Just trying to figure out where you fit in." I fixed him with a stare.

He squinted. "They need someone to keep a lid on things. So I'm along to keep an eye on the deal."

"For Mr. Norton?"

His narrow chest seemed to swell a little. "For the firm. I'm a company man."

I nodded my head and affected a neutral expression. "I see. What do you know about Homer industries?"

He was staring back at me now, just as expressionlessly as I was at him. "I know we're not going to offer more than forty dollars a share." The moral high ground of the more serous businessman was now his.

"Less if we can help it," I stated flatly, leaning back into my chair and fixing him with a stare that said I had the harder nose. I followed up with, "Do you know what we're buying?" The word *even* implied but not stated.

"Of course, it's a metalworking firm." He leaked a long breath, letting it whistle between his teeth.

I shifted gears and made a halfhearted attempt at bonding. "All bullshit aside; tonight you and I are going to have to pitch two perfect strangers on a multi-million dollar deal. Are you ready to work with me on this?"

"What do you think, just because I'm an accountant, I don't know how to schmooze?" He gave me a sour look and shook his head.

"It's not that. I just want you to let me do the talking. What I need from you, and it's for the good of the firm, is to follow my lead and support me with numbers when I ask for them. That's all."

"Look Jack, this is a career maker for me too. I need it as badly as you do. Norton as good as told me I'd get a six-figure bonus if this baby goes through, and I'm not going to let you or anybody else fuck that up. Okay?"

"Okay, Ed. But if we're going to work together we have to pool our resources, play to our strengths. What do you know about John and Winston Homer?"

Ed's face lit up with a grin that almost made him seem likeable. "I'm glad you asked me that, because it leads me to a suggestion about tonight."

"What's that?"

"I think our success with these Homers depends on how much they like us. Everybody on The Street knows they're in play. They're going to be getting a lot of similar offers, and the one they take, all other things being equal, is going to be based on personal relationships. And, well, I've done some checking on them." He leaned back in his chair and let his smile evolve into smugness.

I wondered how he could have done so on such short notice, or had he been in the loop longer than me? "Well?" I said.

"You know how some guys like to make deals on the golf course?"

"Yeah."

"Well my cousin Nathan was a fraternity brother of theirs at Columbia. He says they're both heavy drinkers and they love topless bars. So we get them drunk and take them to a strip club, maybe get them laid . . . it couldn't hurt our position."

This was surprising coming from Ed, "I thought you were a numbers guy."

"I am, but I want this bonus. And since I am a numbers guy, I'm looking for the shortest distance between two points."

By one-thirty that afternoon I was in a black corporate car, cruising up the FDR with Ed Bloomfield, on our way to a two o'clock meeting with Chazz Palumbo, the manager of "the newest, hottest, strip club in town" Golden Dreams. It turned out Arnold Norton also had a notion about the Homer brothers, and more importantly, a connection with the guys who owned Golden Dreams, so he loved the idea. Brad Seaman, eat your heart out. Of course for me this posed a fine dilemma: I wanted to see Lisa again, but not necessarily at the club and this situation put me at risk of breaking my resolve. Of course there was a level on which I did not mind. In some ways I was like a junkie and the faster I saw her and the more powerful I seemed when I did, the more pure would be the high. Seeing her at the club in this context would almost be like mainlining. Certainly though, it was business, and I had no choice. To be honest I was thrilled with the path my life was taking. My career was on an incredible upward swing, and I was on the threshold of my most secret desire.

"Jack! Jack! Are you listening to me Jack?"

I pulled my head out of the clouds and registered that Ed had been talking to me—or rather at me—for some time. "Huh? What?" I replied groggily, "I must have dozed off."

"With your eyes open Jack?" Ed shook his head in frustration as the car turned off the drive near the Fifty-Ninth Street Bridge. "What are you going to say to this guy, Jack? I mean this is a topless bar not a whorehouse."

"Just leave the talking to me. Why don't you give me the petty cash now?" I held out my hand.

"Petty cash? You call this petty cash?" he pulled a thick white envelope from his breast pocket and handed it over with a sour expression, "Five thousand dollars is not 'petty cash.'"

I snatched the envelope from his hand. "I don't know what you're so worried about, this was your idea."

"Yes, but I didn't know how expensive you were going to make it. Do you really have to spend the whole five grand?"

"I'm not really sure yet how much we'll need, but if the deal does goes through, this will be money well spent." I stuffed the envelope into my own inside pocket.

"All I know is, we better get them to sign after spending this kind of dough."

"All I know is they better turn out to be as lecherous as your cousin makes out. Can you imagine if he was wrong and they turn out to be born-again Christians?"

Ed grinned for the first time since getting in the car, "If they turn out to be born-again Christians this is even more likely to work."

The car pulled up in front of the club and we got out, instructing the driver to wait. The front door was locked, but there was a sign listing a delivery address on the other side of the building. We walked around the corner, stopped at a scuffed metal door, and rang the bell. After an annoying wait, the door finally swung inward and the empty space was filled by a large, hairy man dressed in a dirty kitchen uniform. He looked us up and down.

I took a step toward him, "We're looking for Chazz Palumbo. We have a two o'clock appointment."

The man stepped back, "Chazz inside office," he muttered thickly.

We followed him through the kitchen and into the plush club with its three bars, curtained divans, and rows of runways sprouting golden poles. On the far side of the main room there was a door marked PRIVATE.

"Chazz inside." The hairy man pointed then left.

I shrugged at Ed, and rapped gently on the door.

"I'm busy in here, what the fuck do you want?" a hoarse voice shouted from inside.

Ed raised his eyebrows, and I called politely through the closed door, "We're looking for Chazz Palumbo. We have a two o'clock appointment."

"Oh shit," came the voice from the other side, "I'm sorry. Just give me a minute here."

After a few moments the door opened, and a scantily clad woman emerged. She smiled quickly and brushed past us, leaving the door open behind her.

Inside a heavy set, middle-aged man was standing behind the desk, tucking white shirttails into brown suit pants. Pulling up his fly, he walked around the desk and offered his hand. I only hesitated for a second.

"I'm Chazz Palumbo, pleasure to meet you. Why don't you shut the door and grab a seat?" He sat behind the desk and lit a cigarette.

Ed began to cough irritably and I kicked him in the shin.

Chazz leaned back in his chair and blew a couple of smoke rings at the ceiling. "So, what can I do for you fellas?"

"I'm Jack Cole and this is my associate, Ed Bloomfield."

"Cole, right, I spoke to your girl. What's up guys?"

I cleared my throat and decided with a guy like this the direct approach would be best. "We're going to be entertaining two very important clients tonight. I want to arrange VIP treatment for them. Is that possible?"

Chazz leaned forward and stubbed out his cigarette, scattering ash. "Sure it's possible. Anything's possible. What ya got in mind?"

I pulled the petty cash envelope out of my pocket and dropped it on my lap. I removed ten one hundred dollar bills and slid them across the desk, "First we want to be met at the door and ushered in as if we were your most valuable patrons."

Chazz licked his lips and grunted like a dog watching someone fill his bowl.

I counted out two thousand more. "Then I want four of your best looking girls to come and spend time with us, exclusively. Finally, I want our clients to be entertained for the balance of the evening by two of the ladies, in private. You understand what I mean?"

Chazz nodded, his eye on the stack of bills. "What's that, 'bout three grand there?"

"Unless I miscounted."

Chazz lit another cigarette. "Package like the one youse are talking about, I can't put that together for anything under five G."

I counted out five more hundred-dollar bills from the envelope on my lap and dropped them on the pile between us. "Thirty-five hundred. That's what I got." I slipped the envelope with the remainder of the cash under the table to Ed.

Chazz stuck one beefy forefinger into the stack of bills and swirled them around a bit in the center of the table. "That guy you work for, that Norton?"

"Mr. Norton?"

"He's a friend of Ronnie's?"

"Right."

"For a friend of Ronnie's I can maybe work it out for forty-five hundred."

"Chazz, man. I'm out of dough." I pated down my pockets to show how flat they were and then I turned to Ed. "Ed, how much cash you got on you?"

Ed made a show of rummaging around in the pockets of his suit, pulling crumpled hundred dollar bills from various pockets until there were five of them lying wrinkled and sloppy on top of the stack. "I think that's everything." He said when he was done.

Chazz looked a little deflated, like a fat man after a heavy exertion. "Four grand huh?"

I grinned at him, "Take it or leave it, man."

He suddenly grinned back, swelling up quickly like a lawn inflatable and scooping up the pile of cash like a Monte Carlo croupier. "I'll make it work."

Now, with the negotiation out of the way I got back to business. "Most importantly, everything should appear spontaneous. You understand what I mean?"

Chazz snorted. "Yeah, by the end of the night your clients are going to think that the girls want them for their bodies."

I shook my head and said, "Whatever." And then I did something without even thinking about it, the words just poured out of me as if I had no choice in using them. "Oh, and I was told to ask for one of your girls in particular, Lisa something, maybe Clem, something? No, no her name is Charlotte, Charlotte C," I said, trying to pull it off so Ed wouldn't notice.

"Charlotte C," Chazz said, frowning. "You don't want her, she don't put out. That's why I keep her on the stage."

"That's okay, Chazz. Only two of the girls need to put out. Ed and I won't be sampling the wares. But make sure you send Charlotte C, and don't tell her she was requested."

Chazz scratched his head as though confused. "Sure, no problem, but she don't put out, and the price is the same."

"Thank you." I tapped Ed on the shoulder and we stood.

Chazz rose with us, extending his hand again. I took it and he squeezed tight. "You gentlemen have come to the right place. It's gonna be like fantasy island in here tonight for your clients."

It never hurts performance to imply future business, so I said, "This could be the start of a wonderful relationship, Chazz. We'll be back around ten." I let go of his hand.

By six o'clock that evening my erstwhile partner Ed and I were sitting at the bar of the harbor view restaurant in The South Street Seaport, watching the sun set over Brooklyn, and anxiously awaiting the Homer Brothers. I was drinking a little scotch to try and get in the mood, while my partner toyed with a mineral water.

"You should probably have a real drink, it'd loosen you up," I said to him, "If these guys are drinkers, and you say they are, they're not going to feel real simpatico towards you unless you have a drink with them."

Ed stopped picking through the nut bowl and turned to me. "If and when they get here, I'll have a drink. Anyway, I think it's you who doesn't trust me for not drinking. Do you drink alcohol every day?"

"Fuck you, Ed."

"That's not a nice way to talk to your partner." Ed put a hand on my forearm. "Look, they're coming in now."

Ed stood up, and I pushed him back in his seat, "We're supposed to meet them at the bar. We don't want them to think we've been studying their pictures, do we?"

"But we have."

"Just play it cool, boy."

I studied the two men as they approached. They looked very much alike; both were tall, balding, and heavyset, and despite their obvious middle age, they had the jaunty strut of frat boys on the prowl.

They sat right next to us without recognition, and I decided they hadn't been studying our pictures. I didn't introduce myself right away; instead I listened as they ordered their drinks.

"Two Dewar's Rob Roy's, sweet, and tell me, do you permit cigars?"

This was the Go Go Eighties and the bartender shrugged his shoulders. As he turned to make the drinks, I pulled out a lighter and lit the guy's cigar. "You gentlemen wouldn't by chance be the Homer Bothers," I asked.

The other brother leaned in and looked me up and down, "Yes, the infamous Homer brothers. Are you Ed or Jack, or just a fan?"

I extended my hand, plastered my best shit-eating grin on my face, and thought, *what a corny bastard*. What I said was, "I'm Jack Cole, and that's not to say I'm not a

fan—"

One of them took my hand, cutting me off mid-sentence at the same time, "I'm sure you are . . . a Yankee fan."

Everyone laughed. The Homer Brothers I supposed because they were amused, and me and Ed because we were brown-nosing. The brother who had done the talking introduced himself as Winston, and I immediately pegged him for the dominant one.

The bartender placed their drinks on the bar, and John Homer lifted his glass, "I'd like to propose a toast." Ed and I dutifully hoisted our drinks while Winston grabbed a handful of nuts and grinned, "Here's to the girl who lives up the hill. She won't do it but her sister will." There was a dramatic pause before he continued, "Here's to her sister!" Everyone clinked glasses, and I decided it was going to be a long night masquerading as an idiot.

Winston glanced at his watch, "Let's grab a table and get some business in before dinner. I like to talk dollars and cents when I'm hungry, gives me an edge." He turned on his heel, and he and his brother headed for the host stand with Ed and I following in their wake.

We sat down at the table, and Winston proclaimed in a loud voice, "You know Ed, your cousin Nathan was the first Jew we ever let into our fraternity. Did you know that?"

Ed managed strained smile, "No, I didn't realize that."

"Yep, Nat the Shylock we used to call him. That was a reference to Shakespeare." He turned his gaze quickly on me, "Jack, what are your offers?"

"You want me to just jump right in?"

"What the hell, let's get down to it."

The guy was so much like a big puppy dog that I had to remind myself who he was, and to take him seriously. "Well then," I said, "If that's how you want to work it, I'll lay our position on the line. We want to buy your interest in Homer Industries and we're willing to pay a premium for it. The Stock has been trading at around thirty dollars a share for the past six months, what we'd like to do, is buy your interest, which I believe is around fifty-one percent, from you, at thirty-three dollars a share. All cash compensation."

Winston leaned back in his chair and picked up the wine list. "White or red?"

"Either one is good for me," I replied, wondering if the guy had heard a word I said.

Winston ordered a bottle of Chateau Margaux Margaux, and after it was served, fixed Ed with a stare. "Assuming we did accept your offer, what's your vision for the future of Homer Industries?"

I cleared my throat to speak, but Winston cut me off, "I'm asking Ed."

Ed shot me a look of triumph, and began to speak in measured tones, "We're naturally concerned to preserve the integrity of tradition at Homer. We believe this tradition to be the cornerstone of not just Homer's past, but also its future success. Of course we would evaluate its current operating structure to see where it could be streamlined—"

Winston cut him off with a chuckle, shaking his head, "You know, you boys have a reputation at Walsh Dahmer, and I'm sure it's deserved. The Homer family also has a reputation, which may or may not be deserved. I'm a carnivore," he proclaimed lifting his menu, "I think I'm going to have the porterhouse. Does that come with a vegetable?"

"No, just the meat," I answered. "Everything else is a la carte."

"So that means its thirty-eight dollars for the steak, and eight dollars for a baked potato? No shit?" He motioned for the waiter. "I hope you boys have some vicious amusement planned for later. You know, John and I don't come into New York that much."

We pulled up in front of Golden Dreams in the company limo. Through the tinted windows I could see Chazz Palumbo officiating over a long line of would-be patrons. He spotted us getting out of the car and rushed over smiling.

"Mr. Cole, Mr. Bloomfield, what a pleasant surprise. Step right this way," he exclaimed, ushering us past the long line.

As Chazz led us through the ropes, Winston elbowed me in the ribs and whispered loudly in my ear, "Frequent flyer, huh? That's my kinda guy."

We were led to a table front and center of the main runway, where Chazz motioned curtly for a waitress. "You see these guys?" He pointed. "Anything they want, on the house." He turned back to us. "You boys enjoy yourselves. You need anything, you just send for me."

Winston produced another of his seemingly endless supply of stogies and smiled, "May I?"

Chazz flicked open a lighter by way of answer. Then he disappeared.

Winston settled back to watch the dancers undulating across the stage while I turned my head to scan the crowd, wondering where our girls were. I didn't have to wait long. They were gliding toward the table under Chazz's watchful eye.

There were four of them, all dressed in skimpy shifts, two blondes, one brunette, and Lisa, the trip hammer of my heart. They stopped at our table, one of the blondes in front. "You boys want company?" She winked at me.

Winston popped up like a jack in the box, pulling out a chair and patting the seat. "What's your name, dear?"

She gave him her hand, and he kissed it, "My name is Cheri and this is Cassandra, Karen and Charlotte."

"Well, Cheri"—Winston licked his lips—"why don't you sit next to me and tell me all about yourself?" He called for champagne.

Lisa, A.K.A. Charlotte, scanned the group with a professional but decidedly stiff upper lip. Then her glance hit up against me and the stiff upper lip shattered to reveal a sort of shocked embarrassment. Only for a split second though, and I'm sure that I was the only one who noticed it, but there you are. I was the only one who was looking for it. Anyway I looked away first, really just glanced away because I too was embarrassed. Because I felt a little guilty, because I had contrived the meeting in the first place, so I looked away. I guess on some level in shame. And that was all it took. In the split second that I looked away she was gone, disappeared, swallowed up by the club.

An hour went by and she didn't come back. The other girls danced for the Homers, flirting and gyrating, donning and doffing their few garments, their shadows playing shapes against the walls in the flickering candlelight. I found myself shutting down, drinking steadily, and staring into the dark. Ed attempted to carry on a conversation with the brothers, I guess because that appealed to his sense of propriety. He should have saved his breath. John and Winston were distracted by the mounds of flesh before them, and only made a halfhearted return to his corporate speeches and financial drivel. About forty-five minutes into the dancing phase I noticed Chazz Palumbo scoping out the table. He showed up again about fifteen minutes later, then a few minutes after the second recon Lisa reappeared.

She sat next to me, giving me her profile, her expression icy. It was obvious she didn't want to be where she was, that she didn't like mixing with the customers—which was why, I guess, Chazz, had tried to steer me away from her. It took a couple of minutes before I even realized I was staring, and that I hadn't said a word. She seemed to be taking this in stride, regarding me with a little bemused half-smile. I leaned forward, staring straight into those wonderful eyes. They were by the way, the softest velvet brown you've ever seen.

"Lisa? It's Jack," I managed to croak out.

She smiled, showing perfectly even, white teeth. It was a dazzling smile, and she knew it. "I know, you're Chazz's big spender, and I'm supposed to be nice to you. Would you like that, Jack?"

"Don't you remember me?" I blurted out.

She laughed softly, and it was like the sound of gentle water bubbling over smooth stones. She raised her hand to my face. "Well you're not running a fever. I'm surprised at you, Jack. Anyway, I think you have me confused with someone else. My name is Charlotte."

She leaned in close and I could feel her warm, sweet breath brushing my face. Her lips were almost touching mine, and every square inch of my body felt tingly and more alive than it had felt in years.

"All you have to do is tell me what you want."

"Why don't you dance for me?" I was confused; there wasn't any doubt in my mind as to who she was.

She stood and placed her hands on my shoulders. Her hips rocked gently, inches from my face. Her shift was light green and loosely tied with a silk belt. It clung to her slender waist, and I remembered her shape, her scent.

Her hips began to sway gently as a new song began its slow opening. She lifted her hands from my shoulders and stepped back, slowly untying the silk belt, letting it hang from the loops of her shift as it fell open to reveal her breasts, full and plump and firm in the dim light. She had on sheer silk panties, and through them I could see the dark thatch between her legs was groomed in the shape of a heart.

The song picked up speed and so did her dance. She let the shift fall down around her waist, and danced closer so her breasts were within inches of my face. The urge to reach out was almost overpowering. Then she let the shift fall down around her ankles.

She turned her back to me, her long brown hair spilling almost to her waist. She wore only a thong, and her bottom was shaped like a peach. My desire was so strong it physically hurt. I held a champagne flute at my right hand, and I gulped it down wishing it were scotch. The music stopped and she fell into my lap.

"That was really nice," I lamely offered, not knowing what else to say. I don't know what I expected, but this was not it.

Laughing, she slipped off my lap and retrieved her shift. The spell was broken. I looked over to take stock of my companions. John Homer had an idiot grin plastered to his face, Ed Bloomfield sat stiffly in his chair, ignoring the woman next to him and Winston Homer spoke intently to his girl. He broke off when he saw me looking.

"Jack, I want to thank you and Ed for a truly wonderful evening. But I'm afraid we're going to have to cut it short. These two lovely ladies have expressed an interest in seeing the inside of the Plaza Hotel, and it just so happens that's where John and I are staying." He stood and extended his hand to Cheri, helping her to her feet. She whispered in his ear. He smiled, patted her hand. She grabbed the girl dancing in front of his brother and the two disappeared into the club.

John frowned, and Winston slapped his back. "Don't make such a long face, Hoss. They'll be back; they just went to get dressed so they can come back to the hotel with us."

Winston turned his gaze to me, sucked in a deep breath, and retrieved his cigar from the ashtray. "Mr. Cole, it's been a real pleasure to meet you and your partner Ed, here." He gestured with the cigar, "If you can get the price up to thirty-five dollars a share, then aside from a few other small details which the lawyers can work out, John and I are most likely agreeable." He stuck his cigar between his teeth and thrust out his hand. "We're gonna take off. You have someone run the contracts over to the hotel in the morning, and it looks like we got a deal." He turned his back for a second, picked up his briefcase, and turned to stare me in the eye, holding the gaze longer than I felt comfortable with.

I smiled and broke the stare first. Then he said something that stayed with me like a bad aftertaste.

"You know, it's strange you boys went through all this trouble to woo John and me. Everybody on The Street knows we want to cash out, you could have set this whole thing up over a simple lunch." He shook his head, chuckling. "Can't say we haven't enjoyed ourselves though."

We shook hands all around, and the Homers headed for the front door where the girls were waiting, leaving me alone with Ed, Lisa, and the remaining stripper.

As soon as they were out the door, Ed turned to me with a big smile plastered on his thin face. "We did it! We closed the deal."

I smiled back, still wondering about what Winston Homer had said. "Congratulations, Ed, I guess we're in the big time now. How about another bottle to celebrate?"

He stood up, "No, I gotta get home to the wife." He offered his hand. "Goodnight, Jack."

When Ed left, the girl who'd been sitting with him left as well, and I poured Lisa a glass of champagne. "What have you been doing all these years?"

"I told you, I'm not who you think I am."

Frustrated, I decided to play along. "Then tell me about yourself. Where are you from?"

"Virginia Beach."

"Have you been in New York a long time?"

"About three years."

"Do you like it?"

"You ask a lot of questions, Jack."

"How else am I going to get to know you?"

She gave me a mischievous smile, "I can think of other ways. What do you do for a living, Mr. Big Wheel?"

"I'm an investment banker."

"Ooh, you're making me wet," she mocked, picking up her champagne glass and running her tongue along the rim.

"You're very direct."

"I'm a stripper, and we're in a strip club. That's my job." She sounded bitter.

"You do it well. Do you enjoy your work?"

She put the glass down, "Do you enjoy yours?"

"Sometimes. I like the action, the money."

"Do you make a lot of money, Jack?"

"I'm starting to. Do you?"

"Do I what?"

"Make money?"

"Tons and tons of it, but I want to be an actress."

"So why do you do this?"

She looked strained but kept up the banter, "Money. I have expensive tastes," she said.

"Do you?"

"So do you. How much did Chazz charge you for all this?"

"Enough. Do you want to come home with me?"

"You're cute, but I'm working and I don't date men from work."

"I thought that was your job."

Her eyes flashed angrily, and she said between her teeth, "Think again. I'm a stripper, not a whore."

"What about the girls that left with my friends?"

"That's Cassandra and Cheri, and that's their business. Those were the two you paid for. Those were the two who would do that sort of thing. Karen and me, we were just here to strip and to entertain."

"So can I take you on a date?"

"I already said I don't date customers."

"Come on Lisa, why are you playing this game with me?"

"Do you have any idea how many men ask me out every night?"

"A lot."

"Yeah, a lot."

"How many of them were your college sweetheart?"

She stood to leave. "I already told you, I'm not who you think I am." She shook her head as if I was crazy, and I was starting to think I was in the twilight zone.

I couldn't just let her get away again, even though I felt like an idiot pushing the issue. She could have had any of a number of reasons for denying who she was. It didn't matter, though. I was obsessed. "I really have to see you again." God, I must have sounded desperate.

She stood up and offered me her hand. I took it between both of mine and repeated, "I mean it. I want to see you again."

"You think you could afford me?"

"Maybe."

"I dance here three nights a week. You come back and who knows? Good night, Jack." She gently extricated her hand and walked away. I stared at her retreating back. She was who I thought she was. She was lying to me.

FOUR

I arrived at Dr. Schaffer's Park Avenue office at eight A.M. on Monday morning. The décor in the waiting room was warm, wood paneling and overstuffed chairs. As cozy as they might have designed it to be, however, I still didn't feel comfortable. I'd just received too much bad news from doctors over the years, and become too cynical. The receptionist told me to take a seat and I leafed through an old copy of *Time* magazine until a blonde woman in her early thirties, sporting a white lab coat and wire frame glasses, appeared.

"Mr. Cole?"

"Yes."

She smiled, "Follow me please."

I trailed her into a small office off the hallway, and took a seat next to her desk.

She pushed a small sheaf of papers toward me. "They're just standard forms," she said, lifting one by the bottom corner. "You need to sign here, here, and here," she continued, flipping through them one by one.

I signed at all the indicated places, and then pulled out my wallet. She was checking the signatures when I pushed the check toward her.

She lifted the thing in her long nailed hands, "What's this?"

I was surprised, "That's the eight thousand dollars you said we needed, to get started."

"Didn't your father tell you?"

I was further surprised, "What are you talking about?" I said, "I don't have a father."

"Well, whatever." She said, pushing the check back toward me. "Your mother's husband, whatever you want to call him. He paid the bill."

"Barbara, listen to me. I'm going to be as clear as I can. My mother has never been married. We have no living relatives, and for the past five years she has been institutionalized with severe Alzheimer's. Nobody even visits her but me. Will you please double check your records?"

She sighed, "Okay. But it's a waste of time. He was just here a half hour before you showed up."

"Tell me about it."

"He just came in, said his name was Carl Cole, and he was the husband. I told him I'd spoken to you, and you were coming in to sign the consent forms. He said that was fine, he'd just come to pay the bill. And he did."

"He said his name was Carl Cole?"

"Yes."

"I'm sorry, I'm just very confused. Cole is my mother's maiden name, or it's just my mother's name. She was never married, like I said; it was her parents' name."

Barbara took a breath. "Isn't that peculiar?"

"Did he leave an address?"

"No, he just paid the bill."

"Well, did he pay by check? Credit card?"

"No, he paid in cash."

"Didn't that seem strange? I mean, do a lot of people come to your office bearing wads of C-notes to pay for operations?"

"I did think it was strange." Her phone buzzed. She spoke for a minute, and hung up. "The doctor is ready to see you, Mr. Cole."

I got up from the chair and paused, "Barbara, the man who paid the bill—what did he look like."

She wrinkled her brow. After a minute she said, "He actually looked a bit like you. I guess, about your mother's age, tall, like you. In fact he looked a lot like you. Only he had something about him," she frowned some more. "You know he was very powerfully built, and he had what I can only describe as a presence. Like an actor might have. He seemed larger than life."

By the time I got into my office my head was pretty twisted. Between this mystery guy, who I had to assume was, based on his actions and the nurse's description, my biological father, and Lisa's strange denial of our past, I didn't know if I was coming or going. Then there was the deal, and the meeting at Arnold Norton's office, which was going to take place in the next half hour. Well, if this guy was my father, I wasn't going to waste too much time worrying about him; he'd never seen fit to reveal himself before. If he wanted to give me secret financial help, though, I'd be more than willing to accept that. Actually, come to think of it, this was not the first time in my life that I had benefited from an unexpected windfall. Odd that a man would spend a lifetime shadowing me from the dark, provide a safety net for both me and my mother, and yet choose to never reveal himself. Of course, maybe it wasn't odd; maybe that man had something to hide, or something to lose. I thought for a moment about Arnold Norton, the coincidence of seeing him in the club, the nine thousand dollar check the next day, and now this, this deal. I pushed the flight of fancy from the forefront of my mind and continued down the bullet points of my internal agenda. Sometimes you just gotta compartmentalize.

Lisa, I was going to give it a shot. Mom, she was going to have her operation. Me, I was going to get ready for an important business meeting, and put everything else to one side.

I picked up Ed Bloomfield and we arrived together in Norton's office at ten-thirty. He welcomed us from behind his desk and apologized, saying he would need a few minutes to catch up on paperwork before we could begin. We sat on the sofa facing the desk. Me stifling yawns, and Ed bouncing his leg up and down until I stretched out a hand to quietly restrain him. It was like sitting next to a human tuning fork. Finally the great man pulled off his reading glasses and looked up.

"Very good, gentlemen, you seemed to have achieved our purposes in these papers." He gestured to the mound of stuff piled up on his desk, "Now you say the Homers have agreed to the broad strokes of our offer, and are just waiting to review the contracts with their legal staff?"

Good suck ups that we were, we nodded in unison.

Mr. Norton smiled, "Ed, I want you to get these papers sent over to the Plaza right away. As soon as the back and forth is done and we go to contract, we'll set the first installment of your bonuses in motion." He paused, staring at Ed. When Ed made no move, he said, "Ed, you go get that done right away. I need a few moments alone with Jack."

Bloomfield stood reluctantly, annoyed at being excluded. "Thank you Mr. Norton, I'm on my way." He tapped me on the shoulder. "I'll catch you later."

Once he was gone, Norton opened a humidor and took out two cigars.

"Cohiba Espandido, they're Cuban."

I smiled, thinking of the symbolism. "Contraband?"

"Indeed." They were already clipped and he leaned across the desk toward me and lit them. "You're going places, Jack," he said through a puff of smoke. "That was a neat piece of work selling the Homers. Quite frankly, I wasn't sure you had it in you."

I blew a smoke ring and considered the left-handed compliment. "It really wasn't difficult once Ed and I figured out what motivated them, and got them to like us. It's all about empathy, I guess. Anyway, the deal you're offering them is much better than they'd get anywhere else."

"Yes, but I hadn't thought of them as motivated sellers. This was actually something of a fishing expedition, and you really managed to reel them in. That's why I want to make you project manager on this." He paused obviously waiting for a reaction.

I removed the cigar from my teeth. "I'm flattered."

"Then you accept?"

"Of course."

"Okay, this is going to be your baby, soup to nuts. I'll be giving you guidance, but you'll be signing off on every transaction, and your word will be final. Have Doris contact Sandra to have all your other work reassigned to Bill Morris. I don't want you to be distracted."

"Should I be making plans to go to Ohio?"

"I don't think that will be necessary. You should be able to handle everything from New York." He opened a drawer in his desk and retrieved a business card, "I want you to go to this address tomorrow and speak with Tommy Tierney. Mr. Tierney and you will be setting up a holding company unrelated to the firm"—here he paused to give me a meaningful look before continuing—"for the purpose of issuing bonds. We'll be using those bonds to raise cash to pay off the Homers. As soon as this is done, we'll discuss the next step." He stood up straight and offered his hand in dismissal. "I'll touch base with you as soon as we get a response from the Homers. Oh, and start leaking the deal to your broker friends as soon as we have signatures, and not before."

When I got back to my office I told Doris, a grandmotherly secretary who I shared with another analyst in my department, what I needed her to do. Then I called Bill Morris and invited him to lunch. With this out of the way, I got started downloading and organizing files. Halfway through I had another of my unsettled feelings. There was still nothing in writing, no memo, nothing. I switched gears, not that I was really nervous, but because it would make me feel a little bit better. I composed two memos, one to Doris and the other to Bill Morris, both stating "As per Mr. Norton, etcetera . . ." At the end of each I CC'd Norton. Then I opened the journal I'd started and outlined recent events. With this out of the way I leaned back and began to take stock.

At thirty-one it seemed I was on my way, with a six-figure bonus, a new title, and a bright future. I could still taste the cigar in my mouth. Even though I didn't like cigars much, I knew it was the taste of success; 'Come over here dear boy, and have a cigar, you're gonna go far.'

My mind turned back to Lisa. I needed to plan my next move. I tried to focus on more practical matters, but my heart had a stranglehold over my brain, and I kept dunning myself with schoolboy questions: 'What was she doing now?' 'Might she be thinking of me?' 'What did she mean by asking if I could afford her?' And of course, all the un-answered questions revolving around my paternity that had tortured me since I could remember, all that mud on the bottom of my subconscious mind, stirred up again.

The phone rang.

"Hi Jack, its Sue."

"Hi Sue, what's up?" I sort of snapped, not liking her reality intruding on my daydreams.

"We have to talk. Can we meet for lunch?"

"Why can't we talk now?"

"I think we should discuss this face to face."

"Well, I'm booked for lunch, and I'm more than likely going to be stuck here late tonight. So if it's important, you might want to go ahead and give me some idea."

"Jack," her voice was suddenly cold, "I've met someone else, and I don't think we should continue to see one another. Now there, I've said it."

Relief flooded through my body, I was free. But for the sake of form I managed to make my voice sound stern, "How long has this been going on?"

"Nothing's been going on. It's just that my feelings have changed, or maybe it's that they've failed to evolve. And really,

I'm just trying to do the right thing. I met a guy last night, and he asked me out, and I said yes. I just don't want to do it behind your back. So you don't have to get incriminating on me. I'm actually doing you a favor."

"You're right Sue. You are doing me a favor. So I take it dinner is off on Friday?"

"Well, yes. I didn't think, under the circumstances, you would—"

"You're right again, Sue. I don't. But hey, thanks. I gotta go." I hung up without waiting for a response. My ego was actually a little hurt, but overall I felt good. I'd never really thought we were right for each other, and now freedom had come unbidden.

I picked up the phone and called the office number for the home where my mother resided. When the receptionist answered I asked for Ms. Donnelly.

"Hi Jack," she said when she finally got to the phone, "I'm sorry about your mother. What did the doctor say?"

"Well, he said the cancer is operable, and for a certain amount of money, he will spare her life."

"I know it's hard, Jack."

I sighed, Ms. Donnelly was a very nice woman, and I didn't realize how bitter I must have sounded. "No, it's all right Ms. Donnelly, she's going to be operated on Thursday, and she should be okay. I have a question for you though."

"What's that?"

"I had a strange morning. I got to the doctor's office early to pay the bill for the operation, and a man claiming to be my father had been there ahead me, and already paid for it—in cash. The funny thing is, I don't have a father. My mother never even told me the name of the man who got her pregnant with me."

"Isn't that strange?"

"I think so. It's the reason why I called. I need to know if anybody aside from me ever goes out to the home to visit her."

"Hmm, I could check the sign-in book. And Rosa might know more. Let me call you back."

At five o'clock, after clearing out my backlog of work, and with the details of the buyout pending rebuttal from the Homer legal team, I found myself with nothing to do. I was certainly done with work for the day. My plan was to go back to Golden Dreams tonight to see what headway I could make with Lisa, but they didn't open till eight, so I decided to reach out to Brad for happy hour.

When he came on the line he was his usual upbeat self.

"Jack old buddy, how are you?"

"I'm on top of the world, my friend."

"No kidding? Why? What's the dope?"

"Just closed a big deal, got a big promotion, bonus, ECT. How's by you?"

"What deal did you close?"

"Come on now Brad, you don't want me to violate SEC regulations, do you?"

"Why should I care?"

"It'd be immoral and illegal."

"Whoever said business was either?"

"You want to get a drink?"

"Sure. Top of the Sixes at six-thirty?"

"Done."

We hung up and the phone rang.

"Hi Jack, its Emma Donnelly."

"Hi."

"It turns out your mother does have another visitor, a man who shows up on the log every couple of months, sometimes more. The last time he came was the day after your mother's heart episode."

I felt a flock of birds take flight deep in my gut, "What name does he use?"

"Wilbur Sanspitiere. But let me put Rosa on the phone with you, she's met him."

"Hi Rosa, you've met Wilbur?"

"Yes, your Uncle Wilbur. He's very nice, he speaks Spanish."

"Thing is Rosa, I don't have an Uncle Wilbur. I don't know who this man is."

"That's very strange, Mr. Cole."

"You don't know where I could find him, do you?"

"No. He comes and goes. He brings flowers."

"I see. Can you do me a favor?"

"Yes?"

"If he comes again, could you call me right away?"

"Of course."

"Thank you."

I hung up and called for a 'Black Car,' one of the perks of the new position, and something I was not planning to let go to waste. Rush hour traffic was heavy on the FDR, but I still made it uptown by five forty-five. I had the driver leave me in front of Bloomingdales.

I was in the jewelry department staring into a glass case filled with gold and jewels when a pretty saleswoman confronted me. She smiled, showing even, white teeth. "Looking for a gift for that special someone?"

I stared into the glittering case, remembering a Valentine's Day years before, when I'd wanted to buy her a piece of fine jewelry, but couldn't afford it. I'd bought her a sweater instead. I smiled back at the pretty lady. "I'd like to take a look at the gold tennis bracelet in the lower left hand corner, please."

She opened the case and removed the bracelet. I turned it over in my hand and saw the price tag, two thousand dollars. I dropped my Visa on the counter, "You know what? I'll take it. Can you have it gift wrapped?"

By the time I exited Bloomie's on the Lexington Avenue side, the wind had picked up and the gray sky had gathered dark. I remembered they'd predicted snow. In the light of a newly lit street lamp, I could just make out the first flakes swirling and dancing. Turning up my collar to the cold, I hurried across the avenue. I stopped at the corner when a thin and poorly dressed woman with two children in tow stepped into my path.

"Excuse me, mister." Her voice sounded weak and wispy.

I shook my head with the natural instincts of the time and place, and made to move on. The woman stretched out a twig-like arm that barely seemed to fill the sleeve of her thin coat and lightly touched my shoulder. She fixed me with a hollow, brown-eyed stare.

"Please sir," she said, "anything you can give. I need to feed my children."

I paused and took a closer look. She couldn't have been more than twenty-five, but she looked much older. She reminded me somehow of a starving dog I'd taken in and fed as a child. When my mother came home she'd thrown the dog out and yelled at me, saying that; 'We couldn't feed all the stray dogs in the neighborhood.'

I fingered the small vanity in my pocket. How could I justify the money I'd just spent and walk away without giving her something? It felt like moral extortion. I reached in my pocket, found a twenty-dollar bill, and handed it to the woman. I still felt lame. The money was more to assuage my own conscience than to help her.

She didn't seem to care about all that though, and blessed me as I hurried briskly up the cold street, feeling almost worse than if I'd given her nothing at all.

The Top of the Sixes is a bar-restaurant situated on the top floor of 666 Fifth Avenue. Surrounded by windows, it boasts an impressive view of the Manhattan skyline. Because of its glamorous views and upscale prices, it's a favorite watering hole of the Midtown executive set. When I arrived there at six thirty-five, the place was awash in a sea of suits. Elbowing my way politely to the bar, I ordered a scotch. The first sip warmed my belly and blew the disturbing images of hungry women and children from my mind like so much smoke. After allowing myself a few minutes alone with the therapeutical waters, I began to scan the place for my buddy. I caught sight of him sitting on a window ledge, rapping with two conventionally attractive women. Catching his eye, I raised my glass. He grinned and beckoned. He was obviously proud of having the two ladies in tow, and eager to show off. I made my way toward them and pulled up a chair.

"Jack Cole, this is Betty Weisman and Patricia MacDonald, but everybody calls her Patti."

"How do you do?" I replied, smiling around the table. "Do you ladies work with Brad?"

Betty nodded, "I'm his sales assistant and Patti does cold calling. But we're both studying for the Series Seven. What do you do, Jack?"

She was pretty, and I could tell by her tone and body language, she thought I was attractive too. But there was room for nothing else in my heart just then. "I'm in banking."

"Oh really," her eyes lit up. "Commercial or investment?"

"Investment."

"Are you hiring?" she blurted out, laughing. She had a nice laugh.

"Betty!" Brad exclaimed in mock disapproval, "Really, in front of your boss too! No loyalty these days."

Patti giggled into her cocktail. "How do you know she doesn't want to get a job with Jack just so she can spy for you? Couldn't you use some inside information?"

Just silly banter but they were all enjoying it, and it made me feel important. So I made an exaggerated show of looking over my shoulder. "Sh," I put a finger to my lips, "the walls have ears. Any one of these suits could be working for the SEC."

Everybody laughed. Patti stood up, tapping Betty on the shoulder, "I'm going to the powder room. You want to come with me?"

Once the girls disappeared into the crowd Brad punched me lightly on the shoulder and leaned in whispering, "Speaking of inside information, what's the dirt on the big deal you just closed?"

I leaned in close, thinking this was how business was done, and money made, 'On the Street.' Feeling vaguely excited, I whispered, "Homer Industries. We're acquiring a controlling interest in Homer Industries. But you gotta sit on that info till I tell you to make a move. We'll all make more money that way." And just like that, without even leaving my seat, I broke the law.

A smile spread across Brad's face, "For real? I mean this isn't some kind of Greenmail thing?"

"No this is for real."

Brad put an arm around my shoulders, "Jack, old buddy, let me buy you a drink."

At ten P.M. I found myself standing in front of Golden Dreams Gentlemen's Club, fingering the small box in my pocket, and contemplating the wisdom of what I was about to do. Probably because it was Monday and snowing, there was no line out front. I sauntered unhindered to the front door. I didn't bother to ask for Chazz, I just entered anonymously, paying the admission and checking my coat like any other slob.

I sat at a table lost in the shadows near one of the smaller runways and ordered a drink. From here I could observe without being noticed, much. After a few minutes I saw Lisa, and my pulse quickened. She was dancing for a group of three overweight businessmen. This both angered and titillated me. I felt like racing across the room and beating the men with the very chairs they were sitting on, and then ravishing her on the table. I bit my lip, drawing a thin trickle of blood. I had no right to any kind of emotion. Not yet. I had to be cool.

A woman came and asked me if I wanted a dance. I turned her down, and as she walked away, I recognized her as one of the girls from the night before. I sipped my scotch and watched Lisa, as she flowed, liquid, like water, around the table of drooling heart attack candidates. I downed my scotch and motioned for another. The thick, smoky, iodine taste burned my tongue and warmed my belly. Why couldn't I let go of this woman when there were so many others to be had for the asking?

Maybe a good psychiatrist would say it was because of Mother. Mother who, at this moment, was probably staring vacantly at a dark wall. Yes, the shrink would ask me about my childhood and after awhile my resistance would break down. I'd tell him how I'd never known my father, and how my mother worked two jobs to support me. How she'd had a succession of boyfriends. How one night, when I was ten years old, I'd crept out of bed in the middle of the night and seen my mother dancing for one of those men. Yeah, the shrink would tell me it was because of my mother. Well, I already fucking knew that.

Lisa stopped dancing, and one of the men at the table put a bill in her G-string. Another wave of anger swept over me like a hot wind. I put it in check. I had no right to the emotion.

As Lisa walked away from the table, I saw the girl I'd just turned down for a dance whisper in her ear. She smiled, that faith-inspiring smile of the angel slut. Turning my way, she flowed toward me like quicksilver.

I placed the gift-wrapped package in front of me on the table. She looked down, smiled, the soft light played off her auburn hair.

"You want a dance, Jack?"

I leaned forward, out of the shadows. "How much?"

She laughed. "I didn't think money was an object for you."

I drained the scotch from my second drink and rattled the ice. "How much?'

She stretched. "Twenty dollars."

"I'll tell you what"—I pushed the gift towards her—"you can have this, or you can have the twenty. It's up to you."

She picked it up and weighed it daintily in her hand. "Umm, a mystery. What's in this box is worth a lot more than twenty dollars. Isn't it?"

"A token of my admiration and affection. What do you say?"

She let her shift fall to the floor as a new song began.

When the dance ended she sat next to me. She was so close I could smell her perfume. It was light, pleasant, and familiar. Carefully, she untied the bow and neatly sliced the wrapping paper with her fingernail. She opened the lid and let out a small gasp as the contents were revealed.

She leaned forward and tapped me on the cheek, "This is the nicest gift I've ever been offered."

"I never forgot you—" I started to say, ready to pour out the contents of my heart on to the zinc oxide table top.

She placed a finger on my lips before I could get out the words. "Tomorrow night, Six o'clock. Meet me at the Plaza Hotel in the Oak Room Bar."

Without another word she got up and started to walk away from the table, but she turned back. She stood over me, weighing the small box in her hand and staring. I returned her gaze and saw something I hadn't seen the last time—pain, pain and vulnerability. A glimpse of the girl I remembered behind the sensuality. She placed the box carefully back down in front of me and turned away again, this time disappearing into the crowd. Bemused, I picked up the box and opened it. The bracelet was still inside.

FIVE

Tommy Tierney's office was on Front Street, about a block away from Jeremy's Alehouse. The street in front of the dilapidated old building was all cobblestone and tar and the place looked like it should have been condemned. I climbed four flights up and knocked on 4B, where a brass plate proclaimed TIERNEY AND ASSOCIATES. The door opened and I immediately came to the conclusion that if he did have associates, he would have had nowhere to put them. I assumed Tommy himself opened the door because the room was so small it barely fit him. There was a desk, two chairs, a safe, a couple of file cabinets, a beat up shade covering a dirty window, and an old stoop-backed man in a dusty suit.

I stuck out my hand, "Mr. Tierney?"

He smiled at me, and at once I realized why I was there. The clear blue eyes in the craggy face were steady, alert, intelligent, and deeply corrupt. "Yes," he said, "and you are?"

"I'm Jack, Jack Cole," I offered, "I work for Arnold Norton."

"Ah," he responded, "the new boy. Please"—he gestured elegantly toward one of the two chairs—"sit down." As I complied he situated himself behind the desk. An old black, rotary phone right next to him started to ring. He ignored it, staring at me, sizing me up, while the phone rang and rang. It rang more than twenty times before it stopped, and he finally spoke. "So, what brings you to me?"

"I need to set up a holding company."

He leaned back in his chair, tapping his cheek with a pencil. "A holding company, simple. There must be something else."

I cleared my throat, "There is to be a two hundred million dollar bond issue generated by the holding company."

He sat up straight in his chair. "No small amount," he said in a soft voice.

The silence hung in the air for a while. During this time I noticed a clock ticking on the wall, and the sound of my companion's labored breathing. Finally, he began to speak. "Who will buy the Chinese Paper?"

"It's contracted to a broker at Bachman Securities."

"Then what happens?"

"Bachman buys the bonds, and the cash is used as consideration in a deal to buy fifty-one percent of Homer industries."

"How many days has Bachman agreed to hold the paper?"

"I don't know."

"Who buys the paper from Bachman?"

"I don't know."

"Right." He pulled some forms from his desk drawer. "I need you to fill these out, and then have them notarized. When does the transaction need to take place?"

"As soon as possible."

"What's the name of the broker over at Bachman?"

"Johnny Canella."

"Him, makes sense," the old man muttered under his breath. "You can fill those out now. When you're done, there's a notary over on John Street by the Yankee Clipper." He looked at his watch, "If you hurry, we can file by noon."

I stood up and offered my hand. "Nice to meet you, Mr. Tierney."

He took my hand and held it, staring into my eyes, "How long," he asked, "have you been working at Walsh Dahmer?"

"About three years," I replied, releasing the tension from my hand, hoping he would let it go. But he held on.

He stared rather too intensely into my eyes. "Do you like it, Jack?"

I pulled back gently on my hand hoping to regain possession of it. "It's really great," I said.

Rather than letting go, Tierney flapped a second thin hand over mine from the other side, so now he was holding my hand with both of his. "You know, I myself worked at Walsh Dahmer, back when it was Walsh Dahmer, and Palmer. Back before Norton married old man Walsh's daughter. Back before Palmer found himself dead."

I felt uncomfortable and I wanted to go, but at the same time I felt drawn in to the conversation. "Those," I said, "must have been interesting times."

"They were." His voice came out in a coarse whisper like it was filtered through sandpaper. "You said your name was Cole,

Jack Cole," he muttered almost to himself, and then suddenly speared me with his eyes. "Are you any relation to Monique Cole?" he asked in a demanding tone.

My heart skipped. "I'm her son."

Tierney nodded but not at me, to himself as if some puzzle piece was falling into place.

"Did you know my mother?" I asked, almost too eagerly.

He suddenly dropped my hand. "Yeah," he muttered, "I knew your mother. I can even remember you when you were just a baby." He made a point of looking at his watch. "You better hurry up and file those papers, Jack. We're running out of time." He turned back to his desk, dismissing me.

"Wait," I said. "Did you know my father?"

He looked slowly back at me over his shoulder and fixed me with one alert, watery blue eye. "Your father, Jack? Why would I know your father?"

"Because you knew my mother."

"Just be thankful you knew your mother, boy. Be thankful and be careful. Some bones are better left buried." He turned his back and once again began to busy himself with papers on his desk. I stood for a few more minutes under the arch of his crumbling door, but when it became clear that I would get no more I left.

Later that afternoon I sat next to my buddy Ed at the long conference table, gazing across the broad expanse of mahogany at Norton, Grunley, and Petersen, a trio of inscrutability. Arnold Norton leaned forward, staring intently at us. There was a full minute of uncomfortable silence before he began.

"You're going to have to make two filings with our friends at the SEC. One to indicate the intention of Dano Corp. to acquire a controlling interest in Homer Industries, and the other is a requirement for debt issuance, high yield junk bonds. You don't have to worry about underwriting. We're going to do that in house.

Ed made a note on a pad in front of him. "We're going to do this through Walsh Dahmer?" he inquired.

Norton shook his head, "No, Through Dano Corp., a financial holding company, with Walsh Dahmer acting as investment banker."

Ed did some more scribbling. "I see. Who is going to be purchasing the bonds?"

Mr. Norton made a face, "We've arranged with a friend at Bachman Securities to purchase the Chinese paper, under the stipulation that these instruments be bought back from him at twenty percent over his price within three months."

I decided to ask a question, just to show that I was on the ball. I coughed, and Norton looked in my direction. "That stipulation is written into the debt covenant?"

The three Easter Island statues on the other side of the table looked at me as though I'd just farted, and I wished I'd kept my mouth shut. Finally Norton said, "No, of course not. This is a gentleman's agreement."

I guessed Ed hadn't noticed that the environment wasn't particularly friendly to questions, because he looked up and asked, "How do we guarantee that we can re-sell these debentures? I mean the market for junk bonds isn't particularly liquid."

Mr. Norton suddenly grinned, "Ed, you haven't done your due diligence. I'm surprised at you!"

Ed's ears turned red, "I have carefully analyzed the . . ."

"Jack, tell him about the pension fund," Norton exclaimed with the air of a conjuring magician.

As project manager, I'd been briefed on this aspect of the scam just before the meeting. And a scam is what it was, though in my callous ignorance, I didn't fully appreciate it at the time. Not to say I shouldn't have. I was just so blinded by my overnight success that I didn't see too clearly, or didn't want to.

What I said was, "Ed, the pension fund is way overfunded, and there's enough in its portfolio to more than cover the cost of buying up those junk bonds."

Ed dropped his pencil and leaned back in his chair. He pushed his glasses all the way up the bridge of his nose. "I really don't see how that's going to work. I don't mean to appear condescending, but I am going to have to refresh your memories on pension accounting." He cleared his throat, waiting for a challenge, and when no one interrupted, he continued.

"The calculation of pension funding is based on the historic return for safe investments. Actuaries determine the future liabilities of the fund, based on the likely rate of return on T-bills, or top AAA rated corporate bonds. And because for defined benefit obligation plans this is standard across all industries, there are strictures regarding what corporate pension plans can hold as assets. These strictures are not only generated by the governing bodies of public accounting, but are in accordance with state and Federal law. I might also add that in the case of this particular fund, it is set down in the contract between the employees and the employer." Ed took a deep breath and wiped his forehead.

Mr. Petersen, who had been leaning forward with blood in his eye ever since Ed's diatribe began, nodded. "Thank you for that quick overview of pension accounting, Mr.

Bloomfield. It's always helpful to be reminded of what we pay you for. Yes under all the aforementioned strictures, the allowance inside the portfolio for junk bond investment only adds up to ten percent of the total pension assets. And what, you may ask, about the other ninety percent?" He turned and smiled at me. It was not a nice smile. "Mr. Cole, will you please enlighten Mr. Bloomfield as to how we pry the other ninety percent loose."

I was uncomfortable, but taking my cues. "Ed, are you familiar with Guaranteed Investment Contracts?"

He sniffed. "I've heard the term."

"A GIC is a promise, by someone the law recognizes as a qualified guarantor, to pay a sum certain in money, on a specific date. A pension fund may, legally, count a GIC as an investment grade bond. All we have to do is get someone to stamp our junk bonds as GICs, and we're in the clear. And Ed, that's not hard to do."

Ed took off his glasses and rubbed the bridge of his nose, "I see. This is what they call the creative finance. What happens if and when these junk bonds default?"

"There's no reason why they should. And as long as they remain in the portfolio they're held at historical cost," Mr. Norton explained as he reached in his pocket and removed two envelopes. "These are the first installments on your bonuses, gentlemen. There will be three installments, the first two for thirty thousand, and the final payment for forty thousand."

He pushed them across the table and continued, "You'll notice they are unsigned. Mr. Cole is the project manager, and the signature on the account." He looked directly at me. "Cole, you may sign them now. This is what they mean when they say 'write your own ticket,' my boy."

Instead of entering the Oak Room through the hotel lobby, I strolled up Central Park South to the side entrance and peered in the big, bay window. Inside older wealthy men sat in deep leather chairs talking to one another, or to younger, attractive women. I didn't see Lisa, and for a moment I wondered if she would stand me up.

The bar was crowded, but I managed to find a seat where I sat for a while before the old man in the white dinner jacket decided to notice me. He might not have been impressed with my new suit. Someone once told me that these bartenders worked here for decades, and took home upwards of fifteen hundred a week. I wondered briefly how many guys like me they'd seen over the years on the way up, and on the way down.

Finally, the stooped-back bartender crab-walked over to me and deftly flipped down a cardboard coaster, "Evening sir. What's your pleasure?" He had a faint accent, and grinned in a way it was impossible not to like.

"A bottle of good champagne and two glasses. Someone's joining me."

He gave me an amiable shrug. "You want to see the wine list?"

I took a deep breath, "You have Dom Perignon?"

"Sure."

"I'll take it."

After twenty minutes I began to seriously wonder if I'd been stood up for real, but then I saw her. First in the mirror behind the bar, and rather than turn around, I studied her reflection as she made her way through the crowd. Even dressed demurely, in an Irish knit sweater and long, pleated wool skirt, she turned heads all over the room.

She pecked me on the cheek, and a flock of butterflies took wing in my stomach. I hadn't felt this way in a long time.

"Been waiting long, Jack?" she inquired, knowing damn well I had, but looking into my eyes for the first time with recognition of who I was to her.

I stood and offered my stool, as the previously desultory bartender now rushed to pour champagne. "All my life," I answered.

She looked me straight in the eye, "You just wouldn't be put off, Jack. Just couldn't let well enough alone." Flashing eyes, but passionate, not angry.

I shook my head. "No."

Her demeanor softened. "Well Jack Cole, you certainly have gone to a lot of trouble to get me here. I wonder what you want."

"I thought it was obvious."

"I don't think it's obvious even to you." She took a sip of champagne. "Dom Perignon." She smiled sideways. "Are you getting in over your head?"

"You seem so cynical," I replied. "Why did you come?"

She laughed. "Curiosity."

I was starting to feel insecure, like I had ten years before. I hesitated a moment, then decided not to fence. "That's all?" I asked.

She followed me, dropped the bantering tone. "Maybe more like I'm surprised you don't hate me." She looked down.

Win, lose, or draw, this woman had colored my worldview for the last third of my life. "Why did you pretend not to know me?"

"I wouldn't have chosen to see you again, not in the way you found me. We didn't leave each other on the best terms. I don't know what it is you want from me . . . For lots of reasons it just seemed best to put you off." She looked deep into my eyes. "Why wouldn't you be put off, Jack?"

Time to roll the dice, time to be real, I thought. "You really want to know?" I asked.

She inclined her head slightly and crossed her legs, her skirt falling away to reveal a muscular calf above the boot. For a moment I just stared, scripting a response, and then I went ahead and said the first thing that occurred to me.

"See, I never got over you. I don't mean I put my entire life on hold. I've had relationships . . . the thing is . . ." I broke off, pushed my face closer to hers, locked in her eyes, and then continued. "I never told any other woman 'I love you.'"

The look in her eyes took a deeper dive. "I'm sorry if I hurt you," she said.

Something snapped back in my head. It wasn't what I wanted, to bring her down. I knew it wasn't a good strategy. "It wasn't your fault," I said. "It wasn't our time. Looking back I can see how much I was smothering you. I just want you to know . . ." I paused, cast about in my head for a way to express myself. "That wasn't really me. At the time I was just so blown away that a girl like you would even look at me, that I just couldn't trust it. I saw it disappearing all the time."

She stared into her crystal champagne flute. "And now it's different?"

I waited for her to lift her eyes, and then said, "I've begun to trust the things that life is offering me."

She held my gaze. "And you think that I am one of those things?"

I broke eye contact first. "I didn't mean it that way."

"It's okay," she smiled, "it remains to be seen what you get from life, and what you get from me, Jack Cole. Where are we going for dinner?"

The Water's Edge was a restaurant built on a stationary barge in the East River. It was on the Queens side in Long Island City and in order to reach it from Manhattan you had to take a ferry that was provided by the restaurant. It had two stars from the *New York Times* and afforded something no Manhattan eatery could, the Queens perspective on the New York skyline. It could be difficult to get a table any night during the summer, but during the colder months it was much quieter. I slipped the Maître d' a twenty and he gave us a table by the window.

We were in the midst of a very cold winter and parts of the river had frozen over. As Lisa and I sat there sipping cocktails, we watched the ice floes drift down the river in the dark. I reached across the table and took her hand. "You don't wear any jewelry?"

She shrugged. "That's because I don't have any worth wearing."

"Why didn't you take the bracelet?"

"Because my mother told me not to accept gifts from strangers." She gave me a lopsided grin. "I don't take advantage; let's get to know each other again first, okay?"

Subtlety has never been one of my strong points. That, coupled with a lack of patience, caused me to weigh in with both feet and blurt out, "Why did you take a job dancing at the club?"

She seemed to shrink in on herself, to almost squirm. It was the last thing I had wanted and immediately I regretted the question. "I just don't have a choice right now," she said.

"Everyone has a choice," I replied, foolishly compounding my mistake as if I wasn't in control of my mouth.

Her body went rigid. "You're being facile, naïve, and smug. You just don't know." The words rapped out of her mouth like slaps on a taut drum-skin. I winced inwardly.

I jumped into damage control mode. "We can change the subject."

"You've changed," she said and it was declarative.

"Really?"

"Yes, different. It's hard to put a finger on, subtle. More confident I'd say, but also less hopeful."

"What exactly do you mean by that, less hopeful?"

"Just what I said," she waved a hand. "See one of the things I liked most about you, maybe what most attracted me to you back then, was your sense of possibility. I always thought it was part of what made you vulnerable. I mean, you were intelligent enough to know that possibilities could go the other way, but you were still so full of hope."

I shook my head, confused. "Did you ever love me?"

Her eyes tunneled, like they were drifting far away, but fast and straight. "I did, and that's why I left you."

I looked deliberately past her, out to the black churning water on the other side of the windowpane. "That doesn't make any sense to me."

She took in a subtle breath that I noticed, then said, "Maybe not, but you had a lot you needed to accomplish, and you were obsessed with me. Eventually, that obsession would have destroyed you. I had to cut you off like a drunk at a bar."

"Really?" I was a bit incredulous. "May I also say that you too have changed?"

"Of course. It's been ten years. I'm not eighteen anymore. But I'm curious, how do you think I've changed?"

I let my reaction speak without consulting my brain. "Harder, edgier, but also less hopeful, if you don't mind my saying so."

Her body went tight and rigid again. "I get that, but I'm also sure your assessment is clouded by the context in which you found me."

I just nodded.

She relaxed a little and leaned forward. "It's sitting like a rock between us, the place where you found me." She paused, waiting for a response. When I didn't give her one, she said, "It's been a bad year for me."

"Is that how long you've been dancing?" I asked in a neutral voice.

She nodded.

"Do you like it?"

"No. I despise it," she answered quickly.

"Then why—"

She cut me off. "I already told you, I don't have a choice."

I looked deep into her brown eyes. "Why don't you have a choice?"

She pulled in a deep breath. "Do you want to hear my story?"

"Yes."

Now she did the opposite of tensing. Her whole body seemed to sag, like her bones had turned to jelly. When she lifted her head and took my gaze there were tears in her eyes, but I could also tell she was ready to talk. "There was a man, I suppose there always is. He's actually a brilliant playwright, but he's not a very good man." She shook her head. "I'm getting ahead of myself. When you left Hofstra, I changed my major to drama. I decided to become an actress. I came to Manhattan after graduation, to land a starring role in a Broadway show. Remember when we saw *42nd Street*? I think that's the day I took the notion. So it's actually all your fault."

I smiled. The memory was a good one.

"Anyway, when I got here, I took an apartment on the Lower East Side and immersed myself in the bohemian lifestyle. I took a job as a waitress, and acted in off-Broadway shows, and that's where I met Carl. I was cast as the lead in a play he wrote called *Apple Time*. It really was a wonderful play, and it got rave reviews. Overnight Carl became the literary lion of my whole social circle. Everyone thought he was the second coming of Neil Simon. To make a long story short, we became lovers, and when my Aunt Nancy passed away and left me some money, he talked me into investing it in one of his shows. The show actually did well. It made money, but the cash kept disappearing. And finally, so did he. But there were still bills to pay, and I desperately needed to recover my investment, so I borrowed money to keep it going, hoping that would happen. I didn't realize at the time that the play had reached a point of diminishing returns. It had already made all the splash it was going to, and we began to play to smaller and smaller crowds. In the end I lost not only my own money, but also the money I'd borrowed."

"Who did you borrow the money from?"

"That was the problem, actually. You see I didn't borrow from the bank. I borrowed from a guy in the West Village, the kind of guy you have to pay back, or else."

"How much did you borrow?"

"Twenty thousand at four points a week. That's eight hundred in vig I have to pay every week, and that's just to break even. It doesn't pay down the principal at all. I couldn't make that kind of money waitressing, not and have anything left to live on. So I had to figure something out. One of the girls who was in the show was also a dancer, and she suggested I try it. What else could I do? I'm not a bank robber."

"Wow. You still owe the money."

"If I didn't I wouldn't be dancing."

"If you paid him off, would that get you free?"

"Yes."

"I'm sorry." It was all I could think of to say.

The dinner came and went, and the conversation drifted through memories, and news of old friends, and here and there, and everywhere.

Two hours later as the ferry pulled into the dock under the FDR Drive, she took my hand and pulled me close. I hadn't been all that aggressive all night, mostly because I didn't want to scare her off, but now I took the hint. I wrapped my arms around her, and we kissed. Her lips were full and soft, like I remembered. Kissing her felt natural, as if her lips were made for mine, or at least with me in mind, and time had stood still, and we were still nineteen. Her mouth opened and our tongues entwined. Her breath was sweet, tasting of chocolate mousse and breath mints. I held her tight, not wanting to let her go, even as the boat docked.

She suddenly stopped as I led her up the gangplank, tugging me back. "I want to spend the night with you." She sounded oddly shy, nervous.

"You do?" I was surprised.

"I do." She sounded confident again, "I want to investigate the habitat of the North American Yuppie."

I hesitated, remembering the shitty one bedroom I lived in for a thousand a month. I couldn't take her there. That wasn't part of the image I'd been cultivating.

"Sure, but my apartment's being painted. Why don't we get a room at the Plaza? You can leave your sociological field work for another day."

SIX

A lot happened over the course of the next week. Mom pulled through her operation with flying colors. The Homer deal went to contract, and all the financing and backroom dealing was in motion. On a deeper level for me, I had two more dates with Lisa, the old feeling really rekindling. The only issue was, I still hadn't taken her to my apartment. Instead we kept going to the Plaza and she had to be beginning to suspect I was married, or hiding something. But I planned to put an end to that speculation before it reached critical mass. I had an appointment set up with a real estate agent. I was going to put a down payment on a luxury condo and have done with it.

So really, except for the frustration I felt at having come so close to a revelation about my father's identity, everything was going swimmingly for me. Everything, that is, except Ed Bloomfield. Ed had been acting strangely. He was getting thinner and looking haggard. It was very possible, I thought, that he could rock the boat, especially after the conversation I had with him on the morning we went to contract. The door to my office had been open and Ed stuck his head in.

"Jack, you got a minute?"

I looked up from between the stacks of paperwork and nodded.

He stepped in, closed the door, and took the opposing seat at my desk. He remained silent for so long that I decided to break cover first. "Well?"

"I need to know something, Jack," he said in a strained tone.

No good could come of his moral ambivalence. He both annoyed and concerned me. He also made me feel guilty, like I was less of a man because I wanted to keep my eyes shut. "What's that, Bloomfield?" I asked tersely.

He locked his judgmental eyes into mine. "Are you comfortable with the way the Homer deal is being structured?"

I took a deep breath and dissembled, "I don't take your meaning."

"I think it's a scam. I think it's immoral and illegal. I don't think I can go through with it."

I leaned back in my chair. It was worse than I thought; I could see my whole career going up in smoke. I was on the verge of enough—enough to take care of my mom, enough to woo Lisa properly. I was in a lifeboat heading for dry land, and Ed was planning to bore a hole that would sink us all. I needed to talk him off the ledge.

"Ed, you've got to put this thing in perspective. Its just business. Nobody's going to get hurt, not unless you do something rash. We're not taking over Homer to destroy it."

"We're not?" Ed demanded, his voice dripping with sarcasm.

I avoided his eyes, "No, we're going to make it more profitable," I replied in a soft voice.

He fixed me with a cold stare, "You know what's happening here, and you can't be that stupid. We set up a separate company to make that bond issue. A legitimate company buys the bonds themselves. Then we're going to sell to another company just a few months down the road. The first company makes a few payments then goes bankrupt and defaults on the bonds. The third company gets spun off and since its only assets are these worthless bonds, they go under too. The pension fund loses about ninety percent of its value and the remainder is swallowed up in legal fees. You think this is right?"

I sighed. "Dude, this deal is going down with or without us. If you cause a problem, you're only going to destroy yourself. Think of your family. Not only that, but our firm is a reputable one. There's no way Walsh Dahmer would willfully engage in something like you just described."

"Are you really that naïve, Jack?"

I gripped Ed's shoulder. "We're not doing anything wrong, old buddy." I felt dirty like I was lying to Ed. Lying to myself.

After Ed left I sat staring at the wall for a long time, and then I opened my journal and made a record of the conversation.

At four P.M., contracts signed and wire transfers confirmed, the Homers and their legal team left the conference room. A controlling interest in Homer Industries now officially belonged to Dano Corp., the holding company that I had created.

Mr. Norton removed a gold pocket watch and flipped open the cover, "Congratulations, gentlemen, I'm going to authorize Mr. Cole to issue the second bonus payments."

Mr. Grunley coughed. "Your final payments will be released when you have restructured the Homer pension fund to include the GICs derived from Dano Corp.'s junk bond issue." He beamed down the long conference table, "I'd like to see that done by the end of the month."

I looked over at Ed. He'd been very quiet all during the lengthy closing. Now I could see his thin, pale hands noticeably shaking. I really began to worry, not for myself, or the deal, but for him. He suddenly stood, overturning a chair. Inside I cringed. "Gentlemen, I have been trying to control myself now for the past week. I've been telling myself, lying to myself, 'this is the big leagues.' 'This is just business.'

I stared at him, aghast. Ed's voice was alternating high and low, like a kid going through puberty, "But I cannot justify it to myself!" he continued. "I know that many questionable things occur on Wall Street and by and large, I don't make judgments. But this is just wrong. This deal is going to affect the pensions of thousands of people who've worked years for them."

"Be careful what you're saying Bloomfield," Mr. Petersen cut in. "It's slanderous and insulting. If you'd like to resign your position with the firm, I don't foresee any objections."

Mr. Norton put his hand soothingly on Mr. Petersen's shoulder. "Take it easy, Dick," he said, before turning back to Ed. At this point Ed looked as shocked with himself as anybody else in the room. "Mr. Bloomfield," Norton began, keeping his hand on Petersen's shoulder. "I fear you've arrived at an erroneous conclusion regarding the finances on the Homer project. These Guaranteed Investment Contracts are exactly what they purport themselves to be, guaranteed. The junk bonds that constitute the contracts are high yield. Indeed, rather than having a negative impact on the Homer pension fund, these contracts will substantially increase its value."

Mr. Grunley nodded his agreement, and said, "And Bloomfield, if you have any concerns regarding conflict of interest, remember we have set up different—"

Ed cut him off, "I'm sorry, gentlemen." He picked up his briefcase and stood from the table. "I'm a CPA, I'm not a child. With or without legal ramifications, the whole thing is immoral. I'm returning to my office to clean out my desk and tender a formal resignation. Good day, gentlemen."

Ed swept out of the room, seemingly restored to his normal steadiness and color, like that which had been sapped away lately had been restored. For a good few minutes the room remained silent. I spied the faces of the white shoe investment bankers by whom I was surrounded; they betrayed no emotion. Like watching a man bare his soul was something they saw every day.

I wrestled with my own emotions and finally concluded that Ed was a fool, a fool throwing away a job, a bonus, and possibly a career. The boss men at Walsh Dahmer were unforgiving. After offending them the way he had, Ed stood a good chance of spending the balance of his career filling out tax returns at an H&R Block franchise somewhere in Brooklyn. Even so, I had a sneaking admiration for the man's courage. He saw something that went against his values and he wanted no part of it.

It was Norton who broke the silence, "It seems Mr. Bloomfield is having difficulty reconciling his conscience with the reality of the business arena. I think we all applaud his sensibilities but, at the same time, agree they are far too delicate to be practicable in a competitive business environment." He looked at me "Mr. Cole, are you ready to continue alone?"

I didn't hesitate. Even though I'd experienced pangs of conscience when Ed made his speech, I needed to keep things in perspective. I was staying on the team. I mean, I'd climbed onto the field to be a player and, if this was what it took, I was game. Besides, I was meeting with the real estate broker in just a few hours and I needed the bonus. If I'd known then what I know now, I'd have taken my chances with Ed out in the real world, but what I said was, "I'm a company man. Ed Bloomfield notwithstanding, I'll complete the job I've undertaken."

Norton surprised me by coming down to my end of the table and sitting next to me. "I think we're all glad to hear that, Jack." He said. "I understand you're looking to buy a condo?"

I was taken aback, wondering how Norton knew this. Then I realized that the real estate company must have called the firm for references. "Yes, I am. In fact, I'm meeting my broker tonight to look at a place."

Mr. Norton reached in his pocket and produced a business card. "This is the card of a very close friend. He was a frat brother of mine at Harvard. Now he's the president of the Cross-town Savings Bank. Give him a call once you've settled on a place, and he'll have a very favorable mortgage approved for you the same day."

Ed Bloomfield left the meeting and immediately went to his office to clean out his desk. There wasn't much to take: some papers, various odds and ends, a picture of his wife and daughters. He stared at the picture before stuffing it into his briefcase. Going home to break the news of his resignation to his wife was a grim prospect. He loved his wife, but she would think his moral reservations about the takeover stupid, and she would be angry. Whether he chose to admit it or not, Ed was desperately afraid of his wife. Not that he didn't love her, he did—but he walked on eggshells around her.

Now, Ed wasn't a heavy drinker, but he did enjoy an occasional touch of gin. And he couldn't bear the thought of going straight home to Mrs. Bloomfield. In fact Ed didn't plan to go home tonight until after he'd had the chance to tie one on. After ten years of working for Walsh Dahmer, and after ten years of going straight home, Ed was going to do something out of character. Ed was going to stop for a drink . . . or two . . .

Ed hurried across town from Chambers Street, lugging his overstuffed briefcase. He passed by the legion of little Irish bars that dotted the area, and glanced dubiously at his watch: five-thirty. This was happy hour, and too close to the office. He didn't want to be in a crowded bar, and he didn't want to have to talk to anyone he knew.

He hit Fulton Street and decided to follow it all the way down to the Seaport. On a Monday night in the dead of winter, the Seaport would be quiet. He went to Pier 17 and, on the second level of the mall, found a restaurant with a reasonably quiet bar. Dropping a twenty on the wood, Ed ordered a gin and tonic.

The bartender put the drink in front of him. Without looking up, Ed sucked it down and ordered another. The bartender shook his head, fixed another, and stood waiting to see what Ed would do. This time he just took a sip.

The barman put Ed's money in the till, laying the change on the counter in front of him. "You must have really needed that drink bad, mister," he said.

Ed stirred his drink and eyeballed the man behind the bar. "I just quit my job and my wife's going to kill me."

"Well, why'd you do it?"

"Spur of the moment." He drained his glass. "May I have another?"

The bartender fixed another, laid it in front of him. "This one's on me."

The door opened with a creak, and Ed saw a tall, lean, middle-aged man in a suit walk in, an overcoat slung over one arm. Despite the emptiness of the bar, he took the stool next to Ed.

"Pernod"—he held up his thumb and forefinger, slightly parted—"and this much water, little ice." As the bartender moved to fill his order, the man turned to Ed. "It looks like snow. I heard on the radio that it's supposed to be a big storm." His accent was vaguely European, maybe French.

Ed gestured for another drink. "I like snow. Makes things seem cleaner. In a city as dirty as this one, it's nice when things at least *look* clean."

The newcomer smiled wistfully, "I've seen many cities, much dirtier, and some where it never snows."

"I know it's not so bad here. I'm just feeling melancholy tonight." He stood up, extending his hand. "My name's Ed."

The newcomer accepted his hand. "And I am Roget or, if you prefer, Roger. Why so melancholy, Ed?"

Ed looked straight down into his gin and tonic. "Because I just quit the job where I've worked for the past ten years."

"I suppose you will miss it."

"No, I probably won't miss it. I never really liked it all that much. Something about being an accountant and working in an office. You know? Dealing in symbols of reality instead of reality, it always seemed strange, surreal. But I still have to pay the mortgage and save for my children's education, so I guess I'll just have to find somewhere else to sell my skills."

"One place is so much like another," Roget mused.

Ed nodded thoughtfully. "That's true, though it'll be tough to match my salary."

"So why'd you quit? Angst? Mid-life crisis?"

"No. It was a moral issue. You know how they say everybody has a price?"

Roget raised an eyebrow. "Hmm . . ."

Ed's face narrowed to a sharp point focused once again on the gin and tonic sitting before him on the bar-top. "Well, I don't believe that. Some people definitely do have a price. But if you know better, and you want to be a decent man and live comfortably with yourself, then you don't have a price. Not for certain things."

Roget nodded sympathetically. "I see. What was it they asked you to do?"

Ed broke up his staring contest with the gin and tonic and looked Roget right in the eye. "Basically what it came down to was to scam thousands of people out of their pensions."

Roget gestured for another round. "And did they offer you a price?"

"A hundred thousand."

"That wasn't enough?"

"When I really thought about it, the amount wasn't the issue. I just couldn't do it."

Roget put a finger to his lips and pointed to some tables away from the bar. "Perhaps I can help. I know some people who might be interested in your story. Let's go over there and finish our conversation in private."

I arrived at The Water Tower around six-thirty. The real estate agent was waiting and rushed out to greet me as the driver opened the door to the corporate Black Car. I felt like a million bucks.

"Hey, Jack." The agent grinned like he was genuinely happy to see me. "I'm Jeff Cronin from City Lights. We spoke over the phone."

We shook hands. Jeff was tall and skinny, and his hand was sweaty in spite of the cold. I looked up at the Water Tower. The building was tall, maybe thirty stories high. The nearby structures, though very elegant, were nowhere near as large, giving credence to the moniker of *tower.*

"The apartment we're going to look at Jeff, what floor is it on?"

"The top. It has magnificent views of the river, two bedrooms, one and a half baths, and a sunken living room. Maybe I should just let it speak for itself," he concluded as we entered the vestibule and he shook hands with the superintendent.

The super gave him the keys, shook my hand, and then we were in the elevator that was both elegant and obviously designed to complement the huge marble hallway.

"Where are you living now?" Jeff asked as we ascended.

"Uptown, pre-war tenement, walk up," I replied in real estate speak.

"You must have had a big change in circumstances to be looking to buy something like this."

"Yes."

The elevator opened on a small hallway with two doors on either end. We went to the door labeled 31B, and Jeff fumbled a key into the lock.

We entered a small foyer, went down four steps to a short hall that opened out to a sunken living room before branching off into another hall. The living room faced the river, and looked out on a glassed-in patio. The view, especially now at night, was spectacular. Off to the right a dining area and good-sized kitchen bisected the hall. Across from the kitchen was a bedroom with a bathroom and shower, perfect for my mom. Down the hall was the master bedroom. It was huge with its own deluxe bathroom containing a tub so large it resembled a wading pool.

After the tour I walked out on the patio and stared at the river. I wanted the apartment. Lisa would love it, and there was room for my mother. Another deal like Homer Industries and I'd be able to afford a full-time nurse. After a moment Jeff stuck his head out.

"You like it?"

"How much did you say it was?"

"Five hundred thousand, and it's a steal."

"How much down?"

"Forty thousand."

"How much is the maintenance?"

"Now that's a great deal, it's only a thousand a month."

"I'll take it."

"Look," Roget said to Ed, "we should probably take this conversation to another place. I think I can help you, but I also think we could be putting ourselves in danger by discussing this out in the open. Also I think time is an urgency. If we don't begin to make official records of your information immediately, it is more dangerous.

"Once we begin the process, they will leave you alone. Your window of vulnerability is now, between leaving the office today and going to the authorities. Once they realize you have spoken to someone official they will leave you alone. They will restrict their activities to internal damage control." He gripped Ed's forearm "Do you understand?"

Ed stared at Roget for a long moment, the man's face going in and out of focus. The guy made him nervous. He just wished he hadn't had five gin and tonics, then maybe he could think straight. But this man had friends at the SEC; maybe it would be best to listen to his advice. "Ok," he said, "tell me what to do."

"Good. As a precaution, in case you were followed, I'm going to leave first. I want you to wait, and I don't want you to make any phone calls. I want you to wait twenty minutes, and then you leave."

He reached out and gripped Ed's shoulder, whispering in close to his face, "Don't talk to anyone. Don't make any phone calls. Wait the full twenty minutes, and then leave the bar. Make a right on South Street, and walk uptown on the waterside by the fish market. Walk up four blocks, and I'll pick you up in a car. I'll take you to a friend of mine who works for the SEC."

Ed stared at his new friend. He felt dizzy, a little sick to his stomach, but mostly he was afraid. "Okay."

I sat alone in the darkened kitchen of my tenement apartment eating Chinese takeout—orange beef with rice. I ate it right out of the cardboard container using a plastic fork. I was going to have to buy a lot of things for my new apartment. I tried to concentrate on these types of details, attempting to generate excitement for my new lifestyle, but Ed Bloomfield's face kept coming between my plans and me.

What if Ed was right? What if our actions, so far removed from the realities of Homerville, Ohio, were going to cause thousands of people to lose their jobs? What would I have to say to the thousands of people who might one day wake up to discover that the pensions, for which they'd labored their entire adult lives, had been swallowed up in the greedy maw of corporate America?

Well, I told myself, it would happen anyway. Why shouldn't I get my piece? The piece I'd been working so hard for. What had my mother always told me about easy money? What had she left behind but unpaid bills? Look at Ed. I'd never really liked Ed, never respected him, but today Ed took a stand, and me, I took a check. It was a lot of money. It was a beautiful apartment. I threw the rest of my food in the trash. I couldn't eat another bite.

It was cold and winter dark when Ed left Pier 17. Leaving behind the thin crowds at the mall, he walked parallel with New York City's largest—and currently deserted—fish market. The strong fishy smell permeated the cold air. Ed weaved a bit as he walked.

The area, though very close to the financial district and not far from a lower income residential neighborhood, was deserted when the fish market was closed. It was one of the oldest parts of the city and kept in some of the worst repair. On the streets that were not still cobblestone, the cobblestones peeked out of the tar used to cover them over. It was lonely, and even more daunting in the shadows of the Brooklyn, Manhattan, and Williamsburg bridges.

Even though he was still drunk, the cold air sobered Ed up a little bit. He became apprehensive. Maybe it had been a bad idea to meet a stranger at night, in the middle of this historical harbor wasteland. He looked for a cab, but the streets were deserted. He'd already gone three blocks, and he convinced himself that his fears were groundless. He might get mugged, but the nice gentleman in the expensive suit couldn't mean him any harm.

A long black car glided out of the night and stopped in front of him. He saw a man jump out, and allowed himself to feel relieved when he recognized Roget's shape. Ed stopped and waited, smiling half-drunkenly, with his right hand held out to shake. The man from the car, in his long dark coat with his hat pulled low over his face against the night's chill, walked straight up to him and with his gloved right hand reached for Ed's. His grip was powerful and went on too long. Ed looked at him reproachfully but though the man was roughly the same size as the man he had met in the bar, it was not the same man. Ed had only a split second to process this horrifying fact and then the man's left hand came up. The knife ripped into Ed's stomach and up into his chest.

SEVEN

Detective Nat Weston was asleep when the phone rang at four A.M. He reached out a long arm and snatched up the receiver on the second ring. He looked apprehensively over at his wife before he answered but it was too late, she was awake.

He sighed into the receiver, "Hello?"

A brisk, staccato voice sped through the wire at him. "Nat, it's Pat."

"Good morning, Pat," he replied to the lieutenant, who was also his former partner. "It's my day off."

"We just secured a crime scene at the St. Steven Hotel on Fifty-second, looks like a homicide. Chief wants you down here right away."

"All right," he sighed. "Take me bout a half hour. I'll be there."

He looked over, and his wife glared back. "You'll be where in a half hour?" she demanded.

"They got a body turned up downtown, that's where I gotta be." He swung his legs over the side of the bed and rubbed his eyes with a big fist.

"It's your day off, and you promised Darryl you'd take him to Karate at three."

He looked over at his wife with sleepy eyes, "I'll be back in time to do that, baby." He leaned over and kissed her on the forehead, before standing and heading into the bathroom.

Forty-five minutes later Detective Weston pulled up in front of the St. Steven Hotel. A small knot of people stood out front being held at bay by a couple of uniformed officers. He pushed through the crowd, flashed his badge, and went inside.

The St. Steven must, once upon a time, have been a nice place to stay when visiting New York, but not in a long time. Nat knew the old man who owned and operated the place, One Eyed John. One Eyed John carried an unlicensed handgun, and only rented rooms for periods of twenty-four hours or less. If you wanted the room for more than a day, you had to bring your luggage down to the lobby, check out, and then check back in, paying in advance. One Eyed John's bread and butter business was with area prostitutes who rented by the hour, and went in without luggage.

John and two of his employees, along with a dozen or so guests, were in the lobby by the front desk, arguing with a harried patrol sergeant.

Nat caught the sergeant's eye. "Where's the body, Bill?"

"Top floor, fourteen C."

Nat pulled a handkerchief from his back pocket and placed it around his index finger, before pressing the elevator button.

Then he looked back at the sergeant. "Bill, don't let nobody upstairs now. And don't let nobody out just yet either, you hear?"

Nat studied the elevator on the way up, but it didn't have much to tell him. Like many buildings, the St. Steven didn't have a thirteenth floor. It occurred to him that meant that the fourteenth floor, where the body was, was actually the thirteenth. Nat smiled; you could run from bad luck, but you couldn't hide from it.

When he got off the elevator there was a group of people at one end of the hall. At the other end, the door to 14C was ajar. Two detectives he knew stood outside with a uniform officer he'd never met. He walked up to them.

"Hi, J.P., Murray," he greeted the two detectives. They didn't shake hands and he said nothing to the uniform cop. He peered through the door. The bed was made, and the room itself looked clean and orderly, as if nothing had happened. There was a man talking on the phone.

Nat took it all in, and then turned back to the three men. He looked the uniform up and down, locking eyes with him. "You the first officer?"

"Yes sir," the uniform replied.

Young and nervous, thought Nat. "This the crime scene?" he asked.

"Yes sir."

"Who the fuck is that, on the phone, in the middle of the crime scene?" Nat asked reasonably.

The uniform gulped. "He's from the DA's office, said his name is Trent."

Nat turned to J.P. "You know better than this, J.P., letting that guy use the phone in there."

"Sorry. We only got here a couple of minutes in front of you. I tried to talk to him, but he shushed me."

"He shushed you?" Nat shook his head in disgust. "I'm surprised at you, big tough guy like you, letting some pencil neck, paper-shuffling lawyer shush you! Do me a favor, get all those people down the end of the hall into a vacant room, so's we can start getting some statements. And nobody leaves till I say so. Oh yeah, and secure the roof, stairs, and elevator."

J.P. nodded, relieved somebody else was taking charge, and then he and the other detective headed down the hall and began herding the crowd into a vacant room.

Nat turned to the uniform, "What's your name, son?"

"Rossman, sir."

"Body in the bathroom, Mr. Rossman?"

"Yes, sir."

"You told that Fella from the DA's office he couldn't use the phone in there?"

"Yes sir, I did."

"What'd he say?"

"He said he was with the DA's office and he could do what he liked."

Nat winked at him, "That so?" He reached in his pocket and put on a pair of latex gloves. "You just wait right here."

Nat entered the room, careful not to touch anything, and watching where he put his feet. He walked up to the man on the phone and smiled at him.

The man cupped the receiver. "What do you want?" he asked in an impatient voice.

Nat snatched the phone from the man's hand and hung it up, "I want you out of this room and down the hall with everyone else, till the integrity of the evidence has been secured."

"Do you know who I am?" the man spluttered.

Nat, who was already an impressive size, puffed himself up so that he was towering over, surrounding, and invading the young lawyer's personal space all at the same time. "I can figure it out. You look like an agitated chicken, but you're an assistant DA, young enough to be my son and with very little experience, at least you sure don't know what the fuck you're doing at a crime scene. Now get the fuck out of here and down the hall with the others till I call for you. And in the future, you listen to the representatives of the police department when they speak to you and I won't lodge a complaint with your superiors. Now, out!" Nat shouted.

"Are you fucking kidding me?" the man exploded. "You people are lucky I'm here. I was told to come here by your fucking boss, Joey Trucchiero! I was at home, in bed, shacked up with a chick you would not believe, and I got a phone call from your boss telling me the mayor himself wanted me down here to assess this crime scene and you think you can get in my face and talk to me that way?" The assistant DA stepped closer and was breathing hot air almost directly into Nat's face now.

Nat kept his feet firmly planted where they were, kept his eyes leveled down to meet the gaze of the feisty DA and moving not a single muscle other than his hand and forearm, carefully removed a handkerchief from his pocket and wiped his forehead with it.

"What's your name, son?" Nat asked in a softer tone.

"Peter McDaniel," the man answered.

"Well, Mr. McDaniel, I didn't quite understand all the ins and outs of how connected and important you are." Nat continued in a voice so soft that it was almost a whisper, "but the thing is . . . you're a lawyer, correct?"

"Right. I'm with the District Attorney's Office," McDaniel responded in a soft, almost mellow voice.

"Good, good," Nat replied, nodding his head and continuing in his soft tones. "Then you understand all kinds of things, like obstruction of justice and how lack of cooperation with the police can become a real problem. Especially when you get arrested for it and you end up in the Tombs overnight before anyone finds out about your plight. Do you have any idea what could happen to you in just one night in the Tombs?"

Mellow fled the lawyer's voice replaced with strident outrage. "Are you threatening me, detective?"

Nat laughed out loud, "I'm not threatening you, McDaniel. What I am doing is explaining what's going to happen to you if you don't get the fuck outa here before I count to ten, because I'm almost retired and I really don't care who you know. I will put you in jail for the night and you just might get fucked in the ass, and that *will* happen before you get pulled out by your 'friends.' One, Two, Three . . ."

A whole cast of emotions played across McDaniel's face, but it only took a few seconds for them to run the gamut and then he scurried away.

Nat went back to the front door and called out to one of the officers down the hall, "You stay on the front door down there." He turned to Officer Rossman. "Come on in, and tell me what you know."

Rossman stepped over the threshold and pulled a leather-bound notebook from his pocket. "I was on foot patrol on Ninth Avenue. At six forty-three I passed in front of the hotel. At that time the night manager emerged from the building screaming that there'd been a murder. I calmed him down, and radioed for backup, suspected homicide. The man brought me up to this floor, and a hysterical woman showed us the room. I came in the room with them, and they showed me the body in the tub that you're about to see. I then called in to report the body.

"The hysterical woman, who it turned out was the maid, entered at about six-thirty to make up the bed. The room had been rented out several times during the course of the evening, but it was just hookers, and they don't usually stay the night.

"Anyway, the maid came in and cleaned up, made the bed, and then went into the bathroom where she found the body. She immediately ran out screaming for the night manager. And that's it. I haven't let anyone in since I got here, except that guy from the DA's office, and no one's left the building either."

Nat handed Rossman a pair of latex gloves, "The door was open when you got here?" he asked.

"Yes sir."

"The light was on?"

"Yes sir."

"Was the door locked when the maid got here?"

"She said it was."

"The lights, were they on?"

"I didn't ask her."

"You should have." Nat yawned. "All right, let's take a look at John Doe."

In the bathroom, the mangled corpse lay face up in the tub. The fatal wound seemed to be a deep slash, ripped up from the stomach, terminating in the chest. The blood, a dark red color, was congealed around the body. Nat gave a start. The hands of the corpse were missing. There beside him on top of the toilet seat were a hacksaw and blowtorch. Just like the body on Park Avenue. Nat recovered himself.

He sniffed. "Suit and tie, corporate type." He reached down and placed his hands lightly and carefully under the arms beneath the shirt. After a minute he straightened up, "What do you think happened here, Rossman?"

"I don't like to venture an opinion, but it looks pretty plain to me."

Nat crossed his arms. "It does, does it? Go on."

"He picked up a hooker. They came back here and either her or her pimp tried to rob him. There was a struggle, and he ended up dead." Rossman spread out his hands in the universal sign of supplication. "End of story."

"And the hands, what happened to the hands?"

Rossman looked over at the corpse, a queasy expression on his face. "Hadn't thought about it," he said.

Nat nodded. "You think the murder took place here?"

Rossman was starting to look less sure of himself. "Yeah, you don't?"

"Well, when I felt under his arms just now he was cold and clammy to the touch. Man's been dead for more than fourteen hours now. Now like you said, at least four, five hookers been up here with their Johns during that time. You gonna stand here and tell me none of 'em used the bathroom? In all that time?"

"I see."

"Do you? This ain't the crime scene. This here body's been moved. Now go on downstairs and find me two brown paper bags. When you get back I want you to wrap John Doe's stumps in 'em. Like this we preserve the evidence that might be there."

On Saturday morning, while basking in the afterglow with the love of my life, I got a page from Arnold Norton. I returned his call and discovered that I was booked on a three P.M. flight to Miami out of Newark. But first I had to swing by the office and pick up two hundred thousand in cash to take with me. The two hundred K, it turned out, was my budget for bribing a guy named Johnny Zale, the business agent for Union Local 22B, and the man in control of the Homer pension. I was to meet the guy at a hotel bar near the airport, get him to agree to our deal, pay him, and whatever was left over was mine to keep.

That's how I found myself at the bar in the Marriot Hotel near the Miami Airport at eight P.M., nervously looking for a guy who matched Zale's description. I didn't have long to wait. I knew him as soon as he walked through the door: about fifty years old, big and heavy, like a football player gone to flesh. He shuffled into the lounge and leaned up, belly first to the bar, calling for "The biggest beer you got!" I was actually certain it was him because he was still wearing a nametag from the convention he was in town to attend.

I fixed him with a stare until he became uncomfortable and looked back, and then I smiled as if in recognition. "Say, you're Johnny Zale, aren't you?" I said.

"Who're you?" he asked just before he lifted his pint to his lips and made it disappear in one slough. He gestured to the bartender for a refill.

I stepped close enough to shake his hand. "I'm Jack Cole, I work for Walsh Dahmer."

He gave me a suspicious look and a decidedly unenthusiastic handshake. "The new owners," he said.

"Right."

"What can I do for you?" he demanded without getting off his stool.

There wasn't another stool close enough, so I just leaned up against the bar. "Just wanted a few minutes of your time, really."

He looked deliberately away from me, like a tough street guy might from a cop. "For what? You want concessions; you gotta talk to the political leadership. I'm just the business agent."

I laughed good-naturedly and called out to the bartender, "Give us two beers over here on my tab. The biggest you got!"

He was looking at me now, not like we were friends, but he was looking at me. "What did you say your name was again?" he asked.

I grinned at him. "Jack Cole and I've got a proposition for you. A little business. Fix you a golden parachute, so you can get out before the shit hits the fan."

He put a finger to his lips, gestured to the bartender for another drink, and pointed to a back table.

When I got back to New York the next day, I had an agreement for the pension fund to buy GICs from Bachman Securities, and twenty thousand in cash left over from the bribe money, just what I needed to take care of my next order of business.

I met Lisa for brunch in a coffee shop on Twenty-third near the Chelsea Hotel. I went there directly from the airport, without stopping home to change, and the twenty thousand cash was rolled into a couple of pairs of socks in my overnight bag under the table. I ate corn beef hash and eggs while she toyed with a fruit cup.

"I've been thinking about your problem," I told her between forkfuls.

She smiled noncommittally, like her thoughts were far away. "What problem is that?"

"About the money. The twenty grand."

Her smile vanished, "That's my problem."

"Yeah, I get that," I said through a mouthful of eggs. "The thing is that it could be your problem for a long time. The way I figure it, the longer it stays your problem, the more it becomes mine."

She shoved her almost untouched fruit cup into the middle of the table, jarring it up against my plate. "Well it's not your problem."

I let my fork fall with a clank and fixed her with a soulful look. "Lisa, would you deny someone you loved the chance to live out a harmless fantasy?"

"That depends on how you define harmless," she replied in a strong voice.

"Right. Say I want to be your knight in shining armor. Say that's all I've thought about for the past ten years." I reached for her hand, but she kept it just out of range.

She scooted to the edge of the seat cushion as if to leave. "I'd say it sounded like bullshit," she said, almost as if in parting. But she didn't leave.

I had touched a wound and had to speak quickly. "I went down to Miami yesterday on business and I made exactly twenty thousand dollars in cash. It's in the bag on the floor under the table." The words tumbled quickly, chasing one another from my mouth until they lay there on the table between us.

She gave me a funny look but she was stopped dead in her tracks. No longer leaving, staring at the bag under the table. "Did you do a drug deal or something?"

"No. Investment banking, but that's beside the point. What I'm trying to illustrate is that the money came easy. I want to use it to pull you out of debt."

She settled back into the booth. "That's very sweet"—she took my hand across the table—"but I can't let you do that."

"Why not?"

She stared hard at me. "It's a lot of money, and I have learned that there are strings attached to that kind of money."

"Lisa, I love you. I always have. Helping you is a lot more important to me than money. Not only that, but it will be worth it to me to get you out of that club."

She shook her head, "I can't accept it."

"Look, if you want, you can call it a loan and pay me back when you can. I can afford it, Lisa."

She leaned over and kissed me, "Okay, but I'm going to pay you back. I swear I will, every single penny."

It was nearly noon on Monday and I had been hard at work since seven, endlessly reviewing the Homer pension fund statements. I wanted to get my analysis completed before I left the office, but after five hours, my mind was numb and my belly rumbling. I buzzed Doris and asked her to order me up a corn beef sandwich from the deli in the lobby, and when it arrived I spread out *Newsday* across my desk.

Half way through the sandwich I got to the Metro Section, and one of the headlines leaped off the page.

WALL STREET ACCOUNTANT MURDERED!

FOUND IN MIDTOWN HOTEL

> The mutilated body of high-powered CPA Edward Bloomfield was discovered early this morning in a room at the St. Stephen Hotel on West Fifty-second Street. According to the NYPD, Mr. Bloomfield was an apparent robbery victim. The hotel is known to police and area residents as a place frequented by local prostitutes. The body was discovered by a hotel staff-member who went in to make up the room. At this time the police have no suspects.

I chucked the rest of my sandwich in the wastebasket, my appetite gone. I leaned back in my chair and shut my eyes. Something funny was going on, I was certain of that. See, even though Ed and I were never what you would call close, I was almost positive that Ed was not the type to go with a prostitute. Ed had barely looked at the dancers at Golden Dreams. He kept a picture of his wife and two young daughters on his desk. Hell, Ed was so straight he didn't even like off-color humor.

Not only that, but the other day when Ed spoke his mind at the meeting, he had become something of a moral superman to me. That image didn't jive with a sleazy, back-alley tryst ending in sloppy death. I found myself whispering a silent prayer for him.

Other people in the office must have also seen the paper. It was strange that no one had called. I picked up the phone to dial Arnold Norton's direct line and hesitated. I was, I realized, a little nervous. I'd been trying to build up my little, 'cover your ass file,' and I really didn't have anything substantial in it. Now, with things spiraling out of control, it couldn't hurt to give it a little extra oomph. I had a recording device in my desk drawer that could be connected to the phone, so I hooked it up first, and then dialed Norton's number.

"Mr. Norton, this is Jack." I said, hoping I didn't sound as nervous as I felt.

"Jack," he replied, sounding pleased, "I told you to call me Arnold. What's on your mind?"

"Did you see paper today?"

"You mean about Ed?" his tone downshifted to somber.

"Yes."

"Of course it's a terrible tragedy. You know, I think he was in a bad state of mind. I'm not entirely surprised he did something rash. It's an awful blow for his widow, of course. Especially in light of the circumstances under which he died."

"But Arnold," I felt strangely uncomfortable using his first name, "Ed was not the type to go with a prostitute. There must be more to it."

"I know he never seemed that way, but there were things about Ed you don't know. We've been aware of his philandering for some time. Considering the reputation of the firm, we took a dim view of it. We even spoke to him about it recently. And that may, in fact, have been one of the factors involved in his recent outburst."

"Have you given any of this information to the police?"

"No. Out of consideration for the widow, we're going to keep it private. And we're going to pay out his full bonus to her as well. With respect to the firm, we'd sort of like to keep any information on Ed Bloomfield confidential. No talking to reporters and only give the police answers to questions they ask directly. Any speculation, or any type of scandal connected to the firm, has a huge price tag attached.

"So get back to work, Jack, and try to keep this business off your mind. It's a tragedy about Ed, but I have a good deal more confidence in you."

I thought he was full of shit, but I also didn't know what his game was. It certainly wasn't my place to argue with one of the 'masters of the universe.'

Especially one who just might be my father.

The thought exploded across my mind like a confetti bomb. I mean, he knew my mother at the right time. He looked a bit like me only older, though that could be said about a lot of guys his age. Most compelling in my mind though was the interest he was suddenly taking in me. That and the undeniable fact that there had been someone intervening in the lives of both myself, and my mother to make sure we were taken care of at all the critical points. It was a pattern that I was only just becoming aware of.

What I said though was, "Thanks for giving me some of your time, Mr. Norton."

"Arnold, please call me Arnold."

I decided never to call him Arnold again. It just didn't seem to fit.

An hour later I got a call from the Cross-town Savings Bank, to let me know my mortgage had been approved by Norton's frat brother. I pushed the Ed business out of my mind and called the real estate broker to tell him the happy news. We agreed to close by the end of the week. I also asked him to make the keys available for me for the next night so I could show Lisa the apartment.

As soon as I got off the phone, Doris buzzed from the front desk.

"There's a detective Weston here to see you."

I sighed. It was the last thing I wanted to deal with. With Norton nervous, the whole thing had a potential for turning into a minefield, but it could not be avoided. "Send him in, Doris."

I put on my suit jacket and positioned myself behind the desk, trying to establish as much of the home court advantage as I could. The office door opened and a tall, heavyset black man in a wrinkled brown suit walked in. I stood up and reached over the desk to shake hands.

"Won't you sit down, detective," I said, indicating a too-small chair to the right of my desk. "What can I do for you?"

The detective crossed his legs and removed a pen and pad from his pocket. "Mr. Cole, my name's Nat Weston and I'm a detective sergeant from Manhattan South." He lay a gold shield face up on the desk and left it there. "I'm investigating the murder of Edward Bloomfield. Exactly how long did you know Mr. Bloomfield for?"

"I've been with the firm a little over three years. I guess I've known him that long."

"And how would you characterize your relationship with Mr. Bloomfield?"

"I'm sorry, what do you mean by that?"

"Just what I said. Friendly, cordial, professional? Did you get along with him or didn't you? Did you ever go out together socially?"

"All right, I understand. I'd say we had a cordial, strictly professional relationship. I've been out of the office twice with him, both times within the past month, both times on business in a social context."

"I see." He scribbled on his pad, "that's why I'm here, I saw your name and those two recent appointments in his organizer. So, may I ask the nature of this business?"

"Sure. We were pitching two out of town businessmen on the acquisition of their firm. So we took them out on the town to, you know, to entertain them."

He stopped writing, put his pencil down and fixed me with a deliberate stare. "This entertainment, what did it consist of?"

I was sweating now. "We took them to dinner in the Seaport—"

He picked his pencil back up and paused with the nib hovering just above his notepad. "What was the name of the restaurant?"

"The Harbor View."

He fixed me with the stare again. "What else did you do?"

I let out a whole bunch of air I had been keeping in my lungs and answered in an exasperated, fatalistic tone. "We took them to a strip club called Golden Dreams."

"Oh, yeah," the detective grinned like his expectations at last were being met. "Did Mr. Bloomfield have a taste for that kind of thing?"

I shifted my tone into neutral. "I wouldn't say he did. We were there basically for the benefit of the clients."

The detective nodded quickly. "You said you were out with him twice in the past month. Where did you go the other time?"

"Also Golden Dreams . . ." I broke off as the big cop smirked. "Is everything all right, Detective Weston?"

"Sure is. Just you said Mr. Bloomfield didn't have a taste for stuff like that. Seems like a man without a sweet tooth sure is laying into the fudge, is all."

"I see. Our two trips were related."

"Okay. This acquisition, was it successful?"

"Yes."

"Was it what you might call a hostile takeover?"

"No. Management was receptive to our offers."

"Was there anybody who might have been angry at the way the deal went down?"

I kept my face composed, but inwardly I was frowning. I wanted to tell the cop that Ed himself was unhappy about it. But I'd been briefed and my mortgage was approved. What I said was, "Not that I could say."

"What was the name of the company involved?"

"Homer Industries."

"Never heard of it," he mused, scribbling.

"It's in Ohio," I offered.

"Can you think of any enemies or strange habits Mr. Bloomfield might have had? Any at all?"

"No. As I said, we weren't particularly close."

The detective stood up. "Thanks for your time. I have a few more people to interview in the building, and I probably won't be bothering you anymore." We shook hands and he left.

I didn't get much more work done after that. I sat in my chair staring into space for what must have been an hour. I should have told the cop about Ed's misgivings. Should I maybe even pick up where Ed left off, seize the moral high ground?

The phone rang. It was Rosa, my mother's semi-private nurse.

"I'm sorry to bother you at work," she began, "and don't worry, it's not an emergency. It's actually a good thing."

"What is it?"

"It's kinda funny. It almost seems like your mother is getting better. She recognized me today, and not just for a minute, all day. She's been asking for you by name. I thought you might want to come out."

"I'm on my way."

EIGHT

The corporate car dropped me off in front of the nursing home. As it pulled onto the block I could see Mom and Rosa. Mom was seated in a wheelchair, wearing an overcoat with a blanket on her knees. Rosa sat on the bench next to her.

I nodded at Rosa and leaned down to kiss Mom. She surprised me by saying, "Hello, Jack."

It felt strange. I could see recognition in her eyes, and it made me feel awkward. For years I'd seen nothing but empty eyes. Now she was suddenly there again, the woman who tucked me in at night and checked the closet for monsters. I wasn't sure what to do. "Hi, Mom. Rosa tells me you're getting better."

She smiled, "I remember some things, you know. I remember seeing you on Thanksgiving."

Rosa stood, "I have to go now, Mr. Cole."

I smiled and handed her a check. "Thanks, Rosa.

I took her place on the bench.

"You look like you're doing well," Mom said.

"I guess I am." I replied, uncertain how to respond. "Why are you sitting out here in the cold?"

"I'm not sure. I think it's been a long time since I was outside. When am I coming home?"

I smiled sadly. She was better, she was starting to recognize places and people again, but she didn't understand exactly what was going on here. I thought about the new apartment and the bedroom for her.

I took her hand. "Soon Mama. Very soon. I just have a few things to take care of, and I'll be coming back for you."

She squeezed my hand, pulled me closer. "I don't want to die here."

"Don't worry, Mama, I won't let you."

"You know, sometimes I know what's going on. They don't think I do, and I can't show them. It's like being in a dream and not being able to have any effect on anything, just observing."

She stopped talking and stared listlessly ahead to the empty field beyond. I wanted to ask her about my father, but I thought that would be selfish. My mother was fragile now. Even when she'd been strong and healthy when I was a boy, she'd refused to discuss my father. All she'd ever said was that he was a charming, bad man, and she wasn't even sure she knew his real name.

Anyway, by this time I thought I knew. It all sort of added up. Mom had worked for the firm before I was born and then for a little while after. Someone with money had been lurking in the shadows my whole life and helping when it was needed.

Someone who couldn't afford to reveal himself, even when I got recruited for Walsh Dahmer. If I needed any further proof there was my current Cinderella-like ascension to the halls of power. If I wasn't the bastard son of Arnold Norton, then I didn't know what the explanation was.

About a block away from my new apartment I had found a bright, cheery, little pub with a fireplace and what I can only call "Old World Charm." Lisa was supposed to meet me at six-thirty, and here I was at seven P.M. still waiting. I was, in fact, ordering my second scotch when she finally made her entrance. As always, my heart began beating faster when I first caught sight of her. I watched her kicking the snow off her boots in the vestibule and even that seemed graceful.

I stood up smiling, waiting for her. She caught my eye and her whole face lit up in a warm winter smile.

"I'm sorry I'm late, honey. Have you been waiting long?"

"It doesn't matter. I'd be willing to wait a lot longer."

She grinned and rubbed cold hands against my face. "It's positively arctic out there."

I motioned for the bartender. "You want something to warm you up?"

"No. I'm anxious to see your empty palace. Let's go," she grabbed my hand, pulling me toward the door.

"Wait," I laughed, "I haven't settled up." I knocked back the rest of my scotch and dropped a twenty on the bar.

It was a short, close, cold huddled walk to the Water Tower, and it felt so nice to be near her. Just before we got to the building I stopped and pulled her closer.

"You don't have any plans for the evening, do you?"

"We're going to spend it together, aren't we?"

"Yes. But I made arrangements to go out with another couple. I hope you don't mind."

She squeezed my hand, "Why should I mind?"

I smiled through the darkness, "No reason."

The keys were waiting with the doorman, and we took the ride up with the elevator man in silence. Lisa loved the apartment. Shedding her long winter coat and boots, she danced through the rooms barefoot. I followed awkwardly, content to admire her spontaneous movement.

"It's so big and empty. It feels so free like this." She paused, breathless in front of the fireplace. "I wish we had wood and a bearskin rug, so we could build a fire and make love in front of the flames. Just you and me, safe behind the glass with the cold snow falling over the river out there." I walked up behind her and she stopped talking, staring into the cold hearth, imagining future fire.

Suddenly, she fell back and I caught her in my arms. She turned so we were facing. Pressed up against me I could feel her substance, her breath rising and falling. Alive. I kissed her deeply. When we came apart I asked, "How should we decorate it?"

She raised an eyebrow, "We?"

"Well, I thought you might help me pick out the furniture."

"Don't you have stuff?"

"Not much."

She broke away and started pacing, "We have to make a list. One thing I can tell you for sure, this place needs a bed. A big brass bed. You need stuff for the kitchen, couches, a coffee table, dining set, chairs, TV, stereo . . ."

I laughed. She was such a live wire, and she seemed so pleased at the prospect of decorating my place for me. I could see her mind racing. "Electronics I have, it's just the furniture. Can you come shopping with me tomorrow night?"

She frowned. "Tomorrow I have something I have to do, but the night after I'm free."

I was disappointed but what I said was, "That would be fine, but I want to get everything all at once. I want it all delivered next week, because I'm really anxious to move in." I surprised myself by saying, "The other place isn't a home. I want a home."

"Then why don't you take the whole day off? That way we can really spend some time shopping."

"I can probably swing that," I looked at my watch. "We have to get moving. We're supposed to meet my friend Brad and his date at eight-thirty."

We were supposed to hook up with Brad and his date at a place called the Vindaloon Palace. It was in the neighborhood, and when we arrived they were already seated. Brad's date's name was Megan; she was about twenty-seven, petite with curly blonde hair. After introductions and cocktail ordering, Lisa asked who picked the restaurant.

"I did," said Brad. "I love Indian food, but to tell you the truth, I can really only tolerate eating it once or twice a year. Any more and my stomach would rise up in revolt. But I'm telling you I love the stuff. So when I do eat it, it's a gastronomic event, and I wanted my second date with Megan to be special."

"Where did you guys meet?" asked Lisa.

"About a month ago I started taking a course at the Learning Annex. We met there."

I leaned back to give the waiter room to drop the cocktails on the cramped table. "I didn't know you were taking a course." I was surprised and if you knew Brad as I did, you would be too.

"Forgive me for not telling you everything, Jack."

"I'll let it go this time," I said with a straight face. "But what type of course was it?"

Megan leaned in and placed her hand over mine. She looked very earnest, and I was kind of surprised. "It's a course in past life regression," she said. "You and Lisa should take it. It's fabulous."

I couldn't resist giving Brad a sarcastic smile. "Past life regression?"

Lisa kicked me under the table, and then turned to Megan, "What do they do in the course? It must be very interesting."

"They teach you how to meditate and look for clues in your present life to help determine who you were in the past. They also use hypnosis to take you back to a time before you were born, to the 'jumping off' point. They show you how the same souls keep coming back together, over and over again, life after life."

I was surprised. I'd never pictured Brad as being quite so New Age. "So who were you in your past life, Brad?"

He turned red, or at least his ears did. "It doesn't work exactly like that, Jack."

I knew I had him, so I cut him off. "Well, did you find a past life, or didn't you?"

Megan reached over and took Brad's hand, which I thought was sweet, and then she turned to me like a peacemaking mother. "Brad is shy about telling you what he found out, but I think he should be proud. I think it makes him more sensitive to a woman's needs. Why don't you tell them about it, Bradford?" And then she added, "Be proud."

I dipped a piece of Indian puff bread into some kind of cilantro sauce, and gave Brad a look that tipped him he would never live this moment down. What I said was, "Yes Bradford, why don't you tell us about it?" Under the table I received another kick. I looked over, and Lisa's eyes were laughing.

"All right," Brad said, "but if you laugh, you have to pick up the whole check, deal?"

I nodded.

"Ok, I was a slave girl in ancient Rome." He looked defensively around the table, prepared to ward off any sign of mockery.

I didn't laugh. I did smile. "So, what was it like?"

He gave me a dirty look, and Megan looked around the table with shining eyes, "See, that's why he's so sensitive to women in this life."

I nodded, this time with a straight face. "I'd always wondered, now I know."

Probably to break the pattern of my bad manners, Lisa excused herself to go to the bathroom. Predictably, Megan offered to join her, leaving Brad and me alone. Prick that he was, he didn't let the grass grow.

"I've met your girlfriend before," he said.

I licked my lips, feeling suddenly dry. "Yeah?"

"I don't know how to tell you this, but she's a topless dancer. I've seen her working at Golden Dreams." He looked concerned, but I knew better.

It did bother me, and the possibility should have occurred to me before I arranged the double date. Sometimes I can be a little dense, but I'd be damned if I showed that to Brad. "I know that," I answered, deadpan.

"And you don't mind?" He was incredulous, at least that's the only word I can come up with to describe his facial expression, his tone.

"I give stock tips to former Roman slave girls, I date strippers. I guess I'm just not a judgmental man. By the way, were you a harem girl, or just an ordinary slave?"

"Fuck off," he replied, moodily, studying his cutlery. "Say, I read something in the paper about a guy from your firm being murdered. Did you know him?"

I frowned. I'd managed to put it from my mind, mostly, but it bothered me on many different levels. "Yeah, I did. In fact he was my partner on the deal I just closed, and I had to talk to the cops about it."

"Sorry. Were you guys close?"

"No, I wouldn't say close. Listen. Lisa met him once, and I don't want to discuss it with her around, so let's drop it for now, okay?"

NINE

The medical examiner's report was sitting on Nat's desk when he arrived at ten, and it confirmed all of his suspicions. Bloomfield had been dead at least fifteen hours before his body was found. The body had to have been moved, and there was definitely more to this than met the eye. No hooker or pimp would go to the trouble of moving a body in a case like this, and certainly not into their own terrain. Then there was the knife they'd found on the roof, covered with the victim's blood. The victim's blood, and the fingerprints of one Lucas Monroe, recidivist and pimp extraordinaire. Why would a pimp take the trouble to move a body to a place he was known to frequent, and leave a convenient knife close by to incriminate himself?

It all seemed too pat, especially in light of the character references he'd gotten on the victim. According to everyone the guy was an upstanding citizen, straight as an arrow. The only inkling of anything risqué in the guy's resume came from the man he worked with, Cole. Cole said they'd gone to a strip club together, but even he had said it was out of character. Thinking of Cole, something was off about the guy—nothing specific, but Nat's intuition told him the guy was holding something back. He made a mental note to look into it.

The interoffice buzzer rang, "Weston."

"Nat, Joey. Come into my office, I need to talk with you." The line went dead.

Nat sighed. He couldn't stand Joey Trucchiero, the chief of detectives and his boss. Joey had held the job for only six months and, in Nat's estimation, was far more of a politician's sycophant than he was a cop. He was a short, squat bully of a man who tended to spit when he talked. When you went into his office, he was the one doing the talking.

Nat walked slowly down the hall, each dreadful step drawing him closer to the human sprinkler. When he arrived at the frosted glass door, he knocked lightly.

"Come right in, Nat."

The fat man sat behind his desk. He pointed at the chair next to it. "Cop a squat."

"What's up, chief?"

"I wanna check out what's going on with the murder at the St. Steven. Where you at with that?"

"I was just reviewing the ME's report, and it confirms my theory that the body was moved. So I want to keep the case open."

Joey's calm exterior suddenly became agitated. "What are you talking about? The body was found in a whore's hotel."

Saliva sprayed from his mouth. "Ya found the knife with a known pimp's prints on it! I want you to pick up that pimp, book him, and close the case, today!"

Nat managed to keep his voice low key, patient. "Chief, I've got more than twenty years on the job, and every instinct, along with some pretty fair evidence, leads me to believe that there is more going on here than meets the eye."

Joey waved his hand dismissively. "Look Nat, I like you. I do everything I can to make your job easier. I expect you to do the same for me. The word from downtown is *damage control*. This Bloomfield guy worked for some pretty important people, the kind of people who pay big taxes, and make big political contributions. You understand?" Joey paused for a moment, waiting for some sign of agreement or submission from Nat. When he got none he continued in a quieter but more menacing tone. "I want this thing wrapped up today, with a minimum of fuss and muss."

Nat took a deep breath. "Chief, if I didn't continue this investigation, I wouldn't be doing my job."

Joey's skin seemed to ripple and tremble all over, like he was on the point of morphing into something else like some kind of inner beast was about to erupt from within his thin casing of human skin. "Your job is what I tell you it is!" He shouted. "And, if you don't go out and pick up that pimp, today, close the case, today, your job is going to be directing traffic, on foot, in the shittiest part of the South Bronx! Capiche?"

Nat stood up. "Yes sir."

Everything moved pretty quickly for me the day after my double date with Brad. I completed most of the details of transferring the pension fund assets and received my final bonus check before lunch. At eleven A.M. I left work and went to my lawyer's office where I laid down a fifty thousand dollar down payment on my new condo. Then at one P.M. I met Lisa at the apartment. We measured rooms, made lists of furniture, and went out for sushi before embarking on our shopping spree.

Seven hours and twenty thousand dollars later we were sitting in a Turkish restaurant, holding hands and sipping red wine with our menus untouched between us.

Lisa looked shyly over at me, which was unusual for her. "What if I told you I quit Golden Dreams?"

I didn't skip a beat. "I'd say that was terrific."

She studied her cutlery. "But what if I also told you I had to leave town for a few months?"

"That'd make me sad. Are you in some kind of trouble?"

"No. I told you I was an actress. Remember I said I had to work yesterday?"

"Yes."

"Well, I wasn't at the club. I was at a callback for an audition I went on last week. Anyway, they offered me the role," she paused for a moment to take a seated bow. "So I'm going on tour with a regional company."

I forced myself to smile. "I'm really happy for you. What's the show?"

"My Fair Lady."

"I've seen that. What part did you get?"

"I'm just a member of the ensemble. But it's real work, and it pays real money. And I really need to get back in the saddle."

I caught myself frowning unconsciously, and forced another smile.

She squeezed my hand, "Are you okay?"

"Of course. I was just thinking about how much I would miss you, that's all."

She tugged me gently forward and pecked me on the cheek. "I won't be gone forever, just a few months. And I'm not leaving for a few weeks. Besides, you can come and see the show, maybe even stay for a little while."

It was bitterly cold along Eleventh Avenue. In spite of the layers of clothing Nat wore under his leather bomber jacket, the wind cut through him like a knife. His hands, jammed in his pockets, were curled around two police mug shots. One of Lucas Monroe, the pimp he needed to pick up; the other of Georgia Brown, a prostitute known to work for him.

He'd just come from the uptown rooming house where Lucas lived, but the room was empty and the landlady claimed not to have seen him for a while. A friend on the vice squad tipped him to a couple of bars Lucas haunted, but he'd drawn another blank there. Now he found himself out in the middle of the night, peering into the faces of the streetwalkers and whistling the tune to "Sweet Georgia Brown" under his breath.

As he approached the corner of Forty-eighth Street, he saw three young men clustered around a woman. They were hassling her, pushing her around in a circle and taunting her. Nat picked up his pace. As he got closer he could hear them.

"Where you hiding the money, bitch?" one of them shouted, pulling her head back by the hair.

She shook him off and made to move away, but another one got in front of her. "You heard what Jerome said? You wanna get jacked up?"

"You best step back, Trevor. Lucas'll cut you up," she said through tight teeth.

Nat slipped into the shadow of a nearby tenement as the third man stepped behind her and kissed her on the neck. She pulled violently away and he laughed. "Lucas ain't gonna cut nobody up. What I hear, Lucas be cut up hisself."

As the three men laughed, Nat stepped out of the shadows, his Glock pointed at the head of the third man. "Chill out boys, the lady's with me."

The third man turned toward Nat, staring down the business end of Nat's gun. "Got no problem with you. Why don't you walk on back where you came from, old man?"

Nat moved closer, pressed the barrel of the gun right up into the man's head. "You a hard rock, boy?" he hissed.

He brought his knee up quickly between the man's legs, crushing his testicles. The man fell, writhing in pain. Nat turned, pointing the gun at the other two. "Y'all run along now." They hesitated, and Nat gestured with the gun again. "Go on now. Get!" They ran off into the night.

He looked at the woman. "You Georgia Brown?"

She nodded.

"I need to talk to you." The man on the ground got up on one knee, and Nat kicked him in the face. "You see that building there?"

She nodded, scared.

"Good. Go inside the lobby and wait for me. I'm gonna talk some to this boy." She hesitated and he said, "Go on, it'll be warmer in there, and I ain't gonna hurt you."

She disappeared into the building.

Nat looked down at the man bleeding on the pavement. "Roll over flat on your face, and kiss the ground, hard rock."

Nat cuffed him, then dragged him under the awning of a closed deli and propped him against the door.

He put away his gun and sat next to the guy. "What's your name, boy?"

"What the fuck you care, what's my name?" the guy said through a mouthful of marbles.

Nat laughed and smacked him in the face. "See, that attitude man, it's not helping you out. We're all alone here, man. Don't fuck with me. What's your name?"

He sucked air between his bloody teeth. It made a whistling sound. "Name's Max."

"Awright Max, why you bothering Sweet Georgia Brown?"

"Why the fuck you care? She ain't nothing but a ho."

"Cause I'm The Man, Max. And if she ain't nothing but a ho, what are you?"

"What you think I am?"

"I know what you are. You after Georgia 'cause Lucas is gone. You figure you gonna inherit his property. What happened to Lucas?"

"Man, I don't know."

Nat took the guy's nose in his hand and wrenched it. Blood flowed out. "I done told you not to fuck with me, boy," he hissed. "I don't care. I'll take you down. Maybe I'll take you up to the roof and throw you off. You best tell me something."

"Lucas is dead."

"How'd he die?"

"I don't know. They say he cut him up and left pieces all over town."

"Who's he?"

"The Frenchman."

Bells went off in Nat's head. The German guy from Interpol, the corporate hit man, the body in the apartment on Park Avenue. "The Frenchman?" he repeated.

"Yeah, the Frenchman. Now that's all I know."

"When was the last time you saw Lucas?"

"Little more than a week."

"Where can I find the Frenchman?"

"I don't know, man. He come and go. I ain't never seen him myself, I just heard of him."

"Who's seen him?"

"Georgia know him."

Nat pulled the man up and un-cuffed him, "All right, get the fuck outa here. I don't want to see you no more."

The man limped off into the night. Nat went into the lobby, but Sweet Georgia Brown was gone.

It wasn't until the Friday after Detective Weston interviewed me that I saw Ed's widow. I'd met her at company functions once or twice before; I remembered her as a sturdy, cheerful woman. This time I almost didn't recognize her, because she looked so gloomy and bedraggled. Of course that would be expected under the circumstances, but with her I think it went beyond ordinary grief. Anyone would be upset by the death of a spouse, but there are those who share a love beyond ordinary need or familiarity. True love I guess you would call it. Looking at Mrs. Bloomfield I could just tell that sorrow consumed her. There was a noticeable slump to her body as if the bones had grown soft. Her makeup ran, and you could tell the tears came and went in waves by the mascara patterns running down her cheeks. The most pathetic aspect of her visage were the two small children she had in tow—two little girls who just looked deflated, like balloons on the third day out when they begin to shrink.

She was coming out of the elevator just as I was returning from lunch, and I ran smack into her. Not only did she recognize me, she also associated me with Ed's recent work.

"You're Jack, Jack Cole, aren't you?" she demanded without preamble.

"Yes, of course," I tried a sympathetic smile. "I am so sorry for your loss, Mrs. Bloomfield." I couldn't quite remember her first name.

"You know Ed didn't die the way they said. You know he was upset about the deal you were working on, that he spoke up." It was not a question.

I leaned back my head, filled my chest with air and exhaled. "I know Ed had concerns, but I don't believe his death was in any way connected to the firm."

She stepped closer to me, looked me in the eye, the children milling around her skirts. "You can lie to me, Mr. Cole, but don't lie to yourself."

I had no response. After a minute she walked away, leaving me with a stomach full of writhing snakes. I stood by the elevator with my eyes open, realizing she was right. I returned to my office, collected my things, and told my assistant that I was taking the rest of the afternoon off. Twenty minutes later found me sitting on a bench in Battery Park, fingering the business card of Detective Nat Weston, and sipping a steaming cup of coffee from a deli on the corner.

Here was the dilemma: As a man of business, on the cusp of real money, the girl of my dreams, and the ability to do the right thing by my mother, I'd be a complete fool to seek justice against the Golden Goose. I'd certainly be slapping a wet blanket over my prospects, and that would probably be the least of it. I could end up like Ed. On the other hand, the structure of the Homer deal was already making me feel dirty; to turn my head and pretend I didn't see what was right in front of me would be like selling my soul. I took a warm mouthful of the sweet coffee. Of course these two extreme ends were just that, extreme ends. My experience in life told me that situations usually panned out in the middle. If Norton and his boys weren't guilty, they'd never know I spoke with the police. If they were, getting on the right side was not only the right thing to do, but also the smart thing. I made up my mind; the 1st Precinct was on 16 Ericsson Place, walking distance from where I sat.

Fifteen minutes later I stood in front of a desk sergeant who cast a critical eye over my Armani suit and camel hair coat before asking, "Whadda ya want?" in the staccato tone of the native New Yorker. I know because I'm one myself and sometimes have a hard time disguising it.

"Looking for Detective Weston," I replied, handing him Nat's card.

He peered at it for a minute as if it might reveal something unexpected, "Nat's not in today. Can someone else help you out?"

"I don't know," I responded. I hadn't considered the possibility that Nat wouldn't be there, waiting for me.

"Is it about a case?" The sergeant prompted.

"Right, I might have some information for him. He interviewed me last week, and told me to look him up if something else came to mind."

The sergeant raised an eyebrow. "So, something has come to mind?"

"Right."

"Do you have to talk to Nat, or will someone else do?"

I thought about it. It didn't really matter. I just wanted to get it off my chest before I changed my mind. "No," I replied, "I suppose it could be anyone."

"What case does it pertain to?"

"The Bloomfield murder."

The cop nodded his head. "I'll be back in a minute."

The sergeant reappeared in a very short while, followed by a short, squat man in shirtsleeves and a polyester tie. He had dark black hair almost shellacked back on his round head in a Fifties style DA. The two broke their formation as they approached, the sergeant returning to his desk, and the other almost colliding into me. He stopped just before impact, and thrust out a pudgy hand. "I'm Joey Trucchiero"—he sounded like Donald duck with a Brooklyn accent—"Chief of Detectives for Manhattan South." Loose bits of spittle splattered about us.

"Nice to meet you," I said, taking his hand.

"The sergeant says you're looking for Nat?"

"I was."

"You wanted to discuss the Bloomfield murder?"

"Right."

He led me through the squad room and into an office in the back. I didn't think it was his office, or anyone else's for that matter. It contained no personal effects, or proper office equipment. In fact the only furniture in the room consisted of three chairs and a small table. He pulled a chair up to one side of the table and gestured for me to do the same.

"So, whatcha got for me?" he asked in a confidential manner, like I had a gift for him or something.

It was definitely an interrogation room, and something about Joey made me uncomfortable. But I plowed ahead anyway. I started with the Homer deal, covered Ed's involvement and his two outbursts, finally concluding with the feeling I had now that Norton was behind the thing.

Joey listened quietly to my whole story, taking notes and making small noises of encouragement, but overall leaving me to tell my tale without interruption. When I was finished he handed me a legal pad and asked me to commit to paper everything I had just told him. It took me about twenty minutes and when I'd signed, dated, and handed the statement to him, he grinned and shook my hand.

"I'll make sure this goes in the record, and is accorded the full weight it deserves."

I didn't know how to interpret that and just said, "Thank you, detective," and left.

TEN

I spent a romantic weekend fixing up my new apartment with Lisa, and arrived in my office feeling great. As if nothing could go wrong.

"Good morning, Doris," I called out as I passed the secretary's desk, "you look lovely today."

She smiled up at me. "Good morning yourself, Mr. Cole. You seem to be in a good mood."

"I am," I responded, opening my office door.

Before I got all the way in Doris sang out, "Jack, Mr. Norton called ten minutes ago, said he wanted to see you as soon as you arrived."

I favored her with a big grin. "Thanks, let him know I'll be down in five minutes."

I closed the door behind me and dropped my briefcase on the desk. If Norton wanted to see me right away, it was probably good news. They most likely had another project for me to tackle. Another project meant an opportunity to earn another astronomical bonus. God was good, life was grand.

I booted up my IBM. I'd been working on a list of companies I considered to be prime takeover candidates. I was going to impress the top cats with some initiative.

Ten minutes later I was ushered into Norton's office. As soon as his secretary closed the door I knew something was wrong.

Norton, Grunley, and Petersen were all there, along with a man I didn't recognize. They sat staring at me, all in a row. I thought of those statues on Easter Island. No one said a word or offered me a seat, so I stood awkwardly in the center of the room while they regarded me without humor. The silence lasted a good minute. Finally, Mr. Norton spoke.

"Good morning Mr. Cole. This is Mr. Hodges with the SEC." Norton's voice was as cold as his demeanor. The stranger nodded silently at me. "Mr. Hodges needs to ask you a couple of questions," he continued.

Mr. Hodges looked me up and down before he spoke, "Mr. Cole, are you familiar with the role of the SEC?"

I looked him straight in the eye. "Yes sir."

He held my eyes. "Do you understand the definition of insider trading? Do you know the penalties for it?"

"Yes sir," I heard myself croak.

"Are you acquainted with a man named Brad Seaman who is a licensed securities broker with the firm Harrison Schindler & Co.?"

I was starting to see where this was leading, but it didn't add up. Norton had told me to do it, and there he was, staring at me in indignation. I decided it would be best to keep my mouth shut till I saw where all this ended up. So I answered the question, "Yes sir, I am."

"Mr. Cole, I am not here now in any official capacity. This is something of a courtesy call, which I am making out of deference for my friendship with Arnold Norton. Mr. Cole, you are under investigation for, and suspected of, insider trading." Mr. Hodges rose from his seat, inclined his head toward Grunley and Petersen, shook Norton's hand, and swept out of the room.

Mr. Norton finally nodded me to a seat, "Well Jack, it's not as bad as all that. Fortunately Mr. Hodges is an old school chum of mine, and I'm sure he can be persuaded to drop the investigation. So I believe we can consider ourselves lucky, there will be no criminal charges brought."

He reached into his desk drawer and produced an envelope, "I think you must be able to appreciate the position of the firm though. We cannot afford the taint of scandal. Anything involving the SEC could be potentially ruinous. Now, you may not feel this is fair, but in exchange for my intervention with the SEC, I expect you to tender an immediate resignation." He lifted a sheet of paper, "I have written it for you, and I expect you to sign it as is. Your termination will be recorded as an amicable parting; it will go in your HR file that way." He placed an envelope on top of the resignation and pushed them both across the table toward me. "This is a check for a little over fifteen thousand dollars. It represents outstanding wages payable, along with accrued vacation pay, and what I feel is a generous severance on top of that. This is the last money you will see from Walsh Dahmer. After you sign this, I will arrange for a member of our security staff to oversee you as you have your exit interview, and then clean out your desk. I am sorry it worked out this way. I don't expect to see you again after today."

I left the office and walked over to Broadway in a daze. I stopped at Trinity Church and sat in a pew, trying to come to grips with reality.

Everything had been swept away. Not only were my ambitions dashed, but how was I going to keep my head above water? I had about twenty eight thousand, which may sound like a tidy sum, but I had just finished inflating all my living expenses in anticipation of advancement. And keeping mother out of a public home wasn't cheap; never-mind bringing her home to live with me. And since I'd resigned, there wasn't even the prospect of unemployment. I needed to find a job, and fast.

The first thing I wanted to do was get in touch with Brad and find out what had happened. I left the warm pew and headed out onto the cold street. This was in the days just before cell phones, or at least before they were common, so I found a pay phone on the corner, dropped a quarter in the slot, and dialed Brad's office number.

A woman answered, "Brad Seaman's office."

"Good morning, my name's Jack Cole, and I was trying to get a hold of Brad."

"One moment," she said and put me on hold.

After a couple of minutes of Christmas music, a man's voice came on the line. "Hi, how can I help you?"

"I'm holding for Brad Seaman."

"Brad's taken a leave of absence. Maybe there's something I can do for you? My name's Steve Errico and I'm handling his accounts."

"When do you expect him back?"

"I really couldn't say. It's open ended. He had some sort of family emergency. But as I've said, I am handling his accounts, if you need to make a trade . . ."

"No, that's okay. I'll try him at home, thanks." I hung up wondering if they'd gotten to Brad as well and that leave of absence crap was their way of politely dismissing him. I dropped another quarter in the slot and punched in Brad's home number. After four rings the answering machine picked up, and I left him a message.

As I turned from the phone, a raggedy man shook a paper cup in my face. "Can you spare some change? I'm trying to get something to eat." I dropped a few coins in his cup and moved on.

It was cold and I wasn't ready to go home yet. I returned to Trinity Church and sat for a long time staring at the cross. The whole situation was pretty unfair. Norton had told me to trade inside information. He was the guy tapping into that pension fund. He'd even all but ordered me to hinder a police investigation. My anger began to boil. I was their fall guy. Not only that, but I was now certain that there was no way he was my father, no way he had been the man providing help to me behind the scenes. Even in the midst of everything, somehow this felt like a deeper loss.

I got off the elevator on Norton's floor. The receptionist must have been told to deny me entrance, because she immediately put the phone on hold and called after me to stop. I stormed past her.

Norton stared at me over his computer terminal as I spilled into his office, the secretary pecking in my wake.

"I'm sorry Mr. Norton," she said, breathlessly, "he just barged right past me, I didn't have time—"

Norton lifted a hand. "That's all right, Kathy, I'll speak with him. Just close the door behind you." The door closed and he turned to me, arms folded across his chest. "What do you want, Cole?"

Now that I was actually there, confronting him, I felt less sure of myself, but I plowed ahead anyway. "I'm being fired on ethics, and that just doesn't add up. You're the guy who told me to leak that info. You're the guy telling me not to cooperate with the police. You're the guy embezzling the Homer pension fund." I was gathering momentum and I stepped forward and slammed my fist on his desk.

Unperturbed, Norton leaned forward and said, "Don't be an ass, Jack. Your signature is on everything. If there is any impropriety—and I'm not saying there is—in the Homer deal, you're the one who's going down for it. You could already go down for insider trading. I'm protecting you, you fool. Or would you like to spend some time in a small cell with a guy named Bubba? Would you?"

"That's not the point, Arnold," I said through clenched teeth.

"I'm afraid it is, Cole." He picked up the phone, "Kathy, you can call security now." He turned back to me, "Not only that, but if you ever set foot in this building again, I will call the police and have you arrested for trespassing."

Security must have been loitering right in front of the office because they burst through the door just as Norton was finishing his threat.

Rush hour was over, and the cold platform was only sparsely peopled. I leaned up against a pillar and wondered what I was going to do. I knew the worst thing to do was to get depressed. What I needed to do was get out and beat the bushes right away. And how was I going to keep my promise to my mother now? I had to put that out of my mind, had to tackle one thing at a time.

The Uptown Number Six came roaring into the station. I grabbed a corner seat and opened *The Wall Street Journal* to the help wanted section. A man speaking loudly at the far end of the car suddenly interrupted my concentration,

"Excuse me, ladies and gentlemen. My name is Nick Carver and I represent The Kinsale Outreach Center. We are attempting to feed the hungry. Now, I know some of you here today are hungry. If you are, I got sandwiches, juice, and apples. Just let me know, and you got it. If you're not hungry, and would like to help . . . we're not funded by the city, state, or federal government. Anything you can afford to give will go to feed hungry folk. Thank you."

I looked up. He was an elderly, black man, working his way through the car trundling a large bag. I stuck my hand in my pocket and fingered the change, my instinct to donate. But, for the first time, in a long time, I felt like I needed the change myself. It was ridiculous of course, but it somehow made me feel bad, less of a person. All my life I'd associated my personal worth with my net worth, or my ability to achieve net worth. This was how society judged me; this was how I judged myself. I pulled the change out of my pocket and stared stupidly at it, forty-five cents. When the small man with the big bag reached me, I handed over the change. The man thanked me and asked me if I was hungry. I shook my head, wondering if the old man had seen something through the Armani suit.

It was a long walk from the subway on Seventy-seventh and Lexington to my apartment on East End. On the way I passed three liquor stores. I paused at each of the first two. At the third I stopped and bought a bottle. See, I wanted a drink. I also knew it was a terrible idea. I needed to keep my edge, I was about to engage in a race against a negative cash flow, but I also needed to alter my reality somehow. I couldn't exist much longer on this morning's harsh plane of failure.

The doorman handed me my mail, three bills, and a letter from the local Assemblyman. I dropped them, unopened, on my new kitchen table, and poured myself a big glass of scotch. I kicked off my shoes, removed my jacket and tie, and then I lay down on the couch with the bottle of scotch on the coffee table next to me. The first big swig made me feel better. It was eleven-thirty A.M. The only other thing I'd had so far that day was a cup of coffee.

I woke at six P.M. when the telephone rang. My head was thick, and my mouth tasted funny. The bottle was almost empty on the table in front of me. The answering machine picked up: It was Lisa reminding me about our eight o'clock dinner date at Ben Benson's Steakhouse.

I didn't pick up the phone. I didn't know what to say to her. I Wished I had someone in the world with whom I could talk without strings attached. Mother flashed through my mind. I thought about my father, but here the picture was only the memory of a childhood fantasy. I lifted the bottle from the table and finished it off without bothering to pour it into a glass.

Roget Voltan sat in the back room of a very small French restaurant on West Fifty-first Street, absently picking, with his left hand, at a plate filled with cornichon and suasion. Fanned out in his right hand were five freshly dealt cards. A pair of aces, a pair of kings, and a seven.

Gilbert, the chef, pursed his lips and said, "Deux."

The three other men at the table checked. Roget was the last to bet. "Votre deux, et une autre deux." He threw four chips into the pot.

Roget drew one card, another ace. His beeper went off and he absently reached into his suit pocket and shut it off.

This time Gilbert checked and the rest of the players followed suit. When Roget bet two again, everybody folded. Roget's other beeper went off, vibrating at his waist. He raked in the pot and squinted at the read out: Arnold Norton, using his emergency code. *Asshole,* thought Roget, hating to have his poker game disturbed. But he and Norton had a deep connection that spanned decades. When the man called Roget always responded.

An hour later, he was ushered into Arnold Norton's office by a security guard. Neil Grunley and John Petersen were there already. The three of them reminded Roget of the three witches from *Macbeth,* predicting corrupt possibilities that were not what they seemed.

"You wanted to see me, Arnold?" Roget said, ignoring the other two grinning nervously at him. They were afraid of him, Roget knew, and treated him as someone might treat a live grenade with a personality.

"Yes. Why don't you sit down?" Norton replied, indicating a chair at the small round conference table where the rest already sat.

"What's on your mind?" Roget asked, impatient to return to his poker game.

Norton leaned forward, his voice down to a whisper. "It's Cole. He was forced to resign this morning. As per our decision after discovering he spoke with the police. At first it went well, but he came back making threats and behaving erratically." Arnold patted the chair next to him again.

Roget continued to ignore the chair—did not in fact even remove his coat. "How did you force him out?" he asked in a flat toned voice.

"My friend Hodges. Perhaps you remember him from the old days?"

Roget remained silent.

"No?" Norton filled in the response for him, "I don't suppose it matters. Hodges is with the SEC and he's an old friend—"

"Like Tierney?" Roget interrupted.

"Tierney?" Norton asked, truly confused.

"It doesn't matter." Roget took the seat but left his coat on. "What about Hodges?"

"He's an investigator for the SEC now, and he has a snitch named Brad Seaman who works for him, feeding him little bits of information in exchange for his own survival."

Roget sneered, "So?"

"Well this Seaman fellow is a friend of Cole's and Cole gave him some inside info on the Homer deal. Seaman used the info, and then fed Cole to Hodges. I was able to use this to force Cole to resign."

Roget nodded, "I see. So, what's on your mind?"

"Just this: If Cole is going to start developing a conscience he could become dangerous. He could become a real liability and it might, perhaps, be better if he followed Bloomfield sooner rather than later."

Bloodthirsty little pencil pushers, Roget thought, *bloodthirsty and stupid.* "I see. I'm afraid that would be ill advised. I recommend that you wait, just as I recommended you wait with Bloomfield."

"Why? I think it needs to be done as quickly as possible. It needs to be done now." The words poured out of Grunley in a petulant torrent. "Or do we need to look into other means like we did with Bloomfield?"

Roget inclined his head toward the man for a moment, appraising him, speculating as to what it would be like to kill him. What kind of end would he make? Roget stood, "By all means, Neil. Kill him, but if it must be done now, do it yourself, and this time I will not clean up the mess created by your stupidity."

Norton lifted a hand, "Please, Roget, sit back down. Why do you suggest we wait?"

"It is common sense. Bloomfield is dead and the police will eventually conclude that the pimp, Lucas Monroe, killed him in a random fashion. That is good. If you murder Cole too, they may sense a pattern. The reason you chose this young man to begin with was his isolation. If all goes well, he will sink further into isolation. By the time he's taken care of, no one will even know he's gone. But you must wait." Roget turned to go.

"Roget," Norton corrected, "the reason why we chose Cole in the first place was because you recommended him."

Roget paused at the door and looked back. "Yes, of course, Norton. I recommended him. I've recommended a lot of guys to you over the years, and I have never been wrong about any of them."

At eight o'clock Lisa was seated alone at a table for two. She felt better than she had in years. She had finally been able to quit dancing at the club. She'd landed a paying role in musical theater, and she was in love.

She liked Jack for all his contrasts; he tried to be a tough guy, but he was soft with her. He wanted to be a killer businessman, and he seemed to be successful, but she looked into his eyes and saw limitless, sweet vulnerability. No different, really, from the nineteen-year-old she had loved as a girl.

She took a sip of mineral water and looked at her watch: eight-fifteen. He was late and that wasn't like him. Then she saw him, weaving unsteadily across the floor. The headwaiter staring suspiciously in his wake.

He plopped down. "Hi, sorry I'm late," he slurred.

She took stock: Even dressed in his best Armani suit, he looked disheveled. Like an unmade bed, her mother would have said. He needed a shave. His hair stuck up at odd angles. His tie was too short, and his shirt was buttoned unevenly.

"Have you been drinking?" she asked.

He held up his thumb and forefinger, pinched together. "Just a little."

The waiter arrived, "May I bring you something to drink, sir?"

"Double scotch, rocks."

"He'll take a cup of coffee," Lisa corrected.

The waiter looked back and forth, uncomfortably between them. "Which will it be, then?"

"The coffee," Lisa repeated. She reached across the table and took Jack's hand. "What's wrong?"

Conflicting emotions played across his tipsy face. "Nothing, I went to an office party, and maybe I had a little too much. I'll be okay after I eat something. How was your day?"

She pushed the breadbasket across the table toward him. "What was the occasion?"

"Occasion?" he repeated, confused.

"Yes, the occasion for the office party. The one where you got drunk."

"Oh," he said, "It was a retirement party."

ELEVEN

Nat Weston got home late; it was close to ten o'clock when he sat down to eat leftover spaghetti and watch T.V. with Keisha, his wife.

He stared sadly at his plate. "Darryl must have been pretty hungry if this is all he left me from dinner."

"Two of his friends from school came over. They looked so hungry I made them stay for dinner. I swear, I think some of the parents around here don't feed their kids at all. I could heat you up a pork chop."

The phone rang.

Keisha went into the kitchen to answer it. After a minute she called out to him, "It's Pat from the station. I told him you were eating, but he said it's important."

Nat sighed, pushed the TV table out of his way, and strode into the kitchen, taking the telephone from his wife's outstretched hand.

"What's up, Pat?"

"The perp you're looking for, Lucas Monroe?"

"Yeah?"

"I got him."

"Where's he at?"

"The morgue."

"He's dead?"

"No, he's dancing. They opened a fucking dance club here."

"Very funny, Pat. When did they find the body?"

"Looks like the Coast Guard found the body in Jamaica Bay a couple of days ago, but they had a hard time identifying it. The hands had been cut off."

Nat's blood started pumping. The suspicion awakened by the street punk's tales of "The Frenchman" were now confirmed in his mind. "Sweet Jesus. Stay there, Pat. I'm on my way."

"Listen Nat, let me give you a piece of advice."

Nat drew in a deep breath.

"I know you don't want to hear it, Nat, but I'm only telling ya 'cause I care. 'Cause we were partners for ten years. 'Cause I know what you're up against with this. Leave it alone. This is one mystery you should just leave a mystery."

"You think this one could mess me up, huh?"

"Nat, I think this one could bury ya."

"I can't let it go, Pat. That's just not what I signed up for."

Pat was silent for a long minute. "All right. I got your back, if I can, but I just might not be able to help you. It might go that far."

Nat hung up the phone and turned to Keisha, who was now regarding him with a familiar, sour expression. He kissed her on the cheek. "I'll only be gone a couple of hours."

"What about your dinner?" she called as he sat on a bench putting his boots on in the hallway.

"I'll grab something."

He looked up from his feet when a scarf hit him on the top of his head, and she was standing over him. "You better grab it on the way," she said. "You know you never have an appetite after the morgue."

Thirst woke me up. I was on my back with the first gray light of winter dawn creeping through the blind. All the scotch I'd drunk the night before was embedded in my face like hot, fuzzy, insulation just under the skin. My throat choked on dry tissue that should have been moist. I desperately needed a cup of water, but I couldn't bear the thought of getting off the bed.

I lay suffering for about a half hour. When I finally got up, I still felt drunk and unsteady on my feet. I stumbled into the bathroom, knelt in front of the toilet and forced myself to puke until I could puke no more. Then I put the shower on full blast and sat in it for a long time. Finally I crawled out and gulped down as much water as I could. I felt just slightly better.

Lisa was still asleep, breathing softly where I'd left her. I passed through the bedroom and into the kitchen, swallowed four aspirin, and brewed coffee. After the second cup my mind began to function a bit. At first I filled up with regret—regret for the amount I'd drunk the night before, regret for the money

I'd spent. I'd just been laid off with no prospects and, on the same day, put another couple of hundred on my Visa. I could barely remember what else I'd done or said the night before, but those regrets stood out in my mind.

I didn't think I'd told Lisa about my troubles, but I wasn't sure. I wanted to. I needed to share my fear with someone. I needed someone to help me make plans, to give me a pep talk. I needed someone to have faith in me. I'd always had faith in myself, but now that faith was shaken. For the first time in a long time, I needed something from outside of myself to give me strength.

Ironically, this newly lost faith in myself kept me from confiding, as I needed to, in Lisa. I was afraid she loved, not me, but my carefully crafted image of myself. An image I could no longer maintain. I was desperately afraid that if I shattered this image with honesty she would go away. I guess I had no faith in myself, and I had no faith in her. The same mix of emotions had ripped us apart the last time.

She was suddenly behind me, softly massaging my scalp. "How're you feeling, baby?"

I looked up with a weak smile. "Like I poisoned myself."

Her hands dropped to my shoulders. "You did. Why don't you call in sick? I'll stay and nurse you back to health."

So, I hadn't told her. To agree with her now would be the best thing. I didn't have the strength to get dressed and pretend to go to work. What would I do anyway? I was in no condition to go job-hunting today, I could spend the day licking my wounds, gathering my thoughts, and relaxing. Tomorrow I would begin all that much fresher.

"Okay"—I forced a smile—"I just have to call my secretary and let her know."

I picked up the cordless and dialed a seven-digit number at random. Someone's machine picked up and they got my message, they could make of it what they would.

The next morning we woke at seven. After a quick breakfast, I walked Lisa to a cab, picked up a copy of the *New York Times*, and doubled back to my apartment. Once home I laid a notebook next to the help wanted section, brewed a fresh pot of coffee, and sat down to plan my future.

In the ads under Wall Street, there were positions for recent grads, BOH (back of the house), operations, compliance, sales, sales assistants, analysts, stockbrokers. All of these ads seemed to promise limitless possibilities. Some had telephone numbers, some addresses, and some just fax numbers.

I'd never really gone job-hunting before. I'd been recruited for my first job out of college. The job at Walsh Dahmer had come to me through headhunters. I didn't know how to interpret the short ad blurbs, or quite where to begin in general. It came down to five ads that looked promising. I circled them, but it was hard to tell. When I finished with the Wall Street section, I scanned the Finance area and discovered a couple more under Accounting. All together I generated ten leads. I copied them all into my notebook and got on the phone. I knew I'd feel a hell of a lot better if I were at least able to set up one appointment. Four of my leads had phone numbers, the rest were destinations for resume copies, either through fax or mail. My luck was well in, because I was able to arrange two appointments from the four calls, one for two o'clock that same day and one for eight the next morning. That done I reviewed my finances and paid my bills. When I was done I felt better, more in control. I could see that I had a couple of months of good financial steam in me, and all I had to do was get working quickly.

I stared at the ad for my two o'clock appointment.

> WALL STREET
>
> INVESTMENT BANKING
>
> NYC inv. bank specializing in middle market M&A and private placements searching for associate/ analyst. Required: 2–3 years relevant exp. at inv. bank, Big 6 acctg. firm or major corp.: excel financial/PC/writing skills & academic record; ability to work long hours.

It was right up my alley, and I couldn't see how I wouldn't qualify. The salary had to be at least in the high five figures; jobs like that always were. That would be enough to start with. I'd have my foot in the door, and I'd be able to find my own path to the feast. The only thing I'd have to tell Lisa was that I'd switched jobs.

My resume needed work, and I cursed myself for never having bought a PC. Not a lot of people had them at home back then, but they were around and I could have afforded one. I checked my watch; I still had time to go to one of the neighborhood computing centers. First though, I needed to make a couple of calls. I left another message for Brad. I was starting to wonder about that—the guy should have returned my calls by now.

The next call was going to be more difficult. My 'Cover Your Ass' file, including the tape I'd made of my conversation with Arnold Norton the day I discovered Ed Bloomfield had been murdered, was still in my former office. I'd wanted to take it the day I was terminated, but that security guard had been watching me like a hawk to make sure I took nothing but personal effects. I thought Doris, my former secretary, might help me. There was only one way to find out.

"Mr. Cole?" She sounded surprised when I got her on the phone.

"Hi Doris."

"What happened?"

I sighed. "It's a long story. I was forced to resign."

"And then you came back. Everybody's talking about it. Why did security throw you out?" She sounded concerned, which was good.

"I had words with Mr. Norton."

"I see." Her voice became more distant.

I plunged ahead anyway. "Doris, I need a small favor. Can you help me?"

"I don't know. What is it?"

"I left a file there. You'll find it under CYA in my brown filing cabinet. I obviously can't go back to the office, but I need that file. Could you get that for me?"

There was a long silence. Finally she said, "I'm sorry, Mr. Cole. You know I've been with the firm over thirty years. I wish I could help you, but I can't afford to lose my job."

I could feel her slipping away; I also knew it was just a matter of time before those files were cleaned out, if they hadn't been already. "I understand, Doris. But could you at least retrieve it and put it in a safe place?"

She sighed. I could almost see her shaking her head at the receiver. "I'll think about it. Now I really have to go."

Something clicked in my head. "Wait!" I shouted into the receiver.

I must have sounded crazy but it stopped her. "What, Mr. Cole?" She demanded in clipped tones.

"Did you say that you've been with the firm for thirty years?" I know it sounds crazy and self-centered, but until that moment I had never thought about how long she'd been at the firm, and what it implied.

"More like thirty-two. Why is that so urgent to you?" Her voice sounded guarded.

"Did you know Monique Cole?"

"Monique Cole? I haven't heard that name in forever. Are you related to her?" Now it was her turn to sound surprised.

"She's my mother."

"Well, I'll be. Monique and I were good friends. I remember when she had you . . . I mean, that must have been you, the time works out with your age, but that would make you . . ." She suddenly stopped talking.

"You were going to say?"

The line was silent for close to a full moment. "I was going to say, that would make you John Palmer's son. At least I think it would. Your mother got real quiet and secretive about you, you and your father . . ."

"Doris, I'm not real sure who my father was, but I am sure who my mother is. Will you help me with the file?"

The phone went dead.

I sat for a long time after that, pondering the name John Palmer. Could it be true? I picked the receiver back up, and then put it back down. Doris had almost weakened, and then she had forced herself to hang up on me, so she was nervous about something. Chances were if I tried to call her back right now, she wouldn't answer. And if she did I'd probably scare her off all together. No, if I were going to have a chance to persuade her to give me that file, or any other information, I'd have to go do it face to face. Besides, right about now I had to compartmentalize and get myself ready for some interviews.

At twelve-thirty, armed with my updated resume and dressed in a conservative suit, I began the trek to the East Eighty-sixth Street subway station. My heart raced as I negotiated the jostling crowds on the busy streets. Man, I was nervous; I needed a job, today. In spite of the cold my hands were sweating, even after I took off my leather gloves. I needed to get a little more Zen; I tried to invent a good reason for having left Walsh Dahmer.

For a moment I entertained the notion of saying I left because of the death of Ed Bloomfield, but that dog wouldn't hunt, not if I was representing myself as a killer businessman. I thought about saying I had a personality conflict with upper management, but that would have been a classic interviewing error. Finally I decided to say I resigned for personal reasons and leave it at that.

The express was pulling in just as I arrived at the station and got down to the lower level. I arrived at Brooklyn Bridge Station in lower Manhattan just before one o'clock. With an hour to kill before the interview on William Street, I grabbed a cup of coffee and sat for a little while in the park in front of City Hall.

I sat on a cold bench being regarded suspiciously by pigeons, and watching the crowds go by. There were policemen, office workers, executives, students from Pace University, and lots of homeless people. An old man sat down on the bench next to me and smiled. I looked around. Most of the benches in the park were empty, but there he was, sitting next to me.

"It's a cold day for sitting in the cold. Ain't it?" The old man observed, removing a container of coffee from a brown paper bag.

I nodded politely and muttered a perfunctory, "Yep," hoping it would beg off further conversation.

"Yes indeed, cold winter and likely to get colder. But you know, I've seen worse," he proclaimed, waiting for a response. When all I did was nod politely, he continued, "How old do you think I am?"

I didn't really want to talk to the guy, but he seemed a nice enough old man and I couldn't be completely rude so I took a guess. "I really couldn't say, sixty-five, seventy?"

He smiled, showing a few bad teeth and a lot of gum. "Nope. I'm seventy-nine years old. Fought in World War II and spent most of my life working in a factory in Long Island City. Too old to work now."

"So I take it you're retired?"

The old man gave a dry, coughing laugh. "Yeah, I'm retired now. But I'll tell you this, if you don't have money, retirement ain't all it's cracked up to be. You know why I'm out here in the cold?"

"No, I don't."

"Well, I'll tell you why. See, most of the month I live in an SRO." He gave me an inquisitive look like Popeye staring into a camera. "You know what that is?"

"Sure, single room occupancy."

"That's right. But towards the end of the month, when my social security runs out, I gotta put my things in storage and sleep out for a few days. When my next check comes in I go back to the SRO. The same damn room. When I'm not in that damn room it stays empty. But that don't matter, I still gotta move out till the next check comes in."

I looked down at my shoes, feeling a little embarrassed, wondering why the old man had come to confide in me. I thought

I should say something, so I offered up, "That's all the income you have, just Social Security? Didn't the place you worked have a pension?"

"Oh, there was supposed to be a pension all right. I paid into it, but I never saw any of it. It got swindled. I never did understand it, I mean I understood it, there was a bankruptcy and somehow the lawyers managed to pull the fund into the assets of the company and then they raided it to cover their fees. What I don't understand is how they got away with it." He took a sip from the steaming cardboard cup of coffee, and then shook his head in confused disgust like he was re-living the trauma.

I felt suddenly sick to my stomach. I fished in my pocket, found a twenty and handed it to the old man. "Here, take this." I wished him a good day and headed off to my appointment, desperately trying to change my state of mind.

The building which housed Goldstein & Welch must have been quite the office tower back in the nineteen twenties when it was probably built. I took the elevator to the tenth floor and presented myself to the receptionist, who made a call and told me to take a seat.

And I sat; I sat for over half an hour. Finally a young guy, about twenty-five or twenty-six, stuck his head out from behind a door, looked in my direction, and said, "You Cole?"

I smiled and stood up, but the guy just disappeared again. I stood awkwardly for a minute and when nothing more happened, sat back down. Another five minutes or so went by and the guy reappeared and beckoned me. I followed and tried to shake the guy's hand, but when I got close enough he turned his back and hurried down a long corridor. At the end of the hall he turned into an open door. I followed and found myself in a small conference room. As the door clicked shut, the man finally turned to face me.

He took my outstretched hand and gave it a halfhearted shake. "I'm Lenny Pissarro, Jack, the Director of Personnel. I'm sorry you had to wait so long, but I'm very busy, and my secretary probably shouldn't have scheduled an interview today at all."

I felt awkward, unwelcome, but I tried to hide it. "Does that mean you don't have a position available?"

Lenny sat and motioned me to a seat across from him, "No, I do. It just might have been better to meet on another day. Do you have your resume with you?"

I handed it over, and Lenny put on a pair of granny glasses. He studied it for several moments then fixed me with a stare. "Tell me about yourself, Jack."

I forced a bright smile. "What would you like to know, Mr. Pissarro?"

He waved my resume around in the air like it was, I don't know, a worthless piece of paper. "Just tell me a few things about yourself that might not be listed on the resume." He said.

I gave him a nod. "Well, I was born and raised in New York City. I'm unmarried. I worked my way through college, recently completed my MBA, and I'm looking to further my career in investment banking."

"Why?" He demanded in an almost accusatory tone.

"Why what?" I countered, struggling to keep the impatience out of my voice.

"Why investment banking?"

"It's where my interests lie."

"What interests are those?"

There was nothing for it but to bury the man in bullshit. "I'm interested in the dynamics of progress. I'm interested in acting as a catalyst in the business world, as a midwife to new ventures. It helps to give life meaning. I believe we all strive for that."

"I see. That is very heartfelt. What do you feel you can bring to Goldstein Welch?"

"The dedication driven by the sentiments I just described."

The guy laughed. I didn't like the way he laughed. He changed gears abruptly, "Why did you leave Walsh Dahmer?"

"Personal reasons."

"Such as?"

I groaned. Lenny wasn't going to accept my ambiguity on this point. "I wasn't completely in tune with the corporate philosophy there."

"Then why did you stay there as long as you did?"

"It took me a while to realize that."

"What makes you sure you're going to be in tune with our corporate philosophy, here?"

"I know something about your firm and I admire its work."

"For example?"

"The CMC deal," I replied, hoping Lenny would let it go at that. It was the only thing I knew about the firm and I didn't have a lot of details.

"How much do you expect to make here?"

"A minimum of eighty thousand."

"That's what you need to make?"

"Ballpark."

"How many hours do you think you'll be working each week?"

"As many as need be. I'm a team player."

"What do you know about the position you're applying for?"

"I'll be an analyst who also has some responsibility for client liaison."

"That's correct. You'd be reporting to our Middle Markets Accounts Manager. I'll tell you what; you seem like a sharp guy, Jack, quick on your feet. I'm going to forward your resume to Matt Hinckley, he's the man you'd be reporting to if you got the position. If he likes what he sees, and your background checks out, we'll be in touch by next week to set up a second interview." He stood and offered his hand. "I want to thank you for your time."

Nat Weston expelled a deep breath, gathered his papers and walked slowly down the hall to Joey's office. He rapped gently, but firmly on the door.

"Yeah?"

"It's Nat."

"Come in, Nat," Joey responded, his tone annoyed, an unpleasant emphasis on the name.

Joey didn't look up when he entered so Nat stood awkwardly for a moment on the threshold, and then coughed.

Finally Joey looked up, "Why don't you sit down and tell me what's on your mind?" he said, still holding a pen poised in his hand as if ready to go back to work.

Nat squeezed his bulk into the small chair across from Joey. "It's about the Bloomfield case."

Joey dropped the pen and leaned back. "Go on."

"We found Lucas Monroe."

"I heard that. He's dead. That wraps up the case into a nice, neat package. So why are we here, wasting the taxpayer's time and money discussing it?" He was starting to spray, and Nat wiped a fleck of spittle from his cheek.

"You heard the body was found without hands?"

"Yeah, so?"

"Well, some years back there was a gang, used to operate round midtown. Used to sometimes cut off a victim's hands, then use them to plant prints on a weapon when they pulled a job."

"Yeah, I know all about that. Irish gang, what were they called again?"

"They used to call 'em the Westies, in the newspapers."

"Well those guys are long gone. So what are you trying to tell me here?"

"Just that whoever killed Bloomfield also killed Lucas Monroe. He killed Monroe first, then used the severed hands to plant prints at the Bloomfield murder scene. The guy who did this is known on the street as The Frenchman.

"What kinda fairy tale shit are you trying to put over on me here? The Frenchman, my ass! You know what, Weston? I think you're starting to get carried away with yourself. Like all of a sudden, you're Ellery Queen or something. Look, I told you I want this case closed. So take your half-baked theories to the shredder, and close the case. Okay?"

"Joey, I know if you give me a little more time, I can find this guy."

"You're fucking incredible! You just don't fucking listen, do you?"

"Joey . . ."

"No, Nat. You listen to me, and listen good. Shut the fuck up. Get out of my fucking office. Close the fucking case. And if you want to find a fucking Frenchman, go to fucking France!"

TWELVE

On the Monday following my interview at Goldstein Welch, I completed what had become my daily ritual: walking Lisa to a cab and pretending to go to work before doubling back to the apartment to set up interviews. I'd gone on seven interviews so far, two of them directly with firms, the rest with agencies and headhunters. From these last, I'd settled on two recruiters to work with, and I was hopeful that the Goldstein Welch interview would ultimately bear fruit. So there I sat, scanning the want ads and waiting anxiously for nine A.M. so I could phone in to the headhunters.

The first call I made was to Marci at Harold Davis Associates. I was on hold for what seemed like an eternity before she finally came on the line.

Sunshine danced in her voice, "Good morning, Jack. Did you have a great weekend?"

"Very nice, Marci, and you?"

"Good. I don't have any news for you yet, Jack. I'm sorry."

"But I thought you said you'd have five or six today. You said I'd have my pick." I felt like an athlete all pumped for the big game, then told I'd have to sit on the bench.

"I know, but my leads fell through. Why don't you check back with me on Wednesday? We should be able to get some balls up in the air by then." She still sounded perky, but there was a cold undercurrent that hadn't been there the week before. Still I trusted her because she was the headhunter who had recruited me for Walsh Dahmer three years before, so I knew she could produce. She knew she could make money from me.

"Thanks," I said, "I'll do that."

Next I called Keith Sparrow at Sparrow & McCall. Keith had the same basic line as Marci, the same distance, the same lack of interest. It was unnerving. I leaned back in my chair; I had no place to go. Frustrated, I began to create a new list from the Sunday want ads, and ten minutes later I was done and staring at the wall. Time, I decided, to place a follow up call to Lenny Pissarro at Goldstein Welch. But what if it was bad news? I stood up and began to pace. What if it was undecided, and Lenny decided I was a pest for calling? No, he wouldn't think that. He would think it showed aggressive initiative. Lenny seemed like the type of guy who would respect that. Any way, if they wanted me or not, my phone call wouldn't change the fact. And at least I'd know.

I dialed the number.

"Personnel, Lenny Pissarro speaking."

I hung up. I felt foolish, like a kid making crank calls. Why was I afraid to speak to Lenny? Maybe I was afraid of bad news and maybe I was afraid of being rejected by a guy like Lenny. I didn't really like him. During the interview it seemed like Lenny looked down on me. Then again, maybe Lenny just looked down on people when he had the upper hand. Either way it didn't matter, he was a human resources guy. You dealt with guys like him on the way in, and on the way out. That was it, with the possible exception of the company holiday party or a benefits seminar. I picked up the phone again.

This time when Lenny answered, I said, "Good morning Mr. Pissarro. It's Jack Cole."

"Jack who?" I knew the guy was just being a prick, but I remained patient.

"Jack Cole. We had an interview together last week. I just wanted to touch base to see how things were progressing."

"Oh right, Cole. Listen Cole, I'm sorry, but we're not going to be making you an offer. Good luck."

I could feel him slipping away, "Wait," I said quickly, "May I ask why you decided against my application?"

"We just felt you weren't a good fit. Now really Mr. Cole, I have to let you go. I have calls holding." The line went dead.

I looked at the clock. Nine-thirty. Nine-thirty, and already I felt as if I couldn't continue on this plane of reality. I had a bottle of scotch in the cupboard. I pulled it down and poured myself a quick shot. At least I could feel better.

I woke up at four-thirty. I had done nothing, accomplished nothing. I felt like shit. I could not continue to do this. I had polished off three quarters of a liter of scotch on an empty stomach. I'd spent my whole day in a drunken stupor. I closed my eyes; I wanted to go back to sleep, but I was forgetting something. Then it came back to me. I was supposed to take Lisa to the theater tonight. Now that was dumb, too. I was unemployed and about to spend a few hundred on dinner and the theater.

I sat up. It would be okay. I'd land a job tomorrow. So what was a couple of hundred more or less?

I took a shower, dressed, and downed a pot of coffee. When I was done I looked and felt slightly better. Leaving the apartment, I grabbed a downtown number six to Grand Central where I took the shuttle to Times Square. From there I hiked over to a theater on Forty-fourth and bought tickets for the show, *Broadway.* I tried to use my Visa Gold, but it was maxed out. Slightly disturbed, I used my Amex instead. It was a hundred and fifty dollars for two orchestra seats in the fourth row.

I ducked into a bar on Forty-third, ordered a bottle of beer, and gave Lisa a call. By the time she got there I was into my third beer. She sat next to me and ordered a spritzer.

"Tough day?" She took my hand and peered into my face.

"No, I'm fine. Why did you ask that?"

She gave me a sad smile. "You just look a little down, that's all."

"I'm a little tired. How was your day?"

Her face lit up and I felt suddenly jealous. "It was great. I really feel like I'm finally doing something. You know, rehearsing for the show. The people are fabulous too, I'm really making friends, and that's important because we're going to be spending a lot of time together. I couldn't bear the thought of spending months and months with a group of people I didn't get along with."

I groaned inwardly, thinking of her being away so long. Then again, it would give me time to recover. I stared at the green bottle in front of me. She was still talking and suddenly she stopped.

"You're not listening to a word I'm saying!"

"Sure I am. You were talking about other people in the cast, and how much you liked them."

"And what did I say after that?"

I smiled, "I . . . I don't know."

Her look of consternation suddenly blew away, replaced with giggles.

"I'm sorry. I guess I was just daydreaming."

She took my hand and squeezed it. "You're hopeless, Jack Cole."

"I am, you know."

"I know what?"

"Hopeless."

"Hopeless, what?"

"Hopelessly stuck on you, Lisa Clement."

She stared at me for a long moment. Then she said, "You can say it if you want to."

"Say what?"

"You know. What you want to say, but are afraid to."

I suddenly knew what she wanted me to say. "I love you, Lisa Clement."

"I love you too, Jack Cole."

The next day I told Lisa that I had to leave for work early and then I got up at four A.M. After a quick breakfast I hopped the subway down to Wall Street. Around six A.M. I set up shop on a bench in the middle of a traffic island right in front of Walsh Dahmer. Doris, I knew, usually got to work around seven. I hoped to catch her on the way into the building. Spreading out a newspaper, I pulled my hat down low over my head and settled in to wait. After only a little while the sun rose and all around me the financial capitol of the world came to life.

I spotted her crossing the street at around quarter till seven. Detaching myself from the frozen bench, I hurried my cold bones after her. It didn't take long to catch up.

I fell in step with her when she was still some distance away from the building. "Doris, it's me, Jack."

She stopped in her tracks, a pained look on her face. "Jack," she said. "We can't be seen together. Do you know what they might do? Do you know what they're capable of?"

"I do. Do you?"

"Does Norton know that you're Monique Cole's son?"

"He does," I said.

She looked nervously up and down the street. "So you think he set you up because you're the son of his old enemy?"

"I don't know that much about it all. Maybe you can tell me?"

A man passed by and stared at us as we were talking. I noticed Doris go pale. The man nodded at me then continued up the street.

"I did secure the file for you," Doris whispered, watching the man as he made his way toward the Walsh Dahmer building.

"Thank you, Doris. When can I pick it up?"

"Do you know the Heidelberg Restaurant up on East Eighty-fifth?"

"I do."

"Be there at five o'clock this afternoon and I'll send it to you. Be at the bar, and don't be late."

She turned on her heel and hurried quickly toward her office.

The Old Heidelberg is a German brew house and restaurant located in the section of the Upper East Side of Manhattan that all the locals called Germantown. The restaurant is pretty old and I wouldn't be surprised if it hadn't been there since the 1920s. I would hit it every once in a while when I had a craving for schnitzel, or sauerbraten washed down with a Dinkelacher beer in a glass boot. The food really was good, if you didn't mind clogged arteries.

I got there a little after four P.M., just in case. I couldn't resist and I ordered one of those beers, only not the whole boot, and I waited.

Two hours went by. It was now after six and I'd already had the plate of schnitzel. I'd had the conversation with the single geriatric drunk ensconced at the bar with me. Dieter, the bartender had long since discovered an excuse to disappear into the kitchen, and I was beginning to think if I heard one more jaunty polka I'd cut my own throat. I was, in fact, about to leave. It was an hour past the time that Doris had arranged to meet me, and I could only assume that I'd been stood up.

Then the door leading to the sunny street from the dark bar flung open, cold air and bright sunshine rushing in on its heels. A man maybe five years younger than me stepped in and looked around. By this time the geriatric drunk (whose name was Seymour) was snoozing on his stool. Dieter was still buried somewhere in the kitchen. The barroom was separated from the dining room by walls, so I was completely alone with the newcomer. The man stared hard at me for a long moment, so I stared back. It was uncomfortable and went on far longer than I would have liked, and then I noticed the file in the man's hand. It was the file that I had asked Doris for. I was sure of it.

I stood up from the chair and nodded. And the man nodded back, taking a few steps towards me. "You're Jack Cole, am I right?" the man asked.

I nodded.

He dropped the file on top of the bar next to my half-drunken beer. "This is for you," he said. "And now that you've got it, I'd thank you not to bother my mother anymore. She's all set to retire next year and she doesn't need any problems."

I nodded again, my eyes on the file. "You have my word, pal."

He turned on his heel and swept out through the same door, and I was left holding the file. I flipped quickly through the contents: It was all there. I waited a solid ten minutes, finished my beer, and then left myself.

The next two weeks went by in a blur. I was out with Lisa every night, and up, hung-over, looking for work every morning. Both of the headhunters I'd been working with mysteriously stopped taking my calls, and I was having a more and more difficult time landing interviews on my own. But it was getting toward the end of the year and I figured everything would loosen up in January.

Lisa still had no idea I was out of work. Really, aside from the negative cash flow, I was enjoying life. Brad Seaman puzzled me. He never did return any of my calls, so I just stopped trying. I decided he was angry with me for getting us both in trouble, but I wasn't going to lose sleep: He'd asked for the information.

It was the Friday before Lisa was to leave on tour. We were down on Bleeker Street on the way to meet a girlfriend of hers at one of the little rock clubs that dot the Village. I had a hobo flask of scotch in my pocket and I nipped at it now and again, much to Lisa's annoyance. We'd just come from seeing the tree at Rockefeller Center, and I felt a bit maudlin, remembering all the times I'd gone there as a child with my mother. As a kid I'd wanted to go skating, but mom had always shot me down, saying it was too crowded, too expensive.

We arrived at the club a little before show time and it was crowded. The woman who was performing was reputed to sound like a young Joan Baez, and she was popular. I paid the cover to a large, hairy, middle-aged guy in a black leather jacket. He had a dirty red bandanna tied around his skull, and looked like a retired Hells Angel. Inside, a large bar opened into a room with a small stage and picnic-style tables.

A small brunette seated next to a preppie-looking guy caught Lisa's eye and waved. The woman was introduced to me as her friend Mary from 'the cast' and the preppie was her boyfriend, Doug. There were musicians on stage tuning up now. The girls chatted away excitedly about the tour, so I turned to Doug.

"So, you going to miss her?" I asked.

"I miss her already, man."

"Yeah, I know what you mean. Are you going up to see the show?"

"I'd like to go up for a couple of days around Christmas. If I can get the time off work."

"That sounds like a good idea." I turned to Lisa. "What do you think, baby?"

She raised her eyebrows and smiled, "About what?"

"Me coming up for Christmas."

"That's a great idea, I'd really love that."

"You could come up with Doug," Mary chimed in.

Doug nodded, "Yeah, I have a car. We could drive up together, as long as I can get the time off."

"Don't you get time off at Christmas anyway?" I asked.

"Not necessarily. I'm an actor—which you can also interpret to mean waiter—and the place I work is going to be open on Christmas, Christmas Eve, and the day after."

Mary sucked her teeth, "Doug, if they don't give you the time off, just quit. You could find another job like that in a week."

She turned to Lisa. "Doug and I met at the restaurant. It's in Midtown, it's called Le Mark, but I call it Le Crack."

"Can you make good money waiting tables?" I asked Doug.

Doug scratched his head, "The money can be good, anywhere between five hundred and eight hundred a week, depending on business. But it's kinda tough on your ego. I'd really rather do almost anything else, but I need the money and the hours are flexible. You know, so I can search for acting jobs."

The waitress came over and we ordered two pitchers of beer and four shots of Jagermeister. Then the announcer climbed onstage and introduced the first act.

We got home around two in the morning, and Lisa was drunk and amorous. She had me in a lip lock all during the cab ride, which was nice, but I had a little too much on board and it made me dizzy. So many thoughts and fears crowded into my drunken mind that I felt little stirring in my nether reaches, but I knew I was expected to perform.

We entered the apartment and she let her long overcoat fall from her shoulders in the alcove. I took off my coat and hung it on a peg. She stood there with her back to me, looking over her shoulder. She wore a tight, black dress with a zipper in the back.

"Are you going to unzip me, Jack?" she asked softly.

My thoughts and fears melted away and I moved behind her. I pulled the zipper down to where it ended at her waist, allowing my hands to linger a moment on her hips before running them up the length of her slim body to her shoulders. I pulled her dress halfway down and kissed the nape of her neck. She trembled, and then turned to face me. I gathered her in my arms and we kissed. I let my hands travel down her back. She pushed me back and slowly removed my clothing, letting them pile up at my feet and then she let her dress fall completely away.

Nat Weston sat at his desk, his eyes red and strained from reading over witness statements related to a shootout in a nightclub on Forty-third. Three men were in the hospital, one man was dead, and Nat was reasonably sure one of the wounded men was also the shooter.

It was an important case in its way; a challenging case, but his thoughts kept drifting back to the Bloomfield murder. It pissed him off to no end that he'd been ordered to back off, especially when he knew something stank. There were two things in this world that really got Nat's goat. One was being told what to do by someone less competent than he, and the other was an unsolved mystery. He also knew that if he kept working on the case, Joey would make good on his threats. Then again, he could always continue the investigation without Joey knowing.

He pushed the witness statements aside and pulled a legal pad from his desk drawer. Across the top he wrote *The Frenchman?* (Roget Voltan). On one side he wrote *Ed Bloomfield*, on the other, *Lucas Monroe*. He drew a line down the center of the page, separating them. He had two dead men and an enigma. He needed to find Georgia Brown because he had no other witnesses. Then he remembered Jack Cole. Something about Mr. Cole smelled fishy, like he was holding back. If some strange character named The Frenchman had gone to all that trouble to waste a harmless accountant, it was probably related to the accountant's job. He wrote the name *Jack Cole* on the sheet.

He had to get in touch with the guy from Interpol, Helmut Steger. Would that get back to Joey? Would Helmut simply add his voice to the chorus demanding he back off the case, or would he shed light? Nat decided to call Steger, but only after he checked out a few things for himself.

I saw Lisa off on Monday morning. I felt empty. Lisa had become so much a part of my life again that I was faced with a great deal of loneliness. There was nothing to fill the void. No job, no hobbies, no real friends. Somewhere in the back of my head a voice laughed and said, "That's not quite true, Jack old boy. You do have a friend, and he's a lot of fun. His name's Johnny Walker and he's not going anywhere." I shook my head and pushed the voice to the back of my mind.

Then there was mother. I'd committed myself to spend Christmas with Lisa, but I didn't want to leave mother alone. I thought about the promise I'd made her. Bringing her home had seemed like a simple thing at the time, when I'd had money, or thought I did. Now it seemed next to impossible. Still, I had to find a way.

At least now, with Lisa gone, I could stop the charade and begin my job search in earnest. Maybe I could grab a job somewhere waiting tables at night like Mary's boyfriend, Doug. Then I could search for a real job during the day. At least this way, I'd have some money coming in.

I spread a copy of the *Village Voice* on the table and turned to the classifieds section. I hadn't worked this kind of job in a long time. Not since I worked as a bar back before I started college, but I'd certainly eaten out often enough that I thought I could do it, and I could lie about experience. Doug had said it took only a couple of days to land a waiter's job, if you weren't picky. I made a list of seven places, all within walking distance of one another, and began to dream up a list of fictitious references that, with any luck, they wouldn't bother to check.

THIRTEEN

At two o'clock Nat Weston walked into the offices of Walsh Dahmer. The pretty young woman behind the desk looked doubtfully at the large man in the wrinkled brown suit.

"May I help you, sir?"

Nat flashed his gold shield and smiled. "I'm Detective Weston, and I'm here to see Jack Cole."

She consulted her directory and dialed an extension. "Hi Charlie. It's Cindy in reception. There's a Detective Weston here to see Mr. Cole."

She put down the receiver. "Mr. Weston, if you'll just have a seat, someone will be right out."

Nat sat on one of the comfortable leather couches and, after a few minutes, a man he'd never seen before emerged, smiling and extending his hand in greeting. "Good afternoon, detective. I'm Charlie Braverman. I work in personnel. How can I help you?"

"Hi Charlie, I'm looking for Jack Cole," Nat replied, implying he had no interest in Charlie Braverman.

"So I've been told. Mr. Cole's not available, but one of our Senior Partners, Arnold Norton, would like to have a word with you."

Nat gave him the squinty eyeball. "Not available?" Nat repeated as if he didn't understand something.

"No. But perhaps I should let Mr. Norton explain."

Nat sighed. "Lead on, Charlie."

Braverman led him to Arnold Norton's office and turned him over to another pretty assistant. Before she could finish asking him to wait, the office door behind her opened. Norton came briskly out from inside the office and shook Nat's hand warmly. "Please come in. What may we do for you, detective?"

"Well sir, it's about the Bloomfield investigation. I wanted to ask Mr. Cole a few more questions. Is he here?"

Norton pointedly didn't offer Nat a seat. Leaning back against his desk, Norton frowned. "I was under the impression that the investigation had been closed."

Too late, Nat realized his mistake. This had to be the guy who was putting pressure on the mayor's office and turning up the heat on Joey, who would, in turn, royally screw Nat for rocking the boat.

Nat smiled submissively. "For all intents and purposes, the investigation is closed. I just need to sort out some of Mr. Cole's statements for the final report. It's all routine."

"I see." Mr. Norton frowned and tapped his finger along the line of his chin. "I see. Mr. Cole is no longer with the firm." He stared straight at Nat, as if to say, 'You got a problem with that?'

Nat didn't like the look. "Do you have any idea where I can reach him now?"

"Why don't you try him at home. You do have the address, I trust?"

"Yes sir, I do. Thank you for your time, Mr. Norton." He paused at the doorway. "By the way, was Mr. Cole fired, or did he quit?"

Mr. Norton's face glowed red. "I don't see how that could possibly be germane to your investigation."

"Just call it curiosity. Do you mind answering the question?"

"As a matter of fact, I do, Detective."

"So you never worked in New York at all?" the large, dark haired man across the table asked. He tweaked his mustache, and peered at my application as though it were his kid's bad report card.

"No sir. But I can't imagine the service would be all that different from Ohio."

"Well, it is, trust me. But don't worry about it. I prefer you're coming in knowing nothing. There's nothing worse than a waiter who thinks he knows it all. Why'd you move here anyway"—he squinted at the application—"Jack?"

"I'm originally from here, I just came back."

"You an actor?"

"No, I'm not."

"Good. I'm sick and tired of actors; they're always taking off when you need them most. Listen, I'm gonna give you a shot.

Come in to trail tomorrow at three. Black pants, black shoes, white dress shirt, any kind of tie you want."

Nat stood in front of the tenement where Jack used to live, cursing himself for being stupid enough to go directly to Walsh Dahmer. He knew it was going to come back at him in a bad way. He rang Jack's bell and waited five minutes, then he buzzed the super.

A little old man peered out of an apartment door in the hall on the other side of the glass. He didn't buzz Nat in. Instead he called out from the hall.

"Hey, what you want?"

Nat flashed his badge and signed for him to open the door. A minute later Nat was standing next to him in the warm lobby.

"So, what you want?"

"You the super?"

"Last I checked."

"I'm looking for one of the tenants here, Jack Cole."

"He moved."

"How long ago?"

"Few weeks."

"Got a forwarding address?"

"Sure, place I send the mail."

"Can I have it?"

Twenty minutes later Nat entered the lobby of the Water Tower on East End. The doorman told him that Mr. Cole was out and Nat decided against leaving a message. As he walked away from the building, he shook his head, wondering about the change in circumstances that took Jack from a tenement walk up to a luxury building in just a matter of weeks. Maybe he won the lottery, Nat mused. His pager went off. He squinted at the number and it was Joey. There was a pay phone on the corner and he called into the station house.

Joey came on the line. "That you, Weston?"

Nat took a deep breath. "It's me, chief."

There was a moment of silence, then, "Okay Nat, everything's arranged. Come in this afternoon and clean out your desk. Tomorrow you're gonna report to the 101 out in Queens, in uniform, for the night shift. You got it?"

He sighed, kicking himself. "I understand."

Nat got home around five. When he opened the front door, he smelled cooking coming from the kitchen, and heard laughter coming from Darryl's room. He stuck his head in the kitchen, the brown box of personal effects from the office tucked under his arm. Keisha sat at the kitchen table with one of the neighbors from down the hall.

"Hi Keisha, hi Diane," he said, sniffing the air. "What's cooking?"

"Brisket," Keisha replied. "What's in the box?"

Nat gave a short laugh. "Evidence."

"Evidence? You don't bring evidence home."

"This kind of evidence I do. This is evidence that proves what a fool I am." He walked down the hall and stashed the box in a corner of the living room. Then he went into the bedroom and looked around inside his closet. His uniform wasn't there. He walked to the doorway and shouted down the hall, "Keisha, where's my uniform?"

"Why, is there a parade tomorrow?"

Nat sighed and stamped back down the hall to the kitchen. Diane was gone and Keisha was chopping vegetables for a salad.

"What are you doing home so soon anyway?" she asked without looking up.

"Problems at work. Where's my uniform?"

She put down the knife, "What's going on, Nat?"

He went to the fridge, grabbed a bottle of beer, and sat down at the table. "I'm getting transferred out to the 101 in Queens, for uniform patrol duty, starting tomorrow. The night shift." He took most of the beer down in a single swig.

Keisha nodded at the bottle. "You want another one?"

"Nah, maybe later."

"What happened?"

He explained the situation to her and when he was done, she shook her head. "I just don't understand you sometimes. What are you trying to prove?"

Nat stood up and put his arms around his wife. "Baby, I'm a detective. I'm a detective sergeant. There are two unsolved murders. I have a responsibility to do my job."

Keisha didn't shake him off, but she didn't melt into him either. "Not if your boss tells you not to," she said.

Nat kissed her on the cheek. "Now you're starting to sound like Joey. Least you don't spit when you talk.

She gave him a frosty look. "And who are these people anyway? A pimp? Who gives a damn about somebody like that? An investment banker? He was probably trying to figure out a way to make diapers more expensive."

Nat let her go. "Maybe you're right. But damn it! I take pride in what I do. I do my best to protect and serve the people of the

City of New York and I don't sacrifice my self-respect for the sake of some grubby politicians."

She raised a questioning eyebrow.

Nat shook his head. "It's like this Keisha. I might have to answer to Joey, or the mayor, or the chief of police, but at the end of the day, I work for the people of the City of New York. Those political idiots don't own the city and they're not always right. I mean, they sure think they own this town, but someone has to keep them honest. *That's* the true job of a good policeman. If I'm not *that,* then my whole life is a lie!"

Now Keisha put her arms around him. "I'm sorry, baby. You know I'd love you if you were a school crossing guard."

He sat down, pulled her down onto his lap, and kissed her. "Thank you."

She put her hand to his cheek and then got up and returned to the sink. "Is there someone you can go to for help?" she asked over the running water.

He pulled Helmut Steger's card out of his wallet. "Maybe," Nat said, staring at it. He lifted himself off the chair and walked down the hall to the living room.

Nat settled into his recliner with the cordless phone in his hand, closed his eyes for a long moment, and then dialed Helmut's number. A woman's voice answered in German.

"I'm sorry miss. Do you speak English?"

"Yes."

"I'm looking for Eva Schmidt."

"This is Eva. Who's speaking?"

"I'm Detective Sergeant Nat Weston, with the NYPD. I'm calling from New York."

"Yes?'

"I need to get in touch with Helmut Steger."

There was a stifled sob on the other end, then silence.

"Helmut told me I could reach him through you, at this number."

The silence lasted for another long minute, and then the woman's voice came back, composed, almost cold. "I'm afraid, detective, if you need to send a message to Helmut, you'll have to contact a psychic medium."

This time it was Nat's turn to be quiet for a moment. "What happened?" He finally asked.

"He was found last week in Quebec, Canada. He had been strangled and his hands removed." The ice in the woman's voice cracked and he heard another muffled sob on the other end.

"I'm sorry, Ms. Schmidt. I'm sorry for your troubles," Nat muttered awkwardly.

There was a long sniff on the other end and the voice returned. "Please excuse my emotion, detective. This has been a terrible blow."

"Ms. Schmidt, I am terribly sorry."

"It is never far from my mind, detective. What business do you have with Helmut?"

"Well ma'am, Helmut and I worked a case together here in New York. He asked me to contact him if I had any information. He gave me your number for that purpose."

"Yes, I suppose that makes sense, detective. Helmut was afraid that there was a leak at INTERPOL. He would have been afraid that contacting him there would have compromised you, and him. That's why he would have given you my number, because he believed that his own was tapped."

"Do you believe that, Ms. Schmidt?"

"He is dead, detective."

"Who do you think killed him, Ms. Schmidt?"

"The man he was looking for detective, the man you are looking for."

"The Frenchman?"

There was a dry throaty sound on the other end of the line that might have been a laugh, but could just as easily been a cough. Then the voice returned. "I suppose, detective, but then you know as much as I do, so there is no longer any reason for this call to continue. Except I will say, that you should be careful to stay alive and avoid talking to the people at INTERPOL."

"Why?"

"I have told you all I can, all I know, and my phone too may be tapped. Good day, detective." The line went dead.

He leaned back. As shitty as it felt, with Steger dead, Joey wanting the case shut, and his being re-assigned anyway, maybe it was time to leave well enough alone.

FOURTEEN

I arrived at the Pasta Pot a little before three. Devin, the manager, looked me up and down and nodded approvingly.

"Good, you look all right," he said. Then, "What was your name again?"

"Jack."

"That's right, Jack. Okay." Devin looked away from me and yelled into the back, "Gary!"

I saw a very tall, very thin man, with a very long neck stand up from a group of waiters seated around a table near the kitchen. He pointed at himself as if for confirmation, and Devin fluttered his hand impatiently. Gary came across the floor toward us. He moved like a charging ostrich, swaying from side to side. He could have been anywhere from forty to fifty years old.

"What's up, Devin?" he asked.

Devin frowned in contemplation for a split second, and then remembered my name. "Gary, this is Jack. Jack's gonna be trailing you today."

Devin walked away, no W4, no I9, no talk of pay, nothing. Gary looked me up and down, and then circled me, smiling sarcastically. "My, my, fresh fish." He turned and walked toward the back, beckoning me to follow with a long thin finger.

He introduced me to the other waiters, who were eating some sort of pasta dish consisting of noodles floating in a watery sauce.

Gary caught me staring at the food and raised an oddly shaped eyebrow. "Are you hungry?"

"No," I said quickly.

"Did Devin give you a copy of the menu?" he asked doubtfully.

"Last night," I assured him.

"Good, so you've looked it over?"

"Yes."

"Ever work with MICROS before?"

I had no idea what he meant, so I favored Gary with a blank look.

"MICROS, the computer." He smacked a terminal nearby.

Understanding dawned and I smiled. "No, but I'll pick it up."

"Good, then we'll leave it for later. My side work today is the mis en place."

I looked knowingly at him and Gary led me into the kitchen, where he sat me down in front of a huge pile of silverware, with a big pitcher of hot water and a rag. In a half an hour I'd polished it all, and Gary led me out into the dining room. He took me from table to table, teaching me a number for each one, and having me wipe down the glassware as I went. He explained about position numbers, how a particular seat is designated number one, then going clockwise around the table, two, three, four, etcetera. In this way you always knew who got what.

At five-fifteen the first table came in, and Devin let Gary and me take it. As the night progressed and the dining room filled, I followed Gary about, listening and watching. After a while Gary began to assign me small tasks, like clearing tables and running food or cocktails to the guests. In the kitchen, the cooks yelled and screamed at everyone. The bartender made me wait, and launched insulting comments at me when I didn't know what certain things were. All through the night, Gary gently corrected my mistakes. I learned that drinks are served to the right, and with the right hand. That food is served to the left and plates cleared from the right.

I was amazed and insulted by the rudeness of some of the guests. Some snapped their fingers to get my attention whole others wouldn't look me in the eye or acknowledge me when I greeted them. I did notice that they treated Gary with more respect, and some even knew him by name.

At the end of the night we cleaned up the restaurant. When we finished, Devin called me over. Up to this point, he hadn't spoken to me at all.

"You did okay, Jack. Came back tomorrow at three and trail again. After that, I'll put you on the schedule. You want a drink; go grab one at the bar. You're entitled to one shift drink, after that, you gotta pay."

I was very tired. The work was physically demanding in a way I was not used to. There were five or six people at the bar, and I took a seat near the service area. After a good long while, the bartender came over.

"Devin told me I could have a shift drink."

He gave me a sullen look, "Yeah, but just a tap beer and you have to drink it in the kitchen."

I took my beer into the kitchen where Gary and two other waiters, Sammy and Miguel, were sitting on milk crates, drinking. I pulled up a milk crate, and Gary nodded at me.

"Tell the truth," he said. "You've never waited tables before in your life."

I laughed. "No."

Gary and the other two waiters laughed. "So what did you do before this, man?"

"Would you believe financial analyst and investment banker?"

Gary seized my hand and studied it for a moment. "Yes I would," he pronounced.

"Is that bartender always such an asshole?" I asked.

"He's got his problems. See, he doesn't think he should be a bartender. He thinks he should be a Hollywood movie star, but he's just a bartender. Some people are just not happy with what they got," Sammy explained.

Gary drained his beer and asked if anybody wanted to go for a drink. Sammy and Miguel both declined, having a long subway ride back to Queens, and families to support, but I decided to go.

We left through the back door. A few blocks away there was a bright, cheery bar, where Gary knew a lot of people, and I knew Johnny Walker. We sat and drank for hours and during that time I got to know Gary. He was forty-six, he was gay, and he lived alone with his cat in Chelsea. He had a film degree from NYU, but never made much out of it. Rather than pushing for a career, he'd spent most of the white-hot days of his youth tripping the light fantastic in the New York nightclub scene. His eyes still lit up when he spoke of those unrepentant days of debauchery. He was very funny, and a good companion.

A little before four A.M., the bartender made last call, and Gary suggested an after-hours club he knew. I'd yet to drink my fill—and lately, wondered if I could anyway—so I agreed.

The after-hours club was on Eighty-third, in a pre-war building that contained commercial space on the first and second floors, with warehoused apartments above that. We went in a side door, and up a narrow stair. At the foot of the stairs, a man stopped us. Gary told the man he was a friend of Wally's and we were allowed to pass through. Halfway up the stair we were frisked by a big, black guy in a tank top. Finally, at the top of the stairs we were charged five dollars each by a huge transvestite in a polka-dot party dress. It was dark and crowded inside, with a makeshift bar along one wall, a small dance floor, and, on the other side of the room, a blackjack table.

We pushed our way up to the bar where Gary bought two cans of beer.

"I wouldn't drink anything else here," he explained. "You never know what they put in those bottles."

I smiled and took a sip.

Gary elbowed me in the ribs and spoke low, like a conspirator. "Hey, you wanna get some blow?"

I stared at him. I'd tried pot in college, along with everybody else, but coke wasn't really in my vocabulary. Of course, in the Eighties it didn't have quite the stigma attached to it that it does now. And, anyway, I was hitting rock bottom, or so it felt.

I might as well have some experience to justify it. How bad could it be? What I said was, "How much?"

"You give me twenty, and I'll get us something for forty."

So, I handed him a twenty and Gary disappeared into the crowd. He returned a few minutes later and handed me a small package of pyramid paper. That's a kind of a glossy square of paper that jewelers pack loose stones in—and coke dealers, white powder. I cupped it in my palm.

"You go first," he said. "The bathroom's over there."

I waited a couple of minutes on line for the men's room, and when I got in, locked the door. I removed the package and opened it carefully. Taking a key I dipped it into the snow and took a couple of toots. It made my nose numb and it felt good.

Back at the bar, I slipped the package back to Gary and wandered over to the blackjack table. When one of the players left the game, the dealer, a middle-aged guy wearing a wig, asked me if I wanted to play. I laid a ten down and drew twenty-one in the first round. By the time Gary found me a half hour later, I was up over a hundred dollars.

It was eight A.M. by the time I got home feeling more dead than alive, but not at all tired. Indeed I was wired. People everywhere were on their way to work, full of rest, energy and purpose. I felt like an alien. I raised a feeble hand to my doorman's cheerful greeting. I'd made two hundred and fifty dollars playing blackjack, but I'd have given it all up just to get some rest.

I finally managed to fall into something that passed for sleep around noon. I woke up painfully, in a state of regret, my head pounding. My brain felt like a loose yolk sloshing up against a thin shell. It was two o'clock, and I had to be at the restaurant at three. So I took a shower and got dressed, hoping I looked better than I felt.

I got to work on time and Devin told me I'd be trailing Gary again. I walked to the back where the waiters had congregated to eat 'Family Meal' and Gary was there. Oddly enough, he looked and sounded okay. I got a bowl of the pasta everyone was eating and picked at it a little, but after a while gave up. It made me feel like puking. I headed toward the bathroom and Gary followed.

"Jack," he said as he held something out to me in a closed hand. "You should do some of this."

I knew what it was and shook my head.

Gary poked me, "Trust me, I know what I'm saying. Take a little of this and you'll feel better. You'll be able to get through this shift."

I was torn. I should never have done it in the first place, but Gary was right, I was never going to make it through the night. This could be the last time. I accepted the package.

It was very busy between six and eight for the pre-theater rush. I buzzed all around the dining room, working hard, and picking up the rhythm of the job. Gary was right, the stuff had helped, but now I wanted more.

There were no reservations for after eight, and with a snowstorm on the way, the balance of the evening was shaping up to be slow. Devin left early. He sent most of the staff home too, leaving only Gary and me along with the bartender and a couple of kitchen guys to close the place at eleven. A different bartender was working tonight, Lenny. He was a much nicer guy, pleasant, heavy-set, and prematurely gray with a handlebar mustache; he looked like a friendly walrus.

By eight-thirty the place was empty, and we sat at the bar, chatting with Lenny.

"Looks like it's going to be a long night," Lenny said, turning his back to switch Frank Sinatra off and turn on the radio.

"At this point I don't want to see anybody, anyway." Gary lit a cigarette. "Can I get a vodka tonic?"

Lenny made him one, filled himself a tap beer, and then asked me if I wanted a drink. By now, of course, I'd forgotten all about how I'd felt that morning, and I asked for a scotch and soda.

Lenny also lit a cigarette, "Where'd you work before this, Jack?"

"Actually, this is my first restaurant job. I did office work before this."

Lenny nodded like a sage walrus, "Be careful. This kind of work can be a trap, you know."

"No, I don't. What do you mean by trap?"

"The work's easy to get, and you make your cash every night. I mean, the cash isn't great, but it can seem better than what you get with more secure work, and you just get addicted to it. Before you know it, you're working all night and sleeping all day. You start enjoying the nightlife, 'cause you're in it all the time. It can be good for a while, but it's one big lie."

Gary laughed.

Lenny shot him a sour look. "You know how long I've known him for, Jack?"

I sipped my drink. "No idea."

"About twenty years. When he first started out in this life, he had ambitions; he wanted to be a filmmaker. Believe me, I see it all the time. Some kid starts working a job like this, just to pick up the slack while he pursues a career like acting, singing, or even to save money and open a business. Nine out of ten, they end up professional waiters, and in this industry, that can be a bad thing. No medical benefits, no pension plan, no job security. You get to a certain age and no one wants to hire you anymore. What do you do? You're too young for social security, what do you do?"

"You mean if you don't contract AIDS and die?" Gary asked.

I drained my cocktail feeling suddenly uncomfortable. "You guys seem pretty down on things," I said.

"We are." Gary responded quickly. "You want another drink?"

"Yes, please."

Gary sniffed back on his running nose. "Well, you're right Lenny. But nowadays, all that's pretty much true for all types of work. Kids getting out of college today are making like sixteen thousand, that's not enough to live on in New York. You can make more, but people get downsized or fired in corporate shakeups every few years. Medical benefits don't always cover everything, if they exist. Union jobs are going overseas for cheap labor, and the middle class is an endangered species. You know when it all started?" he paused for a rhetorical moment. "When Reagan broke the air traffic controllers' union. Now every corporation in America expects you to work harder for less, almost as if it's your patriotic duty. It's fucking bullshit. I would never work for one of those corporations; they're all about the guys on top."

I stayed quiet, thinking about what my rebuttal would have been just a short month ago.

"And the politicians," he continued, "they're even worse. I can barely bring myself to vote anymore. They don't represent the people. They represent corporations. They represent lobbyists, and people who make campaign contributions. They run the country for the benefit of multinational fucking corporations."

Lenny poured out three shots, "So why don't you do something about it then?" he asked.

Gary sucked his teeth. "I can't even do something about a table that sits down at five till eleven, to keep me two hours late when I want to go home. I am the American people and I am impotent!"

We all did the shot.

The telephone rang, and Lenny picked up. He talked for a minute and handed the receiver to me. "It's Devin," he said.

"Hi, Devin."

"I forgot to speak with you before I left. You got the job. Come in Monday at three, and you'll get your own station."

"Thanks, Devin. I'll see you then."

I ended up with Gary and Lenny in the after-hours. I got the feeling that the political dialogue was one they'd been having for the entire twenty years they'd known each other.

But I learned something about Gary that night. It was Lenny who revealed it to me, and he was real careful about it. He waited until Gary was out of earshot before he leaned in close and spoke in a confidential tone.

"Hey, Jack, I just wanted to let you know something, I could tell you were uncomfortable when Gary started talking about AIDS and dying earlier. You see, the thing is Gary has AIDS; he's been diagnosed for years and for the most part he's been healthy. It's just that lately he's been losing weight and on his last trip to the doctor he was told that his T-cell count is pretty low. He's been on an experimental medicine and it was keeping his T cell counts up, but lately his counts have been going down again. I guess what I'm trying to ask is, if you don't mind, try and help me keep an eye on him so that he doesn't do anything stupid."

I'd only just met Gary, but this revelation made me sadder than I would have expected. "Yeah, I'll do my best," I agreed.

Lenny picked up a girl and left the club around three and I played blackjack until a little after five. I was up fifty bucks, but I still left when everything caught up with me, and I started thinking about Lisa. Gary remained behind.

When I got home there were two messages on my answering machine, one from Lisa. She was settled into the house she'd be staying in for the next couple of weeks. She left the number and said I should call any time, it didn't matter when, that she just wanted to hear from me. I looked dubiously at the clock—five-thirty A.M.—and I decided she meant late, not early. One A.M. would have been late, but five-thirty was early. I'd call her when I got up, and tell her I'd been out of town on business. The other call was from Doug. He'd gotten the time off from work, so we could drive up together and see the girls for Christmas.

FIFTEEN

The day after Nat Weston was foolish enough to rattle the cage of upper management at Walsh Dahmer, he reported out in Queens for patrol duty. The next day a memo came down from personnel, detaching him from the 101 Precinct and assigning him, temporarily, as an "extraordinary liaison" to the transit authority.

The next day, as he drove to downtown Brooklyn to report for his new duty assignment, he tried to figure out what was happening. For instance, what the hell was an extraordinary liaison, anyway? Why was he required to report to a civilian, who he suspected wasn't even a civil servant, but the boss of some nonprofit organization with a city contract? He really must have ruffled some important feathers, and now they were trying to bury him, literally. The Transit Authority, huh? They were sending him underground.

He glanced at his wrist to check the time, and realized he'd forgotten his watch. So he looked up toward the Watchtower clock, eight-thirty. He pulled up in front of the building on Livingston Street, parked the car in a tow away zone, and placed his OFFICIAL POLICE BUSINESS sign on the dash.

Nat walked briskly through the crowded lobby, took the elevator to the sixth floor, and rapped gently on the door to suite 617. A young black woman dressed in jeans and a blue flannel shirt opened the door. She couldn't have been more than twenty years old, but she had a sensible look about her that appealed to Nat.

He smiled. "Good morning, miss. I have an appointment to see Don Mitchell at nine A.M."

She returned his smile. "Good morning yourself. You must be Detective Weston."

"Yes, I am."

She stepped back to let him in. The office was one large room with six metal desks, only one of which was occupied. Nothing fancy about the room at all. The desk was occupied by a man of about thirty-eight, in good shape, speaking excitedly into a phone. A coffee machine sat on a table at the far end of the room, and the girl walked to it.

"How do you take your coffee, detective?"

Nat noticed the question was not if he wanted any, just how he wanted it. He laughed. "Black, no sugar. What's your name?"

She handed him a steaming paper cup. "Tracy Willacy."

The man hung up the phone and, in two long strides, was in front of Nat, his hand outstretched. "I'm Don Mitchell. It's very nice to meet you, detective."

Mitchell's hand was firm and dry, his blonde hair beginning to gray at the temples. Nat decided that he was probably older than he looked. "It's nice to meet you too, Don. Call me Nat." Tracy handed him his coffee.

They all sat down and Don began, "I can't tell you how gratifying it is for us to have a veteran police officer like yourself volunteer for the program."

Nat smiled. He hadn't volunteered for anything, but nobody had to know that. "Why don't you give me some background information on what you do here?"

"Well, as you know, HNCR is a nonprofit organization hired by the city to perform outreach and rehabilitation services for homeless people in the New York City Subway Systems. Our goal is to recruit volunteer labor from local colleges, augmented with a certain amount of professional staff, as our budget allows.

"What we do is get down in the subways and reach out to the people living there, to make them aware of their options and alternatives. We make decisions as to when people living there are at risk, and attempt to come up with working solutions.

"We also link up with Children's Services, and decide what should be done with children we find living down there. Your role in all this, detective, is to act as our liaison with the Transit Police, mediate disputes, and organize support for our efforts within the department."

Nat nodded. "I see."

He was just beginning to realize how deep he was being buried. He was being sent to work with the mole people. That was just about as deep underground as they could push him.

I woke at three o'clock the following afternoon. My head throbbed and my legs felt weak. I hated myself, at least in that moment. I knew I was going down the tubes, and the tubes were greased. I was committing spiritual suicide.

I wandered aimlessly around the apartment for a while, drowning in self-pity. Finally, I sat down to take stock. I loved the place, I'd put everything into it: my hopes for the future, my fairy tale of true love, and my mother. I touched the kitchen table. It was good quality, butcher block, the nicest table I'd ever owned. I wanted to enjoy it, serve dinners on it, and enjoy them with people I loved, or would one day love. I wanted to protect these things. I remembered an ad from childhood, 'Today is the first day of the rest of your life.' I found it comforting. Today, I would not drink. Today I would begin planning for the future. I took a deep breath and felt better. I sat listening to the patterns of my own breathing. I realized that the condo was going to become more and more of a burden. I knew I had to sell it.

I fixed myself a cup of coffee and called Lisa. The phone rang five times, and then a woman answered. Lisa had gone to town with some other cast members. She'd probably be back late. There was a celebration because tomorrow would be opening night. I left a message, and then called Doug.

Doug picked up on the second ring. He had spoken to Mary earlier, and the girls had made reservations for us at the Brookline Hotel in Shropshaven, the town they were performing in up in Massachusetts. We made plans to leave the morning of the twenty-third.

I hung up and had my first tussle with the green-eyed monster. I was jealous of Doug. Why was it Mary was able to get in touch with him, but not Lisa with me? She was out on the town, having a good time, while I sat at home twiddling my thumbs.

I pinched myself; I was really going too far. I'd just missed her call; it was as simple as that. I had no business reading any more into it. Then the malevolent little man inside my head coughed, to get my attention. *Hey pal, remember, Lisa's a stripper, a free spirit. Who's to say she hasn't met somebody else up there, maybe a member of the cast? Maybe she was just calling to tell you not to come, what then? Then you'll really be alone, won't you?*

I stood up and opened the kitchen cabinet. A bottle of scotch sat the shelf. I'd promised myself not to drink, but I had to make the little man in my head go away. I caressed the smooth, glass bottle. One or two wouldn't be a big deal, and tomorrow was the next day of the rest of my life. I poured some over ice.

By eleven o'clock, Lisa still hadn't called. I was drunk and feeling lonelier than ever. The walls in the apartment were closing in on me. She was with someone else; I just knew it. At eleven-thirty the phone finally rang and I seized it like a cat scooping up a mouse. It was Gary, the waiter.

"Hi Gary," I said, trying to sound more sober—and less disappointed—than I felt.

"We just closed up the restaurant and Lenny and I are heading over to the Germantown Brewery. Do you want to meet us?"

I looked at the clock, I wanted to wait for Lisa's call, but I needed to get out of the house. After all, Lisa was out, why shouldn't I enjoy myself too? I needed to embrace the light before my soul fell into a dark hole.

"Sure. What time."

"We're leaving in five minutes from here."

I took a shower and dressed all in black, to match my mood. I left the building and walked up East End to Eighty-sixth. It was a cold clear night, and even in the smog-ridden, light obscured

New York sky, I could see the full moon and a scatter of stars. The further west I hiked, the more crowded the streets became. On Third Avenue the streets were filled with couples walking hand in hand toward the movie theaters. I hated them all.

The Germantown Brewery was fairly new and large, with huge copper vats in the full-length windows. Inside there was a long bar to the left with three bartenders behind it, and they were all moving, it was that busy. Gary and Lenny were already there, standing at a high-top table by a window. They were still dressed in their work clothes. Looking around, I now noticed that a lot of the crowd was similarly dressed. I observed them for a moment, noting their contrasts, Gary tall and thin, with a protruding neck, Lenny, fat with a protruding belly, both of them now in black overcoats. They looked like nothing so much as Laurel and Hardy transported in time to 1989. I bought a scotch at the bar and joined them.

"How was business, tonight?" I asked, not that I cared.

"We were packed, man," Gary replied.

Lenny seemed distracted, staring at the bar, "Look," he said, "three seats just opened up." He grabbed his drink and headed over. We followed and I saw his ulterior motive. Just to the left of the open seats were three attractive women.

We each dropped a twenty on the wood, and Gary ordered another round. Lenny turned to strike up a conversation with one of the women, and Gary handed me a package. "I made a nice score earlier, why don't you help yourself to a toot?" he said.

I hesitated, but it was already in my hand, and Gary's attention had wandered. Why not? It would make me more sociable, and anyway, today was shot already. Tomorrow was a good day for new leaves.

By the time I returned from the men's room, I felt good all over. Lenny and Gary were doing shots with our female neighbors, and a glass was thrust into my hand. It tasted like medicine.

"Jagermeister," said Lenny, then he introduced me to the girls, Lisa, Lauren, and Tami.

When I shook Tami's hand, she favored me with an unmistakable look. It was bold, and appraising, and faintly disguised by a humorous twinkle in the eye. She was about my age, slim, with short brown hair and soft brown eyes, her accent liquid, southern.

"Where are you from?" I asked, trying to imagine what she'd look like without the sweater and jeans.

She flipped her hair. "Virginia."

I dropped my drink down on the wood next to hers. "Do you live here now?"

"No. I'm just up on business, but I'm thinking of moving here permanently. It's an exciting city. And where are you from?"

"Right here."

She raised an eyebrow. "Born and raised?"

"Yep."

"A native New Yorker. You don't meet many of those."

"Not in Virginia, I imagine," I replied and she laughed. "Can I buy you a drink?"

She tossed off the remainder of something fruity looking in a highball. "I'd like that."

I caught the bartender's attention and signaled for a round.

"So what kind of business are you up here on?"

"Smoking." She put a cigarette to her lips, and I rushed to light it for her. "I'm doing public relations work for Phillip Morris. How about you, what's your line?"

"Investment banking," I answered automatically then rushed to qualify, "but I'm between jobs right now."

"That must be exciting." She positioned herself so our knees were touching.

"Sometimes," I replied, not moving away.

She reached out and took my left hand between hers, "You're not married?"

I thought about Lisa. "No, never have been," I said.

"Well, take my advice," she said. "It's for the birds."

She had my left hand in hers and I spared it a glance. There was no ring, but a pale circle where one had once been. "Why? Are you married?"

"Divorced, happily divorced." And the sincere smile she graced me with made me believe it.

I laughed and looked down at her lower half, hanging partly off the bar stool, round and accentuated in her tight, jeans.

She noticed, arched her back, and smiled. "Do you like my ass?"

I was surprised by her directness, but I laughed and said, truthfully, "Very much." And this seemed to make her happy.

"Danny," she said, "that's my ex-husband, he always said it was my best feature. Do you think that's a compliment?"

Lisa's face flashed through my mind, but the coke was making me horny beyond belief. "That depends on the context," I replied.

"That's true. Danny got me pregnant when I was sixteen, and we had to get married. At the time I thought it was for the best, but he turned out to have no ambition whatsoever. I went to college and he was content to work as a mechanic. It just didn't work out and we finally got divorced last year."

"I'll bet you he misses your ass," I said, slipping my arm around her waist.

She put her hand on my leg, just below my crotch. I felt myself growing hard. "He'll miss it till the day he dies," she said.

I looked around and saw Lenny dancing with the girl named Lisa by the jukebox. Gary, looking stoned and pounding down shots with Lauren, the third girl, was grinding his teeth like crazy. I had a momentary pang for Lauren, who seemed to be interested in him. That would have been sad enough considering his condition, but Gary was also gay. Nothing was going to happen for Lauren tonight.

"Where do you know them from?" asked Tami.

"Oh, just around," I replied. She was rubbing up and down the upper portion of my leg now, just underneath my erection, every once in a while bumping into it.

Then she put her whole hand over it and began rubbing. "You like a woman who takes charge, Jack?" she asked.

I was about as horny as I'd ever been and I just nodded, my heart pounding.

"Maybe I'll take you back to my hotel and fuck your brains out. Would you like that, Jack?"

I wanted her, but it wasn't right and I knew it. "I have to go to the bathroom," I managed to croak out.

I slipped off the stool and walked toward the back of the bar, where the bathrooms were. I went in and threw cold water on my face. An overwhelming feeling of sadness and self-loathing overcame me. What was I doing here? I had so much to accomplish to get out of my rut and here I was, acting like an asshole, doing hard drugs, and turning myself into a drunk. There was no way was I going to sleep with that girl. I was in love. I stared into the mirror for a moment; I didn't like the man staring back. I left the bathroom and there was a back door just off to the side. I slipped out and into the night without saying goodbye.

I got home at two-thirty. Compared to what I'd been doing lately, it was an early night. The message machine was blinking and I heard Lisa, sounding a bit tipsy. Once again, she admonished me to call regardless of the time. I dialed the number and she picked up right away, laughing at something as she answered.

"Hi honey, it's me."

"Jack!" she sounded happy to hear from me.

"You were out late," I said.

"So were you," she countered. "Who were you with, Brad?"

"No, some guys from work. I miss you."

"I miss you too, Jack, but I'm going to see you soon. Did you speak with Doug?"

"This afternoon. We're driving up on the twenty-third."

"Mary told me." She changed gears. "You've been out late a lot lately. I've called you almost every night, even before I got the phone; I just didn't leave messages, because you would've had no way to call back. What's going on?"

"Sorry, I didn't know my actions were being so closely monitored." I chuckled a bit to blunt the edge in my voice. "I've been entertaining clients, you know, business, boring stuff."

"Jack honey, when you entertain clients it's anything but boring, remember; I know, and I don't like to think of you doing that kind of entertaining."

"Are you getting jealous?" I was secretly pleased. If she was jealous, she cared, and I knew she wouldn't keep me to a standard she wouldn't up hold herself.

She laughed. "No, I suppose I don't have the right to be jealous. There are more than enough men up here to keep me busy."

I knew she was kidding, but my heart skipped a beat. "What?"

"I'm just joking, don't get all ruffled. I can see your face turning red through the phone line."

"You shouldn't tease me. You're too far away."

She laughed again. "But not for long. You're going to like this place. It's like Christmas Town. It's so quaint. All the streets are strung with lights, and it always seems to be snowing. It's perfect."

"It sounds wonderful, but you know, anywhere would be perfect as long as you were there." She laughed sweetly, like an angel.

"I guess I should let you go, you've got a big day tomorrow."

"Goodnight, Jack. I love you."

"I love you too."

I hung up, really happy I'd left the bar without Tami.

High on the night's conversation, I managed to pass the remainder of the weekend in relative sobriety. Lisa called me after the opening show, and before the party, and the next day.

That afternoon, I hiked down to the jewelry district on Forty-seventh Street and picked out a pair of diamond earrings to give her for Christmas. They cost close to two thousand dollars. I put them on my AMEX. I knew I'd have to pay the bill at the end of the month, but I was feeling less desperate about finding a job. I felt sure I'd find something in the New Year. Everything picked up then.

I arrived at work on Monday at three o'clock, changed, and sat down with the other waiters to eat the family meal. Everyone was somber, silently eating, not interacting in the usual boisterous way. But I felt better than I had in a while. I wasn't hung over. I grinned around the table, but no one returned my smiles. Gary wasn't there, and I knew he was scheduled.

"Where's Gary?" I asked.

Miguel eyeballed me over the rim of his glasses, "You haven't heard?"

"Heard what?"

"Gary's dead."

I looked up sharply, searching for some sign that Miguel was joking, but he returned my stare in earnest.

I'd grown quickly fond of Gary, and a wave of sincere sorrow washed over me. "What happened?" I asked.

Miguel put down his fork and pushed his plate away. "His sister found him yesterday morning, sitting in a chair in his apartment. The doctor said he'd already been dead more than twenty-four hours, alcohol poisoning. Lenny came by yesterday and told us. Said he probably did so much coke, that he drank more than his system could handle, and he just didn't realize it."

I pushed my plate away and went to the bathroom. I turned the lock, and splashed cold water on my face. Gary had been dead twenty-four hours before they found him. That meant he'd been drinking himself to death when I left the bar Friday night. I hadn't said goodbye. I wondered if Gary had known what he was doing. I wondered how it felt to drink yourself to death. I even sort of wondered if Gary had done it deliberately.

It was a busy night at the Pasta Pot. By six-thirty I had eight tables in my station, and I was surprised by how well I was handling things. I was actually starting to enjoy the economy of movement that went along with doing the job effectively, the ability to orchestrate order from chaos.

Devin must have noticed it as well, because he gave me another table, a couple on table seven, by the window. The man's back was to me, with the woman facing the dining room. She looked familiar. I tried to figure it out as I approached the table. I stood in front of them, smiling down, and there, seated right in front of me, was Brad Seaman. The woman was Megan, the girl he'd taken out to dinner with Lisa and me.

Brad was laughing at something Megan had said, but his laugh choked off as he returned my stare. We stayed for a moment, locked in silent contemplation.

"Jack," he finally said, "what are you doing here?"

"Waiting tables," I replied in a flat tone. "What's it look like I'm doing?"

Brad shifted uncomfortably in his seat. "Megan, you remember, Jack? We had dinner with him a while back."

Megan smiled. "Of course I do. How are you, Jack?"

"I'm fine, Megan," I said quickly. "Brad, why haven't you returned my calls?"

He looked uncomfortable. Someone from a nearby table called out "Waiter!" in a shrill voice. I ignored it. "Well, Brad?"

"I don't know what you mean."

"I'm talking about all the calls I made to you after the problems came up with the SEC."

The voice rang out again, angrier this time. I looked over and it was a fat businessman in a cheap suit sitting in front of a plate of ravioli. He gave me a furious nod, which I could interpret as "Come here now!"

"I really don't know what you're talking about, Jack."

Devin eyed my station from across the dining room. I pulled a chair from a neighboring table and sat across from Brad. Out of the corner of my eye I saw Devin stalk over to the ravioli man's table, listen for a moment and walk away with the plate.

"Yes, you do," I said, "you're on a leave of absence from your firm. Why?"

"I just took a couple of days off, that's all."

"What did you say to the SEC, Brad?"

Megan looked back and forth between us, like she was watching a tennis match, "What are you two talking about?"

We ignored her. From the corner of my eye, I could see Devin taking over my station, moving between the tables, catching up on what I'd neglected since Brad sat down.

"I don't know anything about the SEC. I don't know what happened to you, and at this point I don't care." Brad was gathering steam, "Right now, what I want is a bottle of wine. So why don't you get me the wine list, Jack?"

I cracked. *All my bad luck, fuck it,* I thought. *Fuck Brad.* I suddenly knew what had happened. Brad had betrayed me, and the whole thing had been a set up. I stood up, with the water pitcher in my hand.

"Forgive me, Brad." I assumed the waiter's stance, "Did you want regular water or mineral water this evening?"

Brad wasn't all that bright. He leaned back in his chair. "Regular water will be fine," he said.

I lifted the pitcher and dumped its contents over Brad's head. Without missing a beat, I continued, "We have a special on spaghetti tonight. I recommend it." I reached over to a neighboring table and lifted a bowl of spaghetti—the woman who was eating it was halfway to her mouth with a forkful—and I dumped it over Brad's head.

Before I could go any further (cheese and pepper had been on my mind) Devin and the nasty bartender pinned me between them, and gave me the bum's rush out the door. They flung me out, and I ended up sprawled in a pile of garbage. I didn't really blame them, and I really didn't mind. It felt cathartic.

It was cold and I hadn't had time to grab my coat. I didn't think going back was such a hot idea, so I grabbed a cab and returned home, accepting the loss of the coat as the price of retribution.

The next day when I woke up, the situation felt more desperate—a return to negative cash flow. I dialed the number for Jeff Cronin, the broker who'd helped me buy the condo.

"Jeff Cronin, how can I help you?"

"Hi Jeff, this is Jack Cole. You sold me an apartment on East End a little while ago."

"Right Jack, how's the place working out for you?"

I wanted the man to sell it for me, but I was still a little embarrassed to tell people that I was broke and unemployed. "That's what I was calling you about, Jeff. I need you to sell it for me. See, my firm is transferring me to Boston and I can't afford to maintain two separate addresses," I lied.

"Hold on Jack, let me get your file."

After what seemed like a very long time, Jeff finally returned, "Jack, you still there?" He sounded like he hoped I wasn't.

"I'm still here, Jeff."

"Jack, selling your place, at least with the expectation of getting any money out of the deal, is an awkward proposition."

"Why?" I asked. "I made a fifty thousand dollar down payment, that's all I'm looking to get back."

"I understand, and believe me, Jack, if I was you, I'd feel exactly the same way. The problem is the recent downturn; the place has lost some value. It won't last forever, though. The good news is that although you'd probably take a sixty thousand dollar loss on the place if you had to sell it today, in my opinion, if you wait about a year you should be able to make a ten thousand dollar profit."

"I get that, Jeff, but I have to sell now."

"Well, that's a problem, Jack. I mean no one expected this market correction . . ."

"Isn't it possible that somebody else might come along willing to pay my price?"

"Of course it's possible, just unlikely. Have you considered renting it? You'd have to subsidize the rental to the tune of about five hundred a month, but that might be better than carrying the whole burden of the mortgage and maintenance yourself."

"Could you just list it for me and see if it sells?"

"Sure Mr. Cole. We'll be in touch if the fish bite."

He hung up the phone and I knew I'd never hear back.

SIXTEEN

My recent difficulties were affecting my behavior. I felt like an ostrich with my head in the sand avoiding all kinds of things, including my mother. I felt pretty guilty about that and now here it was two days before I was to leave on my trip to Massachusetts, and this was going to be the first Christmas that I would not spend with her. I sucked it up, wrapped the presents I bought for her, and hopped a Rockaway-bound A train. It took close to an hour and a half for the train to spit me out at Frank Avenue, an elevated train station with a view of the beach just two blocks away from the home where my mother resided.

I walked the two cold blocks over and stopped at the security desk to sign in. Drowsily I scrawled my name, with fingers a little stiff from the cold. I almost didn't notice the entry about three signatures up from mine. Another visitor to see Monique Cole signed in under the name of Wilbur S. just thirty minutes earlier. My heart skipped a beat. Not only was this possibly my biological father, the mystery of my life, but also the man was more than likely still there, just three flights above me.

I stifled the instinct to sprint toward my mother's room and headed toward the elevator, swinging my small bag of presents from my hand. The elevator doors opened on the third floor. In spite of the anticipation bursting from my rapidly beating heart, everything in the hall looked just the same as it always did: Phosphorescent lights, the smell of immobility, the occasional resident shuffling by. I walked down the hall, made the right turn and came up on my mother's room. It was dark and quiet, the sound of medical machines humming in the background more an underlying baseline sound than noise. Mother was fast asleep on her bed. Her roommate was absent. I saw no one else. Dropping the gifts on the night table under the small artificial tree I had installed for her the week before, I bent down to kiss her. My lips brushed across her smooth forehead. Something smacked hard against the back of my neck. I felt a thumping, fuzzy, floating feeling and then tripped over the threshold of consciousness.

Something hard jabbed into my shoulder. My eyes fluttered open and the owl-like face of Delores Simmons came into focus. "Are you all right, Jack?" she asked as she retracted the metal cane from my shoulder.

I sat up, rubbing the back of my neck and sensing the beginning of a hellacious headache. "Did you see anyone here?" I asked.

Delores Simmons began to cackle. "No one here but us chickens!!" she shrieked, a crazy toothless grin spreading across her wrinkled face.

I stood up and looked at my mother. She was still asleep, but above her head sat a vase full of flowers that had not been there before—pink, white, and yellow roses. I felt the back of my neck where I had been struck but there was no lump, no cut or abrasion. Nothing left behind to indicate that I had encountered any sort of trauma whatsoever. I stretched just to make sure all the parts were still working then checked my mother again in her medical cradle. She seemed to be sleeping as peacefully and evenly as before. I put my hand to her cheek and her breath brushed my fingertips.

I pulled one of the gift-wrapped items from beneath the tiny Christmas tree and handed it to Delores, "Merry Christmas, Mrs. Simmons."

Her eyes bulged out a bit and she smiled. "Well thank you, Jack."

I left the room and headed down the hall toward the nurses' station, but Rosa wasn't there and the nurses who were there weren't the most observant. They had not noticed anyone entering my mother's room. I decided not to mention the crack on my head, and headed back down to the business office where Mrs. Donley greeted me with a cheerful smile. I pulled out my checkbook and asked her for my balance.

She waived her hand dismissively. "Didn't your uncle tell you?" she asked.

I shrugged a little helplessly. "My Uncle?"

"Right," she confirmed, "Wilbur. He came by just a little while ago. He said he got lucky in Atlantic City playing roulette and he paid for the next six months in advance."

"Mrs. Donley. This guy, my uncle, what did he look like?"

She shot me a funny look, "You don't know what your uncle looks like?"

I shook my head, "It's been a while, humor me."

"Sure, Jack. Big tall guy, about fifty-five, dark brown hair like yours." She shrugged. "I'm not great with descriptions."

I nodded my thanks and stepped outside to stare at the moon. At least now I knew for sure that it was not Arnold Norton. Arnold Norton was balding and while he was tall, he wasn't that big. Of course whoever this guy was, why did he feel the need to protect his identity to the extent that it was worth knocking me out? I was tired of continuing just on the verge of knowing. It was time for me to find out what was going on.

A little after four P.M. I got home and the first thing I did was fish out a business card from the stack on my desk. I sat down in front of the phone and peered down at it, a simple white card with the name TOMMY TIERNEY printed in green script. Underneath the name, the words FINANCIAL FACTOTUM, and beneath that a telephone number in the 212 exchange. There was no other information on the card.

The man himself answered the phone on the first ring.

"Hi, Mr. Tierney. I don't know if you remember me or not, this is Jack Cole. We—"

"Sh," the man hissed loudly into the phone. "Where are you calling from?"

"Home—"

He cut me off again. "If you wish to speak with me you'll have to do it in person."

"Okay. Where and when?"

"Seven P.M., fishy English Pub. Don't call back." The phone went dead.

I let the receiver fall away from my ear then stared at it for a moment in my hand. What was wrong with this guy? He was either talking to me in some kind of code or he was off to the Hatter's for tea, and crazy wasn't the impression I had taken away from the guy at our last meeting. So he was talking to me in code about a place to meet. He could only be doing that because he was scared that somebody was listening. Did he think they were listening to him or me? Of course the first thing I needed to do was figure what fishy English Pub meant. If Tierney was throwing clues at me it had to be something he thought I had a shot of figuring out. So it had to be something related to our one meeting or the location of his office or what he did for a living. Then it hit me: The guy worked near the Fulton Fish Market, so that's fishy. Now all I had to do was locate an English Pub near the Market. But of course I already knew the answer.

The North Star Pub was a tiny place all decked out to simulate an English pub. They had a lot of British Ales on draft, Bass and Watney's and something called Samuel Whitbread's Pale Ale. I'm a scotch drinker so I settled for Black Label on the rocks and took a spot at a small table facing the window. The window fronted South Street and from there I could see the harbor and The Fulton Fish Market across the street. It was already dark and the streets were pretty quiet. Of course it was Saturday. If it had been a Friday at this hour the whole Seaport would have been jumping. But the area around was a commercial district and it wasn't very densely populated. It could be a ghost town on the weekends.

The pub was just about empty as well, with only the bartender and waitress together with a couple of neighborhood drunks crying into their beer to share the space with me. Aside from that there were only two tables occupied in the whole place. I turned my wrist to check my watch: five till seven. Tommy Tierney did not strike me as a man who would come late. I leaned forward in my seat, squinting into the glass at the street beyond.

I didn't have to wait too long. There he was walking briskly down the waterside along South Street. It was a cold night and Tommy was moving fast, a little bent forward. When he reached the corner he made a vertical dash across the street and then he was tumbling into the small pub with a cold wind on his heels.

Tommy was very tall and thin, his cadaverous head sitting atop a long neck protruding from the collar of an even longer black coat. He craned it about left and right, scanning the room. He saw me and smiled, but it was perfunctory and without warmth. I retained my position and watched him curiously as he made his way across the room and took a seat across from me at the small, scarred wooden table.

The waitress arrived almost on his heels and he ordered us two pints of stout before so much as saying hello.

"Your father," he began without preamble once the waitress was gone, "was my best friend."

Something didn't feel right, but it was the only clue I had received in my entire life. "Who was he?" I demanded.

"Jack Palmer."

"Jack Palmer," I repeated, confused.

He leaned forward in his seat. "Yes, Jack Palmer of Walsh Dahmer and Palmer. The third partner."

"How do you know this?" I asked as the waitress returned with our drinks.

He took a long pull from his glass of rich black beer, licking his chops when he was done then pinching the bridge of his nose between his eyes. "We were all young then. We were the Young Turks. Palmer was the youngest of the partners. He had inherited a full partnership from his father, who had been a founding member of the firm. Dahmer had already passed away and Walsh was ready to retire. It was a time of change and transition. Arnold Norton, Jack Palmer, and I had all gone to college together. Jack brought the two of us in when his father passed away and he took his place at the firm. For a while everything went really well." He chuckled, a dry chortling sound somewhere deep in his throat. "Swimmingly really. There was no deal we couldn't make, no company we couldn't reach. We picked stocks like psychics, and we made so much money." He closed his wrinkled eyes drinking deep of his memories. "It wasn't just the money either, the social life, the vacations and the dinners, the clout, it was like a drug . . .

"Anyway, like I said, Arnold Norton was engaged to Walsh's daughter, and the money, the magic, the power, these things were changing him. We didn't realize it at the time but Norton had decided he was going to take control of the entire firm, and the only thing standing in his way was Jack Palmer. You see they had a difference of opinion about how money should be made. Jack believed it should be made honestly and fairly while Norton would do anything to close a deal. As time went by these two men found themselves in conflict more and more. But Jack was a partner—indeed the only active partner at that point—so things went as he said. Arnold became more and more frustrated, and he had yet to wrest power of attorney from his future father in-law.

"There came a day when Norton set up a deal behind Jack's back. It was a shady deal almost as bad as the one you have been working on. When Jack Palmer found out about it he was enraged. So much so that he decided he was going to fire Norton and give evidence to the SEC." Tommy signaled the waitress for another round.

I drained my glass. Leaning almost all the way across the small table I asked, "So what happened?"

"Norton had a very unsavory friend. We all hung out together and this friend of Arnold's began to spend time with us too. Hanging out with us on the weekends at Fire Island or the Hamptons. Meeting us for dinner at the best restaurants in town. He was a very tough guy, big and strong. Norton never missed an opportunity to remind us that the guy had been in the French Foreign Legion—"

"He was French?" I asked, interrupting.

"Yes. And Norton never missed an opportunity to insinuate that the guy was a hit man. He never put it out there in so many words, but it was always implied. It was like he was Norton's dog, and he would threaten you with him, without expressly saying so."

"You think this guy killed my father?"

"You're getting ahead of yourself," Tommy said.

"Why didn't you tell me any of this on the day I met you?"

"Because it took me a while to piece it together, and because the man who killed your father is still a danger today."

"How do you know that Jack Palmer was my father?"

He closed his eyes. "Your mother worked for the firm back then. She was beautiful, a knockout. Jack was married, but it was not a happy marriage. He and your mother spent a lot of time together. Eventually she became his personal assistant and not long after it more or less became common knowledge that they were an item. She would be by his side constantly and most of the employees rooted for them. He was very well liked as a boss and everyone in the company thought highly of your mother. But he didn't leave his wife. He had two young children and he didn't want to break the home. That is, until you came along. Monique got pregnant and it began to show. There was no public scene, no paternity test. On the surface nothing seemed to change. But everyone at the firm assumed that your mother was pregnant with Jack Palmer's bastard, like the lord of the manor and some peasant woman."

I took Tommy's eye square on. "So now he had the choice of two homes to break?"

Tommy snorted. "The second home was born broken. Don't kid yourself, boy. To be born a bastard is not always an easy thing."

I grimaced. It was involuntary, but I couldn't help but feel a momentary twinge. "You believe this friend of Norton's killed him?"

"I do. Like I said, we all knew each other socially and everyone knew the reputation of this French guy. And everyone knew when Arnold and Jack fell out, and when Jack labeled Norton a criminal."

"How did Jack die in the end?"

"The official story? He was murdered in a street mugging while walking his dog in Riverside Park."

The waitress dropped two fresh mugs of stout on the table. I stared morosely into mine for a long moment and then looked up at my companion. "Do you have proof of any of this?"

"Your paternity, no. The thirty-year-old murder? If I did . . ." Now it was his turn to stare into his drink.

"So why are you telling me all this?"

"You have the right to know."

"Why are you so nervous to tell me?"

"Because the man who killed your father is still very much alive. He would kill me if he knew I was telling you these things." Tommy laughed nervously, "Perhaps he does know." He tilted his head back, drained his pint, and then dropped a twenty on the table between us. "I have to go now," he said and walked away from the table. I watched him through the window as he walked away from the pub. I looked down at the table and one of Tommy's business cards sat in front of me. I turned it over in my hand and there was something written on the blank side of the card. *Just beneath the back of the Butterfield lies the Truth*. He did have some kind of evidence and here was another of his bullshit riddles for me to figure out. Well I wasn't going to stand for that. I dropped some money on the table and made for the door to catch up with him.

I paused at the exit, because I knew I couldn't reach him in time. I could see it happening as if in slow motion.

He didn't see the truck speeding down the street toward him. It was a small box truck and it had no markings, no advertising, nothing listed on the thing to make it stand out. It plowed Tommy Tierney down in the middle of South Street, sending his body catapulting into the old fish market building. I ran outside, but at that point there was nothing to be done. There were cops and bystanders crowding the accident scene and I could easily tell that Tommy Tierney was dead.

I thought for a moment of talking to the police and identifying the man for them. But I couldn't see what good it would do and knew it could also 'cause all kinds of complications so instead I slipped off into the night.

SEVENTEEN

I passed the week before Christmas in relative solitude. I visited my mother a few times, though her mental rebound had turned out to be short-lived. She no longer recognized me. At least she had no other visitors to sly rap me when I wasn't looking.

I put a lot of thought into Tommy's clue and got nowhere. It frustrated me that he would choose to communicate in such an obscure way. I spent a little time at the local bar and watched a lot of TV. I even managed to find a picture of Jack Palmer at the library, but after staring at it for some time came to the conclusion that we looked nothing alike. I went so far as to locate his two legitimate children—Mary Anne, whose last name was now

Harahan, and Gerald who was two years older than me. They both lived up in Scarsdale and I could have looked them up, but I wouldn't have known what to say and I didn't yet see the point.

It was still dark at six A.M., when the doorman buzzed to say Doug was waiting for me downstairs.

Doug, tall, thin and defiantly preppie in a toggle coat and Izod sweater, was pulled up in the building's circular drive in an eight-year-old, dark blue Toyota.

He helped me stow my suitcase. "Nice building," he said, slamming the trunk.

"I just moved in about a month ago."

We got in the car, the engine was already running, and it was nice and warm inside. "How big is the apartment?" he asked.

"Two bedrooms."

"Wow. I got a studio I can barely afford. But I got no reason to bellyache, a lot of guys I went to school with are working and can't even afford to get out of their parent's house." He made a right and headed uptown. "We can catch the FDR on Ninety-sixth, Can't we?"

"Yes."

"I figured the Henry Hudson, Throggs Neck, and then I-95 straight up along the coast."

"Shropshaven's up near Cape Cod, isn't it?"

"Yep."

"Sounds good to me."

Doug popped a Grateful Dead tape in the cassette player and cranked up the volume. He proved to be a good companion with a real sense of humor and the hours passed pleasantly enough.

By the time we got up into Massachusetts it was snowing, just a light dusting tumbling from a gray sky but it seemed to promise more.

We entered Shropshaven and I saw what Lisa meant; the town was old, with some buildings that looked as if they might predate the revolution. In the town center, each house seemed to be competing for best decorative effect. They were festooned with lights, and most of the lawns sported Nativity scenes, or snowmen, or elves. One even had a life-size replica of Santa, complete with sled and the entire reindeer team. On Main Street, the effect intensified, each shop and building with its own display. Across from the hotel on the town square there was a forty-foot Christmas tree, underneath which were piled what must have been waterproof Christmas presents. To top it all off, from somewhere concealed in the square, speakers piped out Christmas Carrols.

I turned to Doug, "Did we die and wake up in the North Pole?"

He laughed and eased the car into the hotel parking lot.

An elderly woman behind the front desk took my Amex and gave me a grandmotherly smile as she tapped my info into the computer, "Mr. Cole, I show you registered until the twenty-seventh, so you'll be with us for Christmas?"

"Yes," I agreed.

"You have family up here?"

In New York the question would have felt intrusive, but here it seemed natural. "No," I replied, "my girlfriend's up here. She's performing in *My Fair Lady* at the theater down the street."

"Oh, how nice," she cooed. "You too?" she looked at Doug and he nodded. "Well, my name's Mrs. Stanwick, and I want you boys to feel right at home here for the holiday." She pushed the registration toward me and took possession of Doug's credit card.

I felt eyes in the back of my head, turned around, and there, peeping out of the lobby restaurant, were Mary and Lisa. I tapped Doug on the shoulder and pointed.

Lisa slipped into my arms and for a long moment I just held her close while the rest of the world drifted away. There was only her, her smile, her scent, her closeness.

She stepped gently back and looked me up and down. "Jack Cole," she said, "welcome to Christmas Town. Mary and I are hungry, and the food"—she swiveled around and pointed—"right there, is very good."

I smiled foolishly, "Well, sure. I just have to put my bag upstairs."

"I'll have them sent up to your rooms," Mrs. Stanwick said, handing over the room keys.

We went into the restaurant and sat at a table that the girls had obviously already scouted, next to a roaring fireplace. We all had mulled cider and Doug and I ate Yankee pot roast, while Lisa and Mary had broiled scrod. The food was first-rate. The good people of Shropshaven seemed to be just as serious about food as they were about Christmas.

I looked across the table at Lisa, "So, what's to do around here?"

She laughed, "Well obviously, tonight you and Doug will be attending a showing of *My Fair Lady*, after which we can go out on the town. There are four pubs and three restaurants, including this one. Tomorrow there's the cast Christmas party, and there's also a delightful little church here. I thought we could go to Midnight Mass."

"Listen to this, Doug," Mary chimed in. "It mirrors our own plans."

"When did you get religion?" I asked Lisa.

"It's Christmas Eve. I always go to church on Christmas Eve. And I warn you, I go on Easter too."

"I think I remember that."

Later, in the room, after we made love and Lisa fell asleep, I propped myself up on my elbow and gazed down at her. I was tired, but I didn't want to sleep. I wanted to be conscious of every moment I spent with her. If I could have cast a spell on her to sleep forever with myself woven into the fabric of her sleeping soul, I would have.

Roget Voltan pulled into the parking lot of the hotel a couple of minutes after Jack and Doug went inside. He stopped the car and stared at the hotel, but he didn't turn the engine off. He'd been tracking Jack for a couple of weeks now, and he'd been there in front of Jack's building when Doug showed up that morning. He'd watched them load the car, and then followed them all the way up I-95 to this hotel. Under the circumstances, he could tell Jack planned to be up here for a few days, and he wondered what was here that brought him for the holidays, time he usually spent with his mother. Nothing that connected Jack to this world was good for Roget. In fact, all his instincts told him to turn around and go back to New York. This place was a waste of time. No one could disappear quietly during the holidays and in the midst of friends. He stared at the snow-covered hotel and wondered how clever the 'Sheriff' of Shropshaven was likely to be.

One thing was certain; he had nothing else to do for the holidays. He never did do anything, not in thirty years. He pulled his Lincoln Town Car into a parking space, and went inside. There was no one at the front desk, so he rang the bell. A minute later, Mrs. Stanwick emerged smiling, from the small office behind the counter.

"Good evening." Roget gave up his most charming smile. "Do you have a room?"

She opened a ledger and peered at it, frowning, "Do you have a reservation?"

"No, I'm afraid not."

"Well, I do have one room available, but it's in the older part of the hotel. You'll have to use the bathroom in the hall."

"That's fine. I never did mind roughing it." He slid a credit card across the counter. "You may take an imprint, but I would prefer to pay in cash." He removed a wad of cash from his pocket.

Mrs. Stanwick peered curiously at the money in his hand. "How long will you be staying?" she asked.

"I don't know yet; two, maybe three days."

Roget always kept a suitcase with him. He got it from the car and stowed it in the room before going into the restaurant for lunch.

As Roget sat, Jack and his party were just finishing up. Roget stared openly at them, making no attempt to conceal his interest. Jack noticed and locked eyes with him. Roget raised his eyebrows and smiled. In spite of himself, Jack smiled back, and Roget laughed, calling out to the waitress for a wine list.

I thought about the man in the restaurant as I strolled along Main Street with Lisa. He seemed very familiar, but I couldn't place him and it bothered me. I pushed it from my mind, but it kept coming back, and then I remembered. He was the same man I had seen with Arnold Norton that night at Roebling's not so long ago. Of course that was a huge coincidence, but that wasn't what bothered me. What bothered me was that the man seemed familiar even beyond that night. I just couldn't put my finger on why. I pushed it from my mind again; I wanted to focus on my time with Lisa.

The holidays and the show seemed to have the whole town supercharged, giving Shropshaven a bit of a carnival atmosphere. The streets were crowded and all the stores were open late. I bought Lisa fudge; the town was known for it, and the clerk at the candy store assured me that people from all over the country ordered it through the mail. There were carolers on the street in front of the big tree, and Lisa and I stopped to listen. It reminded me of college. Lisa had been in the chorus at school and she'd dragged me along once when they went caroling at an old folk's home in Port Jefferson. These carolers sang "God Rest Ye Merry Gentlemen" and "Angels We Have Heard on High." They were singing to benefit the Vincent de Paul Society, and I dropped a twenty in their hat. The leader of the group asked if we had a special request and Lisa asked for "The Little Drummer Boy," something she'd called me when we were kids, for some reason. We held on to each other while they sang. Then she had to go to the theater to get ready for the performance, and I returned to the hotel to take a nap.

I met Doug for drinks at the hotel bar, and then we went to a restaurant off the main strip called the Kettle Pot for dinner. It was hearty, unhealthy, homey food, far from the nouvelle cuisine of New York's trendy nightspots.

When we arrived at the theater the small auditorium was already filling up. Our seats were in the third row orchestra. Mrs. Stanwick was seated nearby with a man about her age in tow. He looked bored, but she waved enthusiastically at us, and we waved back. I was happy to be spending the holiday in this friendly little town. For the first time in a long time, it felt like

Christmas. Then I caught sight of the man I'd seen in the hotel restaurant earlier. I found something about him unsettling, and I couldn't say why, but then it came to me, it was the same man I'd seen in the bar with Arnold Norton the night I had drinks with him. I was sure of it. I wondered what would have brought one of Norton's friends up here to Massachusetts? He could be visiting family for the holidays of course, but then why would he be eating at the hotel, and coming to the show alone. Not that my usual Christmas these last few years had been much different, alone except for a mother who didn't recognize me and—before Lisa—a series of girlfriends I didn't really care about. I stared hard at him for a moment, but the man was seemingly oblivious to me, concentrating on the stage. After a few minutes I turned my attention there also.

The show was first-rate. I actually enjoyed it more than many of the Broadway shows I'd seen over the years. Of course I was partial to Lisa, and it was nostalgic for me. I remembered her in our school production of *Kiss Me Kate* freshman year in college, and making out behind the stage after the show.

When the performance ended, Doug and I went backstage. Once again I was put in mind of College Theater; most of the cast was fairly young and this being the last show before Christmas, a lot of their parents were there. Doug wandered off in search of Mary while I stood my ground, searching for Lisa from a stationary position. It didn't take long before she spun out of the crowd, still dancing, still high on the afterglow of the performance. She grabbed my hand and I took a close look. She was still in costume: a red, velvet dress with a hoop skirt, crinolines, and a low-cut bodice emphasizing her breasts. She still wore her hat and held a parasol over her head.

"Did you like it?" she demanded, eyes shining.

I took her hand, pulled her close, and looked into those deep blue eyes. "I couldn't take my eyes off you all night. You stole the show."

She blushed and curtsied. "It's very sweet, but you're just saying that."

"No, I mean it, every word."

She pecked me on the cheek. "I have to get changed. Where do you want to meet?"

"Where are we going?"

"A bunch of the cast is going down the block to a pub. I thought we'd hook up with Mary and Doug, and go over for a while too."

"Okay, I'll find Doug and we'll meet you outside."

I found him and we dipped into a parking lot filled with snow and milling theatergoers. Doug scooped up a handful of powder in a gloved hand.

"This stuff really packs," he said, while I nodded foolishly.

A second later the snowball smashed into my chest and I ducked quickly behind a bush, scooping up powder as I went. We were still bombing each other when Mary and Lisa came walking down the front steps. Doug signaled to me. I crouched low behind the bush while he took up position behind the ledge to the right of the steps. Now neither of us could be seen. Doug whistled and I, taking his meaning, stopped and waited. When the girls descended the last step, we let go a crossfire barrage.

Lisa and Mary scattered, and a full-fledged snowball war erupted with other cast members and sundry persons joining in.

We made love after the party, and we made love again the next morning. In fact we spent all of Christmas Eve morning cuddled under the blankets.

"What are your parents doing for the holiday?" I asked.

The smile of contentment disappeared from her face. "My parents, I don't know."

I found the response odd, and she remained silent for a while so I didn't press. Finally she said, "When they moved to Florida, senior year, they weren't getting along too well. The change was supposed to bring them closer together, but it didn't. My dad walked out on her, and Mom started drinking too much. Anyway, my dad got remarried, new family, everything. Mom, she's never been the same."

I didn't know what to say. My memory of her parents was of a well-adjusted couple. What I did say was, "Sorry."

"You don't have to be sorry," she replied, "I think you're the first person I've trusted since . . . since then."

"I love you."

She grabbed my chin in her hands and stared fiercely into my eyes. "Don't disappoint me, Jack." She started crying, and I pulled her closer, stroking her hair, not saying anything. Not having anything to say, just letting her exorcise her sorrow.

Nat Weston was deep inside the tunnels under Grand Central Station. He was in uniform, picking his way through darkness with a flashlight. With him were two twenty-something kids from the Sociology Program at Hunter College: Josh, pale and thin, with wire frame glasses and a feverish look in his eyes, and Elizabeth, sturdy and idealistic. They were volunteers and it was part of his job to escort them in their search for tunnel people. They called it outreach. Nat called it a hell of a way to spend Christmas Eve day. At least he'd knock off at five and enjoy the rest of the holiday with his family.

Elizabeth stopped and touched his arm. "The turn-off has to be right here someplace. I was told to look for the electrical box at the end of this tunnel." She shone her light up and down the wall till it lit upon a green and yellow box. "It's right there."

Nat went closer and shone his light around it. Just to the left was a ladder leading down into a dark hole. He beamed his light into the pitch-blackness and decided he didn't like it. He didn't like the tunnels to begin with, and going deeper in, he liked even less.

Nat looked back at the two students. "They tell you—" his voice was suddenly drowned out as a distant train rumbled by. He waited for the noise to pass. "—to look for a ladder going into a hole?"

Elizabeth pressed eagerly forward, Josh following reluctantly. "Yes, did you find it?" she peered down.

Nat cast her a dirty look she couldn't see. "Who told you about this hole?"

"A panhandler in the station above, Old James."

"That sounds like a great source for intelligence," Nat muttered, wondering what would happen if they went down and somebody took the ladder away. "You know," he said, "my radio doesn't even work this far down. We are all alone."

The sturdy Elizabeth turned the beam of her light directly into his face. "Detective Weston, there are supposed to be children down there."

Nat sighed. He really didn't want to go down into the hole, but if there were children, it wouldn't be right for him to do nothing. "All right, I'll go down first. Elizabeth, you follow. Josh, you bring up the rear." He swung himself over the side and descended the ladder.

Eleven-thirty Christmas Eve, Roget walked up the front steps of the Roman Catholic Church. He thought Jack would show up. Like everything else in this town, it was festive for the holiday. The front doors were impressive, with large rounded arches edged by carved reliefs of saints and angels. He passed a moment staring at the doors through the falling snow. The choir was belting out "Gloria in Excelcis Deo," and he thought about what a dull place the heaven of these Christians must be. He speculated about what he might do if, for some reason, his file got switched and upon his death he was sent to heaven by mistake. He closed his eyes and saw the great, pearly gate swinging slowly open in smoky twilight. He saw God, a huge, old man with a flowing white beard, smiling down, welcoming him. Then he saw himself giving God a dirty look and brushing past him.

Laughing, Roget entered the church, and as always was amazed when no lightning struck. He scanned the chapel and saw Jack and his friends seated up on the balcony. He took a seat a few rows behind.

Roget leaned back, remembering the last time he'd attended Midnight Mass; it was the first political killing he'd been hired for after leaving the Legion. He'd been hired by the IRA to take out one of their own. They'd outsourced it because no one in their organization wanted the responsibility, or simply no one wanted to do it. He didn't know which, but he'd landed in Shannon Airport on Christmas Eve morning and driven up the west coast till he arrived at the border town of Strabane. He had a photograph of his prey and not much else. He spoke to no one in the town, slept a few hours in his car, had a lousy dinner in a pub one town over, and went to Midnight Mass. His prey was also in attendance, and he made sure to get a seat close by. He'd done that so at the appropriate time he could give him the kiss of peace, because the irony amused him, and because he knew the man was a bomber who had killed innocents, and the hypocrisy did not. After Mass he'd followed the man to a pub a block away from the church, but Roget had not gone inside. He'd already risked too much by going into the church. Instead he'd positioned himself behind a stonewall that the man had to pass on the way home. The wait wasn't very long. The pub closed an hour after the man went inside and when he drifted past the stonewall where Roget waited, he'd killed him silently. The man's drunken friends had staggered on a couple of more blocks before they noticed their companion had collapsed and died.

I sat in the balcony of the town church with Lisa, Mary, and Doug. Both Doug and I had put on suits for the occasion, and the girls wore dresses. We arrived early to listen to the pre-mass Christmas concert that was playing to a packed house. It was a beautiful church; the walls were all white, broken up every few feet by murals depicting the Stations of the Cross, and the windows were stained glass. Surmounting the marble altar, high above the priest and congregation, sat a triptych with Christ enthroned in glory. The smell of incense in the air, Lisa's hand in mine—it really felt like Christmas.

The crowd became still as the choir belted out "Angels we Have Heard on High," and the celebrating priest and his entourage made their way up the aisle in silent ceremony. The celebrant stood in the center, while the rest of the group fanned out.

"The peace of the Lord be with you all!" he shouted.

I don't know quite how to explain it, and I know it's not unique; I hadn't been to church in years, and I was never much of a holy roller, but something about the time and place gave me a spiritual lift. By the time the closing hymn ("Adeste Fideles"), began, I was high on the Lord.

I'd brought a couple of bottles of good champagne with me, and after the service ended, we invited Mary and Doug back to our room to share a glass.

Roget remained as all the others left the church; some quickly, as if they'd stayed too long, others lingering in the aisles, catching up with one another. Jack and his friends were among those who left right away. The boy hadn't really noticed him in the church tonight, not the way he had in the restaurant the day before, and that was fine with Roget. He had wanted to be noticed in the restaurant, but not the church. There was a trick to it, not being noticed, really just a matter of not seeming to notice anyone else. Of course that held true only if no one was looking for you.

In the end, Roget was alone in the house of the Lord, and he made his decision; the stew was not yet ready. Tonight he would simply return to New York. Tomorrow he would take Christmas dinner at Le Perigod. He trailed his fingers in the holy water as he passed the baptismal font. He was, in fact, so comfortable in his strength and his place in the universe that he did something, or rather he at some point that night, had failed to do something. He had failed to notice that as he stalked, so he was being stalked himself.

By the time his finely honed senses at last kicked in and the hair on the back of his neck bristled, it was too late. He saw the shadow just ahead of him in the arch of the nave, the silhouette of a gun in its hand. The man was not close enough to engage and too close to run from. It registered in Roget's head that there was the outline of a silencer attached to the barrel of the piece in the shadow's hand. So this was a professional, a man like himself—in fact, more professional than Roget had been this night. Then the man stepped into the light and revealed his familiarity. Maybe ten years younger than Roget, muscular and well groomed, dressed all in black. Expensive black.

Roget went completely still so as not to telegraph which way he would jump to evade. Also to consider the necessity of doing so.

The man now standing in the dim light of the chapel let his pistol hand drop to where the gun now pointed at the floor. "Bon Soir, mon vieux. Joyeaux Noel."

Roget let the coiled tension in his body fall slack. If Marcel had been here to kill him, he'd be dead already. "Et tois aussie, Marcel. Quad neuf?" Roget responded.

"I am well, Roget, but you. You are not so aware as you once were, no?"

Roget chose not to take the bait. "What brings you here, Marcel? Are you tracking me?"

"Arnold asked me to come up to keep an eye on you. He wants to be sure the job is done." Marcel stepped forward and leaned in close. "Either you do it, or I do."

Roget stepped back and fixed the younger man with a cold stare. "Are you threatening me, Marcel?"

Marcel shook his shoulders in frustration. "Don't flatter yourself. If I wanted you dead"—Marcel tilted his head to the floor—"you would be dead already."

Roget snorted derisively. "Don't be an ass, Marcel. You have proved that you can sneak up on me in the shadows, nothing more. And I will tell you this: It was foolish for you to have killed Bloomfield when you did and it would be a fatal mistake to kill the boy now. If you kill the boy now, everything will most certainly unravel." Roget put his arm around the younger man, "You know Marcel, there is still so much more that I have to teach you. Let's go for a drink, heh?"

Marcel nodded. "I guess so. But if they pay me enough money to kill you, I will not hesitate."

Roget laughed good-naturedly, "Of course not. You are a professional without fear, or emotion, or loyalty. You are a truly marvelous killing machine. What are you doing for Christmas, mon ami?"

The younger man shrugged.

Roget began to stroll him out. "Then you must come with me to Le Perigod—"

The younger man had begun to move, but now dug in his heels. "Attendez Vous!" he hissed. "What about the boy?"

Roget took the younger man's shoulders in his hands. "I told you, Marcel, the time is not yet right. We will do the job when the time is right and not before."

With obvious reluctance, the younger man nodded. "Well, okay, but we will do the job when the time comes?"

"Yes, of course. We will fulfill the contract when the time is right."

"Will they have duck comfit at Le Perigod?"

"Le Perigod, my friend, has the very best duck comfit in all of New York."

I didn't ascend to consciousness immediately; at first I was only aware of my erection. Then I felt her take it in her smooth, small hand, and I opened my eyes. It was warm and she had pulled away the covers. We were naked and she held me in her hand, staring at me humorously from under raised eyebrows, like a child caught with a hand in the cookie jar. She climbed on top of me, easing slowly up and down, and I could only moan, letting her control the action, till we both climaxed and she collapsed on top of me.

"Merry Christmas," she said, her voice hoarse, cuddling closer.

"Merry Christmas," I replied.

She dropped the stocking on my heaving chest.

"What's this?" she asked.

"I don't know. Santa must have left it for you while you were asleep."

"Hm," she said, "You know, I've been an awfully good girl this year. I hope Santa noticed." She pulled out the little scarf first, unwrapped it and smiled, draping it around her nakedness. "I like this. Santa's got good taste." She poured out the candy, feeding me a bob bon and eating one herself. She felt the stocking at the toe, where the little package was. "What's this?"

I just stared. She stuck her hand in and brought out the small jeweler's box. Carefully she undid the string and the wrapping, flipped the lid, and let out a gasp. "They're lovely." She gave me a probing look. "But, you know, I'm beginning to doubt the purity of Santa's intentions, giving me something as expensive as this."

I lunged at her and she melted, giggling into the mattress.

Nat and Keisha Weston hosted Christmas dinner for the relatives, which meant Keisha's mother, sister, and brother in-law, their two sons, and her other sister, who had no husband but did have a daughter. It was a packed house, with a turkey, a ham, and all the good stuff to go with them.

Ordinarily all this would make him happy. He loved his family, he liked Christmas, and he liked to be a host. But this year was different. What he'd seen down in the tunnel the day before had him depressed as hell. There were almost twenty people living down in that hole, like degraded aliens from a *Star Wars* movie. Even that wouldn't have been so bad, though—he was a veteran police officer used to hard sights—but some of those people had been kids, most of them younger than his own eleven-year-old son. It had been hard seeing how those kids were living, and it had been hard taking them away from their parents.

A chill coursed through his body. He wrapped his hand around the bottle of Heineken in front of him and took a long, cool sip. Darryl had been acting sullen all day, ever since he'd opened his presents that morning. Now he could hear him talking to his cousin, Trudy.

"What did you get for Christmas, Darryl?"

Darryl sucked his teeth. "Got a CD Walkman. I wanted Nintendo. CD Walkman, that's something you should just get, shouldn't be a Christmas present."

All this was said low, but Nat could hear it, and he knew, from the way his wife was studying the cutlery that she could too. He shook his head and took another sip of beer. When he was a kid, he'd get something necessary for Christmas. Something he had to have anyway, they'd wrap it up and make a big deal out of it. One year he'd get a winter coat, a new pair of shoes, that type of thing. He'd always been grateful though; he knew how hard things were, how his father went around with holes in his own shoes.

He finished his beer and grabbed another from the cooler. What did those kids in the tunnel get for Christmas? If Darryl was clueless and spoiled, it was Nat's fault. He was the man who was supposed to be teaching him, just like his father had done. He took another long sip from his beer.

Everyone was talking and carrying on all around him. The women were getting up and busying themselves with the table, clearing plates, getting ready for dessert. His brother in-law was bouncing the baby on his knee. The older kids were talking amongst themselves on the far end of the long table. He heard Darryl say the word *cheap*. He didn't hear anything else.

It wasn't Darryl's fault. When Nat was a kid there hadn't been as much TV around, none of this cable TV and MTV stuff. He'd gotten his values from his parents and neighbors, and it was a cultural community then. It was all different now. Darryl got his values watching TV, and he was sharing that with the other kids. They were all watering at the same hole. Even so, Darryl was a pretty good kid.

Nat stood and walked down to the end of the table. He stared down at Darryl for a long minute.

"What's up, Dad?" Darryl asked, a little nervously.

Nat let out a long sigh, "Let's you and me go in the living room and talk."

"Am I in some kind of trouble?"

"Nah, you're not in any trouble. I just want to talk."

We ate our Christmas dinner in the hotel with Mary and Doug. It was nice, but it was anti-climactic. The holiday was ending. The next day I would return to New York and the whole harsh reality waiting for me there. I did manage to cover up my depression during dinner, but I guess not so well later, when Lisa and I were alone. I know because she asked if something was wrong. I really wanted to explain everything I'd recently been through, but in my insecurity I couldn't quite bring myself to trust her enough. So I fobbed her off by telling her, I hated to leave, and I was going to miss her—which of course was not untrue. She seemed to accept this, but we didn't make love on the last night. I just couldn't get myself up for it, and she seemed to accept that too, and we just held on to each other all night.

Early the next morning, Doug and I headed back to the Big Apple. Doug seemed a little melancholy too, and we didn't talk much on the ride home. All together it was a gloomy journey.

EIGHTEEN

When I got home, I walked through the rooms, trying to glean some comfort from my surroundings. It was an impossible task. The place was empty; there was no family, or fellowship in it, not even a pet. Not only that, but I had no history here. Most people, by the age of thirty, have furnished their homes, piece by piece, over the years. Items are well worn and lived in with individual memories connected to the acquisition of each item: This is the couch I purchased with my first paycheck after college. This is the lounge chair I just couldn't throw away, even after the fabric ripped and the stuffing began to hang out. This lamp was a housewarming present from my Aunt Sylvia. I remember when I bought that picture at an Upper West Side street fair. I had no history with any of my possessions; I'd bought everything prefabricated, all at once. This was the house I'd built in an overnight flash. The sand castle I'd constructed, foolishly hoping it could withstand the tide. It was depressing, and I could feel it all slipping away. Even Lisa, although she didn't know it, she was slipping away too. History was repeating, like when I'd run out of money at college and made a hash of it the first time. Only this time I wouldn't wait for her to put me down like a dog. This time I would salvage some dignity. I poured myself a drink.

The warm bite of the whisky made me feel energetic again, made me want to scheme. I really needed to square away a job. That was all I needed, then, with security, I could begin to create the life I wanted. But it was agonizing to realize I had to wait until after the New Year to get started and I realized that what I had to do was survive spiritually through the year's turning. From the day I returned from Shropshaven through the remains of December I drank, and then I woke up on the thirty-first and decided to bring my mother home. It really didn't matter anymore whether I had the resources to keep her; we were both so close to the edge now anyway.

I took the subway to the home. It was a long ride on the A train, a path that wended its way through Manhattan, Brooklyn, and Queens before finally crossing Jamaica bay and ending at the Atlantic Ocean. I got off the train at the sleepy station and walked the few blocks to the home. A short, fat woman walked up and down in front of the Seaside Manor, banging a stick on the pavement. She looked at me with wild, staring eyes as I passed.

I entered the building and checked in at reception before heading to Mother's room. I seemed to be the only visitor in the building—no worries about getting hit over the head today—and the elderly residents either passed by me obliviously, or stared hungrily. It was an eerie feeling. An ancient man in a threadbare suit fell into step beside me. He moved slowly, and as I began to pass him, he tugged at my sleeve. "Slow down, can't you?"

I complied and he caught up. "That's better. Now, who are you here to see?" He had sharp blue eyes that looked almost young in his grizzled face.

"Monique Cole."

He frowned. "Monique, she's not doing too well. You're her son, right?"

"Yes." I stopped moving all together and stared down at him. "What do you mean; she's not doing well?"

"It's hard to say what I mean." His wrinkled face scrunched in concentration like he himself was trying to figure out what he had just said. "They got her on the drugs most of the time. Hard to say, she don't leave the room much."

"So, how do you know she's not doing well?" I asked.

His face relaxed and he looked real deep into my eyes. "She's been here five years, that's almost as long as me, and twice as long as most." He paused again and in a way I could tell he was pleased to have an audience for his soapbox. "You know, most people die here. Yep, this is the end of the line. This is the glue factory they send the horses to."

I hung my head. "Yeah, I know."

"Do you?" He asked almost in a whisper.

I said nothing. There was nothing to say.

"My mother had a problem like Monique," he continued. "Me and my wife, we took care of her till the day she died. No stranger had to take my mother to the toilet to piss, wipe her ass. My kids, they convinced me it would be a good idea to put my assets in their names after my wife died and then they put me in here."

I didn't know what to say to the guy, so I mumbled, "I'm sorry."

"Yeah, good luck with your mother." He walked away.

I grabbed the elevator, walked down a dim hall, stopped in front of my mother's room, and peered in. Her roommate's bed was empty and Mother's curtain was drawn. I entered the room. It smelled of feces and urine. I pulled the curtain. Mother was lying there, drugged and half-asleep. The bedclothes were fouled and I sort of collapsed on the chair next to her. I took her hand and it felt like a bundle of dry twigs. Her eyes were vacant.

I said, "Hi, Mom."

Her brow wrinkled. Something passed through her eyes, and she whispered my name.

I knelt down, kissed her softly on the brow. "I'm so sorry."

Her hand tightened around mine, then went slack. Her body went limp and I knew she was dead. She was lying in her own piss and shit, and she was dead. I started to cry.

When I got home that night I was on the razor's edge. For five years I'd been building a dam to contain my guilt. Now it had burst, and I was drowning. I tried to call Lisa, but she was out. I drank myself to sleep as the old year died alongside my mother.

I woke into the New Year to make funeral arrangements with a hangover. Burying a loved one was something with which I had no experience. There was really only the one loved one, and therefore only the one chance. I was aware that there should be a memorial of some sort, a plot, a coffin, a grave. I decided on cremation. I called the funeral home and made the arrangements.

Later that day, I sat down to pay my bills. After paying the funeral home I only had twenty five hundred left in my bank account, not even enough to cover the mortgage. I decided not to pay any of the bills; I was going to need that money to survive.

Later I tried Lisa again, and after three rings a woman answered.

"Hi," I said, "I'm trying to reach Lisa Clement."

"Oh, Lisa's not in right now. Did you want to leave a message?"

I was really disappointed. I needed to talk to someone. "No, that's okay." I hung up the phone and realized that I couldn't bear to face her now anyway. I poured myself a shot of scotch.

If my life was burning down around me then I had to rise from the ashes before I could reclaim my prize. I didn't know how long it would take me to find my way back, but I couldn't go on lying to Lisa and I couldn't bear to tell her the truth either, so my only solution would be to avoid her.

I felt sick to my stomach. I was like a junkie in the first stages of withdrawal when you just feel a little bad, and it's not unbearable just yet. But there's also a component of dread because you know just how bad it's going to get before it gets better. It's even worse too, because all you need to take the edge off is just a little fix. Just a short backslide, just a small thing to keep the wolf from the door. But of course you also know that the little taste is an illusion; the cold turkey is out there waiting for you.

Of course, probably the worst thing about deprivation of the thing you are addicted to is knowing that the best you can hope for, the other side of the rainbow, is nothing compared to the way you feel during the time you embrace the object of your desire. The best you can hope for, the painless absence of the object of your heart's desire, is mediocrity. Such was my mad, addicted love for Lisa. I stood up and ripped the phone from the wall and trampled it underfoot. Smashing the plastic into little bits, I then cut the cord and line into a litter of plastic confetti. I sat back down on the couch, panting, breathless. I went to fill my glass with scotch, stopped and instead flung the glass across the room. It smashed into a million fragments against the wall. Then I lifted the bottle to my lips and let the fiery liquid funnel into my gut.

NINETEEN

The next month went by in a blur. I decided, even after I bought a new phone and as painful as it was, not to take Lisa's calls. She left messages almost every day, sometimes twice a day, but I never responded. She didn't seem to understand, and that was the substance of the messages she left. And every message, every call was like skin peeled off my heart, but I was alone, alone with my pain. I scattered my Mother's ashes in Central Park, by the lake. Visa and American Express started to call. I told them I was out of work and they suspended my charge privileges. Toward the end of the month, the telephone sort of half shut down my service: I could receive calls, but I couldn't make any. Then the electric company sent a letter threatening to shut off the lights and I made a decision to pay the phone and electric from my dwindling store of funds, since they were real essentials.

All the while I continued to go on interviews but nothing panned out. I was also looking for an apartment. At this point I'd picked up some shifts waiting tables in Midtown and I was making about four hundred a week. If I could just find a studio for seven or eight hundred a month, I'd be okay. Unfortunately, due to my recent financial problems, my credit was damaged, and my applications were regularly rejected. After a couple of weeks I got fired from my waiter job because I refused to work lunches. There was no way I could do that and have days free to interview; I had to get back into the corporate world.

I was terrified: Looking for work was a full-time job, and I was almost completely broke. I was also hitting the bottle pretty hard, and it was getting harder to hide. I'm sure that made me even less attractive to employers. To make matters worse, the Crosstown Bank was starting to apply pressure. Three weeks after I missed the first mortgage payment I received a notice of default and acceleration of the note. Staring into that mess, I realized I was going to need a place to stay just when my blemished credit report was going to make it impossible to find one.

Another month went by, and I received a seventy-two hour notice. One came in the mail, and one was taped to the door. Basically I had three days to vacate before the marshal came to evict me. I only had a few hundred dollars left to my name and I didn't know what to do. I looked up a number for legal aid, and early the next morning went down to their offices on the Lower East Side. There was a long line of people waiting for the doors to open, and when they finally did, they only took the first twenty. I was number thirty-six, and they told me to come back the next day.

The next morning I overslept. Waking up at nine, I knew I had no chance of seeing anyone. I arranged a job interview for the following day and took my remaining money out of the bank. The marshal might not throw me out right away, and I could probably get a room at the Y if I had to. First and foremost, I needed a job.

I woke up the next morning, guzzled a pot of coffee, and didn't feel too bad. I put on my best suit and tie, a pair of Italian leather shoes, and with a Tumi briefcase in hand, I left the apartment at eight A.M.; my interview was for nine-thirty.

The ad described the spot as for a junior analyst, paying in the mid thirties. Just a few months ago I would have thought the job beneath me. Now it seemed like the answer to all my problems. I still can't tell you what I was thinking of that afternoon, but my life had taken on such an isolated, surreal quality that it didn't really seem all that strange.

I arrived at the interview in Midtown with ten minutes to spare and announced myself to the receptionist. She handed me a clipboard with an application. I offered my résumé, but she insisted I fill out the app. I complied, studiously transferring the information from the résumé onto the form.

A few minutes later a young guy in a cheap suit and trench coat, wearing thick glasses, literally stumbled into the room. He couldn't have been more than twenty-two, and was carrying a chintzy vinyl briefcase similar to the one I'd had at the same age. He placed it on his lap and filled out his application. When he was done he glanced over at me and grinned.

"You here for the job?" he asked.

I smiled back, "Yes."

"For junior analyst?" he further probed.

"Yes." He reminded me of a young Ed Bloomfield.

"Then we're in direct competition."

I gave him a strained smile and before we could engage in a deeper conversation, the entrance of a large white-haired man, who stuck his head out the door and called the young fellow's name saved me. I don't know why they called him first, just capriciousness probably. As my companion headed nervously in to his interview, I wished him luck.

About a half hour later the kid came out smiling, light on his feet. I asked him how everything went, and he told me he was getting a second interview. He crossed his fingers and wished me luck. Five minutes later the white-haired man came for me.

"Hi, I'm Don Fidele," he gave my hand a vigorous shake and led me down the hall to a conference room. I sat across from him while he looked over my application.

At length, he regarded me over his spectacles and said, "I'm afraid I just don't understand what you're doing here today, Mr. Cole."

He paused and I knew it was my turn. "I'm not sure I follow you, Mr. Fidele. I'm here for the job."

Fidele waived the application dismissively at me. "I understand that. I'm just trying to figure out why. I mean, you're obviously overqualified; you should have been here seven years ago."

I smiled a tight-lipped smile, I'd been afraid of this. "I understand, Mr. Fidele. It just seems as if I've lost a bit of perspective over the years, and I just felt if I sort of started over, I'd recapture something I lost along the way." I felt myself tense up. It sounded lame even to me.

The man nodded his head. There was sympathy in his face. "Look Jack," he said. "I can understand how you feel. But you and I both know it's impossible to turn back the hands of time. The road of life leads in only one direction. It's unfortunate, but it only goes forward. If I were to offer you a position, I wouldn't be doing you a favor. After a few months you would become bored. The salary wouldn't be enough. Do you understand?"

I stood and offered my hand, "Thanks for your time, Mr. Fidele."

I left the interview in a daze. Somewhere in the back of my head, I knew this was the end of the line. I didn't want to go home; the marshal could come at any time. What was I going to do? Where was I going to go? I tried to come to grips with the path that had led me here, what I had done wrong. I couldn't look within myself, at the fear and loathing, without shuddering. I was so alone.

I began to cry—not to sob, but to cry. I walked along the streets with people giving me odd looks as the tears ran down my face. After several meandering hours, I found myself on Seventy-second and Broadway. The sky above was overcast and steel gray with a fine, misting drizzle falling out of the sky. I wandered into a liquor store and bought a bottle of scotch, taking it out in a brown paper bag.

As soon as I left the store, I took a long sip and immediately felt better. The hot bite of it warmed my stomach and distracted my brain. I wandered west on Seventy-second, past the shops and restaurants, through the milling crowds, and into Riverside Park. For a few moments I stood watching the dog walkers and thought about the fine life of a pampered pet. I walked down the hill, through the little tunnel, and down to the river. Leaning on the railing I watched the river flow, drinking from my bottle. The current looked strong, rushing quickly along. I thought how far away from my troubles it could take me if I were to jump in. But I didn't have the courage.

I walked downtown along the riverside, past the handball courts and railroad tracks. There were people picking through the debris around the old freight yard, some exiting and entering the yawning mouth of the tunnel. I veered away from them, to where old, dilapidated piers stuck out into the water like gnarled, arthritic fingers. I walked out on one of the piers picking my careful, tipsy way over the holes, stepping gingerly where the rickety, fire-scarred boards creaked underfoot.

I sat on the very top of that pier, oblivious to the cold and damp, my Botticelli-shod feet dangling just above the surface of the river. It was almost dark by the time I finished my bottle. It was almost dark, and I was so drunk I felt like I was floating at sea within my own body. Somehow I made it back across the pier without falling in. I left the park and walked for a long way, and at some point, I entered a subway. A train roared into the station and I was grateful to sit. I must have passed out, because I woke as the doors were closing on an unfamiliar station. I looked over and there was an old man sitting across from me.

"Excuse me," I said through a mouthful of marbles, "where is this train going?"

He laughed. His face appeared to be reeling, and there was a vile taste in my mouth.

"Brooklyn," he said.

I was going in the wrong direction. When the train arrived at the next station, I stumbled to my feet and got off. The station was green, dirty, and dimly lit. The platform was empty. The train pulled out, and I realized my hands were empty, I'd lost my briefcase, and I didn't care.

The sign at the end of the platform read TRANSFER TO UPTOWN AND MANHATTAN. I walked toward it, swaying as I went. A staircase led into darkness, and I was afraid to take it, but I couldn't stay where I was, so gripping the handrail, I descended. The bottom was just as dark, but at the far end was a light, and I moved toward it. Something crashed against my skull, I fell, and the whole world slipped away.

When I woke it was freezing cold. I could feel my bare skin against the cold, dirty stones. The back of my head was sticky and wet. Save for my underpants and socks, I was naked. Somewhere water was running. I rose shakily to my feet from the floor of the tunnel. Weak and dizzy, I sat back down. I was scared. I was still drunk, and all I wanted was to go home. To get home I had to make it to the light at the end of the tunnel, but I couldn't find my feet, so I started to crawl. It was a long way along a cold, clammy, grimy floor. When I reached the other side I was able to stand, just barely. I dragged myself up the stairs, my socks soaking wet. I reached the top and held on to the rail till a dizzy spell passed. The platform on the northbound side was empty save for an elderly black man sitting on a bench in a dirty coat. He had a shopping cart parked next to him filled with rags, and he stared at me, shivering and naked before him.

A train plowed into the station, I couldn't bring myself to get on, and it came and went without departures. The old man was still there. He came wordlessly and helped me onto the bench.

"Why didn't you get on the train," I asked.

The man rummaged around in his cart and, by way of answer, handed me some old, dirty clothes. I put them on, and as he handed me two left shoes he said, "Got no place to go. Leastways, no place that train is gonna take me to."

I nodded, understanding.

"I don't have but one coat," he said. "But you can have this." He handed me a thin blanket. "You shouldn't go down those tunnels. Not when they're dark. You're lucky those boys didn't kill you."

He didn't have anything else to say and I sat quietly with him till the next train rocketed in. When it did, I thanked him and boarded.

There were a few people on the train, and they moved to the other end when I arrived. I heard one woman say to the man she was with, "That white bum stinks!"

I must have been pretty deep in Brooklyn, because the train seemed to roar on forever. After a while I passed out again. It must have been the crack I took on the head, because I wasn't feeling all that drunk anymore, no matter how I smelled.

I came to when I felt something being poked into my chest. I opened my eyes, and there was a young, blonde cop jabbing at me with a nightstick. The train was just leaving the Fifty-ninth Street Station. I was almost home.

"Get up you fucking stink ass bum!" the cop shouted.

I was still unsteady, and not thinking clearly. I tried to push the stick away. The cop didn't like this and he grabbed me by the collar and hauled me out of my seat, slamming me against the car doors.

"Hey!" I said, as the train pulled into the Sixty-eighth Street Station.

"Shut the fuck up!" he screamed.

The doors opened and he shoved me out of the train, leaving me sprawled on the platform.

It was a long walk home, lightheaded as I was from the alcohol and rough treatment. I moved slowly, keeping to the shadows, embarrassed, terrified, lest I saw someone I knew, wondering what the doorman would think. I desperately wanted a shower, clean clothes, and a warm bed.

Without a watch, and with all I'd been through, I had no sense of time. It must have been pretty late when I arrived at the Water Tower, though, because the vestibule was locked and I had to ring the bell for the night doorman. When Harry the doorman appeared, he gave me a hard stare through the thick glass of the front door, and made no move to grant entry. Instead he made shooing motions at me.

I stood my ground though, gesturing for Harry to open up. A neat little standoff ensued, until I began to pound on the glass, at which point Harry grabbed a Billy club from behind the counter and opened the door quickly.

"What the fuck do you want?" he roared, brandishing his stick.

"Harry," I said crisply, "don't you recognize me? It's Jack Cole, I live here."

He let the hand with the stick fall to his side. "What happened to you?"

I sighed, letting some of the tension pass from my body. "I was mugged, beaten, they stole my clothes."

"Jesus," Harry said, but still he made no move to let me inside.

"Can you let me in, please? I need a shower and rest. It's been a tough day."

He stiffened, "It's about to get tougher. I'm sorry, Mr. Cole. The marshal was here this afternoon. You've been evicted."

My stomach fell into the ground, "You mean I can't come in?"

"Instructions from management are I can't let you in."

"Harry, I just need to get some clothes, take a shower. I'll leave after that, no one will know."

"I'm sorry, Mr. Cole, I'd like to help, but I can't afford to lose my job." He looked down at his shoes.

I turned away, began walking slowly up the block.

"Hold on," Harry called out, "wait right there." He locked the door and disappeared while I stood shivering. After a moment he came back out with a heavy doorman's coat slung over one arm. He unlocked the door and handed me the coat.

"Take this," he said, "it's better than that blanket." He also handed me a ten-dollar bill. "That's all I got on me, and here," he produced a business card and handed that over as well. "They told me to give you this. Call the number on this card tomorrow and they'll tell you how you can reclaim your stuff." He studied me for a minute, "Do you have any place to go?"

He looked concerned, but I knew there was nothing he could do for me and I didn't want the guy to feel bad. So I said yes, thanked him, and walked off into the darkness of the New York night.

I wandered about for a long time, hiding my face from the few people I encountered. But I need not have bothered; they looked the other way on their own. I was invisible. I needed a shower and some rest. What was I going to do? There was really nowhere for me to turn. I couldn't reach out to Brad. Anyone from the firm would close their door to me. I had no idea now where Lisa was: The theater group had moved on and I'd frozen her out. Gary was dead, though I was sure that if he weren't he would have helped. Susan, maybe Susan would help me. We'd dated for six months, and she must have some kind of feelings for me. Of course it would hurt my pride for her to see me as I was now, but at the moment, getting out of the cold seemed a lot more important. If Susan could put me up for a couple of days, I could find a job and get a place. I allowed myself some hope.

Looking up I saw my wanderings had brought me to Eighty-second and Lex; she lived on Eighty-third between First and York. What time was it? A woman was walking toward me and I asked her the time, she looked at me nervously and hurried away without answering. The time didn't matter. This was an emergency.

Susan lived in a one bedroom, fourth floor walk-up. I arrived and rang the bell. There was no answer. Assuming she was asleep, I leaned on the bell till her sleepy voice came to me through the intercom.

"Susan," I said. "It's Jack. This is an emergency, and I really need your help. Will you buzz me in?"

"Jack?" she replied. "Do you have any idea what time it is?"

"No." I answered truthfully, "Will you buzz me in?"

The door clicked open and I began my weary ascent. I hadn't realized how difficult it would be after the blood I'd lost and the lack of food. When I arrived on Susan's floor, there was a guy in front of her door, about my age, in his underwear. He looked angry. Susan, looking nervous, stood behind him, just inside her doorway.

When he caught sight of me he turned to Susan, "Look at this fucking guy! That's Jack? He looks like a fucking bum!"

I tried a weak smile, but was cut off before I could open my mouth, "What the fuck do you want here?" he shouted. "It's three-thirty in the morning!"

I looked past him at Susan. "You've got to help me. I got evicted and mugged. It's been the worst possible day—" I broke off as the angry man pushed her inside, shutting the door and leaving us alone on the landing.

The man got right up in my face. "Look Jack, she's with me now. There's nothing here for you. Leave now! And if you ring that bell again, I'm gonna come downstairs and break your fucking face!"

There was nothing to be gained, so, without a word, I turned around and left. Once more out on the cold street, I wracked my brain, but couldn't figure out where to go. Funny, but as desperate as I was, what was paramount in my mind was how embarrassed I was that Susan had seen me this way.

I tried to analyze the situation. First, I had no place to go, it was three o'clock in the morning and cold as fucking hell, if there was any recourse for me, it wouldn't be till morning. Very well, I needed a place to rest. I thought about trying a policeman, but after my experience on the train, I decided to steer clear of them. There was a church across the street, and I walked over and tried the door. It was locked.

I continued to wander; growing wearier with each step, until I thought I could lay down anywhere and go to sleep, but it was just so cold. My mind was numb. I had to go to the bathroom, and if I didn't find somewhere soon, I stood the risk of fouling myself. I thought of the Water Tower, of asking Harry to use the bathroom in the vestibule. I was too embarrassed. But desperation has no patience for embarrassment and I almost turned my footsteps in that direction. Then I had an idea. I went up and down the streets trying the front doors of all the buildings. Finally, on about the tenth one, I hit pay dirt: It was open. The lock was taped down—maybe someone had moved earlier in the day and forgotten to remove the tape. Anyway, it was a gift from on high and I didn't question it.

The building was six stories tall and a walk up. On the top floor there was a little landing in front of the roof door, just enough space for me to lie down. I went out on the roof and relieved myself in the cold. I chose a discreet corner. Even as dirty as I was, I felt ashamed that I had nothing to wipe myself with. I went back inside and slept.

Lisa stepped out of the tiny hotel bathroom and into the short hall in front of the room door to get a better look at the dipstick. She stared at it long and hard and then lifted the box the home pregnancy test had come in from the top of the bathroom sink. She gazed back and forth between the chart on the back of the box and the dipstick in her hand and there was no denying it. The two colors matched. A key turned in the lock on the other side of the door and she swept the box and the stick into the little trashcan beside the sink and walked quickly to the bed. Just before she reached it the door swung open and Mary tumbled into the room, wishing a trilling goodnight to someone in the lobby as she let the door shut behind her.

Mary draped her coat over the desk chair and caught Lisa's vibe. "What's wrong girlfriend?"

Lisa was not usually the type to cry, especially not over a man. But Jack wasn't just any man—and now he was even more than that. She didn't sob or wail, but a few tears ran down her face. Her vice choked up a bit as she said, "I just don't understand what happened, why he won't take my calls. Everything seemed fine, then one day he just stopped calling, and then he didn't answer. And now his number's been disconnected."

Mary, who was a bit more emotional, pulled Lisa into an embrace and stroked her hair. "It's okay baby. He'll come around. And even if he doesn't, there are too many fish in the sea."

Lisa gently disentangled herself and sat down on the edge of her bed. "You don't understand, Mary. He's the one."

Mary put her arms back around Lisa. "I'm sorry," she said in a placating tone. "I know he is."

"Mary, that's not all. I'm pregnant."

"What?" Mary jumped like a scalded cat. She pulled a chair around into the space between the two beds and sat down facing Lisa. "How did that happen?!"

Lisa laughed out loud. "How do you think it happened, Mary?"

Mary shook her head ruefully. "I guess I walked into that. What I meant was how did you let that happen?"

Lisa nodded thoughtfully. "It was an accident but I guess on some level, without realizing it, I wanted it to happen. I guess I'm ready to settle down, and I wanted it to be Jack, my childhood sweetheart who recently rode in on his white horse and saved me. My knight in shining armor. My Jack. But now I'm pregnant and I can't get hold of him." She looked down at her feet. "Oh Mary, do you think I scared him off?"

Mary gave what can only be described as a snort of derision. "No way. That guy is yours—hook, line, and sinker. You can see that in his eyes."

"I thought so too, but then why has he disappeared?"

"Did something happen when he and Doug came up for Christmas?"

"No. Well, yes, maybe. He seemed a bit odd—you know, distracted—the last day."

"Distracted?"

"Like he had something heavy on his mind. Like he was hiding a secret."

"But he kept calling after that, didn't he?"

"He did. I just hope nothing bad happened to him. I mean, if something did, how would I know?"

"We're getting a three day break next week. Why don't you go down to New York and straighten the whole thing out, face to face? I'm sure it will work itself out if you do."

"You're right. Maybe that's the best thing."

TWENTY

I don't know what time it was when I opened my eyes. There was a young woman staring at me. When she saw me wake, she screamed and ran. I scrambled to my feet and called after her to say I meant no harm, but she didn't stop to hear me. When I got to the landing I heard a door slam and lock. I felt like a biblical leper, unclean. But I was really just a guy who needed coffee, maybe a donut. Either way I knew she'd probably call the cops so I hurried to make an exit.

Out on the street it was sunny. A New York thaw had set in, which basically meant that the gutters were rivers of slush. Where do homeless people go, I wondered? Soup kitchens, welfare offices, shelters? There must be people out there who would help me get back on track. Remembering the church I'd noticed the night before, I resolved to stop there first. A priest would have to help me. That was his business, after all. I didn't have far to look for the priest. He sat in the sunshine on the front steps of his church, reading a book.

Cognizant of the visage I presented and with the woman's reaction to me fresh in my mind, I approached the clergyman with as much nonthreatening humbleness as I could muster. "Excuse me, Father?"

He was an old, frail man and he looked up at me amiably from his book. It was the first time since the events of yesterday that anyone had looked at me as if I were human.

"You don't look so good, son. Down on your luck?" he asked in a soft, caring voice.

Encouraged by his tone I replied, "In the worst way possible, Father."

He patted a patch of the gray stone step beside him. "Why don't you sit beside me and we'll talk."

I told him something of my tale, and when I was through, the old priest shook his head, frowning. "What kind of help were you looking for, son?"

I bowed my head, "I was hoping you could tell me where someone in my situation goes to get back on track."

He removed a pen and paper from his pocket and wrote down two addresses. "The first," he said, "is for a soup kitchen where you can go"—he checked his watch—"in a half hour to get a bite to eat. The second is for a drop-in center nearby where they can, maybe, give you some help." The priest handed me a five-dollar bill and wished me luck.

Nat Weston was driving back from Queens, where he'd been visiting relatives with his family. He'd just turned off the Fifty-ninth Street Bridge, on his way to the FDR, when he passed Golden Dreams. Since the day of his reassignment, he'd pushed the Bloomfield case out of his mind. It had been bad enough for his career already, and he didn't want to tempt fate further by pushing the envelope.

But there it was, Golden Dreams. Two men were dead, some conspiracy or other had definitely been left unresolved, and a murderer was on the loose. He shook his head and turned onto York Avenue. What kind of detective had he become?"

With his wife sitting next to him he was careful not to let his eyes linger on the club too long, but it was hard to keep the troubled look off his face and she knew him too well. She reached out and tapped him on the knee. "Everything okay, Nat?"

He took her hand and squeezed it. "Just thinking, baby."

I stood in front of The First Church of God Mission, near the L on One Hundred First Street. I was hungry, but I was also embarrassed to go inside. I was filthy. A crowd of about fifty men milled about in disorder, many of them smelling worse than me. Most of them were African-American, and some stared at me with thinly veiled hostility. I would have given anything for my old eyesore of an apartment, a small meal, a little TV, and a freshly made bed.

A red door in the basement of the church opened. A tall, gaunt man strode quickly up the steps, and the crowd fell back before him. He made a brief, grim survey of the assembly.

"All right, ladies and gentlemen," he said in a booming voice. "If you would please form one, single-file line along the gate, we'll begin. As usual, the tickets are green and red. If you get a green ticket, you may go straight in. If your ticket is red, return in one hour." He turned and marched back down the stairs.

A woman appeared and began passing out tickets from a mixed bunch in her hand. My ticket was green, so I guessed my luck was changing and I was privileged to enter immediately. There was surprisingly little noise as we filed in. The room itself was largish, containing a long, metal counter roped off, with a tray stand at one end, and a series of long tables with wooden benches. I turned in my green ticket and was rewarded with a cheese sandwich on white bread, a bruised apple, and a glass of Kool-Aid.

I found a table near the door occupied by older, listless people who seemed less threatening to me than some of the hard-eyed men in the room. No one attempted to speak with me, and I ate my small portion as quickly as I could. When I was done, I hurried out the door. The gaunt man was standing at the top of the steps leading to the street and he grabbed my arm as I passed and placed a pamphlet in my hand. "Praise Jesus," he said.

I didn't know how to respond, so I just hurried away clutching the tract, anxious to get to my next stop and back on the road to a normal life. I glanced at the pamphlet; the cover was plain black, the simple white letters of the title read *When Infidels Die*. I tucked it into the large pocket of my burgundy doorman's overcoat and hurried on.

TWENTY-ONE

The drop-in center was shabby and institutional. I stood in the reception area in my two left shoes while the man behind the desk frowned at my application.

"Oddly enough," he looked down and squinted at the form again. "Mr. Cole, you are entitled, by New York State law, to shelter. That is, if you are truly in need." He paused, waiting for a reply.

Time to dance, "I was evicted, robbed, they stole my clothes. I have no place to go." I felt like I was begging. Could I sink any lower?

The man behind the desk lifted a stamp up in one hand and paused with it in mid-air, hovering just over the form. "You're sure you don't have any friends or relatives with whom you can stay?"

I shook my head. I was ashamed, embarrassed, awkward, but also a bit incredulous. "If I did, do you really think I would be here?" I asked.

The man brought the stamp down on the form with a loud bang, placed another piece of paper on top, and pushed the stack toward me.

"Look, like I said, you're entitled to shelter, but it's not for me to give it to you. You have to go to the evaluation center in Brooklyn. They'll search the system to see where they have an available bed, if they have one, and presuming you are eligible. In the event there is no bed available in the city, they'll send you out to Randall's Island by bus tonight."

I nodded, scared. "How do I get out to Brooklyn?"

"The D train, you got any money?"

I thought about the money the priest and doorman had given me, "Fifteen bucks."

"Good," the man smiled for the first time, "then I won't have to give you a subway token."

Nat Weston set up a lawn chair and a boom box on his fire escape. It was one of his favorite ways to relax. The Stylistics were softly singing "Betcha by Golly Wow" and the weather was unseasonably warm. All he had to do was lean forward and he could see Darryl playing ball with his friends in front of the building, turn his head and see his wife chatting with a neighbor at the kitchen table. He was surrounded by his family and at peace, but at the same time he was alone. His private patio.

He lit a cigar. He only smoked two or three a month, and when he did, he really enjoyed it. As he watched the smoke trail off into the New York sky, his thoughts turned to the Bloomfield case. Someone was going to a lot of trouble to keep a lid on the whole thing. Where to start, he wondered? But the answer was obvious. He would start where he left off, with Jack Cole. Cole could probably answer a lot of his questions. Like where had he gotten the money to move so quickly from the Yuppie tenement slum to the Yuppie high-rise. The guy's shit had to be flaky. Sometime next week he would pay Cole a visit.

In Brooklyn, after waiting on a long line consisting of guys who smelled a lot like me—which was to say, worse than the Fulton Fish Market on a July afternoon—I finally got to see a caseworker. My hopes were high. For the first time in a long while I was inexplicably optimistic. I felt like someone was going to put me back on track and I entered the cubicle ready to tell my story. It turned out I was about ten years too late for the overtaxed social worker to give a shit. The man just wanted to process me on time to make happy hour. At least this time when the man asked me if I had any money, I had the good sense to say no, and he gave me a token, together with the address of a shelter up in the Bronx.

It was dark by the time I arrived at the Armory Shelter on Jerome Avenue, dark and cold. I tailed onto the end of a long line waiting to be granted admission to a warm place. Some were young, some old, most were pretty raggedy, but a few were relatively well dressed, and many looked hard. I was suddenly glad for my unshaven face, even if it was starting to itch. It gave me a rougher appearance, which I hoped helped me to fit in. Truth be told, I was terrified, like I was checking into a prison. I wanted nothing more than to turn away from the line. It was really cold out, though, and I couldn't spend the night on the street.

The line may have stretched out before me, but now it was piling up behind me as well, and many of the men were jostling each other, talking in loud voices and jockeying for position. I pounded my freezing left feet on the pavement, trying to maintain circulation and avoid eye contact with those around me.

A big man in a bubble coat crashed into me, pushing me out of the line. I didn't make a fuss, just stepped quietly back into the line behind him.

For some reason, that wasn't enough. He turned to me and shouted, "Yo!" into my face.

I blinked in confusion.

He clarified it for me quickly. "I said YO! Don't stand so close to me, YO!"

I stepped back, and the old man behind me made a little room. There had been a pack of cigarettes in the doorman's coat when it was given to me, and even though I wasn't a smoker, I decided to light one up. When I did, the bubble coat turned around and gave me a look like I'd just pissed on his leg. "Let me get a cigarette, Yo," he demanded.

I handed one over, hoping it would placate him. He snatched it out of my hand, glowered at me for a long moment, and turned back away. Eventually the line began to move. At the front gate, I was searched, asked for my social security number and date of birth, and given a copy of the shelter rules.

I followed the crowd into the main sleeping area: a huge room about half the size of a football field, filled with cots.

Some had dark, thin blankets, some just sheets. Only about half had pillows. Most of them were already taken, and there were at least as many guys pouring in behind. I staked out a claim on one of the last beds. It was in a corner, near the fire exit.

Once everyone was inside and camped out, one way or another, a guard walked in and shouted, "They serving food down in the basement!"

Most of the guys camped out on the floor left right away and I sat watching. The men, who like me, had snagged a bed, stayed behind. After a little while I noticed them conferring in little groups, haggling. One man, in three or four, would stay behind to watch the beds it seemed, while the others would drift off toward the basement.

I didn't want to lose the bed, so I stayed put, daydreaming about Ben Benson's Steakhouse. After a few minutes, a small, muscular guy watching some beds nearby came over.

He grinned at me and rubbed his belly. "Hey man, you're not hungry?" he asked.

I was a little leery of interacting with him, but under the circumstances I had to respond, "I just don't want to lose my bed, man."

"No problem, bro. This is how it works here. I'll watch your bed for you this time. Next time, you watch mine. One hand washes the other"—he made a little washing motion with his hands—"you know what I'm saying?"

I thought about it. There was something about the guy I didn't trust, but I was hungry. I also didn't want to offend him because eventually they were going to turn off the lights.

I stood up. "Thanks man, I could use a bite to eat."

He stood up too. He was about five inches shorter than me. "Yo, they call me Johnny Five." He held out his hand.

I knew my name wouldn't sound right at the Jerome Avenue Shelter, so I said, "They call me T." I don't know where I came up with it. It just came to me. As to what inspired the choice of the letter T, I don't know to this day.

I left the room and followed the drift of the crowd. There was a stairway on the other side of an arch, and people were already starting to return. I went down. There was a big guard, holding a nightstick standing in front of the door to the cafeteria. He blocked my way.

"That's it," he said. "Eating time is over."

I smiled. "Maybe I could just have—"

He sucked air through his teeth. "I said no more food. What? Is you deaf or something?"

I realized how stupid it would be to continuing arguing, "Sorry, thanks. Which way is the bathroom?"

He sucked his teeth again, and pointed down the hall with his nightstick.

The bathroom was empty, and it smelled really bad. There were some urinals and three toilets, and they were set up loft-style without doors or stalls to separate them. The toilets in these were literally overflowing with feces. I pissed in one of the urinals and washed up at a dirty sink. There was no soap, but there was water and some paper towels.

Two men came into the room. They didn't even spare me a glance. They squatted on the floor by the windows, whipped off their coats, and rolled up their sleeves. One produced a spoon, poured some white powder on it, and started cooking it with a lighter, while the other pulled a syringe from his pocket and tied a belt around his lower bicep. I got dressed quickly and left the room.

I lit a cigarette and walked back up the hall. The big guard was still in front of the cafeteria door, but he was smoking too.

As I passed him, he poked me in the back with his nightstick. "No smoking, Yo!" he said in an angry voice. I extinguished the smoke while the guard took a puff. Satisfied, he let me go on my way.

Someone was laying down in my bed, talking to Johnny Five. I said, "Hey, this is my bed."

The man sat up, looked me up and down, and said, "Fuck you."

From the corner of my eye, I saw three guys, including the Bubble Coat, stand up and drift closer. Then Johnny Five had me by the arm, leading me confidentially into a corner away from the others.

Once we were at a discreet distance he said, "Yo, T, I was trying to do you a favor. You see that's Mark Him's bed. When he saw you in it, he told me, 'I'm gonna fuck that white boy up.' I told him don't do that, man. I didn't want to see you get hurt, so I asked him to let me handle it."

"What are you talking about, his bed?"

Johnny Five's face went from friendly and concerned to exasperated with the speed of a free-falling amusement park ride. "Yo man, I'm trying to hook you up. It's like that Goldilocks and the Three Bears shit. How would you like to come home and find someone sleeping in your bed?"

"That's ridiculous—"

"Yo, you do what you want. I'm just trying to help you out." He walked away and I went off to seek out a quiet spot on the floor.

About ten o'clock the lights went out. All over the big room I saw people lighting up. Some were quick flashes as people lit up cigarettes or marijuana joints and others were long, steady flares as people tuned into their crack pipes. Soon the room took on a pungent smell that wasn't so unwelcome when compared to the all-pervasive body odor. There was an insect-like drone of hundreds of voices speaking all at once, from time to time punctuated by a scream. Then someone put on a radio, then another, and there was dueling rap music. Somewhere out there, someone yelled to turn down the music, and someone else replied, "Fuck you!"

I huddled in a corner, afraid to sleep and grateful for the heavy doorman's coat. It was cold, and the floor was hard. Footsteps approached, and with my eyes adjusted to the darkness, I could make out forms. They got closer, and I identified them as Bubble Coat, Johnny Five, Mark Him, and some other men.

"Yo, White Boy." Bubble Coat kicked me in the side.

I shot to my feet, scared but angry. *Kick 'em when they're down,* I thought through gritting teeth in my mind but said nothing.

Bubble Coat had his head back, and he was staring down at me with that angry look, like I'd done something to him. "I thought you might wanna suck my dick, White Boy." He punctuated this by unzipping his pants.

I stared. *This had to be a joke,* I thought. They can't do this to me. It was like a bad prison movie. My heart raced along at a mile a minute.

"Well?" demanded Bubble Coat, his voice full of rage. His boys spread out behind him. He pulled his penis out and began waving it at me. "Get on your fucking knees, White Boy!" he shouted, while his boys capered behind him, laughing.

This, I told myself, is not going to happen. This is where I draw the line. I stared at Bubble Coat's neck. He had a big, thick Adam's apple. I hated him; I had enough troubles without this guy. He took a step toward me. I balled my fist. With every ounce of weight, rage, and fear in me, I smashed it into the guy's throat. It shocked him, and it choked him. He fell to his knees, clutching his esophagus, trying to breathe. I lit out across the room, tripping over people in the dark, till I hit the door and burst into the hallway. The cafeteria guard was on my heels. He caught up to me.

"That's it," he screamed. "You're making trouble, you're outa here. He grabbed me by the arm and blew a whistle. Another guard appeared and they tossed me out into the cold night.

TWENTY-TWO

The Greyhound bus arrived in Port Authority at noon. Lisa was traveling light, and didn't bother stopping at her apartment. She took a cab straight to the Water Tower, where a doorman she didn't recognize greeted her in the vestibule.

She smiled. "Cole, 31C."

The man frowned and consulted a book on the ledge next to the intercoms. "I'm afraid Mr. Cole no longer lives here."

Lisa bit her lip. "But that's not possible, there must be a mistake. Could you double check, please?"

A heavyset black man in a wrinkled suit and trench coat entered the lobby.

The doorman made a little gesture of futility and flipped through his book again. "No Ma'am, there is no Cole, and 31C is a vacant apartment."

"But there was a Cole here, just a little while ago. You remember?"

"Yes," the doorman held up his hand, and made eye contact with the man who had come in behind her. "May I help you, sir?"

Nat took note of his name tag, "You go ahead and take care of the lady, Howard. I got time."

Lisa smiled at him, "So what happened? I mean, he owned the apartment, is there a forwarding address?"

"I'm sorry, Ma'am. I don't have any more information." He turned toward Nat.

Lisa was not to be put off so easily. "That's ridiculous. There has to be a forwarding address. People like Jack don't just leave a place they've invested that much money in without a forwarding address of some kind. Where do you send his mail?"

The doorman sighed. "Ma'am," he began.

Nat stepped up and flashed his gold shield, "Howard, I'm Detective Sergeant Nat Weston, and I'm also looking for Jack Cole." He looked at Lisa, "Ma'am, I'd appreciate it if you'd hang around for a few minutes." He turned back to the doorman. "Let's have that forwarding address, Howard. Whatever instructions you have, you do not want to be guilty of obstructing justice."

"I'm sorry, detective. I really don't have a forwarding address."

"So what do you do with the man's mail?"

"Not meaning to sound like Elvis, but I write upon it, 'return to sender.'"

"So what happened to Cole?"

The doorman fell back on his stool and folded his arms. "The bank foreclosed on his mortgage and evicted him."

Lisa's mouth dropped open and Nat said, "Really? Do you know anything else?"

"I wasn't on duty when it all happened. Harry, the night guy, he was."

Nat had taken a couple of steps forward and was standing close to Howard now. "How long ago was this?"

Howard's chair was leaned up against a wall, but even so he tried to shrink back, desperate to regain a little personal space. "Last week."

Nat pushed his face even closer to Howard's and asked in a soft voice, "Did Harry tell you anything about the last time he saw Jack?"

"Yeah, he said the guy showed up at like two A.M., and at first Harry didn't recognize him. It was the same day the marshals came and I guess he didn't know he'd been evicted. Anyway, it must have been a hard luck day for Cole all around, 'cause Harry said he looked like a bum."

Nat backed up a little. "How so?"

Howard slumped forward. "Harry said he looked like a bum, a homeless guy. I had seen him earlier that same day and he looked regular, suit and tie, like he always did. But Cole told Harry that some guys mugged him and stole his clothes. Musta beat him up pretty bad, too, 'cause he had blood and bruises on him. Harry couldn't let him in the building, but he gave him the spare doorman's coat because it was a cold night. Said he gave him some money too, and he asked him if he had any place to go."

Nat had backed up, though his interest hadn't slacked, and he was writing in his notebook now as Howard spoke. "What did he tell Harry, did he have a place?"

"He said yeah, he had a place to go and he left." Howard jumped down off the chair, hopeful that the interview was over. He said, "That's all I know. Real shame."

Nat spared a look in Lisa's direction. She felt tears in her eyes. He handed the doorman a business card. "Look Howard, you give this to Harry, and ask him to give me a call. You guys hear anything else; give me a call then too. Thanks for your time."

He turned to Lisa. "Looks like you could use a cup of coffee."

She gave Nat a tight smile.

"Come on, I'm buying."

Ten minutes later they were sitting across from one another at a coffee shop, sipping hot bitter coffee.

Lisa had finally gotten her emotions under control. Jack must really have been keeping secrets from her. She was very concerned because she was finally coming to grips with how deeply she loved him. If she was completely honest with herself, she had been in love with him since she was eighteen. Not only that, but she'd gone to see the doctor just before she left Brattleboro, and he had confirmed the results of the home pregnancy test she had taken.

Detective Weston and she had yet to really speak. Now Lisa regarded him over the rim of her coffee cup. He had a kindly face, even if he did look tough. She wondered what his business was with Jack, and if she should be speaking with him at all. But right now, he was the only link she had to the man she loved. She'd see what he had to say, and then decide how to proceed.

She blew her nose, wiped her eyes, took a sip of coffee, and leaned back against the booth cushion. "So what's this all about?"

"Ms. Clement, I'm a homicide detective. This is about murder." He paused to let it sink in.

She allowed a snicker to escape. "Jack is not a murderer."

Nat kept his voice level. "I didn't say he was, but a man he worked with, Edward Bloomfield, was murdered some months ago. I want to speak with Jack about that."

Involuntarily, she put her hand to her mouth, remembering Ed from that night at the club.

Nat's eyes narrowed, "Did you know him?"

She nodded. "I met him once."

"Under what circumstances?"

"Socially."

"I spoke with Jack a couple of months back. He said he'd only been out socially with Bloomfield twice, both times at a strip club called Golden Dreams." Nat let that hang in the air between them.

It took her a moment to reply. "That's where I met him, very briefly."

"Who?"

"Ed."

A bit of humorous teasing slipped into his tone. "You go to strip clubs a lot?"

"I was working there," Lisa replied in a clipped, flat tone.

"I see. What is your relationship to Mr. Cole?"

Lisa let out a long sigh. "It's a long story. He was my boyfriend in college. I hadn't seen him for a long time, and then I met him again at the club. We were sort of . . . picking up where we left off."

His face softened, "Were you in love?"

"Yes, we were. I mean we still are." She put her head in her hands, took a deep breath, and looked back up.

"How did he feel about you being a stripper?"

"That was a part of my life I'd rather forget. I'm retired. Is any of this pertinent?"

"Could be." He pulled a bulky leather bound notepad from the inside pocket of his coat and dropped it, along with a pen, into the center of the table between them. "What was your impression of Mr. Bloomfield? Did he seem to enjoy himself at the club?"

She watched Nat scratch a few lines into the notebook then answered, "No. You could tell he was uncomfortable, and as soon as their clients left, he told Jack he was going home to his wife. I think he was just there because he had to be."

"I see." Nat pursed his lips and regarded Lisa for a long moment. "How are we going to find Jack, Ms. Clement?"

"You're the detective, Mr. Weston. You tell me."

He laughed. "Touché. We can start with any friends or family he may have turned to."

"Jack's only family is his mother, and she's in assisted living, suffering from Alzheimer's. She's pretty severe; I don't believe she can even recognize her son anymore. He does have one close friend I can think of. Have you tried his office?"

"Long while back. He's no longer employed by Walsh Dahmer. You mentioned a friend, what's his name?"

"Brad. Brad something. We had dinner with him, a kind of double date one night, a couple of weeks before Christmas."

"Brad what?"

She concentrated for a moment. "Seaman, Brad Seaman."

"Where does he live?"

"Up around here, somewhere, I'm not exactly sure, but he works for a firm called Harrison Schindler, that I do remember. Mr. Weston, you don't think Jack was involved in this murder, do you?"

Nat rubbed his temples. He had no official status, and would be conducting this investigation without the resources of the

NYPD. He was going to have to do a lot of legwork and calling in of favors. "You seem like a smart lady," he said at last. "What do you think?"

"I think not. Though something has happened to him and it is probably connected."

"Right, that's what I think too. Listen, Ms. Clement—"

She gave him a smile. "Call me Lisa."

"Okay, Lisa. The thing is, this investigation is closed. Officially a pimp named Lucas Monroe killed Bloomfield, and then got himself murdered during the normal course of his business. Now, of course, I think that's bullshit. See, I am not supposed to be conducting this investigation. What I'm trying to say is, we both are looking to find Jack, so why don't we help each other out?"

After being evicted from the shelter on Jerome Avenue for conduct unbecoming a bum, I spent a freezing night in the basement of an abandoned building, and woke up the next morning itching all over. There was running water in the building, but it was too cold to wash up, and I must have spent my whole first hour of consciousness scratching. I sat on the freezing cement floor and cried. I was starving. I couldn't stay where I was. I had to find food, had to take a shower. I thought about going back to the soup kitchen I'd gone to the day before—maybe there was more help there. One thing I knew for sure, though, I wasn't going back to a city shelter.

I found a subway station and hopped the turnstile on the downtown side. I was actually nervous about breaking the law, but I needn't have worried. No one seemed to care. There were a lot of emotions playing through my head. I felt sorry for myself, the bittersweet, painful images of my life played through my brain like some badly directed film with no conclusion. Mostly I felt numb, and I wanted a drink as I hoped for salvation. It would be so easy to accept my situation, to free-fall into the groove laid out for me, to fall asleep in the snow bank, to curse God and die. But deep down I knew it wasn't true. I was no bum—vagrant maybe but I wasn't really homeless. Oh, I was homeless in point of fact, but in my heart I had a home, I just hadn't found it yet, or built it, or something. I had hope, and hope was going to take me to the next stop.

They pulled up in front of 660 Madison Avenue. Nat placed an OFFICIAL POLICE BUSINESS sign on the dash and looked over at Lisa. "Don't be offended, but since he knows you, I think it's best if I go up alone."

Lisa realized he was right. As anxious as she was to be involved, she knew it would only undermine Nat's credibility if she tagged along. "Okay."

He smiled. She was smart and sensible. "Not only that," Nat said, "but suppose he turns out to be uncooperative? If you call him separately to make inquiries he'll probably tell you things he wouldn't tell me, or give something away through inconsistency."

The receptionist pointed out Brad who was pacing around a desk much like the twenty or so others in the room, talking on the phone, and tossing a baseball up and down in the air as he pitched a client. Nat sat down in the chair next to Brad's desk and made eye contact. Brad stopped pacing and tossing, but continued pitching. Nat discreetly flashed his badge, and Brad told the client he'd call back.

Brad sat behind the desk and leaned back in his chair, crossing his legs, "Did you want to open an account, officer—?"

"Detective, Detective Nat Weston. No, I want to discuss Jack Cole with you, Mr. Seaman."

Nat noticed him tense momentarily, but he recovered and said, "Okay. But let's find a more private place."

Brad led him to a client conference room and closed the door, but he remained standing. "So, what is it you would like to know, detective?"

Nat didn't respond right away. Instead he waited a few seconds to be offered a seat and when that didn't happen he just took one. He removed his leather-bound notebook from his big inside coat pocket. "Mr. Cole is no longer in residence at his last known address, and since you and he are friends, I thought you might be able to help me locate him." He gestured Brad to sit.

Brad ignored the proffered seat. "Why are you looking for him?"

The chair Nat had offered was on wheels, and now he nudged Brad gently with it. "I need to question him regarding the Bloomfield case. Are you familiar with it?" Nat patted the seat of the chair.

Brad caved in and allowed himself to sink into the chair. "Just what I read in the papers," he replied with a heavy sigh.

Nat scratched a couple of lines into his notebook. "Did you ever have occasion to discuss it with Jack?"

"I did ask him about it at the time, but he didn't seem keen to go into the details, and I didn't press the issue."

"I see. Did you know Mr. Bloomfield?"

"No."

"Do you know where I can find Mr. Cole?"

"I haven't seen him in quite some time."

"Do you have any idea why he left his job at Walsh Dahmer?"

"No clue."

"Were you ever privy to any details"—Nat pulled a pair of glasses from his pocket and looked at his notes—"concerning a deal involving a company called Homer Industries?"

"Just what I read in the papers."

Nat peered at him over the top of his glasses, "You gentlemen were pretty close. How is it you haven't been in contact?"

The bored expression on Brad's face deepened. "Just getting older, I guess. I'm involved in a serious relationship, and so is he. We just don't have the free time we used to."

"By serious relationship, you mean girlfriend?"

"What else would I mean?"

"I'm not judgmental, Mr. Seaman. I have no idea what lifestyle choices you've made."

Brad gave him a sour look.

Nat laughed, lifted a pen over his notebook. "What's her name, do you know offhand?"

"You mean Jack's girlfriend?"

"Right."

"I only met her once. I think its Lisa something." Brad leaned forward confidentially. "She's a stripper, you know."

"You don't say? Where does she strip?"

"Club called Golden Dreams."

"Can you think of any other friends or acquaintances of Mr. Cole's who might be able to help me find him?"

Brad stroked his chin. "Not off the top of my head."

"Really?" Nat gave Brad the hairy eyeball from over the top of his spectacles.

Brad clenched his jaw and stared Nat down. "Really."

Nat dropped his pen and notebook onto the tabletop. "Okay, then, I'm going to need a record of all the trades you've made in the past six months."

Brad sat bolt upright in his chair. "Really?"

Nat nodded slowly and responded in a tired voice. "Really."

"There is one person," Brad conceded in a low whisper, "his ex-girlfriend. Her name is Susan Stern."

"I see. Would you happen to have her address or phone number?"

Brad wrote something down on a post it and slid it across the desk toward Nat. "That's her number. She lives up in the East Eighties. Maybe she can help you."

Nat stood up, and so did Brad who held out his hand. "Do you still need a record of all those trades?" he asked, holding on.

"Not at this time," Nat replied, knowing he wouldn't be able to get them anyway, not without a warrant.

"Thank you. I can't tell you how embarrassing that would be."

"Right. Just one more thing, Mr. Seaman, do you have any idea where Jack got the money to leave his rental, and buy into that Water Tower building?"

"Bonus, promotion, something like that. I guess it didn't work out for him, though."

Brad was a cool customer, but Nat noticed his palms were sweating.

Lisa and Nat were seated in the living room of Susan's tiny, one bedroom apartment, sipping instant coffee from Disney souvenir mugs.

"So," Susan said, sinking into the loveseat after she served the coffee, "this is about Jack. Is he in some kind of trouble?"

"No, not necessarily. My partner and I"—he'd elevated Lisa's status for the evening—"need to speak with him regarding the murder of one of his coworkers, Ed Bloomfield."

Susan nodded. "I read about that in the papers. Jack isn't a suspect, is he?"

Lisa eyeballed Susan. She thought the woman had big teeth, big hair and wore too much makeup. "No, we just need to get some information from him and are intrigued to discover that he cannot be located. We were actually hoping you might be able to help us find him. When was the last time you saw him?"

Susan hung her head as if she were embarrassed. "Last week. He came to me for help, and I didn't give it to him." A small tear trickled from the corner of her eye. "I feel very bad about that," she sniffed.

Nat leaned forward in his chair and put his hand on her knee. "What kind of help?"

"It was late, like three o'clock in the morning. My boyfriend was here." She stared for a moment into her cup. "I feel so guilty. I should have tried to help him." She paused.

"Go on," Lisa encouraged.

"He came to the apartment, and he looked terrible, like a homeless person. He was dressed all in rags and he was wearing this funny brown coat, like a toy soldier or a nutcracker or something. He smelled really bad, and I think he was bleeding. He wanted to stay here overnight or something, but Tony, my boyfriend . . . he's so jealous, he didn't give Jack a chance. He threw him out, and by the time I got Tony calmed down it was too late. I really should have done something for him. I mean Jack wasn't a bad guy . . . he just wasn't for me. You know?"

Nat straightened up, "Do you have any idea where he might have gone?"

Susan shook her head sadly. "I don't think he had any place else to go. I mean, I should have been the last person he came to."

Bitch, Lisa thought.

Once back in the car, Nat turned to Lisa, "I'll drop you home now. I think we've done all we can for one night."

"But he's out there, God only knows where. We've got to find him."

"We are reasonably sure of one thing. He's homeless. I've got some connections, but I won't be able to get in touch till tomorrow. Tell you what, though, I'm gonna take the whole week off to work with you on this thing."

Lisa gave him a sharp look. "I thought this was your job."

"It is and it isn't. I told you the case is supposed to be closed. There are a lot of powerful people who don't want anyone stirring up the mud here, and I've already gotten into a lot of trouble over it. I'm really not supposed to be pursuing this."

"So why are you?"

"I think the Bloomfield murder is part of something much bigger, and I think your boyfriend is a victim too. It's pretty odd that he was evicted as fast as he must have been. Usually takes a lot longer than that." He paused for a moment then shook his head. "It's almost like someone was trying to make him unavailable. Anyway, I'm a detective, I like uncovering secrets."

TWENTY-THREE

bout a week after the incident at the Jerome Avenue Shelter, as I was leaving the soup kitchen at The Catholic Worker on East Third, I met Carlito.

"Hey man," came a voice from behind me, "wait up."

I turned my head to see a small, thin Hispanic man of about fifty, limping quickly up behind me. I'd actually noticed the guy inside at lunch. He was pretty well dressed (for a street guy anyway) and he had an intelligent face. So despite the trepidation I felt for most of my companions in misery, I waited.

The little guy caught up and smiled, leaning on his cane, which oddly enough was good quality wood and topped with what appeared to be a solid silver death's head. "Hey, I seen you around, man. What's your name?"

Thinking about what my conversation with Johnny Five led to, I took a moment to reply. Finally I said, "I'm Jack."

He shook my hand. "Carlos, but everybody calls me Carlito. You haven't been out too long, have you?"

"I don't understand what you mean."

"Out, like out on the street. That's what I mean, Bro."

"No," I replied cautiously.

"I could tell, I can always tell. It's in the eyes. Most guys, when they been out a while—if they're not crazy to begin with, that is—they got something in their eyes. Like in The Nam, they used to call it the thousand-yard stare. It's like that, but not quite."

It had been so long since I had a normal conversation with anyone that I didn't know quite how to respond, but I found myself warming to Carlito. So I asked, "You were in Vietnam?" just to keep the conversation going.

"Yeah, but that was a long time ago. But hey, let's walk and talk." He started moving, and for a man with a limp he moved pretty fast.

"How 'bout you, you been out long?" I asked.

"Me?" he laughed, "I'm not out at all, man. I got a squat. In fact that's what I want to talk to you about—a squat, a squat and a job. We turn left up here," he said, pointing with his cane as we reached the corner.

"What's a squat?"

He didn't answer right away. Instead he slapped hands with a big Latin guy sitting on a stoop. "What's up Izzy?" he said. "Hey, I want you to meet my new partner, Jack."

So I slapped hands with Izzy too, and as we moved on down the block, I said, "What do you mean, partner?"

He chose to ignore the second question and tackle the first. "Jack, a squat is an abandoned building, usually something owned by the city or a bank and just left there. People move in and fix them up to live in. Mine even has electricity, water, heat, all that shit. What I'm offering you is a spot in the squat, and a job. You interested?"

"What kind of job?" I asked warily.

"Vending, selling used books." Carlos answered in a light tone that seemed to tell me he knew I was skeptical and he understood. It also seemed to say not to worry.

I still needed some reassurance though. "Why me?"

"You? 'Cause you ain't been on the street too long, because I think I can trust you, because maybe I'm your angel, Bro. Anyway, the squat's on the left up here on the next block. You in?" He pointed with his cane again.

I thought about it. I'd been showering at the Salvation Army. I'd even gotten some clean clothes there, and I was starting to learn my way around the soup kitchens. But I couldn't go back to the shelters, and I was sick of sleeping out. It was just a matter of time before it started to warp my mind. Maybe Carlito's program was just the thing to help me get back on my feet. I gave him my hand and said, "I'm in."

The squat was a on a dilapidated, tenement-lined street in Alphabet City. The first four buildings on the block still served as rental housing, and there were groups of people on the stoops in front of the buildings. They all seemed to know Carlito and he greeted them like he was the mayor. These were people with homes—not rich, but not street people like me. Still they seemed to accept me because I was with Carlito.

After we passed these first four buildings there was a trash-strewn lot next to which was what appeared to be an abandoned building. The front door was bricked over and the windows on the first floor were covered with metal sheets.

Carlito led me through the lot to an alleyway that linked the block's row of tenements. There were people staring and talking out of the back windows, and a group of kids playing stickball. There was also a back door that led into the abandoned building; in front of it sat a man in a wheelchair. The man was about Carlito's age, and had the arms and shoulders of a body builder on steroids, but his legs were shriveled and useless. Carlito introduced him as Julius. Julius smiled. He seemed genuinely happy to meet me.

Inside the lobby work lights were strung out along the length of the passage and tacked into the ceiling. The whole place smelled strongly of cleaning products.

Carlito leaned up against the wall. "Let me tell you about the squat, bro. I opened this building up ten years ago. The apartments are usually full, but occasionally, one opens up and I find a guy like you to fill it. Basically, I try to give people a chance to get their shit together. But there are rules. Everybody helps out with the upkeep, and no drugs. You can drink, as long as you're not a drunk, and nobody brings strangers here. We have a business selling books. You can start working with us, you keep fifty percent, and the community gets fifty percent. If you find another job, you can take it, I don't mind.

"Julius, the guy out front, he's the full-time doorman here. He lives on this floor. Me and him, we were in 'Nam together, he's cool people. You cool with all that?"

"Yeah," I replied, starting to feel like my luck was changing.

He gave me a big grin. "You ready to check out your apartment?"

Carlito led me to the end of the corridor where a staircase should have been, but there was no staircase. At some point it had been ripped out; instead there was an iron ladder secured to the landing above. We climbed up, and this time the stairs were where they should be. We climbed two more flights and stopped in front of a door marked 4C. Carlito pulled a ring of keys from his pocket and opened the door to reveal a tiny, one bedroom apartment. It was furnished too, with a couple of couches, a table, and two chairs in the living room. The small, galley kitchen had just a hot plate and a tiny fridge. Off to one side there was a small bedroom, containing a cot and nothing else.

"The stuff in there," he told me, "belongs to the community, but you can use it, and you can add to it when you start earning money. The shower works, but there's no hot water right now. We're working on the problem." He handed me a key. "Okay, I'm gonna leave you for a bit, but I'll check on you later. Why don't you take a shower"—he held his nose—"you stink."

Lisa took a leave of absence from the theater company so she could work with Detective Weston to try to locate Jack, but the first week came and went for the partnership of Lisa Clement and Detective Weston and there wasn't much to show for it. They visited fifteen men's shelters, including the one on Jerome Avenue, where they discovered Jack had stayed for a night. Unfortunately, no one there remembered him, and he had not reappeared in the system since.

It was the end of another fruitless day, and Lisa sat at her kitchen table, mulling the possibilities. It was just so frustrating that they were running out of ideas. Searching for one man in a city so large was like searching for a needle in a box of needles. She glanced at the clock on the microwave: six-fifteen. Nat was fifteen minutes late. It's six-fifteen, she told herself; do you know where your Jack is? A vision of the Jerome Avenue Men's Shelter crossed her mind, and she shuddered. What a horrible place that was. That was no place for Jack.

The bell rang.

She opened the door and Nat was standing there in an NYPD windbreaker. The weather was much warmer now.

Nat sat down at the table. "You want a beer, Detective?" Lisa asked as she opened the fridge.

"Yes please," he answered. She put the beer down in front of him where he sat staring at the telephone. "That phone have an extension I could listen in on?"

She put her hands on her hips. "There's one in the bedroom. Why?"

"Brad Seaman. I don't know why, just call it a hunch, but I think that boy knows more than he's letting on. Remember when we went to visit him and you waited in the car so he wouldn't know we were connected?"

"Yes."

He put a scrap of paper on the table. "That's his home number. I want you to call him, tell him you're looking for Jack. Don't act too concerned, just see what he says. You could even flirt with him a little. I'm gonna listen in to see if he tells you the same non-story he told me."

The bedroom was right off the kitchen and Nat went inside, coming back with an old-fashioned rotary phone in his hand. The cord stopped just outside the door, so he pulled a chair into the archway and sat down. Lisa, remaining at the table, dialed the number.

After two rings, Brad picked up.

"Hello, Brad?"

"Yes. Who's this?"

"This is Lisa Clement. We met once through Jack Cole."

His voice softened. "Yes, I remember. How are you?"

"I'm fine, Brad. I was wondering if you could help me with something, though."

"Of course, if I can. What's up?"

"I've been out of town, and I can't find Jack anywhere. At the office they say he's no longer with the firm, and he doesn't seem to live at the Water Tower anymore. Have you heard from him?"

"It's a sad case about Jack, you know. There was some sort of impropriety, and he had to leave the firm."

Lisa looked over, and Nat was shaking his head. "When was the last time you saw him?" she asked Brad.

"The last time I saw him was just before Christmas. You know the poor guy was actually waiting tables. It's hard to see a friend turning into a loser. Are you still dancing at the same club, Lisa?"

She paused to swallow the revulsion. "No Brad, I quit months ago. How did you know about that, did Jack tell you?"

"No, I was there a few times, and once you danced for me. You don't remember?"

She let the husky drop into her voice, "I do. I did the night I met you, but with everyone there, well I couldn't say much, anyway, I hope you enjoyed it."

"I did, very much. It's too bad you quit, you were really quite talented."

"I'm glad you noticed. What restaurant did you see Jack working at?"

"Place called the Pasta Pot. Listen, Lisa, why don't you put Jack out of your mind, and let me take you out on a date?"

Nat motioned for her to put the phone on hold, Lisa gave a short trilling laugh, "Can you hang on a minute, Brad?" she asked. "I have to check my calendar and see where I can squeeze you in."

Nat mouthed at her, "Tell him maybe, but you'll have to call him back."

"Hi Brad, you still there?"

"Right here."

"That might be fun, but I'm going to have to call you back."

"Tonight?"

"Maybe. Bye Brad."

She hung up and Nat did the same, "What a sleaze-ball!" she exploded.

Nat shook his head in sympathy. "He's a liar too. He told me some different things. I wonder what it is that Mr. Seaman is trying to hide."

"Well, what's next?"

"First we check out the Pasta Pot, verify the information. If Seaman is lying to you for his own sleazy reasons that's one thing. If he told you the truth, then he was lying to me, and that's a whole different ball of wax."

Carlito had an old, beat up Volkswagen bus, the kind hippies used to drive around in the late Sixties, and I don't think this one had had a tune-up since then. On days when it wasn't raining, Carlito would load up the van with books and drop them off with different people from the squat at strategic corners around town. There was Henry, an elderly man who had been put in a nursing home by his children only to run away.

Jarvis was an African-American guy in his late thirties who was mildly retarded. Roseanne, who seemed to be middle aged but it was hard to tell, was recovering from an addiction to crack cocaine and was one of the thinnest women I'd ever seen. Rich was another Vietnam vet who'd been over there with Carlito and Julius. He had gone out on patrol one morning at the start of the Tet Offensive, and he was the only one who came back. This I heard from Carlito. Rich barely, if ever, spoke.

My spot was on One Hundred and Tenth and Broadway, near Columbia University. Each morning I'd set up my folding table under a thin tree and arrange my books just so. I had an eclectic mix: popular fiction, classics, reference books, and even a select group of rare first editions. Carlito bought them by the pound from a couple of different dealers out in Brooklyn, but he selected them carefully. The popular stuff and classics he'd label. The rare books he'd set a minimum price for. I'd get dropped off about eleven and then picked up again around six in the evening. It wasn't too bad. It gave me regularity and I was making a few bucks.

Prior to hooking up with Carlito, my mind had been so preoccupied with survival that I'd had no time to consider the future or examine the past. I also was no longer drinking, and my mind was clearing. It was amazing how fuddled with alcohol and despair it had been, even before I'd ended up on the street.

Now, with the smoke clearing, my thoughts began to return to Lisa. I now knew how foolish I'd been not to speak with her after my luck started to change. You see, looking at it sober, I knew she loved me and that was nature's protection, the reason couples hooked up in the first place was to look out for one another. Now she was lost to me, and thoughts of her filled my mind, memories of her filled my senses. Now every woman I saw was a pale shadow of some remembered aspect of her. It was like this when I lost her the first time. How many guys get a second chance? Would I get a third? Then I'd think, I wouldn't want her to see me this way, and I'd turn my thoughts to schemes of success, so that I might one day be worthy again.

I'd think of my mother and I thought I'd go insane with the guilt. How I'd failed her, but what else could I have done? The mystery of my father, whoever, whereever he was, it didn't matter. He'd committed sentimental acts in the shadows, but he'd never taken enough interest or responsibility to step into the light and identify himself. It really wasn't worth the effort to consider, but still the mystery consumed me. The last words of Tommy Tyranny—what was it I would find underneath the Butterfield? What was the Butterfield? Finally, there was Walsh Dahmer and the masters of the universe. It didn't matter that they'd done the dirty to me. What mattered was that they were responsible for Ed Bloomfield's death, and possibly, my biological father's, if Tommy was to be believed. And if all that were true, then that I was responsible for not pursuing justice. I felt a tremendous urge to confess, to expunge my sins, but I couldn't go to a priest and I hadn't committed the crime.

That night, after returning to the squat, I went out and bought a six-pack. I knocked on Carlito's door and invited him to have a drink with me on the roof. It was a fine night out, about sixty-five degrees, with a low wind on the tenement tops. The roofs of these buildings were close together and you could literally hop from one to another, and people often did. Many of the nearby roofs were occupied, but Carlito and I were alone. We sat on rusty, folding chairs, drinking Budweiser from the can, while I poured out my tale. Carlito listened to the whole thing and didn't interrupt till I was finished.

"You feel better now?" he asked at length.

"I don't know. I guess I'm just trying to find some meaning in it."

"Ah," he said, nodding his head, "in my generation, they would have said you were finding yourself. But of course my generation was full of shit. They took this country that had, like, this thin veil of manners, hiding this system of lies, and they lifted the veil and exposed the lies. But you know, bro. The lies were always there, and always will be. The only thing protecting us was the veil. It's like a pale guy at the beach, covered in suntan lotion, saying to himself, 'the truth is, the sun is hot and the sun burns and this suntan lotion is a lie.' So he wipes it off, and the stupid bastard gets burned.

I mean, bro. I don't know exactly what the truth of the matter is, but I do know that before the so called 'Flower Children' of the Sixties came to power, before that generation took over, we didn't have homeless like we do today. We didn't have athletes making eight million a year, and we didn't have anybody telling you not to expect your Social Security check when you get old. People took care of each other, not like today. Today people are fucked up.

"So it's not really all your fault. You were raised on the media telling you to go out and get yours, and fuck everybody else. That's what you were taught, that's what passes for culture and religion around here. It's all artificial shit, we're taught to live an artificial life. I guess you just had to go through all this to learn how to be natural, man. Now you're learning about community. Without community, we ain't nothing but a pack of hungry dogs snarling at each other over some dead meat, and that's the lucky people. Some of us, the homeless, we're just living in the shadow of the pack. Not even close enough to the meat to fight for it.

"You know when I came back from Nam, I was proud. I wore my uniform and went out expecting people to offer me a job, or buy me a drink, like they did for the World War Two vets. But instead, I got college kids spitting on me, calling me a murderer. You know, I thought, I got drafted because I couldn't afford to go to college. Those college kids, it was basically their parents who sent me off to war, to protect their investments in Coca Cola, or some such shit. But they didn't send their own kids to war, no, they sent 'em to college, and those kids called me a murderer. And those are the people running the country now.

"Fifteen years ago I was a stone cold junkie, living in the shadow of the dog. A total reject of society, but I know my mission in life is to help my fellow man. I believe that's everybody's mission." He cracked another beer. "How do you like life in the squat so far?"

I grinned. "I like it just fine. I'm really starting to put my life back together."

"Good," he said. "Once you find yourself, maybe you can start helping other people. As for the woman, if it's truly meant to be, fate will bring her back to you. That and maybe you got to start thinking about slaying the dragon."

Lisa and Nat sat across a desk facing Tracy Willacy and Don Mitchell at the HNCR.

Tracy studied the photocopy portrait of Jack. "This is the man you're looking for? You do realize he may look quite different from this now?"

"That's a fairly recent photograph," Lisa replied, "How much could he have changed?"

Nat put his hand over Lisa's forearm to get her to settle down. "What Tracy is trying to say, and it makes perfect sense," Nat said in a soft voice, "is that it is more than likely that Jack is carrying himself differently. If he's homeless now his posture is bound to be less confident and he most likely has more facial hair, if not a full beard."

"That is what I am trying to say," Tracy agreed. "I'm actually pretty good with portraits, so with your permission I'm going to make a couple of sketches based on this photo."

"Thank you."

Don Mitchell pulled a bound book of data printed on perforated computer paper from under the desk and pushed it toward Nat. "That is the week-to-date data for clients who have checked into city shelters, but I don't see any record of a Jack Cole."

Tracy was staring at the picture. "This guy, he's wearing a pretty nice suit in the photo, and this is his first time on the street, isn't it?"

"That is correct," Nat replied, listening attentively to what the young lady had to say. He had learned long ago that insight and wisdom could be found in the least expected places and that included the mouths of twenty-year-olds.

"Well, we can keep checking these registers but I'll bet you the guy isn't using the shelters, not more than one time anyway. I also doubt he will continue to use his real name out on the streets. But he has to stay somewhere, so if I were you I would start checking with the mole people, or some of the other non-traditional homeless settlements downtown."

Lisa didn't like being confused, and she certainly wasn't ashamed to admit when she was ignorant. "I'm sorry, but you lost me toward the end there. What are Mole People and what do you mean by nontraditional homeless settlements?"

Don Mitchell paused for a composition moment, and then leaned forward in his chair. "Mole People, Ms. Clement, are people who live in the tunnels under the city."

"What tunnels?"

"Ms. Clement, the city is full of tunnels. In fact there is an entire"—he paused for a moment, mentally groping for a word—"shadow city if you will, beneath the streets of New York."

"There are literally thousands of people down there, Nat knows about it," Tracy chimed in.

Lisa looked over at Nat and he smiled awkwardly back. "I do know about them, but that's not to say I know them intimately or have a tremendous amount of experience with them—"

Tracy cut in, "I think the tunnels make Nat a little uneasy, but more like a phobia than a fear. Something he has overcome in the past and can do so again in the future."

Lisa gave Nat an encouraging smile and asked, "What about nontraditional homeless settlements? What are those?"

Don Mitchell pushed his glasses up the bridge of his nose and smirked. "The least likely thing possible. Squats and shantytowns, but it's highly unlikely that a guy as fresh on the street as this Jack fellow would have the wherewithal to get into one of those communities. To get into a squat you have to be connected." He looked Lisa square in the eye. "Kind of like getting a rent controlled apartment."

Tracy nodded in agreement. "I agree with Don, I'd be willing to bet that your guy is right now with the Mole People."

"How would we go about finding him"—and Lisa found herself involuntarily looking down at the floor—"down there?"

Don Mitchell stood up and took a lap around the small room. "Tracy," he said when he sat back down. "Would you be able to hook Detective Turner up directly with Old James?"

"Who is old James?" Lisa asked.

"Old James," Tracy replied, "is going to be your ferryman across the river Styx."

"When can we arrange a meeting?" Nat asked.

"Could take up to a week," Tracy replied, "depending on how long he takes to locate, but I should be able to set something up in the next couple of days, assuming he's easy to find."

It was another couple of days of dead ends for Lisa and Nat. They both wandered the streets, and every so often, Nat checked the hospitals, and—unbeknownst to Lisa—the John Doe's at the city morgue. It was this big zero that Nat contemplated as he sat waiting for Lisa at the bar in Pete's Tavern.

Nat had come to the conclusion, that, while continuing to search for Jack, they also had to come at the actual murder investigation from a different angle. As he sat staring into the green beer bottle in front of him and mulling the possibilities, Lisa walked in.

She gave him a chaste kiss on the cheek. "Hi, Nat."

"Hi, want something to drink?"

"Just a diet coke."

"How come you never have a real drink?"

"I'm pregnant."

"Pregnant?" He looked her up and down. "It doesn't show."

"Thank you."

"It's Jack's?"

She nodded.

"Well that explains a lot." He signaled to the bartender. "You know, I've been thinking. We're hitting a stone wall, so maybe it's time to beat the bushes and see what breaks."

"What do you mean by that cryptic suggestion?"

"I think it's time for you to take Brad Seaman up on his offer of a date."

"Wait a minute. He's a pretty creepy guy, and I don't think he knows anything, anyway."

Nat lifted his hand. "Hear me out first. Number one, you don't have to do anything more than spend a little time with the guy in a public place. Number two; I think this guy has got some connection to the murder and to Jack's problems. Now, if he does, he's obviously not alone. Hold on to that thought. I further believe that your boyfriend's misfortune and the Bloomfield murder are both related to the last deal they worked on together, the Homer Industries acquisition. What we need to do is goose him a little. You go out with him and let slip some kind of information that makes him nervous. Then all we gotta do is sit back and see who he runs to."

She wrinkled her nose. "What kind of information?"

"Oh, we'll figure something out."

TWENTY-FOUR

I took a day off to go down to The Coalition for the Homeless. They had a program a guy told me about where they set you up with a phone number and free voice mail. That was a really important step for me, because without a phone number I couldn't even start looking for a regular job. But after waiting several hours to see a caseworker I was told that they had more requests than available numbers. The upshot was, I was going to have to return and see her again the following week, which was okay with me. I was learning patience and had a feeling the caseworker was for real.

By the time I returned to the squat that afternoon, it was almost four o'clock, and there was a big crowd gathered around

Carlito near the back door. As I drew closer, I could see almost all of Carlito's people were there, and he was reading aloud from a copy of *The New York Post*. I just caught the tail end of it, something about seventy-two hours.

"What's up?" I asked Carlito, who'd now put the paper aside to stare at the grim faces surrounding him.

"I never should have let that fucking legal aid lawyer handle this thing. Now I'm going to have to go to court tomorrow. The law says we've got a right to be here."

"What's all the fuss about?" I asked.

He held up the front page of the *Post*, and there was a picture of our thin-lipped mayor, looking more severe than usual—and he usually looked severe. The headline said MAYOR TO SQUATTERS: NO MORE FREE RIDE!

I licked my lips. "So what does that mean to us?"

"That means, that in three days time, the police are going to come and throw our collective asses in the street, because it burns the mayor's prissy ass that we got a place to live without having to pay some rich cock-sucking slumlord who contributes to his election campaign for the fucking privilege!"

"I thought that once you stayed in a squat long enough without someone throwing you out, you got the rights to it," I said.

Carlito shook his head in disgust, "That's supposed to be the law. But lawyers can twist anything around if they want to. They're saying the living conditions are unsafe, so they have to take over the squats and renovate them for middle-income housing. They say it's unfair that we get to live here while people wait on lists for years to get into public housing."

I picked up the paper and scanned the article quickly. "So what are you going to do?"

Carlito let out a frustrated huff. "I have to go to Housing Court in the morning to try and get what they call an Order to Show Cause. That's like an injunction to keep them from throwing us out."

"What if that doesn't work?"

"Then they're going to throw us out." He turned on his heel and stormed into the building, Julius rolling along in his wake.

I felt like one big popped bubble—everything was about to fall apart again. But not without a fight this time. When Carlito went to court in the morning I planned to be there with him.

Roget had gotten the call the week before. Norton explained what was needed, and seemed to imply, apropos of nothing, that it would be an easy task because the guy was homeless. Bullshit—it might be easier once he found Jack, but finding the guy would be a pain in the ass. It was a rare fuck up, losing Cole's trail following the eviction. Of course, with or without Norton he was going to find the boy.

After struggling with the problem for a few days, Roget came up with a simple idea. Spread some money and a description around several homeless communities in the city, and imply there was more money to come. Like fur trapping: Once the traps were baited and set, all you had to do was check on them periodically. The checking was what brought him to Grand Central on the day that the mayor declared war on the squatters.

Checking the traps involved walking through crowded, sweaty terminals and waiting to be approached by one of the men he'd encouraged to search them. After spending more than an hour in Grand Central, he shuttled over to Times Square, stepping carefully over the gap between the train and the platform as he disembarked, and walking in the direction of the A train. Just as he passed the stairs leading to the Downtown R, somebody tapped him on the shoulder. He turned to see a tall, muscular young Hispanic guy with a tattoo of a snake ringing his powerful bicep. Roget recognized the guy. He'd given him a twenty a day or two before, and told him he was looking for his cousin and shown him a photo of Jack. As he looked at the guy now, Roget decided he was either hiding from the cops in the tunnels or was recently released from prison.

"Yes?" Roget smiled with all his teeth.

The man looked quickly both ways as if to make sure no one was listening. "Yo man, I know where your cousin is at."

Roget rendered up the expected smile. "You do? Where?"

"You got some money?" The man rubbed his thumb and two fingers together.

Roget pulled a thick wad from his pocket and gave the man a peek. "Show me where he is and I'll give you a C-note."

"Money first."

"Money after I see my cousin."

"Awright, follow me."

The big man turned on his heel and down the steps towards the One Train with Roget following carefully behind. At the edge of the platform there was a little stair leading to the track. For about a hundred yards they followed the path the track workers used until it branched off on the left into another dark, trackless tunnel. The old service passage, lit only by distant signal lamps, went on a long way.

It didn't take long for Roget's vision to become accustomed to the dark. It was ridiculously easy to see when the big man in front of him stopped and pulled the knife.

"Now you gonna give me all your money," the man hissed.

Roget smiled in the darkness. He enjoyed killing the strong ones. "You're a very stupid man," he said. Roget laughed, backing up a step.

The man came quickly, but Roget could feel his motion. He sidestepped and quickly swept the man's feet out from under him, crashing him face first into the packed earth. Then Roget was on top of him, smashing his knee into the small of the man's back and punching his fist into the hand that held the knife, snapping the man's wrist. The big man tried to wiggle underneath Roget, but the pin was solid. With his right hand, Roget picked up the knife, and with his left, pushed the man's profile into the clammy ground. In the distance he heard rats scurry by.

Roget pressed the knife a little way into the man's ear. "Where is the man I seek?"

The strong man groaned under Roget's weight. "I don't know. I just wanted to rob you."

"I believe you." Roget pushed the knife into the man's ear, right up to the handle. He left the body where it lay. The rats would do the rest.

About halfway back down the dark tunnel walk he remembered the hands. The hands would be useful, since he did have something else coming up. With a sigh he turned back around toward where he had left the body.

I went down to housing court with Carlito the next day, and it was a grim affair. Jeremy Staub, the legal aid attorney representing the squatters, was hopelessly overmatched. Carlito hadn't managed to scrape together the necessary money to refute the expert testimony of the city-hired structural engineer. In the end Carlito's Order to Show Cause was rejected by the judge on the basis that the action to evict was not related to anything but safe housing standards. As far as the squatters were concerned, that was a lie. The squat wasn't the Ritz Carleton, but it wasn't unsafe, either.

Over the next day or so, I followed the story as it unfolded in the newspapers. By and large, they were unfavorable. The media championed the mayor and vilified the squatters. They said the squatters were living rent-free, in apartments that should be available for ordinary New Yorkers in a tight housing market. They said the squatters were abusing the system. Now maybe I'm partial, but I never saw any of those reporters come to the squat to interview the people involved, so I'm not sure what their sources were.

On the third day the police came. We knew they were coming, and Carlito had us organized, along with some sympathizers, to protest the eviction. The strategy was civil disobedience. We would refuse to leave and stage a sit-in, in the style of the 1960s campus rebellions. Carlito felt this was the most effective way to buy us time and draw attention to our plight. What Carlito and the rest of us failed to understand was that we were not rich, young college kids who were going to capture the imagination of a nation. We were the flotsam and Jetsam of society, and the last thing the country wanted was to look at us. Once a year at Thanksgiving was more than enough. With the gentrification of Alphabet City, traditionally a hard luck neighborhood, these long-abandoned tenements were suddenly valuable.

The police arrived with the dawn. I was keeping watch with Carlito and about six others on the roof. First came two flatbed police trucks, from which muscular cops began to unload wooden barricades, the kind they use to line parade routes. They used these to block off the street. There were three other squats on the block, and through the early morning mist, I could see others on their roofs, also looking down. Two phalanxes of police arrived, one from the east and the other from the west, each group about twenty strong. They wore riot gear: helmets, body armor, shields, and clubs.

Jay, a young anarchist from the neighborhood who had come out in solidarity with us, let out a long whistle. "Man, they look real serious."

I studied him for a minute: pale and thin, all dressed in leather, with a purple streak in his hair, and about a half dozen rings in his eyebrows, he was really quite a sight. A year earlier and I would have dismissed the guy as a freak. Now I was standing here shoulder-to-shoulder with him. "You could say they're serious as fucking cancer, Jay," I replied to him. He nodded nervously back at me.

Papi, a thin old man who lived with Julius on the first floor, shook his whole body like a pogo stick, and nervously shouted. "Where is the press, Carlito? Man, you said there was gonna be press!"

Carlito didn't answer, and I knew why. The police came deliberately at this hour, when they knew they weren't expected. If the press did show up later, they weren't going to even get on the block. The police were going to clear out the squats by any means necessary, and they didn't want witnesses. Squad cars pulled up behind the barricades on both sides of the street, uniformed patrolmen taking up position behind them as the shock troops advanced slightly.

The two phalanxes ranged opposite one another, stopped motionless. It looked like some crazy game of red rover was about to break out. From one of the other squats across the street I could hear shouting, and then it got quiet as a uniformed lieutenant walked into the middle of the street with a bullhorn.

"The people residing in 307, 311, 322, and 324," he bellowed. "This is the police. You are directed by court order to vacate immediately. You have ten minutes to comply before you are removed by force. The time is now 5:33 A.M.," and he disappeared back behind the police lines.

For a long moment everything was completely still. You couldn't even hear the birds. It was like the pigeons themselves, the ultimate New York squatters, were holding their breath. Then the two squats across the street erupted in a hail of bottles, rocks, and other missiles.

Jay, the young anarchist, reached down for a beer bottle, but Carlito grabbed his arm. "Bro, this is to be a nonviolent thing. Civil Disobedience, that's all."

Jay looked pissed, "But look what's going on!" He pointed. A detail of police had entered the first squat and was dragging people out roughly, in handcuffs.

Carlito pulled the bottle gently from his hand. "We don't need to give them an excuse. You think we have a prayer of beating them that way? We're making a different kind of point here, man."

If nothing else, Carlito's strategy bought our building some time. We hadn't thrown anything at the police, so for the time being they ignored number 322 as they cleared the other buildings. Our group watched as glass broke and rocks were hurled. I saw one fat policeman with the visor of his riot helmet up get smashed in his exposed face with a rock and collapse to the pavement. That really seemed to rile up the boys in blue. I watched as they chased the squatters down the street, beating them with their billyclubs. One hugely fat man wearing a T-shirt that said LIFE'S A BEACH turned on a pursuing cop and smacked him down to the ground. He didn't have long to savor his triumph; four cops were instantly there, beating him into the pavement with their clubs like Neanderthals in some caveman ritual.

Papi, who was staring over the side of the roof facing the alley, began to shout, "Here they come!"

I looked over, and about fifteen police in riot gear were storming through the alley. I could see Julius sitting defiantly in front of the door in the alley, the wheels on his chair locked. As I watched, police grabbed his chair from either side. Cuffing his arms to it, they unlocked his wheels and spun him off down the alley.

My heart was in the ground. I knew they were coming, and with bad intentions, but no one made a move to leave. I stood my ground with everyone else. A few minutes later the door to the roof burst open and six cops poured through. They formed a line, clubs in hand and we faced up to them, in our own pathetic line, our backs to the parapet. For a moment, we faced off in silence. Then Carlito stepped out of line, his hands open in supplication.

"We offer no violence," he said. "This is our home."

For a moment there was no movement, then one of the cops punched his nightstick into Carlito's gut, doubling him over onto the tar. All hell broke loose. Everyone started running in different directions, and I hopped over to the next roof. Looking over my shoulder I could see the cops beating and cuffing my companions. So far, no one was paying any attention to me. Over one more roof to the right, there was an old water tower. I steeled my nerve to make the next jump. This jump was wider than the last, and I almost didn't make it. As it was, I twisted my ankle and cracked my head, opening a cut over my eyebrow. I picked myself up and shambled over to the iron ladder leading up the face of the water tower. I climbed all the way up to the platform, and hunkered down to watch the rest of the drama unfold.

Nat Weston leafed through a magazine at a Newsstand in Times Square, near the One Train, where two female outreach workers were supposed to meet him for an expedition underground. The plan was to try and convince some of the Mole People to forsake their subterranean haven for the dubious upgrade of the city's shelter system. Nat wasn't looking forward to the excursion. It would be depressing, and his radio didn't work that far under.

There was a tap on his shoulder, and he turned to see an old homeless man looking quizzically at him. The guy could have been anywhere between sixty and eighty. His face was so scarred it was hard to tell.

"You're Nat, ain't you?" the man said.

"Ah, yeah."

"I'm James. Tracy, the girl what helps the kids. She told me to look you up."

Nat put the magazine back in the rack and smiled. "What's up, James?"

James screwed up his face, taking on the appearance of a black Popeye. "Strange things, Nat, strange things."

"What strange things is that?" Nat asked, handing the newsguy fifty cents for a candy bar. "You want one?" he offered.

James smiled, showing mostly gums. "Nah, bad for my teeth."

Nat nodded, "Walk with me, I gotta meet two kids by the Forty-second Street entrance."

"Sure. Tell you what, though. The kids can wait. You walk with me, strange things to see."

Nat stopped in his tracks and waited for James to follow suit. It took a few seconds and James had to double back. "What strange things?" Nat asked once they were reunited.

"Body."

"Dead body?"

"Yep."

"Something stranger, though?"

"Yep." James started off in the direction of the One Train again.

"What's the stranger thing?" Nat asked, hurrying to catch up.

"Hands." Old James laughed. It wasn't a humorous laugh.

"Hands?"

"That's exactly right. What about the hands? Ain't no hands. There's a body down that tunnel, ain't got no hands."

The bell in Nat's head rang. The Frenchman.

TWENTY-FIVE

When I came to it was dark and I was alone. My head ached, my ankle hurt, and I was hungry. I stuck my hand in my pocket, and fingered the reassuring fold of bills. Sixty dollars, my entire savings, all the money in the world.

It was an overcast night, and for a while I watched the moon peek through the mist and clouds only to disappear again, glowing yellow behind them. I slipped through the roof door, down the stairs, and out onto the street. The stoops, normally teeming with life, were empty. There were cops camped out in front of the vacant squats, and I wondered where Carlito and the others were. I'd been reading a lot while working for Carlito selling books. A line from the *Rubaiyat of Omar Khayyam* came to mind, "as under cover of departing day slunk hunger-stricken Ramazan away." I don't know why it occurred to me, I guess it fit. Actually quite erudite for a homeless guy, I thought.

Once more alone upon the street—where to go, and what to do? I would not go to a shelter. I thought about the Catholic Worker on East Third. A man could rent a bed there cheaply, if one was available. I fingered the wad in my pocket, not really all the money in the world, and it was a temperate night. I decided to get a bite, then walk up to Riverside Park and sleep al fresco by the river. Tomorrow would be a new day, back into the fight. Maybe tomorrow I could go down to the Coalition for the Homeless and see a caseworker. There's a good day coming, I told myself, just around the corner. Lisa was still out there. Somewhere my dreams were alive.

Jack began his trek to the Hudson River at about nine P.M., just around the same time that Lisa was sitting at the Bar in Ruth's Chris Steakhouse on Fifty-first Street. There she was, sipping on a diet coke and ignoring the appraising stares of loud, drunken Yuppies. Just waiting for Brad Seaman to show up. In fact, Jack passed within a block of Lisa. At one point, as she waited, the bartender told her a gentleman wanted to buy her a drink, and then pointed at a big blonde guy in a sharkskin suit, smoking a cigar and staring at her with an open, almost disturbing lust. She declined. When the man received his rejection, his friends jeered him. Brad Seaman was not only creepy, she thought, but late. This awful, chauvinistic atmosphere reminded her of him. It was egotistical, she felt, to make a woman meet you in a place like this; it was like a locker room with suits. All the men smoking cigars and talking in loud voices about their important business, and how much money they made. Sooner or later she expected them to all piss collectively in a corner to mark their territory. She was suddenly very glad that her mission tonight extended no farther than rattling Brad's cage. All she had to do was be a little nice to him for about ten minutes and then turn on him, implying that she knew more than she did. After that, Nat said, all they were going to do was see where he ran to.

Then he walked in. She watched him as he made his way through the crowded bar, blending in. She wondered briefly how Jack would have blended in here. Brad finished scoping the joint, bellied up and gestured arrogantly to the bartender for a drink before turning to her.

"I'm sorry I'm late, but I got caught up with a client, and with the amount of money I make off this guy . . . Well, I don't have to tell you, there wasn't a thing I could do." He broke off to take a long pull of the beer the bartender had left for him.

An hour later they were sitting in the dining room eating meat. Brad had just finished telling her about a golf trip he was planning for the summer, and she was bored out of her skull. Not only that, but he was trying to play footsy under the table, and she felt like puking up the meat. It was time to poke her stick in the hornets' nest and run like hell from the tree. Suddenly his hand was on her knee.

She jerked her chair back from the table and his hand slipped away, "Look Brad, I didn't come here tonight because I think you're charming or cute, so get any idea that you're getting lucky tonight out of your head right now. I only agreed to come out with you tonight because I have something to tell you." He stared hard at her and she focused on a piece of spinach dangling from his lower lip. "I want to find Jack," she continued,

"Jack is not around because of something to do with Homer Industries. I know all about your role in the Homer Industries deal. He told me about you, so if you don't want trouble, you better find Jack for me." She stood up.

An ugly expression passed over Brad's face. "You're threatening me?"—his tone was incredulous—"because let me tell you something, sweetheart. Don't you realize that it doesn't matter who you tell what? The SEC nailed me a long time ago, sweetheart. Now it's me who wrecks lives with testimony. How do you think they got on to Jack in the first place?"

It wasn't ladylike, and it cost her a few stares from the crowd, but Lisa spat on the ground near Brad's feet. "You know how to reach me. I assume you're picking up the tab. Have a great night." She didn't look back as she made her way out, but she knew he was staring in shock, and it pleased her.

I had grown up in a big rambling apartment on Riverside Drive. The building itself was crumbling and in disrepair. All the plumbing and heating systems in it were vintage. They were on their last legs when I was a kid, but the space itself had been pretty big and comfortable, even if sometimes the broiler broke in the dead of winter and we froze for a few days. Most of the time it had been pretty nice and a lot of the memories were good. I guess that's why I found myself wandering up the west coast of Manhattan Island bound toward my childhood home.

It was a long walk against the bitter wind blowing off the Hudson, but I didn't pay much attention to my physical discomfort. Something must have been lurking under the surface of my brain, though because as I walked forward the words of Tommy Tierney came back to me. He had told me that the secret to my father's death—or at least the secret to the death of Mr. Palmer—was hidden beneath the Butterfield. I hadn't understood at the time but I thought I did now.

It took more than two hours and by the time I got to 122nd Street the hunch had turned into a certainty, at least in my mind. I had grown up at the foot of a hill on Riverside Drive and 124th Street in West Harlem. Nestled between Spanish Harlem and Columbia University it was a neighborhood of true diversity, with wealthy intellectuals and middle class families living side-by-side with recent immigrants from all over the globe. I had lived at the bottom of that hill in the New York City tenement version of the House of Usher: a building that had been grandiose and expensive in its day, fallen into disrepair and bargain rents. At the top of this hill was International House, living quarters for foreign students and faculty. Riverside Church with all of its significance in the American Civil Rights Movement was another neighborhood edifice. The area was rich, poor, and pregnant with meaning. But most significant of all, at the top of that hill, right above my boyhood home, was a small park that had been gifted to the American people at some point by the Japanese. I'm not exactly sure how it all went down, but at some point the Japanese had financed this small green space next to International House, planted it over with cherry trees, and gifted it to the City of New York. What was interesting about the park was that at some time during the Civil War, the Union had conscripted a brigade of local boys from Harlem Heights, and they had put this brigade under the command of one General Butterfield. There was a statue of General Butterfield in the center of Sakura Park.

I hadn't been there in years but of course the way hadn't changed. The park was still there. It was dark with just a few neighborhood people walking their dogs under a full moon when I arrived. I examined the statue, and the front part where you could actually see the general. I quickly decided that was a dead end because the front part was all display, with a stone-wall and floors encompassing the statue. Around back was a different story. There was green grass and soft earth and opportunity there. But it was a good amount of space to dig around in without tools.

I ran across the street to hit up Riverside Park for a few thick, heavy branches from a tree to assist me in digging up under the statue. Along the way I had to pass through the grounds of Grant's Tomb. I got lucky there: A landscaper must have forgotten a shovel from the day shift. It had been left leaning against a mosaic bench behind the monument.

I dug for about an hour and managed to unearth a small metal box secured by a heavy padlock. When I hefted the box I cringed at the thought of carrying it far, but I knew it wasn't a good time to stick around. Whatever mysteries were contained in the box, they could keep until I found someplace safe to pop it open and eventually bury it again. Either way I needed to get away from Sakura Park. I stuck the box under my coat and headed back downtown along the built up side of the avenue. I left the old neighborhood and headed south, firmly resisting the temptation to sit down somewhere and open the box. There would be time enough for that later. What I had to do now was find a safe place to stash the box and get some rest, so I headed downtown.

I entered Riverside Park on Seventy-second, and walked down the hill and through the tunnel. On the other side a staircase led to the lower park, and directly ahead was a small track.

To the left lay the old piers and freight yards. It was very quiet and still. I chose a spot in the corner of a small field near a concrete wall and laid some cardboard boxes on the wet grass. On the other side of the wall were the freight yards, and it was unlikely that I would be disturbed. I had taken the shovel with me when I started my hike back downtown. Now I pushed the box up against the wall and took a couple of swipes at the padlock, but I made no impression on it. I leaned down close to it and examined the hinges of the box in the moonlight. There was no way I would get into that thing until I was able to get my hands on some tools.

I sat down on my haunches and considered what was best to do. It was frustrating. Tommy had seemed to indicate that a lot of my mysteries or problems could be solved if I could just get into that box, but it wasn't going to happen tonight. Finally I decided to take a patient approach and wait. Being homeless had at least taught me a bit about patience. I picked up the shovel and dug a shallow hole in an obscure corner of the field and there I buried the box again, covering it with a heavy slab of concrete at the end.

I bunched up my jacket for a pillow and laid down to rest. All in all not too bad, like camping in the Boy Scouts. I smiled at the memories. Someone had paid for me to go every summer to learn shooting and fishing and woodcraft. Maybe someone whose name was in that box under the concrete slab just a few feet away. I hadn't been drinking lately, but tonight, after the riot at the squat, I'd treated myself to a bottle of cheap scotch. Now I took a long sip. In a few minutes the world slipped away and I was dreaming.

Nat was waiting in a car across the street from the restaurant. When he saw Lisa emerge he unlocked the passenger side door.

"Well?" he asked.

She got in. "I dropped the bomb and he pretty much told me that he gave Jack up to the SEC."

Nat thumbed through his notebook and scribbled a few lines. "Did he tell you for what?"

"No, because the way I was playing it, I was acting like I already knew."

Nat let the notebook drop into his lap. "Right. What do you think he gave him up for?"

"Insider trading. No?"

Nat fiddled with the radio. "I guess."

Lisa adjusted her seat back. "What now?"

"Now we wait." Earlier in the day, Nat had slipped into the bar and put the pay phone out of commission."

"What if he has a cell phone?"

"If he did, you would have seen it." This was long before they were common and only the wealthy really had them.

Nat stared moodily at the bar door. Lisa asked, "What's wrong?"

He rolled one eye over at her, keeping the other firmly fixed on the restaurant. "Tough day at the office. Guy murdered down in the tunnels under Times Square. Difficult to identify, guy had no hands."

"What?"

"Sick, huh? Whoever killed him cut them off." Nat didn't go any further into it. He didn't wish to disturb her with the connection.

There was a pay phone right out in front of the restaurant. Nat had had a friend at the phone company come by earlier to make sure the redial button worked. "What if he goes in the other direction?" asked Lisa.

Nat stared straight ahead. "He won't."

"What if somebody else gets to the phone first?"

He shifted his gaze over to her. "Lisa, have a little faith."

The restaurant door opened and Brad walked out. He looked both ways, and you could almost see him homing in on the pay phone. Nat pulled his hat down over his face. "Get down," he said, giving Lisa's elbow a tug.

After a few minutes Brad hung up the phone and stepped into the street to hail a cab. "All right, kid, you're on," Nat said as Brad sped away. Lisa slipped out and Nat eased his car into the street to follow Brad's taxi.

Lisa picked up the receiver and hit redial. A recorded voice asked her for a dollar seventy-five. She was ready with a fistful of quarters and put seven of them into the slot. After four rings a man answered, "Norton residence."

For a second she hesitated. "I'm sorry I must have gotten the wrong number. Could you please tell me what number I have reached?"

"Check your number and try again, miss."

He was about to hang up so Lisa said quickly, "Please, I don't want to disturb you again, could you please tell me what number I've reached?"

"I'm afraid not, miss. This is a private number." The voice on the other end hung up, leaving her with just a dial tone.

Lightning cracked suddenly in the west. A few seconds later, thunder rolled. Lisa hung up and hailed a cab.

The thunder woke me up with a start. I leaned forward to the river and saw lightning briefly illuminate the Jersey sky. Then it started pouring. I thought about the tunnel above me that connected the upper and lower levels of Riverside Park. It would be relatively dry there, but I decided against it. People walked back and forth through it and I'd be vulnerable. I stood on shaky feet, covering my head with my jacket.

Behind me were the freight yards and a long tunnel leading away from them. The thought of going into that darkness was scary, but I couldn't stay exposed to the driving rain. There was a hole in the fence with about a three-foot drop to the tracks below. Clutching my bottle of scotch, I hopped down.

The great gaping mouth of the cavern was dark and forbidding, but in the distance I could see lights flickering in the wind. They looked like campfires. I took a swig from my bottle and entered. A rat scurried across my feet. It was like entering the underworld in some kind of ancient fable.

The flickering lights mitigated the darkness somewhat. After a while my eyes became accustomed to the point where I could make out shadows. To the left and right along the walls, there were what looked like small lean-tos. I could sense, more than see, eyes upon me. The further along I got, the further away the fires seemed, like something desired in a dream. I kept going, feeling less threatened by the fires than by the darkness, or by the shadowy people who lived in the shacks along the walls.

I reached the first fire, just a small pit with a metal grate flames burning within. Along the walls I could see small tents made from tarps and sticks, and shacks made of plywood, a 1990-style Hooverville. I remembered something my grandfather, who had been a traveling salesman, once said. "Nothing is so comforting to the tired man, than a light seen through darkness." I was cold, tired, and wet. I was at the point where I didn't care whose fire it was, and I just sat down. There was an open, barred window high up on the wall of the tunnel, and the wind whistled in, making the flames dance. I took another swig from my bottle.

My eyes closed and I must have dozed off for two or three minutes, because when my boozy eyes opened again I was surrounded by dark shadows hovering just outside the perimeter of light. I counted seven.

"Hello," I called out and the word echoed back at me.

One of the shadows stepped forward assuming the form of a grizzled, fifty-something-year-old man in a flannel shirt. He was heavily bearded with broad shoulders.

"What do you want?" he demanded in a voice filled with proclamation.

I stood, scotch bottle in hand. "My name's Jack. I'm homeless. I'm looking for shelter."

For a long minute the man stared wordlessly at me. Then I offered him my bottle and he accepted, taking a long pull. Other shadows stepped into the light, four men and two women. The bearded man passed my bottle around, and it was almost empty when it returned to me.

After another moment the man said, "I'm Tim. You're welcome here."

I sat back down in front of the fire and stared into the flames, thinking about the road that had led me to this place.

TWENTY-SIX

Nat sat in a Chinese joint on Ninth Avenue waiting for Old James to show, and thinking about the events of the previous night. He'd trailed Brad's cab, but the guy had just gone home. After an hour or so his lights went out and Nat threw in the towel. Lisa hadn't knocked it out of the park either, but at least they now knew for sure that Brad was involved. The guy he'd run to when he got his tree shook was Arnold Norton, Jack's old boss—the same guy who'd put all that pressure on the department to close the Bloomfield case. It was nothing that could be used in court, but it was, Nat felt, significant validation for the pursuit of their private investigation.

Old James finally limped in. They ordered lunch and Nat got down to business. "What you got for me?"

Old James stared at the plate Nat had ordered for him. "The body's got a first name," he replied, looking around for silverware. There was none on the table.

Nat ignored his distress. "Yeah?"

"A Dominican guy from uptown. They say he just got out of Riker's after five years and come down to the tunnels to coop awhile," James replied while scanning the room for a waitress.

"He have a name?"

Old James stared anxiously at his plate. "Hector. That's all anybody knows."

"Anybody know what happened to him?"

Old James tipped an almost empty bottle of soy sauce over his food. "Could you ask them for extra soy sauce and maybe a fork and knife? How do they expect a guy to eat without no fork and knife?"

Nat pushed a pair of chopsticks across the table toward him.

James stared at the chopsticks as if they were snakes. "What the fuck is that, you expect me to eat with a couple a twigs?"

Nat laughed. "The Chinese do it."

Old James sucked in a breath to expand his chest. "Well I ain't no Chinaman. I am an African American and I eat with a fork. Do you mind getting me a fork and some soy sauce, please?"

"Sure." Nat got the sauce and a plastic fork from the counter and returned to his seat. "There's your sauce. You gonna answer my question?"

James poured the rest of that bottle over his food, too. "Well, nobody knows for sure about this. But there was supposed to be some foreigner, a white guy. He was looking for his cousin or something. Seemed to think his cousin went on a bummer.

Anyway, this guy was spreading money around, looking for information. Hector told some people he was gonna take the guy off."

Nat stared at the soupy bowl of food in front of James for a long moment and then said. "The guy have a name?"

Old James stuck a forkful in his mouth and shrugged. "I dunno."

"Who told you all this?"

Old James put down his fork and stared Nat direct in the eye. "Now you know I can't tell you none a that. I gotta live down there."

Nat broke eye contact first. "Yeah, right. Listen, can you keep tabs for me in case this foreign guy shows up again?"

Old James piled a load of food on his fork. "I can do that."

Nat stared out the window while James finished his chow fun. When he was done, Nat asked him, "If you were from Manhattan and pretty fresh on the street, how many different places are there you'd go?"

Old James pushed his plate forward. "All depends on who I was."

"Young white guy. Guy with big problems, maybe on the run."

"Might go to the shelters. Once. Used to be squats. Have to know somebody. Tunnels, lots of tunnels out there."

"Any Yuppie tunnels?"

Old James guffawed. "No such thing as a Yuppie on the street."

Nat smiled just to show his appreciation of the humor. "Humor me. What tunnel would a Yuppie go to?"

Old James frowned for a long time, thinking. "You know, maybe the old freight yard tunnels by Riverside. Maybe. Then again, they got some places down under the Village. I never been there, but folks call 'em the condos. They tell me it's nice."

Lisa still had a little money in the bank, and she wanted to keep it that way. But she had vowed to never work in the clubs again. The quickest, most respectable way to fast money she knew was waiting tables. That's how she found herself leaving DiAngelo's at closing after a long shift on the floor. It was a little after midnight, her feet were tired, and it was a long walk between Park Avenue South and Twenty-first where she worked, and Twenty-sixth and Ninth where she lived. But there was no mass transit alternative that was any easier, and she didn't see any cabs. It wouldn't be so bad she told herself. Spring in New York is the nicest of seasons.

Even in a city as flush with beauty as the Big Apple, Lisa was striking. As a matter of course she was stared at on the street. She affected to ignore the ogling and as a result was sometimes a little insensitive to what went on around her. But when she turned the corner on Twenty-sixth, she noticed a dark shadow crossing the street from the other side. The same dark shadow had been moving parallel to her ever since she left work.

She crossed Park Avenue South, going toward Madison. This area, primarily a business district, was empty at this hour. The dark, still quiet was so intense she could hear the echo of her footsteps as she strode along the lonesome pavement. A figure stepped out of a doorway in front of her and she took a sharp breath, but it was just a porter emptying trash. She recovered quickly and continued to the corner of Fifth Avenue, cursing softly as she came to the park separating east from west. She'd forgotten about it. The park was a nice stroll during the day. At night she'd just as soon avoid it, but that meant doubling back to Twenty-third, across town to Broadway, and then back over. As she stood debating the options, someone tapped her gently on the shoulder. She jumped and turned to confront the stranger. He was a tall, lean, powerful man, dressed in a suit and tie. Everything about the man's appearance told you he was safe, okay. But there was something menacing just the same.

"You gave me quite a fright, mister," Lisa said, because she had to say something. He didn't respond. She didn't like that and after a moment said, "Can I help you with something, Buster?" She didn't want to stand and talk. She wanted to turn and run, but something told her that if she did, this man would make things much worse for her.

"Are you Lisa Clement?" English was not his first language.

She took a step back. "How do you know my name?"

He smiled. "I need to speak with you, Lisa. Will you accompany me?" he offered his arm with the grace of a Versailles courtier.

She feinted to the left and took off across the park. A car hurtled past, slowing him down for a split second. When she reached the far side and turned, he was gone. Then she noticed the police car; if it hadn't been there, he would have gotten her. In that moment she knew that when she had her baby and told him about the boogieman, she wouldn't be lying. She'd met him tonight. The guy, she decided, must have something to do with Jack, and Brad, and the Bloomfield case. The guy, she realized, must be the killer Nat was hunting—and now he was hunting her. She had to get a hold of Nat right away.

Roget had sensed something was wrong, sensed that Marcel was up to something on his own, and that was why he had been watching his apartment. It paid off, too, because he saw him leave the building late that night, and that type of nocturnal activity was unusual for Marcel—that is, unless he was out on a job. Roget shadowed him down to Park Avenue South where he watched his sometime partner stake out an Italian steakhouse called DiAngelo's. That too was odd because it was late and the customers were all gone by now, which could only mean that Marcel's quarry was one of the employees.

It all made sense to him when he saw her leave the restaurant through the front door—Jack's girlfriend, Lisa. It must have been that she was working there, and Marcel must have it in his head that he could somehow get to Jack through her. Roget shook his head sadly. Marcel had become more and more of a disappointment to him lately. Not only was he becoming too big for his britches, playing that stupid game that he did on Christmas Eve. Imagine, the little shit who owed his training and his fortune to Roget's tutelage, playing a game of getting the drop on him just to prove that he could. That was dangerous because a rehearsal is a rehearsal—a training for something, and not for nothing. Hadn't Roget explained to the little shit that it was a bad and dangerous idea to tempt the hand of fate in this affair? In fact the more he thought about it, the more he realized that if he did nothing and just let the little shit continue to evolve on his own, it could turn into a fatal problem for himself. All this he thought about as he followed Marcel, as Marcel followed the girl.

Roget was about a block behind his protégée, who was in turn, less than a half a block behind the girl. Roget was still hurrying to catch up to Marcel when he made his first move. It would have been bad if the girl had not shaken Marcel free and torn off into the park. Roget also got lucky in that there was a cop car in the middle of the park and Marcel had hesitated. These two setbacks gave Roget the seconds he needed to catch up.

There was no one else on the street and the cop car was too far away to really see anything. Roget latched on to the back of Marcel's collar with one hand while pulling a knife with another. He pinned the blade to his partner's throat.

"What are you doing here, Marcel?" Roget demanded, one strong arm wrapped around the man's chest while the other pressed the blade till a trickle of blood seeped from his throat.

"I am trying to do some work, old man," Marcel hissed.

Roget pushed the blade a little deeper into his friend's throat. "What is it you want from the girl?"

"Ease up on the blade, old man, and I'll tell you," Marcel replied through clenched teeth.

Roget swung him around and pushed him a little down the street. There was a small space between two buildings, in the center of which sat a small, green dumpster. He pulled Marcel's coat over his head, swept his feet out from under him and dragged him behind the dumpster. Then he let go of the coat, and as Marcel scrambled to free himself and struggle to his feet, Roget drew a pearl-handled Colt .45 from an armpit holster. There was a silencer attached to the barrels end. "Okay, mon ami. I have eased up on the blade, so tell me. What do you want with the girl?"

Marcel wiped blood from the front of his neck, close to his Adam's apple. "Shit! You fucking asshole! You didn't have to fucking cut me!"

Roget tossed him the silk handkerchief from his suit breast pocket. "Stop being a baby and answer my question."

"That girl, that's Jack Cole's girl. We need to find Jack Cole. We take the girl, we find Cole. It's very simple." He paused and looked down at the blood-soaked handkerchief.

"I told you, it is not the right time to go after those people. You know you are creating danger, and not just for yourself? That by itself would not bother me, but you are creating this danger also for me. This I will not tolerate." Roget took a quick step back. "I am sorry about this."

"You know we have a contract, and you're going to kill me for trying to fulfill it?"

There were suddenly voices and footsteps in the alley behind him and Roget spun quickly around to cover the source of the noise. There were two homeless people in the mouth of the alley pushing a stolen grocery cart piled high with returnable cans. Roget registered the situation in seconds and began to turn once again to his old friend when a bottle smashed against the side of his head. He didn't lose consciousness or his grip on the Colt, but he got dizzy and felt a blinding moment of pain, and that was all it took. Marcel rocketed past him, flashing into the dark of the New York night.

Nat picked her up at a twenty-four hour coffee shop on Twenty-third, and it was almost two A.M. by the time they arrived at Nat's apartment on Van Courtland Avenue in the Bronx. Nat pushed the door open. The hallway was dark but there was a light at the end. They found Keisha in a recliner in the living room with her eyes closed. A full minute passed before she opened them.

Then she said, "Who's this, Nat?"

Nat sighed audibly. "Honey, I told you already . . ."

Keisha straightened the recliner and stood up. "Yes, you did. But I didn't get much of a chance to give you my opinion before you were out the door, did I?"

"Look Keisha. Her life is in danger."

"First you get yourself demoted over this, and now you're bringing the danger of your work into this house with your wife and son?"

Lisa had heard enough, and she turned and left. She was in the lobby waiting for the elevator when Keisha, dressed only in her nightgown and robe, caught up with her.

"Listen, your name is Lisa, isn't it?"

Lisa nodded.

"I'm sorry, Lisa. You need to know that all that noise in there was about keeping Nat honest, not to make you feel unwelcome. Come on back in, I know it's all Nat's fault. We'll keep you safe."

Lisa shrugged raggedly. "No. I understand how you feel. It was wrong of me to even consider imposing. I'm just going to leave."

Keisha reached out a hand and shook Lisa's arm. "Don't let your pride make you a fool. It's dangerous for you,"—she gave Lisa a pointed look and continued—"for both of you, out there."

"I think Nat can take care of himself," Lisa replied.

"I wasn't speaking of Nat. He did tell me you were pregnant though. If I forced you, and that baby you're carrying, out and something happened . . . Well, I'd never be able to forgive myself. So you're coming back inside would be a favor to me."

Lisa smiled, "Thank you."

I spent a few days with Tim and his group of Mole People in the west side tunnels. The old freight tunnels went all the way uptown before emerging into the light of day and continuing north beyond New York City. All up and down the tracks in the city lived small colonies of people, and each colony had its own characteristics. Some were composed of gay men, others of drug addicts. Some were whole families with children. The most dangerous were composed of ex-cons and people on the lam. There were a lot of different ways to enter and exit the tunnels and Tim showed these to me, explaining it was better not to cross into other people's territories uninvited. Tim was a little crazy himself: A self-styled urban survivalist, he was a former high school teacher who'd gone around the bend when his wife left him. Eventually he'd become too eccentric for the classroom, so he got fired, ran out of money, and came underground to prepare for what he called "the inevitable revolution."

Tim and his little band of followers were eccentric, but likely harmless if left alone. I stayed with them because they provided me with a measure of protection, something I'd learned to value. Thus I bided my time with them while I plotted my next move. In the meantime, just to survive, I hit up the soup kitchens for sustenance, and collected tin cans for the money that was in it. I couldn't quite bring myself to share meals with Tim and his band. Very often they ate squirrel and "track rabbit," (the large rats you find down in the tunnels). I hoped never to become that wild.)

I also made it back down to the Coalition for the Homeless, where they told me I'd have my voice mail set up within a week. This cheered me up for about ten seconds, and then the caseworker pointed out that I'd have to begin the work of getting documents in hand, and that was going to be a process. I needed proper ID, social security, and driver's license at a minimum before I could really start looking for work or reclaiming the possessions I had lost during the foreclosure. I hadn't thought about all that; first I'd have to write to the County Clerk for a birth certificate. They'd receive that at the coalition for me, and once I had that in hand, I'd have to take it to the Social Security office to get a new card, etcetera. This was all going to take a couple of weeks, and I decided to spend that time in Tim's Tunnel.

On the second day after joining his band, I told Tim about my mystery box. It may seem odd that I'd be willing to trust a man like Tim, and on such short notice. The reason for my trust was a blend of desperation and a gut feeling I had about the man himself. I could tell that he was mad as a hatter, but at the same time I sensed that a large component of his madness stemmed from his extreme ethical beliefs. Odd, but I think his ethics, his sense of right and wrong, were so intensely one dimensional, rigid, and important to him, that not only would he never violate his own code, but it shocked and amazed him when others did. The man could not be dishonest or tell a lie. He had no social filters, which made society perceive him as mad, but also made him someone you could trust. Anyway, I was pretty sure he had tools and could help me open the mystery box.

Once Tim agreed to help, I trudged up to the surface, exhumed the box, and carried it below the earth to present to him where he sat by the fire. He took it from my hands and placed it atop a large flat stone and examined it from a few different angles before standing up and walking off into the darkness of the tunnel. When he returned he had a pair of bolt cutters and a hacksaw. He leaned the box up against the stone, flipped the lock over so that he had an angle from which to saw, and then he began to draw the blade slowly back and forth against the haft. The lock was made of thick metal. It took a while before Tim had made a groove in it deep enough, but when he did he snapped the lock off with the bolt cutters and popped the top.

I don't know what I expected. Perhaps that light would explode from the box and a giant hand would pull me inside and down into another world where everything made more sense and life worked out for me, or that the contents of the box would reveal some answer or some magical transcendence. Of course none of this happened. The box opened and I was still a homeless guy standing inside a dark tunnel next to a madman holding bolt cutters and a hacksaw.

Tim produced a small flashlight and shined it into the little box. There was nothing in there but a tiny tape cassette, a scrap of paper with the name Boyce Lander written on it, then a series of numbers. There was also a small canister of what looked like film.

Tim placed the saw and the bolt cutters down on the rock and peered into the box. "What is that stuff, Jack?" he asked.

I shook my head. "I'm really not sure, Tim, something to do with my father. Do you have someplace safe where I can hide it until I figure it out?"

He nodded.

Later that night as me and the other six members of the troop sat around the fire, Tim stood up—his countenance glowing in the firelight, his wild hair blowing in the draft—he began to harangue us.

"The fall of the Soviet Union and World Communism was just the beginning. Capitalism cannot stand on its own unchecked in the world. The balance is gone. Pandora's box is open, and with the oppression of the people, anarchy will be unleashed on the world. Race wars will follow in North

America. When we have been weakened by internal strife and the collapse of the government, the Chinese will come!"

I looked around at the others and they were staring at Tim like he was Christ preaching the Sermon on the Mount.

"It is against that day," he continued, "that we must remain underground gathering our strength, and increasing our numbers. We must avoid the race wars to come, hone our survival skills, and prepare for the day the people call upon us to face the Chinese!" He paused, looking around at the assembled, taking stock of our faith. "My people," he said at length, and in a quieter voice, "we have a new convert among us."

He could only be talking about me, and under the circumstances it was best to agree, so I nodded sheepishly. This seemed to satisfy him, for he continued. "People, the time has come to share our strength!"

Everyone seemed to agree, because they all stood. Tim had a thick stick he had prepared with gas soaked rags, and this he lit in the fire for a torch. Without further ado, he took off down the tunnel, the rest of us shuffling after. After a few hundred yards he stopped, waiting for us to catch up. At this spot the walls were piled high with dirt. Two of the group, Mel and a guy everyone called Lefty, dug their hands in and began to pry something back. The loose dirt fell away to reveal a wooden board. When it was pulled away there remained a short, narrow door secured with a padlock and chain. Tim produced a key, opened it, and stepped inside, beckoning me to follow.

I entered a small room, which must have been used to store tools at one time, and was now being used for a very different purpose. It was filled with guns. There must have been two dozen of them, pistols, rifles, and a couple of sawed-off shotguns.

Tim handed me a 9-millimeter Sig Sauer P220. I recognized the pistol because I had spent a good amount of time shooting as a teenager in the Boy Scouts and had maintained an interest in guns for most of my life. As impressed as I was at his arsenal, I was in no way ready for what he said next. "When the time comes, this will be your weapon. In the next few weeks you will learn to use and maintain it, and when the time comes, you will be ready."

I managed to smile weakly, muttering, "I'm honored."

Tim thrust out his big hand for a shake. "Welcome aboard," he said, and then they were all around, patting me on the back.

Old James appeared right on time, materialized right next to Nat, like a phantom, on the steps of the New York Library's main branch, next to Bryant Park.

He grinned at Nat, "So, we gonna be dining al fresco today?" he asked.

Nat nodded. "You want a hot dog?"

James raised an eyebrow. "Two, with mustard and sauerkraut."

"Two?" Nat cried in mock incredulity. "Why should I buy you two?"

"When you hear what I got to say, you gonna wanna buy me the whole fucking stand."

Nat got the hot dogs, and then waited while James gobbled them down. "So?" he demanded, when the old man had pushed the last of the dirty water dogs down his gullet.

"So, I found the guy you're looking for."

Nat narrowed his eyes, "How do you know?"

Old James wiped a smudge of mustard from his lip. "You said he was a Yuppie-type, white guy, early thirties?"

"Yeah."

Old James reached over and patted Nat on his shoulder. "Yeah well, maybe I didn't find the guy you're looking for, but I did find a homeless, yuppie-style, white guy in his early thirties, who goes by the name of Jack."

Nat pulled a pack of gum from his pocket, smacked up a stick from the bunch and proffered it to James. "No shit, where at?"

"Freight yard tunnels in Riverside Park, by the Boat Marina."

Nat was already on his feet, "Let's go."

"Where?"

"Take me to him, man."

Old James nodded, licking his fingers, "All right, but you gonna buy me dinner tonight too."

"Yeah, sure."

TWENTY-SEVEN

I sat on a bench beside the river. It was a sunny afternoon with the light reflecting off the water. It seemed a perfect day, and I had a powerful sense of a good time coming. I was realistic, though. I knew I'd have to stay with Tim and his people in the tunnel for a while longer. My most pressing concern was managing to become and remain clean and presentable, so that I could look for work. Maintaining personal hygiene is one of the most difficult stunts for a homeless man, but I knew I would have to be equal to the task.

I closed my eyes, basked in the warmth of the sun, and began to chase my thoughts back to Lisa. As much as I tried to keep myself from dwelling on her, my thoughts always returned to her. Sometimes it was a smile from a good memory, or a glimmer of hope that all would yet come out right in the end. But more often than not, it was a sad longing, a wild, uncontrollable regret that shook my whole spirit till I trembled inside, like a love junkie going through the pain of withdrawal. It was just no good. Even if I did see her again, she might not want me. I'd changed. Maybe it was better to just live with the memories than to risk rejection at her hand.

Even after I got back on my feet, I felt I would not attack life as I once had. Carlito had taught me something about goodness, and I would never be the same. The new Jack Cole would work hard and take care of himself, but he would also help his fellow man. If I would seek redemption, I had a lot to atone for.

"There are men back in the tunnel looking for you." With my eyes closed and the wheels of my mind turning, I didn't notice Tim beside me until he spoke.

I opened my eyes. "Men looking for me?" I asked.

"Yes," Tim responded, staring out toward the river like a man in a trance.

"That's strange. I didn't think anybody knew me anymore," I muttered.

"Somebody knows you. I don't know if it is good, or bad. One is a cop, the other"—he spread out his hands—"is like us, a damaged pot, marred in the making."

"Did they say what they wanted?" I asked, still staring out towards the water, following a tugboat with my eyes as it chugged across toward the Jersey side.

"Only that they needed to see you. If you don't wish to see them, we can hide you. The policeman told me to tell you he was a friend of Lisa's. He seemed to think that would mean something to you. Does it?"

"It does." I stood up. "Let's go."

I saw them from a distance, sitting on milk crates around the cold fire pit: a small, elderly black man with the look of the street about him, and a big man in a windbreaker. He was the same man who interviewed me after Ed Bloomfield was murdered. I even remembered his name, Nat Weston. He stood as Tim and I approached and we stared at each other for a good while. Finally Nat spoke.

"I been looking for you a long time, Cole." He paused, and then added, "You've changed."

At one time I would have been nervous, now I was only curious. "Why have you been looking for me, detective?"

Nat pointed at a milk crate. "Why don't we sit down?"

We sat, and I opened. "You told my friend something about Lisa. Is she okay?"

"Yeah, she's okay. She's in danger, but she's okay."

"Why is she in danger?" I asked quickly.

"Because of you," Nat responded in a tone, grave like tolling bells.

Confusion welled up within me. "What are you talking about?"

"You know what I'm talking about." Now Nat sounded like a cop.

I pulled into a shell. "No, I don't."

The tones of the hardboiled cop picked up steam and pressed forward. "I'm talking about the Homer deal, about Ed Bloomfield's murder, your problems, Brad Seaman, Arnold Norton, and some fucking French guy. Does any of that help?"

In spite of the edge in his voice, I opened up a bit. "Maybe, a little, like pieces of a puzzle you never saw the picture for."

He must have felt me opening up, and he was no fool. He knew he had to give a little. "Okay, I'll give you my half of the puzzle, if you give me yours," he replied softly.

A picture of Johnny Five telling me how hands wash each other at the Jerome Avenue Shelter roared through my mind. Then Lisa's face in Christmas town. "Okay, you first," I said.

Nat sighed. "To begin with, I'm not supposed to be investigating this case anymore. Officially, this case is closed. However, I believe that Ed Bloomfield was murdered by a man named Roget Voltan, also known as The Frenchman. And I believe this guy works for the bosses at Walsh Dahmer, at least some of the time. I also believe all of it is related to the Homer deal and I believe your pal, Brad Seaman, is involved somehow. Okay, a while back I set out to find you, and I bumped into Lisa, who was also looking for you." He broke off for a minute and favored me with some hard eye contact. "And by the way, that woman really loves you." He broke the stare. "Now I'm told this Frenchman is looking for you right now, in the homeless community, and this guy don't wanna just talk to you, this guy wants to kill you." He paused as if waiting for questions from the audience, but I just wanted to hear him out, so I said nothing. After a minute, he continued.

"I found your buddy Seaman, gave him a little interview, and decided he was full of shit. Then I sent Lisa in to see what she could get off the guy, and he gave her a different line of shit. So Lisa went back out, and this time she kinda rattled his cage, implied she knew things about the Homer deal. A day or two later, a man I believe to be the Frenchman tried to abduct her. Now what can you tell me?"

I told him everything I knew about the Homer deal, about the meeting where Ed flipped out, and about all my experiences since. When I finished, Nat whistled.

"I need your help, Jack. I need your help to trap a Frenchman. Are you with me?"

I nodded, "There's something else, too, Nat."

"What's that?"

"I kept a file when I was working at Walsh Dahmer. In the file is paperwork related to the Homer deal, and a journal detailing Ed's misgivings and Norton's behavior. There's also a tape of a conversation I had with Arnold Norton. I made that tape on the same day you came to interview witnesses at the firm. And then there's a box with some other info that goes pretty far back in time. It's a tape, a tube of microfiche, and a numbered bank account from the Swiss bank Boyce Lander. I haven't been able to listen to the tape or look into the account or at the microfiche, but I'm pretty sure it all pertains to a thirty-year-old murder"

Nat leaned in toward me. "Whose murder?"

I gave a sort of involuntary chuckle. "I think it has to do with my father's murder."

"Who was your father?"

"I'm not sure. I was told he may have been the founder of Walsh Dahmer, a man named John Palmer."

Nat rubbed his temples. "So what's on the other tape, the one you made?"

"Mr. Norton telling me to withhold evidence. Or at least to not cooperate fully with the police."

Nat stroked his chin and nodded. "That could really help our case, once we have other evidence. Where is the file?"

"I don't know."

"Great."

"I can tell you who would know."

"Are we playing games here, Jack?"

"No. It would be my former secretary, Doris Colon."

Nat started laughing.

Confused, I asked, "Why are you laughing at me?"

"If you could see yourself, standing where you are, looking the way you look, you'd laugh too."

Roget walked down Forty-second Street, thinking about how much its dark soul appealed to him. The street was alive, real and intense. Porno theaters and smut shops lined the Deuce. The street fairly bristled with bad men and women, selling bad things, and Roget felt at home, like he did in certain parts of Marseille and Casablanca. It was not like the rest of America where Mickey Mouse was omnipresent and the hypocrisy of the Walt Disney Company covered the streets like cheap perfume masking unwashed flesh. One thing of which Roget was sure, the dark spirits of Shakedown Street could not be exorcised.

As comfortable as he was with where he was though, and in spite of his best efforts, he had yet to locate Jack. Ever since he'd killed the bum in the tunnel, the homeless community had avoided him. It was both good and bad to be feared. Maybe he'd have to spread around some more cash.

He stared into a store window and thought, not for the first time, that the Americans would eventually turn their entire country into one giant mall. He saw the old man come into the reflection of the window, and thus it came as no surprise when he felt the tap on his shoulder. He turned to face the little old man with the scarred face. He was reasonably dressed, but something about the guy told Roget he was homeless.

Roget smiled. "Yes?"

The old man regarded him for just a little too long and something tingled in Roget's cerebellum. "You the guy looking for his cousin?" the man asked.

"I am." Roget smiled wider, displaying even rows of white teeth.

"I know where he's at," the man stated in a flat voice.

"You do?" Roget stared deeply into the man's eyes, weighing him, judging him. The man looked like a hard case, definitely a street man. He was also too old to be a threat, though Roget could tell by the way he stood, and the types of scar tissue the man carried around his brows, that he'd once been a fighter.

The old man held his stare and after a moment said, "Cost you a hundred dollars, up front."

"Really?" Roget replied, allowing a little incredulity to slip into his tone. "Okay, but first you tell me what he looks like."

The man stole a quick glance behind him then rattled off, "Thirty something, white, six foot. His name is Jack. He's educated, and don't fit in. That enough?"

Even though he knew he was being set up, Roget was hooked. He was also sure he could handle whatever lay in front of him. He nodded slowly. "Yes. Where is he?"

The old man thrust out his right hand palm up into the standing space between them. "Got to take you there, but I ain't taking you nowhere without the fare."

Roget ripped a hundred dollar bill in half. "Half now, half when we get there."

The old man didn't argue. Roget stuck his hand out for a cab, and didn't notice the man who ducked into the shop across the street to make a phone call.

TWENTY-EIGHT

It was pretty dark in the tunnel. I was alone with Nat, as it had been arranged. I wore a bulletproof vest under my shirt, and had a tape recorder shoved into the pocket of my coat—which I wore not because I was cold, but in order to hide all the necessary apparatus. It wouldn't be strange though, even on a hot day. Homeless people were known to be eccentric.

I wanted a gun, but Nat wouldn't hear of it. I thought about the Sig Sauer I had been issued by Tim, to one day fight off the Chinese.

"You ready?" Nat asked for about the tenth time.

"As I'll ever be," I replied, also for the tenth time.

His eyes were skeptical. "You know what to do?" he asked.

"Yes," I replied, wearily.

Nat was sitting on top of one of the big rocks by the fire and now he leaned forward. "Tell me."

"Again?" I asked.

"Yes."

"You're going to be covering me from behind that pile of trash. When the Frenchman arrives, I'm going to be sitting right here, where I am now. If he tries to take me out right away, you're going to shoot him before he gets the chance. Otherwise you want me to press record on the tape machine and get him to talk. When he's done talking, you're going to arrest him."

"Good, very good. Now remember, you got to get him to talk a lot. He's gonna think you're toast, so he might be willing. If he is, get him to tell you not just about what he's done, but also who he's done it for. Definitely try to get him to implicate Norton. You got any questions?"

I gave a sort of snorting laugh. "Yeah. What's the backup plan for me if he kills you?"

"Well, son, if he kills me, then he's gonna kill you too."

"Thanks for the comforting words, doctor."

"No problem, I'm here to help."

We were quiet and it grew later in silence. In the distance I could hear water dripping, and rats fucking. I was a little tense. I didn't want to die. Even with everything I'd been through, there'd never come a point where I wanted to just give up.

"Where's Lisa now?" I asked, breaking the silence.

"She's at home with my wife, probably learning how to cook southern food."

"She doesn't know you found me, does she?"

"No, but I got my reasons for that. You know, she's a wonderful, warm, strong, loving woman, Lisa. If she'd known you were here, there would have been no keeping her away. And I'm not having that. Anyway, suppose something happens to you down here. Do you want her to witness that?"

"I see your point."

"Do you?"

Footsteps sounded in the tunnel. Nat moved into position with surprising speed for a man his size. I squinted into the gloom; it was Lefty, coming forward at a run. I called out the all clear to Nat and he came back to the circle. Lefty was huffing and puffing, and he nearly collapsed at our feet, gasping for air. Lefty was a dramatic guy.

"You," he said pausing for breath, "got about twenty minutes. I got the call and came right away."

Nat nodded. "All right, then. You head on back where you came from." When Lefty had shuffled off, Nat turned back to me. "I'm gonna get back into position. Don't forget your role."

I sat for what seemed a long time, staring into the shadowy darkness. After a while two figures appeared at the mouth of the tunnel and headed our way. I glanced over to where Nat should be. My hands were shaking, but not in fear, in anticipation. I looked back toward the tunnel mouth, and now there remained only one figure advancing. The other was in retreat. I pressed RECORD.

It was still daylight in the outside world. A narrow beam of light shone through a ventilation grate high up on the wall. A large figure stepped into this ray of light. It was the same familiar man I had seen, many, many times before, and now I realized something else too: I had not only been seeing him recently, I had been seeing him all my life. Unhurried, he studied me quietly from the circle of light.

"Who are you?" I finally asked.

He continued to stare for a long minute, and then said, "Jack, I'm surprised at you. You're an intelligent man. Haven't you figured anything out yet?"

I looked sadly down at my hands, playing my part, "The only things I figure out these days are very basic. What will I eat, where will I sleep?"

He shook his head with a sort of impatient sadness. "Then you don't know why I've come?"

I looked him in the eye. "I don't even know your name."

He laughed at me, an odd but gentle sound. "You won't get off the hook that easily, you know. My name is Roget Voltan." He smiled.

My, what big teeth you have, I thought. What I said was, "Did you kill Bloomfield?"

"No," he answered quickly, "but many others."

Roget stepped closer to me, his hand in his pocket. "Then who did?" I asked.

He ignored my question and stepped deeper into the light and my personal space, leaning his face into mine. "Do I look familiar to you? Look closely."

"I've seen you before, more lately, but for some reason, I feel I've seen you even before all this."

He took a step back and dropped himself onto the rock where Nat had been sitting earlier. "Yes, you've seen me many times, but I don't think you would remember the first time you saw me." His voice took on a very soft quality. I had to lean forward to hear.

"Were you in disguise?"

Roget laughed again, "No, but we were both much younger. Come on, look hard at me!" His voice now tinged with frustration. "Can't you figure it out?"

I engaged his eyes again. "No."

He didn't look away as he responded. "Then I'll make it plain for you. The first time I ever saw you, you were covered in blood and shit, you were crying, and a nurse put you in my arms."

I stared hard, my head reeling. The man was familiar, and now I knew why. He was older, stronger built, but the face was very similar to the one that stared back at me from the mirror every day. My hands shook. I took a minute to get myself under control, and then said, "And you've come to kill me?"

He edged even closer, staring hard into my face. "I killed my own father, you know," he said at last, without obvious emotion.

I shifted involuntarily back. "What?" Over the years I'd dreamed up countless scenarios for conversations with a father I thought I'd never meet. Now here he was, and I didn't know what to say.

Suddenly Roget, the Bogie Man, my father, just looked tired. "Yes," he said, "your Grandpa Pepe, M. Luger Voltan. You know he was a Nazi collaborator during the war?" He paused, seeming to wait for a response, but when I offered none, he continued. "That by itself wouldn't have been such a terrible thing. A lot of people were, and if he'd just moved away to a place where no one knew him, it would have been okay. But Luger, for his own stubborn reasons, refused to leave. He was a strange man, my papa. He never had much to say to anyone. My mother though, she was a kind and timid woman. And she never even considered leaving, even though she despised him. He knew it too.

"This tension continued for years with very little said and less change, but it was a deceptively quiet little volcano, my childhood home. And it was lonely for the collaborator's son. I don't even know what it was that caused the volcano to erupt.

I only know that it came on a beautiful, crisp autumn day with the leaves changing all around. I was seventeen and coming back from school. I remember, I stopped in town to pick up some baguette for my mama, and it was tied to the back of my bicycle with a little string. Very cliché. I remember the ride home, cycling down the dirt road, whistling and feeling happy, until I came to the shadowy lane that led to my father's farm. I knew right away something was very wrong. It was the time of day when that shade of bright, dull light filters through the trees, heralding the end of sun. There should have been birds, but I could hear none. The whole farm seemed to hold its breath. The front door was open and it was dark within. I let my bicycle fall in the yard with the loaf of bread and everything lying in the dust and I entered the house."

"Why are you telling me these things?" I interrupted.

For a moment, Roget seemed at a loss, and then said, "Because I have never told anyone of this, and even with you I waited till I was sure you had nothing better to do." He broke off, and then chuckled. He seemed embarrassed. "Perhaps I should not go on?"

But I needed him to keep talking, and I was drawn in. I told him to continue and this seemed to please him.

"There was no one in the house, and then I saw her through the kitchen window. My mother was tied to an old wagon wheel, leaning over a stump of tree, and she had been beaten bloody. At first I thought she was dead, but when I got to her, I could see she was still breathing. My father was nowhere in sight. Even though he'd never before laid a hand on her, I knew immediately, that he had done this . . . that the volcano had erupted. I carried my mother into the small house; I cleaned her wounds and made her comfortable in her bed. Then I sat down on the front steps with a jug of apple brandy, and I waited. I waited as the shadows of evening drew themselves across the sky, and as the first stars came out, I waited. Finally, as the moon rose over the little house, my father came, weaving his drunken way down the lane to our home.

"He stopped at the foot of the stairs, and as dark as it was, as drunk as he was, he must have seen it in my eyes. But even so, he just stood and waited. I knocked him down. He didn't resist me and some of the rage faded from my heart, but still, I knew what needed to be done, so I knelt beside him in the dirt and I strangled him. It was hard to do for a boy of seventeen, but I continued. I continued because I knew he needed to be put from his misery. I knew that it was my duty to carve for my father, an exit from the hell he'd made for himself in this life. Before the sun rose again I'd left for Marseilles. Strange, but no one ever came after me. No one ever sought justice for the collaborator." He rubbed his eyes and searched my face for emotion, or reaction, but I was numb.

I was incredulous. "You're my father?"

He nodded.

"And you've come to put me out of my misery like you did your father?"

Roget shook his head.

"So I can relax? That's good. Why did you leave?"

"I never left, I was always watching."

"The money—that was you?"

"Right. And there was always more money if she needed it. She knew it, too. She knew that all she had to do was go to the garage anytime she needed and it was always there for her."

"What garage?"

"The garage under the viaduct bridge, where she kept the car." He answered, in a tone that implied I was a fool for not having put it together myself.

I remembered the place where my mother had kept our old Rambler station wagon and I nodded.

"You see," he exclaimed. "You were always provided for, both you and Monique."

I could tell that the words, the need for justification was very awkward. Here was a man who, I could tell, had never asked for permission in his life. And from the way he almost breathed my mother's name, I could tell that he loved her still.

But I wasn't going to let him off the hook. "So, if you cared so fucking much, why didn't you ever show yourself?" I demanded.

"It was complicated. There was another man, a man she loved more than me. And I had to kill him. Your mother banished me when you were just six months old. I respected her wishes. She was the love of my life—the only woman I ever loved. I was never far. I waited till she could no longer recognize me, and only then did I visit her. I didn't wish to cause her pain." His voice seemed to tremble with emotion.

"Was that you who hit me on the back of the head at the home?"

"It was me."

"Why did you do that?"

"Because your mother was right. No good could come from us having contact."

"What harm could it have done?"

"I would not have you share Bloomfield's fate."

I shrugged. "Then don't kill me."

"It's not so simple as that. Norton, Grunley, and Petersen—they killed Bloomfield, I refused to be their murder weapon.

But believe me, if they find one tool does not work, they simply find another."

"Did they have you kill Palmer?"

He smiled, "Ahh, so you do have some clue, some sense of the buried bones."

"I spoke with Tierney. Did you kill him too?"

Roget shook his head. "No, that too was done with another weapon. I would not have killed Tommy."

"Why not?" I asked quickly.

Roget looked almost offended. "Because Tommy was my friend."

"Why would Norton want him dead?"

"Because Tommy and Norton and the rest of them, they all believe that you are Palmer's son, and they suspected that Tommy was going to tell you, and to give you some evidence."

"What kind of evidence?"

"Evidence that they killed Palmer. They had me kill Palmer so they could take over the firm." He rubbed his temples, "It is one of the few killings I have done which I regret. I have almost never killed a good man." He leaned forward again, staring into my eyes. "But Palmer . . ." He paused. "You see, I agreed to kill him so that I could pluck him from your mother's mind, but it was wrong."

A shot rang out from somewhere out in the tunnel and it grazed The Frenchman's shoulder. I saw him flinch and blood quickly flowed but he only swatted at it as one might a fly.

Suddenly, Nat's voice rang out, "Police! Freeze!"

Roget spun around, gun in hand, arm straight and steady like a railroad signal. Two shots rang out and I saw Nat sprawled on the floor of the tunnel. He was still moving.

Roget stared at me for a second too long and I acted on instinct. I couldn't allow my father to put the death bullet into

Nat's head. I grabbed a handful of dirt from the ground and flung it into Roget's face. One hand went to his face, but the other held tight to his weapon; he would recover quickly.

I needed to draw him off. I took off down the tunnel. The old man was in good shape, and I was weak from my time on the street. Just as I thought I couldn't run any more, a strong hand pulled me into a side tunnel I didn't know was there. I couldn't see, but I knew it was Lefty. Roget stopped at the spot where I had disappeared. We remained motionless, waiting. Then he spoke.

"You're around here somewhere, Jack." There was a pause, "Why don't you come out? We have so much to discuss." Silence, waiting, and then a long sigh. "It's ridiculous you know, sooner or later I'm going to find you anyway." Another long sigh. "Okay, I'm going back to kill the cop. He's not dead yet, you know, but he will be. He would put us both away, and then we'll never have the chance to make up for all the lost time . . ."

Another shot rang out and from where I was hiding I saw my father go down, thrashing in the dust of the tunnel. But that couldn't have been Nat. Nat was lying in the dust a few hundred feet further down the tunnel.

Suddenly there was another voice echoing in the dark cavern. "Jack, why don't you come out? I had no idea you were his son. Now I understand. Why don't you come out and we can talk? I'm sure all this can be ironed out." This voice was also strongly accented in French. I knew that it must have been the voice of the man who had just shot my father.

I remained quiet. Time passed as the voice in the dark waited in vain for my response. "Okay," it finally intoned. "I'm going back down the tunnel to kill the nigger. You can wait here and I will be back shortly, or you can come out and make a deal."

I could tell from the way his vice was traveling away from me that he was heading back into the direction where Nat remained lying in the dust. Adrenaline coursed through my veins. Fight or flight, I wasn't going to let Nat die. I surged, Lefty pulled me back, hard. "Wait," he hissed into my ear.

We crept to the end of the cavern, and there was a ladder leading up. In a matter of seconds we were up it, through a grate, and on the surface in Riverside Park. There was sunshine, and joggers, and nannies pushing strollers. We moved quickly, along the wall above them, perpendicular, along the wall housing the tunnel. We were going to beat this new Frenchman to the punch. We could move more quickly in the light of day than he could in the dark tunnel. Up ahead there was another grate leading down, and Tim and his mole people were gathered there, just above the spot where Nat lay. We pulled the grate out and jumped in, landing one after another onto a small mound of earth about seven feet down. We slid down the mound until we were on the floor of the tunnel. Nat was moving slightly, softly moaning. Above him stood a man, gun in hand. He was surprised though, by the large group that had suddenly formed around him, some, brandishing weapons of their own like Tim. But he kept his focus on the man lying on the floor beneath him. I could sense his calculation: His best chance was still to kill the cop, kill the cop and he would most likely walk out of the tunnel and live to fight another day. It was unlikely to him that the shadowy men before him would kill him, or attempt to hold him. His full attention shifted back to the man in the dirt, he took aim . . .

"No!" I screamed, as loud as I could and the man turned to face me. "Don't kill him. You don't have to," I said.

"I'm sorry, Jack, but the man must die." He turned back to deliver the coup de grace.

I tumbled and rolled at him, crashing into his legs. His shot went wild, and I came up underneath the man, crashing him onto the ground. He came up like a jack in the box and cracked me on the head with a pistol. I fell and swooned for just a second, and as my eyes came back into focus, I could see he had returned to his grim work, and his gun was once again pointing at Nat. Then I heard the sound of a shotgun being pumped very close by. Nat's gun lay very close to my hand and I snatched it just as the man shot Tim right between the eyes. I aimed Nat's gun, and with the last vestige of consciousness I possessed, pumped off two shots. I saw the man fall. Then everything went black.

TWENTY-NINE

My eyes opened. I thought I was still dreaming, spilling from horror to sweetness in the twinkling of an eye. I was in a clean, comfortable bed and it smelled nice. I'd forgotten the wonder of comfort. Something told me I was home. I didn't sit up, but looked around from where I lay. I knew I'd never been in this room before, but it felt right.

The door opened and Lisa walked in. "Am I in heaven?" I asked.

She laughed like an angel and said, "Nowhere close, you're in Chelsea."

Images rushed in on me, and I remembered. "Is Nat okay?"

"Better than you, but we'll have time to sort everything out soon enough." She stroked my forehead. "You're home now, and as long as I live, you'll always be home."

I took her hand. I felt weak and my head ached, but I felt joyous too. The gods had given me another chance.

Nat came to see me that night. He sat in the chair next to my bed, the back of his head shaved and bandaged. "How you making out, Cole? I'm sure they would have kept you longer in the hospital if you'd had some insurance."

I smiled through the dull aching pain. "Not bad. Not great, but not bad. You look good for a guy who just got shot. I thought you were dead."

"Body armor. He shot me in the chest, but I was wearing a vest and all it did was knock me down and bust a couple of ribs." He rotated his head and pointed at the back. "Cracked my skull up pretty good, though when I fell. I think I'm getting too old for this shit. I've been eligible for retirement for a couple of years now, and I think I'm going to do just that, as soon as this case is over."

I winced, thinking of all the loose ends. "What is going on with the case?"

Nat sighed, "That's half the reason I'm here. Where is the box you told me about, the one you dug up from underneath that statue in Sequoia Park?"

"Buried again, this time in the tunnel where you found me, the tunnel where Tim died."

Nat reached out and patted me on the knee. "Look, I'm gonna need that box."

I started to sit up like I was going to get off the bed and he pushed me gently back. "Relax, I don't mean right this second. We have time. I'm going to need it to see if it will help me to build a case against Arnold Norton."

"Of course. What about the tape we made in the tunnel?"

"Sure, that would have helped me make a case against Voltan, and then I could have used him against Norton, but that's all out the window now. I guess the good thing is that the other Frenchman met his reward. You killed him and saved my life. Did you know that?"

I should have felt more emotion. I just felt numb.

"Bad thing is," Nat continued, "Ah, maybe it's not a bad thing, but it is. There are a lot of important people who just want to see the case dry up and blow away."

"What do you mean?"

"Well, for starters, Voltan's body was taken away, and now I can't even track where it went. Then the tape you made disappeared from the evidence room at the station. There isn't even a record of its ever being there at all. And finally, your old secretary, Doris whatever, who's supposed to have your file?"

"Yeah?"

"She's moved out of state."

"So what happens next?"

"Whatever's in that box might help, and then maybe we can use that stuff to lure Norton out, make him talk, talk to you and you catch it on tape. If you've got some real evidence in that box about him murdering Palmer . . . well there's no statute of limitations on murder. But the real important thing is to get him to expose his role in the Homer Industries scam. If we can pull that off maybe we can help those people recover some of their pension money?"

I flinched, the guilt slapping me in the face. "I'll help in any way I can," I said. "How can I do any less?"

Nat reached out and squeezed my shoulder, "Thank you." He said.

"What do you think will happen to me after all of the investigation is done and my part in the scam is revealed?" I hated to ask the question. It felt so self-serving, but I needed to know.

Nat considered. "You're cooperating so they should make you a deal, but you probably don't need one even then. I think the judge would look at the totality of your experience, the good that your help has done, and grant you immunity. In fact, I'll try and work all that out for you."

I felt a spasm of pain and nausea and closed my eyes.

"Are you okay?" Nat asked in a tone of genuine concern.

In the distance I heard Lisa puttering in the next room. "How has she been?" I asked.

Nat let his gaze wander in the direction of the noise. "You know she's pregnant, don't you?"

THIRTY

The box had contained three things: The can of film that turned out to be microfiche containing financial records that detailed kickbacks and payoffs. A detailed record of the financial mis-dealings that led to Arnold's annexation of the firm and the fraud that had allowed him to cut Palmer's family out of all but the tiniest share in the future profits of the firm. There was also a numbered account at Boyce Lander Bank. Nat had a friend who was involved with investigating financial crime for the NYPD look into it, and he discovered that you could get financial records from the account just by using the number. In fact that was the only way you could get financial information from the account. The last item was a small cassette tape.

The tape was old and worn and at first did not play, but after receiving a little love from the techno geeks, it went on to sing a beautiful song, at least from the point of view of the guys gathering evidence against Arnold Norton.

The tape contained about a five-minute conversation between Arnold Norton and my father, discussing the death of Mr. Palmer and how it would be implemented and then covered up. I tried to get Norton on the phone to set up a meeting afterward, but he never spoke to me. He hid behind his secretary and didn't return my calls for about two days. On the third day I phoned and asked for his voicemail. I played a bit of the cassette tape's content into his answering machine. Not enough to incriminate him if someone else were to hear it, but certainly enough to pique his interest. A couple of hours after I left the message, my phone rang.

I answered on the third ring.

"Hi, Jack." It was the same soft, suave voice that I remembered.

"Long time, Arnold. How've you been?"

"Good." His answer was short and clipped. "I understand that you want to speak with me?"

"I do," I responded in a flat, declarative tone. "I assume then that you received my message?"

"The piece of that old conversation you played on my voicemail? Yes I did."

"Do you want to meet somewhere?"

He sighed. "That may be for the best. But first, can you give me some idea of what you're looking for?"

"What do you mean by that?" I asked.

"A dollar figure." He responded tersely. "What's it going to cost to get that tape?"

"Oh," I responded. "That's something we're going to have to discuss face to face."

"Where and when?" his voice rasped through the wire like a file.

"You know Lonnie O'Grady's on West Fifty-fifth?"

"I can't say that I've eaten there," his voice fairly dripped in disdain, "but I'm sure I can find the place."

"Good." I replied. "Be there at six P.M., I'll meet you in the bar." I hung up the phone.

Lonnie O'Grady's was an Irish steakhouse that catered to the midtown office crowd and also did a good pre-theater business. When I entered the place at six that night it was pretty packed. I scanned the faces in the lounge and after determining that none of them belonged to Arnold Norton, I bellied up to the bar in a thrift store suit and dropped a government expense account twenty on the wood.

The bartender was busy and didn't get to me for a while, and in that time I scoped the bottles on the back bar, admiring their sleek polish and bright lettering sparkling in the dim light. All around me well-dressed people sipped on colorful cocktails and chatted in cheerful animation. My eyes stopped at the row of scotch bottles lined up on the shelf. There was a light shining behind them and it really made them pop. Johnny Walker red, black, and blue. Cutty Sark, Dewars, Chivas, Pinch, Glenfiddich, Glenlivit, MacCallan. The list went on and on, and I could feel my mouth watering in anticipation. But when the bartender finally confronted me with a flick of a beer stained coaster all I could manage to croak out was, "Pellegrino with a twist of lime."

She gave me an eyeball that said she was wasting her time on a non-drinker, and then moved politely down the bar to fill my order. She was efficient. Within a few seconds the green bottle was standing beside a clean wine glass with a fresh hunk of lime hanging off the rim. She snatched my twenty away from the wood and replaced it with a pile of singles. A few seconds later I saw Norton walk into the taproom. He was wearing a sharp gray shark-skin suit over a powder blue shirt with a pink and royal blue polka dot tie and matching pocket-square. I was seated at the far end of the bar. In the dark of the room and I was able to observe Norton for a few minutes without him noticing. I could see through him like I never had before. Where once I looked up to him and feared him, now I despised him and sought to trap him. The mask that for years had obscured his true nature from me was now gone.

I watched as he exchanged a few words with the girl at the podium, and then observed him from the shadows as he made his way across the dining room. And then he caught my eye, flashed me a fake smile, and headed in my direction.

He looked at the Pellegrino in front of me and raised a quizzical eyebrow, then ordered a Dewars and soda when the bartender showed up.

He looked me in the eye over the rim of his glass and said, "Why'd you do it?"

I was confused and I let it show. "Do what?"

He took a pull from his highball and laughed. "Come on, Jack, you know."

I just shook my head.

He pulled up a free barstool and sat down close to me. "Well I suppose you took it hard when the SEC showed up and we had to pretend to fire you."

I was suddenly speechless, but only for a moment, "What the fuck are you trying to pull here, Norton? You didn't pretend anything. You had me escorted out by security."

"Where did you get the tape, Cole?" He growled, the genial mask slipping from his face.

I shrugged. "Does it matter?"

There was a bowl of nuts sitting on the bar and Norton pulled it closer. "I suppose not." He mused, and then suddenly he was upbeat again. "So how much then?"

"What makes you think I want money, Norton?"

Norton gave a snort of disbelief. "What else could you want?"

I leaned my face in close to his, "Tommy Tierney told me that Palmer was my father. The tape I have is you planning and hiring someone to kill Palmer. What do you think I want? I want some answers. Why did you set me up with the SEC and why did you decide to use me as the fall guy on Homer deal?"

Norton downed his drink and signaled to the bartender for another. "Look. Jack. A lot of people did think Palmer was your father. Your mother had an affair with him that went on for a number of years, but he was a married man and it was never going anywhere. He was just using her and they broke it off at least six months before she became pregnant with you. So me, I don't believe Palmer was your father, I don't believe it for a minute. In fact now that I think of it, I do think I know who your father was, but I'm only just realizing that now, and when I say now, I mean right this moment."

"We'll get back to that," I interrupted. "Right now what I'd like to know is why me? Why did you pick me for the Homer deal and why did you set me up?"

The bartender put a fresh drink down in front of him and he sighed. "Look, my intentions for you and the Homer deal were good. At least they started out that way. You were the son of an old friend, two old friends actually, and I wanted to put you in a position to make some money. Some serious money. I wanted to see you do well. But of course no one makes money honestly in this world. It really wasn't my fault, the firm made a few bad bets and we needed to raise some quick cash to cover them. The Homer pension fund is not the first, nor will it be the last to be raided by a corporation."

I nodded. "I get it, but you had me set up shell companies through Tierney's office. You had me bribe a union official. I mean you had us basically destroy an entire company and the pensions of five thousand retired workers just to cover a few bad bets that you and your buddies made."

He gave me a crooked smile like he was proud of who he was and what he had done. "Yeah, that's about the size of it. But you're not young or stupid either, Cole. Don't try to pretend you are somehow holier than thou. You did all that stuff willingly for us, just to get your slice of the pie."

"Why did you kill Bloomfield, Norton?"

Norton took a big sip off his highball then wiped his lips with his sleeve. "For the same reason why you had to go down and why I should have had you killed right after Bloomfield. Because both of you were going to go to the cops. At least now I think I know why it was so hard to get Roget to agree to kill you."

I stood up from my stool, counted three singles off the top, dropped them onto the bar-top, and stuck the rest into my pocket. I left the room without saying goodbye and with a queasy feeling in the pit of my stomach.

It wasn't until I hit the sidewalk that I realized why Norton had been so open and honest with me. There was a delivery van parked by the front door, along the side of which was painted a golden crown hovering over the head of a steer. There was also a name stenciled above that, Empire State Meats. Not in the least bit out of place to see something like that parked in front of a restaurant. It wasn't the van that bristled my shorthairs though. It was the two short haired, muscular guys loitering next to it. They were on me from the moment I stepped out of the bar, crowding me on either side.

"Hey buddy," the one to my left said almost affably as he steered me toward the open back doors of the van. "You got to check out what we got in the back here."

"No thank you," I mumbled, and tried to step forward and out from between them.

Then the one on my right grabbed my arm, twisting it quickly behind my back while the guy to my left jabbed the barrel of a gun into my ribs and whispered softly in my ear. "Just step into the van buddy, and every little thing is gonna be alright."

I was only a couple of feet away anyway and within seconds I was being shoved into the dark, metal cargo hold. The guy who had been twisting my arm let me go suddenly and as we slipped apart he stuck a needle in my leg, right through my suit pants, and then they pushed me down onto the floor of van and I heard the slam of the back doors. There was no window and I found myself lying there in the dark as the van started to move and the darkness began to spin. I felt myself nauseous and I knew that I was slipping down the rabbit hole of consciousness.

When I came to it was in darkness and warmth. I couldn't see around me and I was bound in place by something that felt like duck tape. I had no way of knowing where I was, but it felt like the inside of a dog's mouth, it was that humid.

Without access to a clock, or the sun, or any other means to mark the passage of time, I don't know how long I sat there, but it seemed like a long time. It seemed like forever.

When a door was finally opened and a light finally switched on, it was both what I expected as well as a huge surprise.

Of course I expected that when someone did finally show up that it would be Arnold Norton. What I did not expect was that I would find myself in the little garage under the Viaduct where my mother had kept her car all through my childhood.

Arnold Norton was alone, and he hunkered down on his heels so he could speak to me where I lay, writhing in my bonds on the floor. There was duck-tape sealing my mouth shut and there was a pistol in his fist. He shook his head ruefully back and forth. "You didn't think I could let you go?" He asked.

I mumbled back at him through the tape and he reached over and ripped it away from my mouth. "What the fuck?!" I exclaimed, my mouth spluttering to life.

Norton shrugged. "I said, you didn't think I could let you go, did you?"

I spat the taste of glue from my mouth. "I didn't think it was up to you!"

He lifted a small tape up to my eyes. "You didn't think I knew you were taping our conversation in the bar?" He asked.

"Then you must know that the police were listening in, and right now they're looking for you-me-us . . ."

Norton cut me off with a laugh. "You were taping on your own, Jack. Don't you think I know that? You were taping on your own and there is no cavalry going to come over the hill. The police have been warned off this investigation. The only one who could possibly be helping you is that renegade, nigger detective, and if he shows up here . . . then he's going down too."

"So what is it you want?" I asked.

He considered me for a long moment. "What I want is the rest of the evidence. Everything that Tommy gave you."

"I don't have that with me." I croaked through dry lips.

Norton spun the pistol around on his palm so that the barrel was in his hand with the grip poking out the other side like a club. He sucked his teeth then smacked the grip quickly and hard against the side of my face. I felt the dry skin of my lip crack open like brittle paper and I tasted warm, salty blood in my mouth. "What the fuck did you do that for?" I spat out at him, and I think I spat out a tooth with my words.

Norton put the gun carefully back into his pocket and took a step back away from me. "I know that, you idiot. What you need to tell me is where it is."

"So you can kill me?"

"So I don't kill your bitch and the pup she's carrying."

I was doing a lot of calculating, but I needed to respond quickly. "It's complicated, you'll have to take me with you." I struggled in my bonds trying to sit up.

Norton lifted a well-shod foot and kicked me back down. "No, I think you'll stay here, Cole. But I'll tell you what, if you don't tell me how to find it I'll kill the girl, and the child she's carrying."

I almost levitated off the floor, but I kept my cool. I had to buy some time, time and opportunity. I looked him in the eye. He obviously believed I still had control of the evidence. If he had thought I'd given it over to the police I'd already be dead. "If I do tell you, you'll leave her alone, you'll let me go?"

"I'll leave her alone, Cole. Just as I left your mother alone, but I'm not going to lie to you. I'm not going to let you go-I can't. As soon as I find what I'm looking for, I'm going to come back here and kill you, put this whole thing to rest once and for all."

I knew he meant it. All of it. "Okay, Norton." I said deciding to stick as close to the truth as possible. "The old freight yards in Riverside Park. The entrance is just under that little tunnel near the old piers. You enter there and count down twelve ventilation grates along the wall on the left hand side. When you come to the twelfth you'll see a big, black stone sitting at its base, you dig there for maybe a foot and a half and you will find a metal box. The stuff you're looking for is in there." For Norton it would be a wild goose chase, but it would buy me some time, and just maybe, with some luck, the chance to save Lisa and my unborn son.

Norton nodded. "Thanks. How long do you think all that's going to take me?"

I stared at him. "A few hours, maybe more." Hopefully more.

He laughed. "Then that's how long you have to live."

He left, shutting the light and locking the door behind him so that I was once again in total darkness. But now I knew where I was, and I knew the space better than he realized I did. I waited until he had been gone fifteen minutes and I struggled to my feet. In one corner of the old garage I knew that there was a broken metal sash that had been a part of a long bricked up window. Its edge was sharp, I knew this from having cut myself on it accidentally as a child. With great difficulty I managed, after some time, to hobble over into the corner where I knew the sharp edge would be, and after casting around unsuccessfully for some time, finally struck up against it. It still took awhile sawing my duck tape bound wrists across it, but little by little, the layers fell away, until finally my hands were free. They weren't of too much use to me right away. My arms were still bound tightly to my body and my hands had very little range of motion. There was also a great deal of pain, because the blood flow had been cut off for quite awhile. Still, I gritted my teeth and pushed on my bonds as I sawed up and down against the sharp metal edge of the exposed sash. The tape slowly rent and after more struggle I managed to get my arms free. I dragged myself over to the light switch and pulled myself up to flip it on. Immediately I saw more possibilities. In one corner of the room there was a box cutter and this I used to free my legs. The first thing I tried to do was stand up and I fell over immediately as the newly flowing blood coursed into my legs giving me the most excruciating sensation of pins and needles that I had ever known.

I sat for a long minute to allow the feelings to pass and then I tried the door, but of course it was locked. The lock was such that you needed a key to open it from the inside or the outside, and my mother had always hidden two spares one on the interior, and the other on the exterior of the small room. I just couldn't remember where, but the contemplation got me to thinking. Odd that I'd never thought it strange as a child, that a single mother in a situation like hers would have the luxury of a car and garage space on Manhattan island, no matter how far uptown. Something else suddenly rang a bell for me. My father, on that only day I'd spent with him in the tunnel, mentioned this garage. He told me that my mother had always known that if she needed, there was always something for her in the garage. There was probably also a key wherever he left the other stuff for her. The floor and walls were made of cement that seemed pretty solid, and I couldn't see there was much of any place to hide anything in it. And then I remembered the window that had been bricked up. I walked over and started pushing on the bricks. At first they all seemed pretty solid, but then I touched one that moved, just a little at first and then I was pulling it out of the wall and a lot of others besides. When I was done there were eight of them out of the wall and I had uncovered a large hollow space within. There was a key there, and there was also a bowling bag. I opened the bag and there was a lot of money inside. I didn't have time to count it though, there was no telling when Norton would be back, and I hoped the key worked. It did.

The door opened into sunshine and I knew I must have been there all night. I stood there blinking and flexing my sore joints and muscles. My mouth was dry and foul tasting, but in spite of the way I felt I allowed myself a few seconds of optimism. It didn't last though, coming towards me down the hill were Norton and his two crew cut goons. They were pushing Lisa before them and they didn't look easy. My first instinct was to tense up for a fight, but I knew it wouldn't answer, I couldn't win and it would put Lisa at greater risk. They were now only about thirty feet away and one of the two crew cut guys gave Lisa a tremendous shove in my direction. She bowled forward across the distance, stumbling a bit, then moving quickly forward on her own. At the last minute she tripped and fell into the dust at my, feet. I reached down to help her up just as Norton slammed into me. I teetered for a second because it was unexpected. Out of instinct I shoved him back, then lifted Lisa out of the dust. I got her to her feet and then his two goons were on me, giving me the bum's rush back into the garage. I ended sprawled on the concrete floor. I looked up and they were dragging Lisa in. Norton slammed the door shut.

"You motherfucker!" He howled. "You sent me on a wild fucking goose chase!"

He was waving a pistol in the air and all I could think of to say was, "Calm down."

He stopped dead in his tracks. He looked like he'd been slapped. "Calm down?" He repeated in an incredulous tone. "How's this for calming down asshole?" He pointed the gun at

Lisa. "If you don't tell me where that fucking evidence is right now, I'm going to shoot your little girl friend here right in the fucking stomach. Right where your little pup is hiding out. How do you like that?"

I lifted my hand in the air, thinking fast, trying to figure a way out, and all I could think of was to rush him. But I didn't. Suddenly there were sirens and the sounds of engines and cars squealing into the parking lot, and Norton shifted his focus. Both of his goons were suddenly looking nervous.

A voice, a familiar voice, called into us through a bullhorn. "This is the Police. We have you surrounded. Come out with your hands up!"

The guys with the crew cuts were looking uncertainly from Norton and then back and forth between themselves.

"Looks like the end of the line." I said to Norton in as gentle a voice as I could muster and this seemed to snap him out of his reverie.

One of the two crew cuts kicked open the front door and they started out into the light with their hands over their heads.

"End of the line? We'll see." Norton muttered. "Maybe for you, motherfucker!" He suddenly shouted and made a lunge for Lisa, with the pistol cocked in his hand.

All that pent up tension, all that fight or flight, all that worry for Lisa and my unborn child. I don't recall exactly, but I must have practically levitated from the floor. I remember colliding into him and grabbing the hand that held the gun by the wrist. It must have been some adrenaline rush because I felt and heard the crack as I snapped his wrist broken and the gun fell to the floor.

Six months later and I was working, doling out meals at a soup kitchen where I volunteered three nights a week after turning in my cab. The duffle bag had contained fifty thousand dollars, it had been enough to help get Lisa and me on our feet, but not enough to retire on. Driving a cab was daily cash, and I'd yet to decide what I'd recycle into. Anyway, it was deep into the dinner hour, we had a full house, and the room was quiet except for the sound of forks clinking. The door opened and a small man limped into the room and up to the line. Without looking up, I began to ladle food onto a plate, placed the plate on a tray, and the tray onto the counter. The man looked me in the eye and he didn't touch the tray. I stared back. It took a second; he'd grown a full beard and was wearing a hat.

"Carlito?"

He cracked a smile, "People tell me you're doing well."

"Okay, I guess. I got married."

He pointed at the ring on my finger. "I see that."

"What happened to you? I mean, since the last time I saw you?"

"That day I had a real hard time. I was beaten and arrested, but I moved on to bigger and better things. Can we go somewhere to talk?"

"Hey Tommy," I called out to the other volunteer working the line, "I gotta step out for a few minutes. I'll be back to help you clean up." Tommy waved me off and I went outside with Carlito.

It was a fine autumn evening, cool but not cold. The sky had a purple cast to it. We sat on the church steps.

Carlito patted me on the knee. "Its good to see you, bro, and it's good to see you helping others now that you're off the streets."

"I'm trying. I got a lot to atone for."

"You're working?"

"Driving a cab."

"That's work. I came down here tonight to see you. One of the guys from the neighborhood recognized you from the squat and let me know you were here."

"So what's on your mind?"

"You used to be an accountant, right?"

"Not exactly. I have a degree in accounting, but I worked as an analyst."

"That's close enough."

"I guess."

"How come you're driving a hack? Don't you like working with numbers?"

"Oh, I do. I'm just not quite ready to go back to the corporate world. I'm not sure I ever will be."

"You know, about a week after the eviction I ran into a buddy of mine from Nam. He's a big construction contractor now. Anyway, I started working with him and we got tight again. His name's Jim Jacobs, he's into liberal politics, and he's got friends on the city council. Not only that, but he's got a lot of like-minded friends who go in for charitable causes of one type or another. To make a long story short, he helped me get a little project off the ground, just barely, but it is off the ground, and I figured you might want to help out."

"I'll sure do what I can."

"Basically, we're building homes for the homeless, and we're using homeless labor and teaching guys a skill in the bargain. This is just a start, I got big plans."

"I don't know much about construction. How would I fit in?"

"I need a guy who understands finance and bookkeeping. Thing is, I can't afford to pay a lot, so you'd probably still have to drive a cab to support your family."

"I'll help you out if I can." We shook hands, and in that same instant, my beeper went off. I jumped up, "He's coming!"

Carlito squinted at me. "Who?"

"My baby. I gotta get to St. Luke's."

Carlito stood. "Come on. I got the van parked down the street, I'll drive."

As Carlito turned the key in the ignition he said, "This is a night you'll never forget, huh?"

"Yes, Carlito, you're right. This is a night I'll never forget."

Lisa was sitting up in the hospital bed finishing her lunch when there was a knock at the door. She couldn't get up because of the stitches from the episiotomy the night before and I was in the bathroom, so she called out, "Come in," in a soft voice, hoping not to disturb the baby sleeping in the bassinet close by.

The door opened to reveal a small, bald, middle-aged man in an expensive suit with a bright green visitor's pass pasted over the front pocket. "I'm sorry to disturb you," he said with a slight French accent, "but I'm looking for Jack Cole. I was told I could find him here."

"Jack Cole is my husband."

The little man's face brightened. He came closer, peered into the bassinet with a smile. "Congratulations," he said. "A boy or a girl?"

"A boy," she replied

"A lucky boy," the man said.

I was a little surprised to find a stranger there when I emerged from the bathroom in a T-shirt and jeans, two days' stubble on my face.

The man gave me an expectant smile. "Jack Cole?"

"Yes."

"Please excuse me for barging in on you at a time like this."

"It's okay. Are you a doctor?"

The man frowned as if he'd forgotten something. "I'm sorry," he said, "I'm a bit jet lagged." He offered his hand for a shake. "I'm Claude Rachou."

I shook with him, and he handed me a business card, "I'm a lawyer," he explained. "My firm represents the estate of Roget Voltan."

I let that sink in. "What does that have to do with me?" I asked suspiciously.

"Everything, Mr. Cole, M. Voltan's estate is worth in the neighborhood of ten million dollars, and you are his sole heir. You are his son, are you not?"

I collapsed into a chair. I thought about refusing the money, but only for a minute. I looked up at the little French lawyer. "Forgive me I'm just a bit overwhelmed. You see, I had no idea . . . my father and I were never what you would call close."

He nodded and smiled. "I see. I'm staying at The Pierre. Why don't you get some rest and call me there in the morning?"

I looked over at Lisa, who gave me thumbs up.

"I'll do just that, Mr. Rachou."

THE END

Made in United States
Orlando, FL
21 November 2022